The Burning Men

WILL SHINDLER

The Burning Men

HODDER &
STOUGHTON

First published in Great Britain in 2020 by Hodder & Stoughton
An Hachette UK company

1

Copyright © Will Shindler 2020

The right of Will Shindler to be identified as the Author of the Work has been
asserted by him in accordance with the Copyright, Designs and Patents Act 1988.

A CIP catalogue record for this title is available from the British Library

Hardback ISBN 9781529301694
Trade Paperback ISBN 9781529301700
eBook ISBN 9781529301731

Typeset in Plantin Light by Hewer Text UK Ltd, Edinburgh
Printed and bound in Great Britain by Clays Ltd, Elcograf S.p.A.

Hodder & Stoughton policy is to use papers that are natural, renewable
and recyclable products and made from wood grown in sustainable
forests. The logging and manufacturing processes are expected to
conform to the environmental regulations of the country of origin.

Hodder & Stoughton Ltd
Carmelite House
50 Victoria Embankment
London EC4Y 0DZ

www.hodder.co.uk

For my mum who said I would, and continues to make editorial comments on my life Karin Finn-style. And my dad – who'd have been chuffed.

I

Five Years Ago

It roared as it burnt. A monster lighting up the night. They saw it long before they got there, the usual banter tailing off as the scale of the blaze became clear.

'Are you sure that's empty?' someone almost whispered.

'Should be,' replied Martin Walker. 'It's just a building site, however big.'

One Pacific Square was supposed to be a game changer, a multi-billion-pound regeneration project straddling the Battersea/Clapham borders. Well, the game was certainly changing. The foreign investors would have to wait a lot longer before they saw their money now. They'd be lucky if the unfinished structure of angled steel and glass was still standing by the time this was finished.

Stuart Portbury dragged the Mercedes-Benz Atego fire engine to a halt and the four other men disembarked. The wall of heat hit them instantly, their ears taking a second to adjust to the thunder of the flames above. Gary Elder and Adesh Kaul began pulling out the hoses while Phil Maddox fetched the Halligan bar – part claw, part blade, part tapered pick. It would get them through doors, padlocks, windows and anything else in their way. Walker could hear other sirens homing in on the site, bees buzzing to a gigantic hive. There'd be about thirty before long, coming from across London. Anything up to a hundred and fifty firefighters would be dealing with this before the night was over. And probably the next day too.

'Third floor, top left.'

It was Kaul who was shouting. It took Walker a moment before he saw it, a figure – male, by the looks of it – frantically waving from a window. Walker strode to the cab of the fire engine.

'Persons reported. Call it in, Stu.' This would trigger the dispatch of an ambulance, a command unit and a station manager. It also just complicated the job. The priority would now be search and rescue before fighting the fire.

Walker ran back to join Elder and Kaul at the pump. The man on the third floor was no longer visible, smoke billowing out of the window he'd been waving from. A second fire engine was pulling up behind them. Walker recognised Sarah Connelly, his counterpart from Lambeth Station, jumping out.

'Looks like we've got one trapped on the third floor, Sarah.'

'What are they doing in there? It's a construction site, the place should be empty?'

'I want to send a four-man breathing apparatus team in,' said Walker. 'Gary, Phil, Adesh and me.'

'I'd be happier with a two-man team. Why so many?'

'The size; that's a lot of floor space to cover and there might be more people in there.'

'Alright, Marty . . . it'll be a stage two entry control. You'll need a crew manager – which I guess will be me. I'm calling for extra pumps at this section as well. We'll need them. You know the drill; you don't go in until there's an emergency crew in place.'

Connelly headed back to her vehicle to fetch the electronic control board which tracked their oxygen levels. Walker could still remember the old days when you did the maths on the job.

Walker, Elder, Kaul and Maddox began strapping on their air cylinders. Connelly was directing her crew to break open a padlocked door. Advertising hoardings proudly boasting *Opening in 2016 – Book your appointment now!* hung above it.

'That door is our entry control point. Your target's an individual on the third floor and a potential search and rescue for anyone else who might be up there,' Connelly said for the record. She wrote their names on to the control board as Walker and his team went through the rest of their safety routine – checking their air supplies, pressure gauges and radios. A third fire engine screeched in, two more firefighters jumping out and immediately going through the same procedures. The man hadn't reappeared in the third-floor window. He was either looking for an exit, or he'd been overcome by the smoke. Walker contained his frustration as he waited for the go-ahead. Finally, the other crew manager signalled she was ready to Connelly.

'You're clear, Marty.'

All four men fitted face masks and pulled down their hoods. Connelly checked them over and waved them on. Sprinting forwards, Martin Walker momentarily pictured his wife Christine – as he always did when he ran into a burning building. Just in case.

2

Six Months Ago

Detective Inspector Alex Finn walked out of Alexanderplatz station, smiled at his dying wife and wrinkled his nose.

'It's a bit like Croydon, isn't it?'

Karin Finn, wrapped in a metallic green gooseberry of a Puffa Jacket, turned and looked. She'd spent her teenage years here in Berlin. Even thirty years on, everything was broadly as she remembered. The trams jangling under the railway bridge, the steady stream of shoppers going in and out of the cuboid Kaufhof building, the tourists staring up at the Fernsehturm . . . even the unseasonal nip in the air. And she'd wanted it to be cold. You can keep your Paris in the spring – Berlin was always a particular kind of bitter.

'I prefer to call it Stasi chic.'

'Well, exactly. Have you ever been to the Whitgift Centre?'

He looked at a street vendor by the entrance to the station, doing a decent trade in currywurst, and inhaled. 'How much fun can you have with curry powder and ketchup, anyway?' He glanced down, satisfied to see the side of her mouth curling into a smile. At six foot four he dwarfed her, which always gave him a sneaky advantage when it came to gauging her mood.

It was Karin's idea to come to Berlin. Her parents lived in Stralsund, a three-hour train ride away, but she'd been brought up in the capital and wanted to see it one last time. The tumour in her head, a magnanimous assassin, was granting them a brief window to 'put her affairs in order'. She hated the expression, along with all the other clichés that came with terminal illness, and was already bored of being told what a 'battler' she was. As far as she could see it was an invasion, the enemy already here and the terms of surrender agreed. There'd been no battle, simply a journey and a destination.

She'd broken the news to her husband over a meal. They'd had osso buco – his favourite – then she'd told him the facts as simply as she was able. There'd been a twitch of the jaw, but his long face remained impassive and his grey eyes inscrutable. Finally, he'd drained the last of his wine, leant forwards and kissed her. The questions came later; his reaction to her impending death more or less the same as it was to any other logistical problem which came his way. First, there was slow methodical probing, then a period of assimilation, succeeded by a laying out of the facts, each one studiously re-examined for any nuance he'd missed.

There'd followed a trip to the hospital to talk to the consultant, which Karin found unexpectedly entertaining. Two quiet, cerebral men, each trying to out-calm one another, condensing language down to a series of exchanged statements. Finally, like one of those souvenir penny machines, out popped a perfectly pressed plan. A strategy to deal with her final months on planet Earth. It was, naturally, faultless. If anyone could draw up the perfect timetable for a terminal illness, it was her husband. It was a skill that could probably make you a bit of money if you were so inclined, she thought; *planmydeath.com* or something.

She'd known from the beginning she wanted to die at home in London, but she also knew the decision would be out of her hands. Her parents both reacted differently to her diagnosis. Her mother was clear; she wanted her to come back home to Germany. It was her father's response that took her by surprise.

When she rang it was always Mum who answered. When she asked after him, he'd invariably be 'dropping a book back at the library' or 'giving the dogs a trot around the block'. When he was dragged to the phone, there was just an awful bonhomie and some awkward words of encouragement followed by stultifying long silences. She'd been his princess, and would be again – afterwards – but clearly this long, suffocating corridor in between was more than he could bear. Understanding his reaction didn't stop it hurting, and she also knew he'd bitterly regret it after she was gone. She wasn't going to allow that.

Tomorrow she'd take her father for a walk to Stralsund's city forest and try and get through to him. Today, though, was about her and Alex. Her father wasn't the only stubborn introvert she knew.

'So where do you want to go?' Finn said.

'Nowhere in particular. Let's just mooch.' She took his arm.

'Mooch?'

'Did you want to see the sights? We could do one of those boat trips along the Spree?'

He shook his head.

'A decent bar with some decent food will do for now, then we can plan some structured mooching.' She smiled.

They found a quiet cafe under the railway arches close to Hackescher Markt and ordered a toasted sandwich each. They ate in silence, and not for the first time she thought her husband could easily be mistaken for an academic. His light brown hair was tightly shaved around the back and sides with a carefully managed fringe on top. He wore a pair of horn-rimmed designer glasses that bridged pronounced cheekbones. The Ted Baker shirt, dark Armani jeans and carefully moisturised skin merely completed the deception.

She'd met enough police in her time to know he didn't fit the archetype of a hardened murder detective, and often wondered how his workmates viewed him. He took figuring out, which meant getting to know him, and he wasn't one to make the process easy. Karin knew well enough that what people couldn't understand they often shot down, but if there was ever a problem he never mentioned it. His mood was always calm as he came through the front door, whatever traumas the working week was inflicting. Somewhere in the journey from his desk at Cedar House to their comfortable two-bedder in Balham, it was all ironed out.

She took a sip of her tea, then took the pin out of a grenade and lobbed it.

'So, here's my thing: I'm worried about you.'

He feigned a look of irritation.

'Don't be.'

'I can be, I'm dying; the usual rules don't apply.'

'The usual rules?'

'When I say I'm worried about you, you don't get to change the subject, use humour to deflect unwanted questions, or fiddle around with your phone.'

Finn sighed, and the warm smile on his face gave way to something else. The stress of the last few weeks was just about visible for a fleeting moment.

'I'll cope. I don't really have a choice, do I?'

'I know you'll cope, you'll be brilliant – that's the point.'

His expression didn't change, but that didn't mean anything. With Alex, fireworks could be going off in there and you'd never know.

'It's day one I'm thinking about.'

He looked at her quizzically.

'The first morning afterwards. The day you put your suit back on, and go back to work. Every time I think of that . . .'

She broke off, the emotion catching her. He instinctively took her hand across the table.

'You'll bottle it up, and for God knows how long, and I don't want you doing that. Let yourself emote, you silly sod.' He looked down into his *weissbier* but didn't reply. 'I don't want you to be alone.' It wasn't the idea that Alex couldn't live without her that bothered Karin, it was the idea that he could live only too cheerfully on his own.

'A bit early to be thinking about that, isn't it?'

'When would you like to talk about it, Christmas?'

He looked upset. 'Not funny.'

'Alex, I haven't got long, and there's some things I can't put in a will. I need you to listen.' She held his gaze a moment, and finally he nodded.

'Alright, I promise at some point I'll download Tinder and go on some appalling dates with a few divorced mothers of four.'

'What did I say about the rules?' He held his hands up in mock surrender. 'I'm serious. I want you to meet someone, and I want you to have children one day.'

'Jesus, Karin; you haven't gone yet.'

His reaction to the suggestion of children was interesting. She'd been a duty solicitor when they'd first met and it was frequently a bumpy professional relationship. She would be called down to Cedar House at all hours of the day and night, and as their jobs demanded, they'd routinely slipped into adversarial positions. Just as she'd formed the opinion he was so far up his own arse he'd probably need a torch to navigate his way out, he'd surprised her by asking her out on a date. Even then, she was amazed they'd made it to a second and a third one. He seemed arrogant to the point of unpleasantness until she understood he really possessed no concept of how he came across. What took longer was working out what was going on underneath. She'd taken the time and discovered a warm, principled man, at odds with the brusque exterior.

As things progressed, marriage and children went from being part of the plan, to being part of *a* plan, until finally there didn't really seem to *be* a plan. They'd settled into a routine they were both comfortable with, and the deep bond between them was enough. It was only in the last year she'd sensed something else bubbling beneath the surface. The odd dropped comment, his irritation at friends who did have children – just enough for Karin to sense something was stirring. It had led her to re-evaluate her own feelings on the subject. At the time, she'd been surprised at how annoying the idea of getting pregnant made her feel. She'd wondered if it would ever change, what it would take to inject some urgency into her maternal instinct. Now, there was genuine regret at time which couldn't be clawed back.

'Do you regret we never had any?' she asked him.

'No.' He shrugged. 'If we'd really wanted them, we'd have done it. We are where we are.'

'I don't believe you,' she said, and his eyes automatically flicked away. 'I want you to have them though. Some day. With someone. But have them. Go out there when you're ready, find someone, and impregnate the fuck out of them.'

He smiled at the words, but what she said next made him laugh out loud. And months later, just hours after she'd been cremated, as he sat alone in a quiet bedroom in south London, it made him laugh out loud again.

3

Today

Adesh Kaul looked up at the custom-made wedding mandap and smiled contentedly. They'd looked hard to find a hotel in south London with a high enough ceiling for the structure. It was his brother Ajay who'd found this place in Morden and it couldn't have been more perfect. He'd married Stephanie under the mandap just a couple of hours before, and the party was in full swing. The room was now a swirl of rainbow colour as the guests danced and mingled. Ajay was holding court trying to impress one of the waitresses, while simultaneously packing an oversized slice of wedding cake into his mouth. Their mother was sat at a nearby table with four equally stern-looking women of a certain age. They were all watching his little brother with horror, and Kaul couldn't help chuckling at their appalled expressions.

He scoped out the hall, looking for Steph, and saw her in deep conversation with Josh, her best mate from work. She was wearing her bright red wedding dress, garlands of flowers around her neck, while the gold she was bedecked in glistened and shone every time she moved. She looked spectacular. He watched the pair chat. Predictably, the wedding was proving only a minor distraction to the constant flow of gossip passing between them. He stared across, determined to catch her eye, and was rewarded with a look of surprise which morphed into a warm, private smile. He wondered if life would ever feel better than it did right now.

Since leaving the fire brigade he'd built a world around him he was proud of. It helped he'd always known what he wanted to do. Forming his own business – a fire risk assessments consultancy – was a natural progression. It allowed him to use the expertise he'd built up on the job, without having to put his life on the line every day. Steph deserved a proper wedding and he'd spent big on it, probably more than was sensible. He owed it all to one night a long time ago. He owed it all to Pacific Square. Everything was as he'd designed it to be.

The man at the back of the room sipped his drink and pretended to study his phone intently. There'd been no problem slipping in. He was just another body in a packed room. Since arriving he'd spent some time looking around carefully, always aware of where Adesh Kaul was and what he was doing. There was something about the guy, he conceded. The wedding too – a *class* of sorts. You could feel the joy in the room and it nauseated him.

He peered up carefully from his phone, making sure his head was still tilted down towards the screen so as not to attract attention. He watched Kaul make two young children laugh and shake their parents' hands. The family moved on and Kaul paused for a moment before striding out into the corridor that led to the toilets. This was it. The man pocketed his phone and stood up.

'I know my brother . . .' said Ajay Kaul to the waitress. 'If I was a betting man, I'd lay odds by the time you're serving breakfast tomorrow I'll be an uncle-to-be.' He woozily tapped the side of his nose and gave her a knowing smile. 'Let's just say I'm not anticipating any particular delay to that development.' He winked, and the waitress smiled before taking his empty plate and politely making her excuses. He downed his champagne, belched and patted his stomach. A quick piss then some more food.

He followed the signs to the toilets and walked down a small corridor until he found the gents. He reached down, fumbling for his flies, when he stopped in his tracks. Someone was smoking in one of the cubicles, he could smell it – see smoke rising above the door.

'I wouldn't, mate. You'll have the alarm and sprinklers going off in a minute . . .'

There was no response and Ajay frowned in irritation. 'Listen, it's a wedding – you don't want to spoil it for every-one, do you?'

There was still no reply. He could hear what sounded like birds' wings flapping behind the door. He stood nonplussed for a moment, wishing he hadn't drunk quite so much so quickly. The smoke got thicker, and the odour was becoming acrid and unpleasant. On cue a loud, shrieking alarm started to sound and the sprinklers kicked in, neatly saturating every-where inside the small space except the one place that mattered. Ajay noticed that the door wasn't actually locked from the inside, just ajar. He pushed it open and jumped back as a wave of heat surged out.

He was greeted by a sight that would never leave him. Adesh – slumped on the toilet seat, the top half of his body completely alight. His hair was almost entirely burnt off, the skin on his face boiling and melting, leaving nothing but the impression of a vacant rictus grin.

4

Karin chose a humanist service as she wasn't remotely religious. She'd organised it herself. One last project to throw
herself into. They'd met a funeral celebrant in December, an
unctuous man who'd irritated Finn from the off. Karin was
pleased enough by what he'd told them and following his
advice, she'd drawn up her own itinerary for the service from
her hospice bed. The melancholy second movement from
Beethoven's 'Emperor' concerto greeted the mourners as they
arrived. Her best friend Cally opened the proceedings with a
small speech and a quote from Winston Churchill: '*Life is a
whole, and good and ill must be accepted together. The journey has
been enjoyable and well worth making – once.*'

Her father read Auden's 'Funeral Blues'. Unsteady on his
feet, and inaudible at times with his heavy accent, it was almost
as painful to watch as it was to listen to. But an unexpected
smile at the very end made it the most memorable part of the
whole day, Finn thought later. The old man's eyes, dead for
the past seven months, suddenly alive and urgent again.

Finally came Finn's speech. A collection of memories and
stories about the woman he'd loved. It was the one thing Karin
hadn't wanted to know anything about. She'd just said, 'Make
them laugh – after Dad, they'll need it.' But he hadn't managed
anything of the sort, the words falling out of his mouth like
dying slugs. There'd been nothing memorable about it; no
anecdote people would take away, no turn of phrase that

would stick in the mind, not even an emotional breakdown to mitigate its mediocrity. Just a disjointed and wholly inadequate tribute to the one person who'd genuinely changed his life. He took some solace from the fact Karin would have found his car crash of a ramble extremely funny.

The wake was awkward too. People he'd known for years suddenly felt mutually disposable. He doubted he'd see or hear from many of them again, which was odd because by and large these were good and decent people. Finn knew it was Karin they'd found so alluring; they admired him, but they'd *loved* her. He'd always struggled with friendships, largely because the concept ran counter to his natural personality. Letting people in didn't come easy to him. It's not that he was without friends, but you could count the real ones on one hand and they'd earnt their place in his life. These people were Karin's friends. He liked nearly all of them, but could already feel himself detaching. There was no animosity to it, but like it or not he was entering a new phase in his life now. They sensed it too; there'd been an unspoken finality to the goodbyes as they'd left.

The same could not be said of Karin's parents. To his own surprise he'd formed a genuinely close relationship with them over the years. His own parents were both dead and while they didn't fill that void, they certainly rented some space in that area. For all their quirks, Otto and Olga Bergmann were old-fashioned people of principle. It was something he couldn't help but admire, just as he'd admired it in Karin.

Finn's boss at the Cedar House murder squad, DCI John Skegman, also came to the service. A thin, wiry man with a sweep of black hair, he could often strike people who didn't know him as a little shifty. His demeanour didn't help, a natural stillness coupled with narrow eyes which were constantly moving. Finn knew differently though; a mutual respect having built between them over the three years they'd worked together. In reality Skegman was a straightforward man who'd let you know if he wasn't happy and support you to the hilt if he felt it was warranted. He also possessed the hide of a rhino, seemingly unbothered by angry superiors and resentful juniors alike.

'Call me, when you're ready to come back to work,' he'd said as he left, though Finn knew it was more a courtesy than an offer. The DCI's interpretation of the Met's compassionate leave regulations had already been more than generous.

Now, several hours later, Finn was finally alone. He was sitting in his bedroom at home drinking up the stillness of it, warming himself in the sunlight blazing through the windows. There was just the quiet ticking of the bedside clock to let him know the world was still turning. He'd almost been defeated as he'd come through the front door, the effort of keeping himself together finally releasing. He felt like an elephant heading for some mythical graveyard in the jungle, ready to lie down and surrender.

'*It's day one I'm thinking about,*' she'd warned him, all those months ago in Berlin.

Now it was here Finn realised he didn't know what to do with the rest of the evening, never mind the rest of his life. He remembered the other thing she'd said that day.

'*Throw my underwear out last.*'

He'd taken it as a joke and laughed, but she'd picked up his hand and said with a twinkle, 'I'm serious.' He'd known then she'd said it for a reason. Unbidden, an image of Karin giving him a glare over her reading glasses came to mind. It was something she'd frequently done, usually after he'd said something pompous. He couldn't help but smile at the memory and wondered how many more times, in the years to come, this virtual-reality Karin would emerge to put him in his place.

He walked over to the chest of drawers in the corner of the room, stopping for a moment to catch his pallid reflection in the mirror, then pulled open the second drawer down. He lifted out a selection of knickers and bras, halting as his eyes suddenly started to prick. He'd got used to this, unexpected tears set off by unexpected triggers.

And then, there it was. Sat at the bottom of the brown wooden drawer was an envelope with his name written on it. He perched on the edge of the bed again and looked at the neat, small handwriting on the front. He could smell perfume and he held it to his nose, getting a blast of Elie Saab Rose Couture. Carefully he opened it and pulled out a solitary piece of paper. There were just two sentences written on it.

'How far will a blind dog walk into a forest?'
Work it out – it's important! x

Oh, for fuck's sake, Karin, he thought. A riddle? That's it, really? And then there she was, peering over her glasses at him again. Off the top of his head, he'd no idea what it meant. He suspected a few minutes on the internet would solve it, but the note said, quite specifically, *'work it out'*. She'd clearly wanted him to think it through. One last challenge to him. He could feel the tiniest of unexpected smiles forming.

'Alright, love – you're on,' he muttered to himself.

He took the note downstairs and sat in the kitchen pondering it over a bowl of corn flakes. Why a dog with impaired eyesight would be wandering around some woodland, and what message of great import this held for him, his brain didn't seem ready or willing to decipher. He glanced at the clock on the wall – it was ten to five and the silence in the flat was already oppressive. He turned on the radio. A woman was wittering on about dog kennels. He stuck with it more for the company than any great interest, until the five o'clock news. There were some soundbites of the prime minister and the leader of the opposition trying to out-smug each other in the Commons, reports of a children's hospital being bombed in Syria, then a story about a man's body being found at a wedding in Morden the previous afternoon. The victim died in a fire at a hotel and police were now investigating. The newsreader's wording was deliberate; not found dead *after* a fire, but in a fire *at* a hotel. For a moment the semantics of it were a glorious distraction.

He couldn't help but let his mind wander. His colleagues at Cedar House would now be fully mobilised. All three emergency services would have descended on the hotel in a chorus of blues and twos. CCTV footage would have been gathered and scrutinised, the hotel staff and all of its guests would be in the process of being interviewed. Forensic teams would be working the scene. It would be chaos – sodden and smoking chaos, with the charred remains of a human being at the centre. It also occurred to Finn how easy it would have been for Skegman to have given Karin's service a miss this morning. With the DI on compassionate leave, the last thing anyone would have needed was the DCI also out of the office for most of the day.

He switched the radio off and picked up his phone. He held it in his hand as if weighing it. There was no question his head wasn't in the right place for work yet. On the other hand, the prospect of another day sitting around this flat was soul-destroying. His fingers made the decision, and Skegman's name flashed up on the display.

'Alex?'

'I just heard on the news about the death at the wedding. I wondered if you could use a hand?'

17

'For Christ's sake, you only cremated Karin this morning.'

'I know how it sounds, but I need to be doing something. I can't see any point sitting around here.'

'Not a chance. And that's it. No argument.'

'What kind of fire was it?'

'*Alex ...*'

'You're also dealing with that stabbing in Thornton Heath, aren't you? From last week? I saw it in the paper. On top of the ongoing workload you must be spread pretty thin.' There was a short silence before Skegman answered.

'You're not thinking straight. You need time off. You need to heal.'

'I'm guessing you've barely got enough senior officers to go round.'

'You know better than anyone what this kind of investigation involves – the level of work, the intensity of it, *the clarity*. You're in no state for it right now.'

'So it wasn't an accident then?'

Skegman sighed and there was another pause. Finn knew him well enough to know he was considering it. For all his protestations, two new investigations on top of everything else *would* be spreading them thinly.

'I wouldn't suggest it if I didn't think I was up to it.'

'The dead man . . . it was the groom. It's looking like someone deliberately set him alight in a toilet cubicle.'

Finn didn't respond, but he could feel the familiar stirrings of curiosity.

'Sleep on it, and if you still feel this way in the morning, come in and we'll have a chat, but I can't promise anything,' said Skegman.

Finn knew what he was thinking; the DCI wanted to look him in the eye, copper to copper, then make a judgement. He thanked him and said he'd call in one way or another first thing. A good night's rest and he'd be ready, he thought. He'd make himself ready.

And suddenly there she was again, sat in the chair opposite, peering over her glasses – *'Who are you kidding?'*

5

Martin Walker wasn't brilliant at speeches, but it didn't matter, he decided. Sometimes you didn't need to be one of life's wordsmiths. Say what you mean, mean what you say; he'd always lived by that and it was a good fallback on days like this. The fourth annual Sundridge Park Retro and Vintage Jumble Sale wasn't the most prestigious charity event in the country, but it was for a cause that meant something to him.

'If you don't see anything that takes your fancy, then I commend to you Janice Barnard's excellent table of cupcakes, fondant fancies and Bakewell tarts. This year one pound will buy you one of each, am I right, Janice?' He glanced over at a beaming woman in oversized spectacles. 'Now all that remains is for me to declare this sale open, and God bless all of you for every penny that's raised.' There was a smattering of applause from the dozen or so familiar faces stood in front of him in the small church hall. He went over and joined his wife Christine whose wheelchair was parked next to some of the stacked pews at the side of the room.

'You've got them eating out of the palm of your hand again, Marty.'

'Don't be daft – everyone likes a bargain, that's why they're here.'

'You should listen to your wife when she pays you a compliment,' said a ruddy-faced man, approaching them with a smile.

'Thanks for coming, Colin, appreciate the support.'

'Don't be stupid, mate. You deserve it – all the work you put in. Not just this, all the events you put on.'

'It's just a jumble sale.'

'Oh, come on. It must take a lot of time to set up – cost you a fair bit too, I should imagine.'

'Nonsense, the church lets us have this space for free, and if you count Janice, then the catering doesn't come to much either.'

'I'm not just talking about today. The charity dinners, the auctions, the sporting events, not to mention all the travelling you do; that's proper commitment. If they ever find a cure for multiple sclerosis, we'll all know who to thank. Don't tell me you're not putting your hand in your pocket for all that.'

Walker was well versed in deflecting the question. For a start he'd always exaggerated the size of his fire service pension. At the age of fifty-nine he looked about the right age to have taken early retirement. The unexpected wealth he'd come into five years ago was under lock and key in multiple covert locations around the capital. He'd drip-fed it as and when he'd needed to, finding different ways to mask its use. It hadn't attracted attention and after all this time he'd even managed to convince himself it never would.

He did miss his old life though; he'd loved being a fire-fighter. He'd joined straight from school and in those early years never gave much thought to the day it would have to stop. But then Christine was diagnosed with MS, and along came Pacific Square.

What took place that night changed everything; from the quality of Chrissie's care, to the lives they'd been able to lead since. It also spurred him to raise money the right way. To do the right thing. There were lots of people like Colin in this world, people who looked up to him. They all saw a fine, upstanding member of the community, who cared for his wife and raised money for charity with unstinting energy. They saw a good man. But none of it helped when he woke in the middle of the night and remembered. His reputation was built on a lie and he was certainly no hero.

'We're fine. Made some good investments when I was younger and I'm reaping the rewards now. Feels right to pump it back into something that matters.'

'Stop making his head swell, Col, you'll turn him into a monster,' said Christine.

'No chance of that, I bet you keep his feet on the ground, Chrissie.'

'Be nice if he did cut loose from time to time – wears the weight of the world on his shoulders, this one. Always has done,' she said.

'You wouldn't want me any other way,' said Walker.

'Honestly, you two are something else. What's your secret?' said Colin.

'Vodka,' said Christine, and they all laughed.

The day went well and both Martin and Christine stayed for the duration, as they always did. The clearing up process was underway when the call came. Walker didn't recognise the number, but he certainly knew the voice. It was one he'd hoped he'd never hear again.

'Hello, skipper,' said Phil Maddox. Walker groaned inwardly. Whatever he wanted needed to be closed down fast. He turned to his wife and smiled pleasantly.

'Just got to take this – I'll only be five minutes. Grab us a Bakewell before we go, eh?' He winked at her and headed out of the back door into a small courtyard at the rear of the church.

'I thought we'd agreed to go our separate ways, Phil?' he said, trying hard to keep his voice light.

'Have you seen the news?'

'No, I've been out all day. What news?'

'It's all over Twitter . . .'

'What is? I'm not on Twitter.'

'*Someone's* been killed – at a wedding . . .' He sounded frantic now. 'Adesh's wedding.'

Walker licked his lips; they felt as dry as old leaves.

'Do you mean Adesh has been killed?'

'I don't know; the police haven't said. But the word on Twitter is that it might be the groom.'

'But you don't know for certain?'

'They're saying he was burnt to death . . .'

Walker tried to process what he was being told. He breathed hard, but couldn't focus.

'Twitter's full of bollocks, just kids in their bedrooms spreading second-hand gossip.'

'Someone *knows*, Martin . . . knows what we did.'

'We didn't do anything.'

That wasn't true, but it felt like the right thing to say. Paranoia may be kicking in, but he wasn't going to admit to anything. Especially to a weak man he hadn't spoken to in five years. For all he knew Adesh Kaul was sipping a pina colada on a beach somewhere right now.

'Don't you get it, Marty? Someone's found out. They've tracked him down and killed him for it.'

'Get a grip, Phil. We don't know anything about it, even if it's true. It's just speculation on the internet.'

'I'm telling you because I thought you'd want to know. You or me – we could be next . . .'

Walker's mind was racing. Whatever worst-case scenarios Maddox could come up with, his own brain was already fanning out like a pack of cards.

'Stay calm, panicking's not going to help.'

'What do you want to do?'

Maddox sounded like a little boy, thought Walker. If someone *did* know, then the last thing any of them needed was a
present-day trail linking them to the past. He needed Maddox
to go away.

'I'll be in touch, Phil.'

6

Maddox looked out of the window and beat down a wave of nausea. He already regretted ringing Walker, but hadn't known what else to do. He looked at the view from his window. He could see the blue shimmer of the Thames, and the four rebuilt chimneys of Battersea Power Station in the middle distance. For once the vista did little to settle his nerves. Walker hadn't taken him seriously. Nothing new there then; he hadn't shown him much respect back in the day either. But this *needed* to be taken seriously, because Adesh was dead. He was quite certain of it now.

He breathed in deeply and forced himself to think. Tomorrow he'd change the locks – perhaps look at putting in a reinforced security door. He'd always felt relatively safe here; it was one of the reasons he'd bought the place. The front door to his flat was the only cntrance and three floors up there was no way for someone to break in. He went over to his desk, sat down at his computer and brought up the London Fire Brigade's Twitter page, but it hadn't been updated. There was nothing on the Met Police Twitter either, so he flicked to the London Ambulance page and immediately found what he was looking for:

London Ambulance Service @Ldn_Ambulance
We responded along with our colleagues @metpoliceuk to an incident this afternoon at the Manor Park Hotel in

Morden. Sadly, there was one fatality. We have treated two other people and have taken them to hospital.

There it was in black and white – official confirmation. It might not have named Adesh, but it as good as rubber-stamped what he'd read earlier. Maddox unplugged his phone from its charger. He found the number he wanted and waited for the call to connect. An answerphone cut in.

'This is Gary Elder. I can't take your call right now but if you leave your name and number and I like the sound of you, I'll call you back . . .'

Maddox cut the call off without speaking. If Walker was still exactly the same pompous arse he'd always been, then Gary hadn't changed either – still a facetious twat apparently.

He found another number, breathing out as a familiar voice greeted him.

'Stu . . . it's Phil Maddox.'

There was a beat of silence on the other end, before finally Stuart Portbury replied.

'Phil . . . ?'

He sounded bemused, as if unsure whether to encourage the conversation.

'I know we said we wouldn't contact each other, but something's happened. I think we may be in trouble, mate. I think it might be connected to Pacific Square . . .'

7

YoYo's Cafe was a familiar haunt for officers at Cedar House. Sat directly opposite the station, it was a place where DC's and DAC's alike could enjoy an uncomplicated cup of coffee with the unwritten rule that stripes were checked in at the door. Finn reckoned Yolande, the proprietor, could probably make a half-decent inspector herself given how much police business she'd soaked up over the years. At half past seven in the morning, there were only a few stragglers left from the overnight shift as Finn walked in to meet the waiting Skegman. The DCI was sat in the corner looking out of the window like a man lost in his own world, but Finn knew him better than that. Those darting eyes wouldn't have missed much; who was in the room, what titbits of gossip were being exchanged. There was a lazy assumption from a few junior officers that Skegman didn't know what was going on at shop floor level. There was a reason they were wrong.

Skegman's eyes bored into him even as he flashed a brisk smile of welcome and it told Finn all he needed to know. The game within the game – the assessment of his emotional suitability to return to the front lines – was already underway. Now the moment was here Finn wasn't quite as bullish as he'd felt the previous evening. He was tired from what felt like the umpteenth night of fitful sleep. Bereavement was *wearing*, he'd come to realise. Over the years he'd perfected the art of parking his emotions. He firmly believed the more dispassionate you were, the better the police officer it made you. But that approach didn't allow for the tidal wave of grief currently washing over him, which couldn't simply be waved away. It certainly wasn't the best preparation for the kind of scrutiny he knew Skegman was about to put him under. For a fleeting moment he'd considered calling their meeting off, but as he'd picked at his breakfast he'd felt the walls of the flat closing in on him again. Exhausted and hurt he may be, but he also knew sitting at home wasn't going to help.

Yolande hobbled over, her bad back still causing her to wheeze, with a jug of filter coffee in her hand and a disapproving look on her face.

'You shouldn't be back so soon,' she said, pouring out a stream of hot black liquid into a mug. 'And you shouldn't be encouraging him,' she said to Skegman, before refilling his cup and shuffling away, not remotely interested in a reply. Both men smiled, and Finn let the DCI break the ice.

'Nice service yesterday. Can't have been easy. I shouldn't think last night was much fun either.'

'No. But I'm glad it's out of the way.'

'She has a point. It's less than a week since Karin died.'

'I began grieving when she was diagnosed, to be honest. Think I was all cried out by yesterday evening,' he lied. 'If it's a choice between sitting at home or getting on with things, I know what I'd rather do.'

'If it's a choice between you sitting at home or screwing up an investigation, I know what I'd rather you did.'

'Grief doesn't work like that, or at least mine doesn't – I still have my faculties.'

'It's more your focus than your faculties that concerns me, Alex.'

'So give me something to focus on; tell me about this man who died.'

28

Skegman sized him up for a moment.

'I'm going to repeat what I said yesterday – have you really thought this through? You know what an investigation like this will ask of you ... the hours you'll need to put in. How early you'll need to be here, how late you'll be leaving. Then there's the levels of concentration required. Now marry that with how you're feeling and ask yourself if you can give of your best.'

'Tell me about the man who died,' repeated Finn.

Skegman ran his tongue around his cheek for a moment, then reached a decision. The game within the game, again.

'His name was Adesh Kaul. He was thirty-seven years old and married his fiancée Stephanie Clough just hours before it happened. He's a former firefighter with the LFB and left the service five years ago to set up his own fire safety consultancy. From what we can gather there were a lot of local businesses on his books: offices, restaurants, shops, that sort of thing.'

'Ex-firefighter, running a fire consultancy ... who gets immolated at his own wedding. Dissatisfied customer?' said Finn.

'Extraordinarily, the same thought occurred to us. We're going through his business dealings with a fine-tooth comb.'

'Can't be a coincidence though – the manner of death?'

'We're keeping an open mind. Early indications are that he was a popular man; everything we're getting back suggests a much-loved son and brother, with no obvious enemies.'

'Well, there was at least one   torching someone on their wedding day feels pretty personal to me. If you just wanted the guy out of the way you'd pick something a little less showy.'

When it came to these things, Finn came armed with experience – over twenty-five years in all. Murder nearly always tended to boil down to one of the four Ls: Lust, Love, Loathing or Loot. Every now and then there was one that defied categorisation; the actions of a sadist or a madman. More often than not though, the motivation was more straight-forward, and instinctively that's how this felt to him. He watched a tired-looking uniformed PC in the corner slurp at his tea, as he mulled it for a moment.

'Someone somewhere hated this bloke – *really* hated him. They picked his wedding day for a reason. I'd want to have a look into the bride – see if there's any dodgy exes lurking somewhere. Also, check out her workmates; look for any potential stalker material. How have the interviews at the crime scene gone? The hotel staff and the wedding guests?'

Finn was talking matter-of-factly now, as if he'd already accepted an offer to lead the investigation. Two could play that game. The small hint of wry in Skegman's expression told him the other man knew precisely what he was trying to do.

'Nothing much is jumping out so far. Everyone's still in shock. The bride's been under sedation since it happened, as have several members of Kaul's family. But there were nearly two hundred people there. It's going to take a while to get through them. The hotel staff said it was one of the smoothest events they'd ever handled. The two families were easy to deal with, things went quietly on the day – everything was pretty tame until . . .'

'. . . someone burnt the groom to a crisp,' said Finn, more thoughtfully than the words suggested. 'If he was thirty-seven, then he quit the fire service at thirty-two . . . that's quite young. Any idea why?'

'The word from his station manager was that he wanted to do something less hazardous. He'd been under pressure from his family to find something else.'

It wasn't unusual, thought Finn. The same happened to police as well. You never forgot you were putting your life on the line every day, but it was true you could become used to the feeling. It was different for your loved ones. Karin never stopped worrying.

'What's your take on it?' Finn asked. The DCI rarely offered opinions this early in an investigation, preferring to wait until enough evidence and facts were gathered. It never hurt to ask him though. In his own way Skegman was as methodical as Finn, which is probably why the two men worked so well together. *Two cheeks of the same arse,* Karin once described them in exasperation.

'Like you, this feels to me like someone sending a message, and whoever did it was good. No one seems to have seen anything out of the ordinary.'

'Have we got a list of everyone who was there, including the hotel staff?' he asked.

'Yes. But I can't guarantee it's exhaustive,' said Skegman.

'Then you can't rule out the possibility someone managed to slip in unnoticed. Sometimes the easiest place to hide is in a crowd. This could be a professional hit.' While Skegman digested the idea, Finn decided to go on the front foot.

'Who'd be in my team? I'd like Jackie Ojo if she's free?'

'DS Ojo's working the Thornton Heath stabbing. But someone's just transferred in who I think you might find interesting.'

Interesting was one word, thought Finn. Unexpected transfers held the potential to be political or expedient, and were frequently both.

'Her name's DC Mathilde Paulsen. We've got her from Dunlevy Road, where she was very highly regarded by DI Bullen.'

'So why's she moving on?'

'Her last investigation was into a suspected paedophile. I don't know the ins and outs, but apparently it affected her.'

Finn nodded. That was fair enough; he didn't know an officer who hadn't gone through something similar at some point. Sometimes a transfer was a way of wiping the slate clean.

'She's something of an enigma,' Skegman continued. 'I get the sense she's lost her way a bit. I think she could use some direction.'

Finn thought about it, then shook his head.

'With respect, I don't need a project, I need a good detective.'

'You're dictating terms now. So you're coming back then?' said Skegman. 'We've agreed this, have we?'

Finn smiled. Skegman didn't.

'You know what I mean.'

'There's nothing straightforward here. Not with the case, not with Paulsen, and not with you. I'll be honest, all of that makes me feel uncomfortable.'

'It's your call. I'll respect whatever decision you make.'

Skegman stared hard out of the window for a moment.

'Alright, Alex, we'll see how it goes. But I'll be watching – any sign your attention's elsewhere . . .'

Finn acknowledged the warning with the smallest of nods. The truth was he couldn't tell how he'd cope, but he needed this and it felt a relief.

'If I can't have Ojo, how about Gemma Danson?'

'Also on another job. I'm afraid you don't have a choice. You said it yourself on the phone yesterday, we're stretched. DC Paulsen may not be what you want, but she's what you've got.' There was another pause and Finn could see Skegman was still very unsure.

'I'll be fine, John,' said Finn.

Their relationship had always been solid, and it was honest too. Finn felt the assurance was sincerely given. At least he hoped it was. Skegman stood up.

32

'DC Paulsen starts tomorrow morning. You can meet her then.' He picked up his bag and hooked its strap over his shoulder.

'Do *you* rate her?' asked Finn.

'I think I've already answered that, haven't I?'

'Not really.'

'Alex, I wouldn't put her with you if there wasn't *something* there.' He smiled enigmatically. 'You'll see . . .'

8

The sun shone down on Regent's Park as Mattie Paulsen glared daggers at the screaming toddler hurtling towards her. A quick sidestep meant she dodged the melting ice lolly being wielded in a flailing hand. A few steps behind, her partner Nancy Deen also weaved out of the way, giggling at their near miss. They both watched as the little girl's mother caught up and began to chide her.

'You were like that once,' said Nancy.

'I was *never* like that.'

'Bollocks. Bet you were the tantrum queen . . .'

The vaguest hint of a smile began to form on Mattie's face, and she turned her head to hide it. Nancy grinned.

'I see you.'

Mattie flipped a large pair of sunglasses down from her head and stood for a moment to enjoy the warmth of the sun. On a beautiful day where plenty of people were out dressed up for summer, she still cut a distinctive figure. Paulsen was twenty-six, with a short bob of jet black hair, a wide mouth and high cheekbones. Her mixed-race heritage meant she didn't fit the usual Scandinavian stereotypes, even if her slightly lilting accent tended to betray her.

In twenty-four hours she'd be starting at Cedar House, and in the strange hinterland between jobs it felt good to be out enjoying the sunshine. Events at Dunlevy Road still weighed heavy on her mind. They weren't the sort of memories which would disappear quickly – the things that happened on that other summer's day, not so long ago, remained vivid. She exhaled and turned to Nancy, burying the thoughts once more.

'So what do you want to do then?'

'Can you not make it sound like a chore? We're supposed to be having fun.'

'I am having fun.'

'You don't seem very relaxed.'

Mattie sighed and forced a smile.

'I fancy an ice cream. You know – one you actually put in your mouth and not jab at passing strangers.'

Nancy smiled back.

'There's a cafe somewhere up ahead.'

Nancy reached for Mattie's hand and let their fingers entwine.

'PDA . . .' muttered Mattie, but they stayed hand in hand as they strolled on and ten minutes later they were sat overlooking the park's boating lake. Mattie was attacking a small tub of overpriced chocolate ice cream with a wooden spoon, while Nancy sipped thoughtfully at a lemon and ginger tea. They'd both thought a day in the park would be a good idea. An extended weekend before Mattie threw herself back into work. Nancy wasn't sure it was having quite the calming effect she'd hoped.

'So how are you feeling about tomorrow?' she asked, not quite managing to disguise the concern in her voice.

'Okay, I suppose. Do we have to talk about it now?'

'I just want to know why you're so tense.'

Mattie resisted the temptation to bite her partner's head off, largely because it would have confirmed her point.

'A new nick means a whole new load of bollocks, doesn't it?' asked Nancy.

'Sexist bollocks, you mean?'

'In part.'

'It's just another nick, that's what you've been saying all week. What's the big deal?'

Mattie's worries weren't easily explained to non-police. In her line of work, you needed to hit the ground running. There was a pressure on new officers to prove themselves fast, especially if you were a woman. It was true that even the thickest of male hides understood the old sexist days of the Met belonged to the past, but it didn't mean the problem was eliminated. It was still there, just subtler and more nuanced. If you bothered to stop and count the moments, they were still unacceptably high. And Mattie was one to stop and count.

There were other concerns too. The canteen talk was full of stereotypes; you could be *'one to watch'*, a *'smart cookie on the fast track'*, or alternatively someone who *'the penny hadn't dropped with'* or even *'a liability waiting to happen'*. There never seemed to be much middle ground. Paulsen knew the jungle drums would be beating. Different nicks were linked by not so much a grapevine as a full-on vineyard. You could bet there were people at Cedar House who'd believe they knew all about her already. But they'd be wrong.

'You've got to seize this, Mat. It's an opportunity,' said Nancy, still relentlessly searching for the positive. Mattie's ice cream was melting in the heat and a dollop dribbled down her spoon on to her sleeve. She scowled and grabbed a paper napkin.

'You know what it is, Nance. What it *always* is.'

'I thought that was the point though? "Starting over" as the Americans say.'

'Like that just washes everything away.'

'You've got to make a choice. Move on, or go under . . .'

'I did make that choice. I *keep* making that choice. But tell my subconscious. It's not listening.'

Nancy groped for a response but couldn't find one and took another sip of her tea instead. Around them children laughed and families strolled in the warm weather. Mattie looked over at Nancy, but she was deliberately looking away now. Mattie tossed the wooden spoon into the empty ice cream tub and turned to do some people-watching of her own. It wasn't the first time she'd managed to bring storm clouds to a sunny day.

9

Gary Elder took a swig of his beer, then checked his phone for a second time. It was an automatic reaction – he could guess why Phil Maddox was trying to get in touch. He'd stumbled on the news about Adesh almost by accident, the radio in the local One Stop casually revealing it while he'd been buying a carton of milk. The weirdest thing was that he wasn't sure yet how he felt about it. It was certainly shocking; he hadn't seen Kaul in years. He'd liked him though – back in the day. Liked him enough to go into business with him briefly. It was funny how people drift in and out of your life, and there was a genuine sadness. But it was the kind of sadness you felt when you heard about the death of a celebrity you liked. The kind of sadness you got over.

It was hard to know what to make of the circumstances of his death too. The police hadn't given much away. Was it an accident? If so, how the fuck did he manage to burn to death at his own wedding? And if it wasn't accidental, why would someone do it to him? An obvious answer was lurking at the back of his mind, but it wasn't one he fancied exploring. It was an impossibility, for a start. No one could possibly know what they'd done at Pacific Square. It was years ago. Any evidence was surely buried by time, burnt to ash.

His train of thought was interrupted by the doorbell. It made him jump, sending his beer can flying and soaking his designer jeans.

'Shit.'

He wiped the excess liquid off, grateful the dark material helped disguise the damp patch, and went to answer it. As he reached for the handle, he felt a sudden irrational doubt. He stopped and looked through the spyhole. The delivery man was already starting to fill out a card.

'Hold on,' he shouted and quickly opened the door. The man looked at him apologetically, tucked the card in his pocket and handed over a large parcel. Elder signed for it and closed the door. He already knew what was inside: a poncey new toaster for his mother's birthday. He'd almost forgotten ordering it. He dropped the parcel absently on a side table. The adrenaline was still pumping. Just for a second he'd been genuinely worried about who was waiting outside. He needed to get some air, clear the cobwebs; a run would do him good.

He changed into a T-shirt and shorts and grabbed his sunglasses. Normally he'd have something loud pumping in his ears, but it didn't feel right. He didn't want to cut himself off from the world today. He wanted his wits about him. He stepped outside, looked around tentatively and frowned. He was being ridiculous, he thought, and he set off.

The man in the car on the other side of the road watched him go, amused by the concern he'd seen on Elder's face. He'd looked nervous and that was good. He watched him run up the tree-lined street for a few seconds, moving now with a good tempo. The former firefighter looked muscular, still in good nick. Not someone who'd necessarily back away from a confrontation. The man smiled and started his car.

Once upon a time he'd have been invited to Kaul's wedding, Elder thought as he increased his pace. They'd been that close. He felt strangely hurt by the snub, which made little sense in the circumstances. The boy must have grown up. The Adesh he knew was shy around women. It was Elder who'd encouraged him to come out of his shell back then. Every so often he missed those days – out on the lash with the lads after a hard shift. He couldn't help but wonder what they were all doing now. Walker's wife was probably in the grip of her MS, the poor bugger. He could picture Maddox doing something in computers – he was always a bit of a tech geek. Christ alone knew what Portbury was up to. He shook his head; none of it mattered in the slightest.

A car suddenly hurtled past, the roar of its engine making him jump. He stopped and watched it speed into the distance, then looked around uneasily. The street was empty, the noise echoing away. He was just being jumpy, and really needed to snap out of it. He began to move again, his steady gallop turning into a hard sprint.

'I'm so sorry for your loss.'

Finn looked at the woman in front of him, and momentarily wondered why the English language offered such limited vocabulary to cover bereavement. His hopes of returning to work without fuss were already over. As he'd made his way through the corridors of Cedar House he'd been intercepted by several well-wishers wanting to pass on their condolences. The effect was counterproductive. He knew it was a touch naïve, but he'd come back to work to get away from the reminders. The woman worked somewhere in IT support, and he thought her name might be Carol, but wasn't sure. He forced a smile and walked on.

'I mean it, you know. I *am* sorry,' she said.

He turned and saw she was looking almost offended. Was there etiquette to how you received these comments too? Were the sentiments even genuine? He wasn't really interested in whether Carol from IT, who'd never even met Karin, was sorry for her death. People said this stuff for their own benefit. They didn't want to be seen as insensitive and he didn't really care whether they were or weren't. He nodded in acknowledgement and smiled with as much warmth as he could produce. Her face brightened. She'd got the little moment of intimacy between them she'd been searching for, and went on her way.

Finn knew he wasn't the most popular person at Cedar

House. In his time there he'd consciously made little attempt to socialise or even integrate with his colleagues. He firmly believed that just because you spent the day working under the same roof, it didn't automatically mean friendship could be assumed. In turn, many of them found him arrogant, even plain rude. He didn't mind, never being particularly one to get exercised by others' opinions of him. But there was another layer to it too. Finn looked every inch the Oxbridge graduate he was. Add a certain coolness of attitude, and there were the ingredients if not for a class war, then certainly an underlying skirmish. For those who noted his reluctance to join the Friday night drinking clans, there was the reward of a slowly developed mutual trust.

Finn preferred people of substance, and he liked even more those who took the time to work him out. It helped professionally as well. Those in the team who judged quickly and superficially were likely to bring the same qualities to their work. His way of operating produced results, and people who tried to conflate a personal disregard for him with a professional one found it didn't gather much traction. Every police officer respects competence; it gets you home on time. More importantly, it keeps you alive.

He'd used the previous afternoon to familiarise himself with the evidence gathered so far. The evening was then spent percolating. He'd ordered, then ignored, a pizza as his appetite continued to fail him. He'd then forced himself to go through the evidence again. And it *was* an effort. In the normal run of things, he was meticulous in his absorption of information. It was a skill most police officers acquired naturally over time, and Finn prided himself on it. But as much as he trained his mind on the details of Adesh Kaul's wedding, it was the random details of Karin's funeral that kept resurfacing. Grief wasn't just tiring, it was merciless too. There seemed to be no activity – washing, eating, sleeping, working – that wasn't visited by it.

He walked into the large open-plan office of the incident room and took in the familiar low-level hubbub of chatter and ringing phones. He was pleased at the lack of heads turning to register his presence. Maybe he was overselling his own importance. One exception was DS Jackie Ojo, who was at her desk leafing through paperwork. She greeted Finn with a warm smile. Known almost universally as Jackie O, Ojo was one of Finn's solid citizens. For those officers at Cedar House who found Finn a bit too much like hard work, she was the perfect antidote. Ojo was a single mother, but rarely talked about her private life. If she found combining her job with raising a child on her own difficult, there was no clue. She always looked immaculate, and Finn could never shake the sense of a swan; serene on the surface but working furiously underneath to survive.

'Good to have you back, guv. You okay?'

'It's better than daytime TV, I suppose. Is the boss in?'

'Yeah, in his office.'

'What about the new girl?'

Ojo looked awkward.

'DC Paulsen's not here; she hasn't rung in either. I don't know where she's got to, to be honest.'

Finn arched an eyebrow. Hardly an auspicious start, and punctuality mattered to him. If he was required to be somewhere at a certain time that's when he'd arrive, bang on the dot.

'Have you met her yet?'

'Briefly, she came in for an induction last week.'

'And?'

'Seems smart. Quiet though. Hard to get to know, I think, but it's early days.' This chimed with what Skegman told him in YoYo's. Smart was good, distracted was not.

'What are you working right now?'

'The Thornton Heath stabbing. Looks on the periphery of gang-related stuff, but we haven't handed it over to Trident yet.' Trident was the Met's department for tackling gang violence, and if it did come under their jurisdiction, it would usefully free Ojo up.

'The periphery?'

'Sounds like a fight over a girl involving some gangster types. Whether they're actually part of anything and who was actually there, we're still trying to establish. Usual bollocks.'

'Keep me in the loop – it'd be good to have you on board though.' Ojo nodded, and Finn moved on down the corridor towards Skegman's office.

The DCI occupied a reasonably sized glass box of a private space. In theory it allowed for openness, but the way he sat there – stock-still, eyes darting around lizard-like as he stared at his screen – always reminded Finn irresistibly of Blofeld from the old Bond movies. He felt his phone vibrating and frowned when he didn't recognise the number on the display.

'DI Finn? It's DC Paulsen. I know you were expecting me at the station this morning but I've gone straight to the crime scene. I'm at the Manor Park Hotel.'

The voice was distinctive, with a hint of an accent. Dutch possibly, he couldn't tell. But it was the tone which surprised him; brusque, on the borderline of rude.

'And why have you decided to do that?'

'Something struck me overnight. Can you get down here?'

He really didn't like the sense of being summoned, and by a rookie DC at that.

44

'Well, I was intending to come down today at some point anyway.'

She didn't reply.

'Paulsen?'

'Sorry, just saw someone I need to talk to. I'll see you when you get here, sir.' The line went dead. As introductions went, it was different, thought Finn.

An hour later, he was parking up in the surprisingly busy forecourt of the Manor Park Hotel. A couple of days on, the area around the banqueting hall remained a crime scene but there was a steady stream of people passing through. The hotel was taking in guests again after being given permission to reopen for limited business. The matter of a gruesome death over the weekend clearly hadn't put off its clientele. Businessmen and women mainly, Finn noticed as he walked towards the entrance. Heads buried in phones, they seemed neither interested in nor bothered by the police presence.

The first thing that struck him was the smell. It was all pervading as he entered the lobby. Sour and rank, he was guessing it was a cocktail of the fire brigade's work, the hotel's sprinkler system and the charred micro fibres of what was left of Adesh Kaul. A slightly haunted young woman was sat behind the reception desk, while a uniformed police officer stood protecting a sealed-off passageway. The PC recognised him and pulled a cardboard box from behind the desk. Finn helped himself to blue plastic overalls, disposable gloves and bootees and slipped them on. He walked down a darkened corridor with the stench growing noticeably stronger until he arrived at a set of large double doors. There was a sign pointing the way to the toilets and he could hear the low-level conversation of the scenes of crime officers at work around the L-shaped corridor. Deciding he'd only be a distraction for

45

now, he pushed the doors in front of him open and entered the deserted banqueting hall.

It was hard not to be affected by the scene inside. The room was untouched since its sudden evacuation over the weekend. Flattened rose petals were strewn over the floor beneath the mandap. Plates of food were still half eaten on tables, broken glass littered the carpet and even the wedding cake, part demolished, sat sagging still on its display table. The smell was now inside his throat, and he started to cough.

'You'll stop noticing it after about ten minutes,' said an accented voice behind him. Finn turned and saw a tall, slightly gangly woman with a black bob. Even under the forensic apparel he could see she was distinctive, her face catching his eye. Part rock chick, part academic, it made you look twice. He made a mental note to cut that out straight away, not entirely sure where it'd come from.

'DC Paulsen?' asked Finn.

'DI Finn? I'm sorry for your loss,' she said formally.

'Thank you, it isn't necessary though.'

She looked uncomfortable, as if unsure whether she'd been inappropriate.

'So, what brought you down here? I was expecting to meet you at the station this morning.' He was trying to keep the irritation out of his voice, but she'd already managed to get under his skin. Her first choice on her first day was a minor act of insubordination.

'Some of the wedding guests were due back today. They were staying here for the ceremony, but then left after what happened. The hotel told me they were coming back this morning to pick up their luggage so I wanted to catch them. They've had forty-eight hours for the initial shock to wear off and I thought that that, plus seeing the hotel again, might

46

spark something. Bring back a memory or a small detail they'd forgotten in the immediate aftermath.'

When she spoke it was quickly and efficiently, and despite himself he found he was nodding. Not so much insubordination as initiative, it turned out.

'And have you found something?'

'Not from anything anyone's said, but ...' She looked around the room again. 'It's all this. It's lavish, very lavish – bells and whistles, and some.'

Finn took in the room properly this time. She was right; add the cost of hiring the hall to everything else and you weren't talking thousands, more like tens of thousands.

'Rich parents?'

'That's just it. One of the bride's friends told me Kaul paid for the whole thing.'

'His family paid?' queried Finn.

'No. Just him. *He* footed the bill for all of this, out of his own pocket.'

'Interesting. He could just be boasting though – people never like admitting their parents helped them out. We need to have a look at his finances, see how well his business was doing. At the very least we should establish how he did manage to fund this. How much more work needs to be done on site here, by the way?'

'Forensics should finish off later but the fire and the water in the toilet area hasn't made it easy. I'm not sure how much they've got.'

'Alright, I'll go and talk to them – see where they're at. What about the fire investigation team?'

'Been and gone – we should get something back fairly soon from them. There's still a lot of people who were here on the day who we need to take witness statements from. Quite a few of them have already disappeared into the wind.'

'We've got a complete guest list though, haven't we?'

Before she could reply she was interrupted by her phone ringing. She answered it and listened for a moment.

'Okay, thanks for letting me know, we can be there inside half an hour,' she said, before turning back to Finn.

'Stephanie Kaul, the bride – she's awake and wants to talk to us.'

Finn and Paulsen set off across south London to St George's Hospital in Tooting, after Finn had checked in with the forensic team in the burnt-out toilet. The scene was a mess and he didn't envy them their task. It was hard not to consider the irony of Adesh Kaul's last moments – surrounded by firefighters whose uniform he'd once worn.

Roadworks meant the journey was taking considerably longer than it should. Sitting behind the wheel, Finn could feel the frown on his face beginning to ache.

'Better call the hospital and let them know we're running late,' he told Paulsen, who was staring absently out of the window. She nodded without reply, and made the call. He refocused on the road. Paulsen certainly hadn't made any extra efforts to ingratiate herself since they'd left the hotel. Over the years he'd seen every kind of response from a new officer on their first day. There were the eager-to-please puppy dogs, the measured ones who kept something back and the loud brash types keen to impress. She was giving him something new. He'd spent most of the journey trying to figure out whether it was an affectation or genuine. With the traffic reducing them to a slow crawl, he decided to test the waters.

'So how are you settling in?'

'Hard to say – first morning of the first day. But I've only heard good things about Cedar House so it's good to finally get started.'

'Your accent – I can't quite . . .'

'Father's Swedish, mother's from Croydon. I grew up in south London, so not as exotic as you might think.'

'Holiday romance?'

'No, they're both scientists. They met on a research project.'

'Not tempted to follow in the family footsteps, then?'

'No. But one of the things I like about detective work is the methodology. Investigative work of any kind has a lot of shared principles with the sciences. Besides . . . I like fast cars.'

She said it in the same quiet monotone as before, and it took him a moment to register. He glanced across at her, and was rewarded with an unexpected lopsided smile, as she gestured at the non-moving traffic ahead of them. He smiled back, despite himself.

Half an hour later they arrived at St George's, and after another ten minutes working through a maze of identical corridors, they arrived at a small reception area. A youngish doctor with a mop of red hair was sat studying an iPad intently.

'Doctor Edwards?' said Paulsen.

Edwards stood and turned.

'I'm DC Paulsen, we spoke on the phone earlier. This is DI Finn—'

'How's she doing?' asked Finn, skipping the pleasantries.

'Not great, as you can imagine. You know what happened?'

Finn turned to Paulsen for a steer.

'When she heard what was going on in the toilet she ran to try and help her husband. She suffered some burns in the process.'

'There was smoke inhalation too. We've given her a lot of painkillers and kept her sedated for the most part,' said Edwards. Finn nodded.

'Probably no bad thing.'

49

'This morning she expressed a wish to talk to the police. She hasn't said a word since. She's refused food, but she's drinking water at least.' Edwards paused. 'I appreciate you've got a job to do, but her mental state is extremely fragile so please use some common sense, eh?'

Finn nodded in acknowledgement, and the doctor led them into the ward.

There was only one bed curtained off from the rest of the room, and Edwards pulled the curtains apart to let Finn and Paulsen through. Just for an instant, Finn's thoughts turned to another woman in another hospital bed, but there was no time to dwell. His eyes narrowed as he saw the condition of the woman lying there. Though they'd been warned of her injuries, it was still shocking to see. There was a dressing over the left side of her face and on her left arm. Both her hands were bandaged and the hair on the left side of her scalp was scorched away. What struck him most wasn't the physical injuries, it was the look in her eyes – dead and expressionless. Terrible as her injuries were, she looked as if she was barely aware of them. Barely aware of her surroundings even.

'How bad are the burns?' whispered Finn to Edwards as they approached.

'She should make a full recovery, but the next few weeks are going to be painful.'

That was an understatement, thought Finn. He tried to imagine how the woman in front of them would have looked on Saturday afternoon. In her wedding dress, committing to the man she loved. They were supposed to be in Bali now – lying on a beach without a care in the world. He walked carefully over and took a seat next to the bed.

'Hello, Stephanie, I'm DI Finn and this is my colleague DC Paulsen. How are you bearing up?'

50

She stared ahead, as if she hadn't heard him. He recognised that expression; when your mind was working so hard to absorb something, it was almost impossible to articulate anything. He'd felt like that himself enough times recently.

'How's Neeta?' said Stephanie eventually in a dry voice. Finn glanced up at Paulsen quizzically.

'His mother,' Paulsen whispered in his ear. She turned to the woman in the bed and smiled reassuringly.

'She's being looked after by the family.'

Neeta Kaul, by all accounts, hadn't stopped sobbing for the first twenty-four hours after her son's death. The family liaison officer said she was sat alone in her bedroom rejecting all attempts to console her. An awful lot of trauma counselling was going to be needed and Paulsen wondered whether it would ever be truly enough. Finn gave Stephanie a gentle smile.

'I'm told you wanted to speak with us?'

'Who did this?' she said finally.

'We don't know. We're still looking into the circumstances.'

There was truth to that too, thought Finn. There was still a possibility it was all some sort of tragic accident. It was highly unlikely though. Adesh Kaul neither smoked or vaped. The early forensic work showed no evidence of a phone or any other electronic device which might have exploded, and nobody was seriously going down the spontaneous human combustion route.

'Someone did this to him, didn't they?'

'It's a possibility. We're not ruling anything in or out at this stage. We'll wait and see what evidence the forensics give us and also what the post-mortem shows before we start building a picture.'

'What do *you* think though?'

'I don't. Or at least we don't. It's a misconception from movies and television that we throw around theories and

51

hunches. The reality is we try to be guided by the facts and by evidence, then let that direct us.'

Paulsen was watching Finn as he spoke. His voice was so quiet she could barely hear him, and his tone was easy and conversational. If you'd walked in on them then you might be forgiven for thinking he was family, or at least a close friend. It struck her randomly how smart his appearance was – the closely trimmed hair, the crisply ironed shirt, the carefully moisturised skin. She reminded herself this was a man who'd just cremated his own wife. If he was falling apart, it wasn't showing. Outwardly, anyway.

'But you think he might have been murdered?' said Stephanie.

'Like I say, until we know more, nothing's off the table. Did he have any enemies you can think of?'

'No. That's just it . . . Adesh was the most easy-going guy you could ever meet. He never really lost his temper.'

'There's nobody – no situation – you can think of then?'

She stopped to properly consider the question, then shook her head.

'Is there anyone who might have had a problem with the wedding?'

'No, why would there be?'

'An ex-boyfriend maybe? Someone else who liked you?'

'No, nothing like that either. And both our families were just thrilled to bits. There was no one who was opposed to the marriage, quite the opposite.'

'Did Adesh have any financial problems?'

'No. His business was a success and we were all so proud of him. It was a big risk when he quit the fire brigade but it turned out to be the best thing he ever did. He loved being his own boss.'

She started to cough suddenly, clearly in some discomfort. Edwards poured her a glass of water from a jug on a side table and passed it across, giving Finn a warning glance as he did so. They all waited a moment while Stephanie gulped it down.

'Why did he quit the fire service?' asked Paulsen.

'Why put your life on the line every day when you've built up the expertise to earn good money much more safely?'

'Some people don't like the quiet life?'

Stephanie shook her head.

'There was one fire . . . it was quite traumatic for him, I think. It wasn't the reason he quit but I think it helped make up his mind.'

'Can you remember anything about it?' asked Finn.

'He was one of the first responders at One Pacific Square.'

Paulsen saw Finn react.

'What was it about that one that was different?' he asked.

'A man died. They were too late, I think . . .'

Finn nodded, but Paulsen could see an intensity about him now, as if a switch had been flicked.

'One more night . . .' said Stephanie, almost as if to herself.

'I'm sorry, I don't understand,' said Finn.

'We wanted a baby, and we always said that the most magical thing would be to conceive our child on the night we got married.' The tears were beginning to come now, streaming down her face as she spoke. 'Now it can never happen and I've got nothing.'

Finn nodded his understanding. He was looking her right in the eye as he did so, making a point of it, Paulsen noticed. He wasn't just here acquiring information; he was acknowledging her pain. That it mattered.

'I'm not supposed to make promises. It's the first rule of my profession; never make a promise you might not be able to keep. But I'll say this to you: we'll do our utmost to find out the truth. You have my word on that.'

His words seemed to have the desired effect and she found her equilibrium again.

'The wake is tomorrow. I'd like you to come. You need to see. Then you'll understand. Everyone loved Adesh.'

II

When they returned to Cedar House, Finn assembled his team in the incident room for a briefing. It was his first opportunity to address them as a group since he'd returned, and he was keen to show it was business as usual. More importantly he wanted to pull together the disparate strands of the investigation and work out a plan of attack.

He looked across at Paulsen who was standing awkwardly on her own, her head buried in her phone. It was the first time she'd properly met the rest of the team, and she was showing precious little interest in integrating. Finn could see the disquiet on some of the older faces around her. There was a protocol to such situations which she was wilfully ignoring. It would need watching. Rub people up the wrong way early on, and she'd have a problem for the rest of her time here. More positively, he was grateful to see Jackie Ojo in there. The Thornton Heath murder was now in the hands of Trident, which meant she was free to link up with Finn on the Kaul investigation.

He tried to read the room as he waited for everyone to gather. With the exception of Paulsen, they were all officers he'd worked with for some time. While not all of them necessarily *liked* him, there was a relationship of mutual trust there. Police officers respected results and he'd led them to enough of those over the years. He watched as they drank their coffees and chatted among themselves. He could sense an undercurrent; his bereavement provoking an unspoken discomfort. He'd led countless briefings over the years, but this time he felt strangely uncomfortable. He looked down at the forensic report he'd just been handed, focused on it and took a discreet breath.

'*Kick some arse,*' whispered Karin, and he looked up, cleared his throat and waited for the hubbub to quieten down.

'Right – forensics have given me their preliminary findings. I've also spoken to the fire investigator. There were traces of an accelerant in the hotel toilet cubicle. Not enough to say for certain it was thrown around, but their working theory is the victim was doused in it. We'll know more after the PM.'

There was a ripple around the room. 'That's what happens if you bring cheap booze to a wedding,' said a voice at the back to a few random chuckles, but most were now concentrating. If there'd been any remaining doubt this was somehow an accidental death, it was now gone.

Finn continued. 'That means somebody reached him, overpowered him and soaked him in petrol before setting him alight. All within a matter of minutes. The victim wasn't somebody frail or infirm. This was a former firefighter who'd kept himself in shape. Whoever did this was a match for him.'

He looked around the room and let the implication sink in, then turned and gestured at the whiteboard behind him. There were two photographs of two different men pinned up. On the left was a youthful picture of Adesh Kaul taken from his firefighting days.

'This is what we know about Kaul. Born and bred in Harlesden, he was with the LFB until five years ago, when he quit to set up his own fire risk consultancy. Early indications are that it was a success. He worked on his own, but given how he died, I'd like to know if he made any mistakes. Any major blazes where someone died or was put out of business, for example. So let's talk with the LFB and cross-check with his client list.' He took a sip from the glass of water on the table next to him, his earlier nerves starting to dissipate now he was in full flow. 'Let's also have a dig through his personal life. Sami, I'd like you to look into the family. See if there's been any issues. I'm not specifically thinking this is a hate crime, but let's establish if they've had any problems recently.' A young DC sat near the front nodded and started to scribble furiously in his pocketbook.

'What about the widow?' said one of the older men who'd been viewing Paulsen with such suspicion earlier.

'Stephanie Kaul, or Stephanie Clough as she was known up until the weekend, works . . .' he looked uncertainly down at his notes, '. . . as a content manager for some firm in Fitzrovia. You all know me well enough by now to know I haven't got an effing clue what that involves.' There was a murmur of laughter which buoyed him a little more. 'But Rog, can you go and pay them a visit – see if she had any admirers who might not have liked the idea of her getting hitched.' He turned to face the room again. 'One further detail: Adesh Kaul quit his job not long after attending the blaze at One Pacific Square.'

'He was *there*?' said Ojo immediately.

Finn nodded.

'I doubt there's a connection, but it's worth noting he was one of the first responders at the scene, one of the first who actually went into the building.'

He looked around the room again and noted the raised eyebrows on one or two faces. He wasn't surprised.

Most people remembered or knew the story because it was a cause célèbre at the time. One Pacific Square was supposed to herald a new commercial dawn for London. Its lofty ambition was to expand the financial service sector south of the river from its traditional home in the Square

57

Mile. The skyscraper at the centre of the complex was intended to become as iconic as One Canada Square in Canary Wharf. So it was more than just the semi-built tower that the flames destroyed – a dream of sorts died too. There was a rebuilding project after the fire, but it faltered as fears over Brexit gave its investors pause for thought. When it was finally completed two years late and over budget, One Pacific Square was no longer the new economic hub once imagined, but was confined to the single high-rise building that bore its name – home to a handful of finance firms, but no more than that.

'For those unfamiliar with what happened, the fire took place while the tower was under construction. The cause was an old kettle being used by workmen which was left plugged into an even older extension cable. The fire burnt for nearly two days and it took over two hundred firefighters from stations all over the city to extinguish it. There was just one fatality though . . .' Finn pointed to the second picture up on the whiteboard. It looked to have been taken somewhere on the African continent. A bare-chested man with curly golden hair was standing proudly with a rifle, next to the bloodied corpse of a dead giraffe. He was staring down the camera lens with a barely disguised leer.

'As many of you may recall, the dead man was an individual called Erik Whitlock. Whitlock was well known to police at the time as a money launderer, and a good one as well. He was widely believed to be the same individual who'd laundered the proceeds of a high-value raid on a security van in Hertfordshire earlier that year.'

'The Stansted heist?' said a voice at the back. It belonged to Dave McGilligott; a young, slightly facetious detective constable, who in truth wasn't one of Finn's favourites.

'Come on, Dave – you been on Mars for the last five years?'

said someone. 'You've got to remember Dave's only twelve years old,' said another, and the room sniggered.

'Yeah, Dave, the robbery that was plastered across every newspaper in the country for a month,' said Ojo.

'Oh – *that* one. Course I've heard of it,' said McGilligott with a wide grin, and then began to sing.

'Who can rob at sunrise?
Sprinkle it with gold
Cover it in diamonds and a miracle or two?
The Handyman. The Handyman can . . .'

The room winced at his out-of-tune warbling, and Finn waited for the laughter to subside. It wasn't the first time he'd heard this bastardisation of the old Sammy Davis Jr. classic. The crime remained unsolved and with each passing year it became more of an urban legend. It was up there with Brink's-Mat and Hatton Garden now in its notoriety. Despite numerous arrests over the years, none of the major players had ever been caught. There still remained a debate whether they'd even been accurately identified. The investigating team were a laughing stock while the robbers were the subject of endless colourful speculation.

As the room quietened, Finn gave McGilligott a glare of sub-zero contempt.

'I don't want to hear that again. Not even as a joke. That goes for all of you – we're not breathing life into that old fairy story.'

'I don't understand,' said Paulsen suddenly. 'Who's the Handyman?'

'A myth,' snapped Finn. 'Supposedly some all-powerful underworld figure behind the Stansted heist, but he doesn't exist. Current thinking is several well-established career criminals teamed up to do it. There's a unit in Hertfordshire still dying on its arse trying to follow the money. You know how the papers like to spin this stuff – they want you to believe there's a Michael Caine type leading a team of loveable old rogues. But it's bollocks. There is no "Handyman" – probably just a bunch of ex-cons sipping sangria by the Med now.'

'What's this got to do with Kaul?' asked Paulsen. Whether she was aware of it or not – and Finn's money was on the latter – she was getting more of those side glances again.

'Quite possibly, absolutely nothing. But did he come into contact with Whitlock that night? Is there a connection? Also the manner of Kaul's death suggests the killer was no amateur. It's more the sort of killing you'd associate with Whitlock's mates. It's an unlikely link, but let's keep an open mind. It's a line of inquiry, until it isn't.'

'Have we spoken to his old station?' asked Ojo. Finn nodded.

'Uniform put in a call earlier, and haven't flagged anything up. Kaul's wake is tomorrow and I'm going. If any of his old crew are there, I'll reach out to them. In the meantime, Jacks, I want the names of everyone who was at the wedding – who we've spoken to, and who we haven't.'

Ojo nodded, and Finn turned to a man in his late forties, another of the older officers who seemed less than impressed by Paulsen.

'Let's check where we are with the CCTV coverage and ANPR. There's cameras in the hotel forecourt, and there's some I spotted on the surrounding approach roads too. Uniform were rounding it up.'

He then turned to a young woman draining the last of an instant coffee from a heavily chipped mug.

'Nishat – keep in touch with SOCO and the fire investigation team. See if anything else comes out, and I'd like to know more about that accelerant they found. Ring the pathologist as well, find out exactly what time the post-mortem's been scheduled for.'

With that, Finn signalled the end of the briefing. The room started to disperse with quiet efficiency and Paulsen found herself alone.

'What do you want me to do?' she asked Finn.

'Look into Kaul's fire consultancy and see how well it was doing. Stephanie seemed to think it was pretty successful. Keep looking into his finances. If he paid for the whole wedding let's find out how he managed it. It was a good spot earlier . . . now follow it up. See where it takes you.'

Paulsen nodded and headed off, glad to have a mission and a compliment. For a moment Finn took in the incident room; it was how he liked it. Everyone focused, everyone clear. He turned on his heels and left them to it.

'The fucking Handyman? Do me a favour,' said John Skegman, holding his head in his hands. 'The link's spurious to say the least, and the Pacific Square fire was five years ago. That's a whole lot of time for Kaul to have made any number of enemies. You might as well blame Donald sodding Trump.'

Finn was standing in Skegman's office. He'd never realised before how awkward the DCI sounded when he swore.

'He was with the crew who found Erik Whitlock's body. There were hundreds of firefighters there that night, but Kaul was one of the four who went in first.'

Skegman thought about it with the expression of a man with badly trapped wind.

'It's that Cambridge education of yours, Alex. Makes you overthink stuff,' Skegman muttered. Finn rolled his eyes, and didn't mind letting it show. Skegman hadn't gone to university and was oddly prickly about the fact. It wasn't the first time he'd made a crack like that and Finn doubted it would be the last. He suppressed his irritation and smiled politely instead.

'I'm not proposing to put it at the centre of the investigation. I'm just flagging up the link, however tenuous.'

'The Stansted heist is a Pandora's box – ask any senior officer in the country. You're talking five years of taxpayers' money that's been chucked away by Chapel Row.'

Chapel Row was the station in Hertfordshire where the unit charged with investigating the robbery was based. Their lack of progress was a standing joke within the police service. It was a smaller team these days than at the outset, in line with their reduced funding, but it would remain operational. The investigation was too high-profile to simply be forgotten. The general feeling was they'd missed their moment and the trail was, if not cold, then certainly lukewarm.

'Look, I don't believe in him either, but there've been a number of deaths,' persisted Finn. 'On the periphery. People who knew people connected to suspects. The suggestion's always been it was the so-called Handyman tying up loose ends. It's how he earnt his name after all.'

That much was true. The first victim attributed to him was stabbed through the eye with a screwdriver, while the second was battered to death with a claw hammer. It was the tabloids who'd come up with the name because he seemed to be working his way through the toolbox.

'Someone was behind Stansted,' continued Finn. 'And they were good – it was well planned and well executed. Whoever was responsible was a pro, and I'm happy to call him the Handyman or the Bogeyman or whatever you want. The manner of Adesh Kaul's death, the fact there's a loose connection to Erik Whitlock . . . don't we have to look into it? If for no other reason than to rule it out?'

Skegman thought about it for a moment and then sighed.

'Alright, talk to Chapel Row. See what their take is on it.

The sooner we can move on from it, the happier I'll be. How's Paulsen getting on, by the way?'

Finn considered his answer, and Skegman smiled.

'Yes, she does rather have that effect.'

'There's definite signs of potential, but I'm not sure she's going out of her way to make friends. It's an interesting approach on your first day.'

'Why don't you send her up to Hertfordshire? Someone who can get under their skins might not be the worst thing. I imagine it'll be the most excitement they've had in ages.'

If Skegman was expecting a smile in response it didn't come. The pause made him look up and search out Finn's face.

'And what about you? How are you bearing up?' There was warmth to his tone but a steel behind the eyes.

'I'm fine, sir. It's good to be back. Honest.'

He met Skegman's gaze, then turned briskly and walked towards the door without waiting for a reply.

'*Liar*,' said Karin.

12

The village was as English as an English village could be. There was a green, a small row of shops and even a working red telephone box next to the war memorial. It possessed one small pub which was packed every night. You could call it sleepy, but those who lived there would proudly tell you otherwise.

In one of the small houses a street or two behind the green, an alarm clock rang. A slightly built man in his late fifties with greying hair swung his legs out of bed, picked up his glasses from the bedside table and rose.

The sober tones of the *Today* programme on Radio Four chattered in the background, as he washed and groomed. He used an old-fashioned shaving brush, with shaving cream delivered directly from his favourite barber in Mayfair. He Brylcreemed his hair, ensuring not a single strand was left untouched. His neatly ironed and pressed clothes were laid out where he'd left them the night before – a crisp white shirt with silver cufflinks, a pin-striped waistcoat, dark corduroy trousers and immaculately polished black leather shoes. As always after dressing, he flicked open the gold pocket watch laid next to the clothes, listened to the mechanism ticking in perfect harmony and fastened it to his waistcoat.

Breakfast consisted of a grapefruit and two slices of heavily buttered thick brown toast, slathered liberally with strong

English marmalade. He drank tea from the pot; a milky Assam which he sugared the way his mother used to, taking a small silver spoon and holding it just beneath the surface, circling it around the cup to enable the maximum infusion of flavour.

A copy of *The Times* was delivered every morning, and after breakfast he allowed himself the luxury of forty-five minutes before work to read through it properly. In his view it didn't just pay to be abreast, it was critical. Scrutinising the front page, he tutted to himself as he read the Governor of the Bank of England's latest fiscal predictions. There'd likely be a general election before the end of the year, he mused. Another headline caught his attention:

'Blaze kills groom at own wedding'.

As he read through the article, one line in particular stood out:

'Kaul was one of the first firefighters to attend the blaze at One Pacific Square, and resigned from the fire service not long afterwards.'

He read the article for a second time to be sure he'd assimilated all the information correctly, then carefully closed the newspaper and ran his tongue across his lower lip. It was probably nothing, but he was not a man who liked loose ends, however insignificant. He strode into the living room where there was a large mahogany desk at the far end.

The sun was shining through the windows and it looked like it was going to be a glorious day. He took a set of keys from his pocket, and unlocked a small drawer at the side of the desk. Inside were at least seven different mobile phones piled on top of each other. Selecting the one he wanted, he turned it on and tapped out a text.

We need to talk – call me.

He peered out of the window and nodded to himself approvingly; it was indeed shaping up to be a beautiful morning.

13

Paulsen took the train to Hertfordshire, stopping briefly to grab a sandwich at Liverpool Street station. She'd resisted the urge to call Nancy for a whinge while she wolfed it down. She was sure she was being sent on the schlepp simply because she was the new girl. She'd seen some of the dinosaurs sizing her up in the incident room and wondered if they were now enjoying a laugh at her expense. They were different with Ojo she'd noticed, but then she was a detective sergeant. New station, same old nonsense.

Finn was adamant a phone call wouldn't suffice – she needed to see the evidence Chapel Row possessed in person. So a day which began in deepest south London was now taking her to the Essex–Herts borders. The police station was based in the bowels of an industrial estate just outside Bishop's Stortford. Before setting off she'd spoken on the phone to a DI Andy Warrender, the man currently charged with leading the investigation into the Stansted robbery. He'd been courteous, but she detected an underlying suspicion after she'd explained her reasons for calling. In person, Warrender was in his mid-forties, with straight blond hair and jowly pink features. He'd made her a cup of tea in a messy kitchen area, before leading her through to a narrow corridor of small offices where his team were based. They were one floor up from the station's main CID, but she sensed the divide from the rest of the place immediately. They might as well be in Scotland.

'Explain to me again why you think there's a connection with your homicide? Suspected homicide,' Warrender corrected himself sharply. Paulsen explained Adesh Kaul was one of the first responders at Pacific Square and Warrender nodded.

'Erik Whitlock is a man we've thoroughly investigated, of course. You think your man might have crossed paths with him that night?'

'It's one line of inquiry. We're trying to track down some of the fire crew on the same watch who were with him. My governor sent me up here for thoroughness' sake, I think. To help us rule out the connection.'

'So you've got a man who might have crossed paths with Whitlock on the night of the fire, then five years later gets burnt to death at his own wedding . . .' He weighed it up. 'I can see why you might want to ask the question at least. What do you want to know?'

'Tell me about the Handyman for a start?'

Given the way Finn described the man – part urban legend, part tabloid invention – she wasn't sure what kind of reaction to expect. But Warrender nodded, as if he'd been half-expecting it.

'It depends on who you believe he is. What you read in the papers tends to be a mix of the truth, bad journalism and out-and-out bollocks. The fact is, there's several people who fit the bill. We've ruled most of them out for one reason or another and narrowed it down to one man. If you want to call him the Handyman, knock yourself out.'

'And who's that?'

'Patience. I'll come to that, but first we need to go back to the beginning. Let me take you through what happened on the day.'

He took her over to a wall in the main office, whose entire

breadth seemed to have been given over to a pictorial reconstruction.

'A security guard and a driver were transporting cash belonging to a Swiss bank from a cargo depot at Stansted Airport to a British bank in central London. Armed men intercepted the van on an A road only a few miles into their journey. The sacks of cash were transferred into a red Subaru, while the van's guard and driver were tied up and dumped out of the way.' As he spoke he pointed at blurry CCTV images of the Subaru, and a patch of scrubland where the two luckless men were left.

'The robbers did their homework. They knew exactly where the most vulnerable part of the route was. They were able to wait in nearby woodland, while a motorcycle rider trailed the van ready to give the signal. They also knew the names of the guard and driver's wives and children. They knew which care home the driver's mother was living in, and they knew what colour outfit the guard's wife was wearing when she dropped off her three-year-old at nursery school that morning.'

Warrender ushered her over to another wall, and Paulsen couldn't shake the feeling it was like being in a museum. It felt as if she was being shown carefully preserved exhibits rather than the kind of live investigation she'd seen in the incident room at Cedar House earlier.

'The burnt-out wreckage of the Subaru was found in a side street in Ipswich two days later. The stolen motorbike we found in a car park in St Albans.'

'What do you think happened to the money then?' asked Paulsen.

'Well, I'm as convinced as I can be that Erik Whitlock dealt with that. He was an experienced money launderer – almost the go-to guy in the UK at the time for a job of that magnitude.'

69

'But the money disappeared?' asked Paulsen.

'Yes. The key question has always been whether Whitlock managed to launder it before he died, or whether his death forced the robbers into doing something else. If he did manage to take care of it, then my strong suspicion is most of the cash is no longer in the country. If he didn't, then it's likely still here in some form.' Warrender crossed his arms.

He looked and sounded defensive, Paulsen thought, and she remembered Finn's words from the briefing. This investigating team was one of the most derided in the country. She felt a sudden sympathy for Warrender. It was easy to mock from a distance. As if reading her mind, he smiled unexpectedly.

'We're following leads in both directions, here and abroad. Which all brings us back to your first question about the Handyman.'

He ushered her to a corner of the wall in front of them, and pointed at a small black-and-white photograph of a man. He looked like an old-fashioned tailor. The face was heavily lined, with Brylcreemed grey hair.

'I've got good reason to suspect this is the man in question. His name is Raymond Spinney. He's a career criminal who started out as a pickpocket, graduated to house burglaries, then finally on to armed robberies. He was behind a series of raids over a three-year period on post offices in Holloway, Clapham, Leyton and Ealing.' Warrender waited a moment as Paulsen worked it out.

'North, south, east and west London?'

'Exactly. One after the other – never in person. But the gang members we've managed to nick over the years have built an interesting picture. Spinney planned the raids with expert precision. Every eventuality was thought through. Who was likely to be inside, how fast it would take an armed response team to get there, all of it. Nothing was left to chance.'

'And you believe he's behind the Stansted robbery because of his previous MO? That it fits?'

'In part. I don't think it's a huge stretch to think he got bored of robbing post offices and wanted a crack at something bigger. The facts support it too – those post office raids came to a halt just months before the Stansted heist. I can also directly connect Spinney to Erik Whitlock: Whitlock was the man who laundered the proceeds of the post office jobs.'

'Hold on,' said Paulsen, cutting in. 'If Whitlock was such a known launderer, why wasn't he was in prison?'

'He was, at various stages, but he was smart. There's a reason why he was regarded as the best in the business – because he learnt from his mistakes. By the time he died, pinning anything on him was pretty much impossible.'

'So have you found anything that directly connects him to the Stansted money?'

'All I can tell you is this: within weeks of the Pacific Square fire, Ray Spinney disappears off the face of the earth. Not a trace of him. His launderer dies, and Spinney goes to ground. Go figure.'

Paulsen tried to take it all in. A huge heist, where both the money and the prime suspect disappeared, with the one man who could connect it all long dead. She didn't envy Warrender.

'If I knew where Spinney was I'd be ninety per cent closer to solving this. So that's my story, DC Paulsen. Does any of that help?'

Paulsen frowned. The truthful answer was not really, but she didn't want to return to Cedar House empty-handed.

'My DI said a number of people connected to the Stansted heist have been killed over the last few years?'

'The so-called "Stansted curse", you mean, as our friends in the tabloids like to call it?' He walked over to a desk and pulled out a file, which he passed across to her.

71

'You're welcome to wade through this. Lewis Huxton was stabbed through the eye with a screwdriver outside his house over the May bank holiday. He'd done time previously for one of the post office raids in Leyton, linked to Spinney. Terry Wu was battered to death with a claw hammer in Hackney in 2016, Wayne Francis was stabbed after a row in a car park in Bromley and Jerry Ademola was found face down in the bath of a B&B in Harlow. I can link all these men tenuously to Spinney. Can I prove anything? No.'

Paulsen started to flick through the file.

'These men were either all criminals, or known associates,' she said. 'That's the difference with Adesh Kaul.' She frowned. 'Did you ever look into the fire crews who attended One Pacific Square?'

'Why would we have? There were over two hundred of them on the night.'

'The fire killed one of your key players. Weren't you interested in talking to at least the first responders to find out exactly what happened?'

'We were interested in what Whitlock was doing there, but as everything was incinerated, we'll never know. Some routine interviews were done, but that was the extent of it. Nothing significant came from them, from what I recall.'

'You must have thoughts of your own about why he was there?' Paulsen persisted. Warrender shrugged.

'My best guess has always been he was meeting someone. But like I say, it's a secret he took to the grave with him.'

Paulsen felt overloaded, as if a picture was building but she couldn't see quite what it was yet. There was also a strong possibility that there was nothing there at all.

'There could be any number of reasons why your man was murdered,' said Warrender. 'Just as likely, there's a psycho ex-boyfriend of the bride who didn't want her getting married. You've got a long way to go before you can draw a line between your dead firefighter and Ray Spinney.'

Paulsen glanced at a clock on the wall. It was a long way back to Cedar House. She needed to ask one more question and she'd deliberately left it to last.

'I'm sorry to bring this up but as I'm sure you're aware, there's a lot of speculation the robbers have always escaped arrest because they've got an inside man. Someone within the police service?'

Warrender pulled a face of tired irritation.

'Not a chance. Again, tabloid bollocks. As far as this team's concerned, every officer's been vetted by me personally. I'd vouch for any of them.'

In an office across the corridor, DS Mike Godden swore out loud to himself. He was sat peering at his computer screen wondering if he needed new reading glasses as he looked at the figures in front of him. Squinting at these sodding screens all day just gave him a headache. The job hadn't always been like this; he was sure of it. He wished he was a few years closer to retirement age.

'Who's that with the governor?'

The voice belonged to young DC Jim Farmer. He was new, on attachment from uniform. Worse, he was *keen*. Like an effing Labrador. Always bouncing around just behind you. Godden peered over his glasses at the attractive woman with the dark hair Warrender was escorting out of the building. She gave the DI an unexpectedly radiant smile before shaking his hand and departing.

'She's fit – I'll say that,' said Farmer conspiratorially.

'Don't go all laddish on me, Jim. It doesn't suit you.'

'Like you hadn't noticed, Mike . . .'

73

Before he could respond Godden heard a noise which made the retort die in his throat.

'Yeah, you're not wrong,' he said with a wink, waiting as Farmer laughed before mercifully sauntering away.

Godden paused a moment to make sure he was alone, and then took a mobile phone out from his drawer. His own personal device was sat charging next to him on his desk. He looked down at the pay-as-you-go in his hand, which rarely did anything except sit in his drawer, ignored. But it was always with him, always fully charged. He'd heard it vibrate with an incoming message and the sound chilled him to the bone. It was a reminder. There was a message on it from much earlier in the day, and he'd missed it. He felt his mouth dry up as he read the six words on the screen.

We need to talk – call me.

14

The following day Finn woke in a state of woolly amnesia. As consciousness slowly returned, with it came an awareness of something fundamentally wrong. Then came a hazy confusion about precisely what, until finally the memory kicked in again: *Oh, yeah – that.*

He reached across the bed to the empty space next to him and let his arm rest there. He thought about the wake he'd be going to later, so soon after Karin's. But he'd asked for this, almost begged Skegman for the opportunity, so there could be no room for self-pity. And he'd been pleased with his first day back. It felt good to be in the thick of an investigation again, back to his daily patterns. In routine he found order, and in order he found focus.

After rising, Finn always drank a pint of tap water, followed by a quick shower and then a double espresso, grinding his own beans – Ethiopian Yirgacheffe by preference. Then, over a breakfast of granola and fresh fruit, he perused the BBC News website on his phone and flicked through Twitter. He was a voracious follower of events on social media, and when violent crime spiked in the capital he monitored the electronic fall-out closely.

Adesh Kaul wasn't the only fatality that week; a sixteen-year-old boy was dead after a stabbing in Tottenham, and a seventeen-year-old had been gunned down in Stratford. As usual the Mayor of London was criticising the government for the cuts imposed on the Metropolitan Police. Equally predictably, the government's response was to highlight their investment in anti-knife and gun strategies. It would have taken press officers at City Hall and Whitehall mere minutes to draft their standard statements, he thought. As someone at the sharp end, the cuts *did* make a difference. Nobody leading a murder investigation would say otherwise. He and Karin used to discuss it at length, their respective jobs giving them unique perspectives on the problem. They both agreed something fundamental needed to change, but neither of them were optimistic it was going to happen anytime soon. He'd sat in interview rooms looking into the eyes of too many fifteen-year-old killers. Nobody was giving them a reason *not* to carry a knife, and all he saw was an increasingly lonely and lost generation. He stared at the image of another bloodstained crime scene, then looked over at the empty chair opposite; he really wasn't helping himself.

On the other side of south London, in a small but beautifully maintained house in Richmond, Mei Tsukuda opened her front door and greeted the man outside with a polite welcome. Stuart Portbury was carrying his toolbox and smiled pleasantly. She led him through to her bathroom and his heart sank; he'd been dreading this. The wall behind the toilet was peeling badly. Something somewhere was leaking and he hated fixing toilets. Kitchen sinks were bad enough, but the likelihood was that once he started to trace the leak, he'd be knee-deep in shit. Literally. But this was Mei, so he'd make sure the job was done to perfection.

'Would you like some tea first?' she offered politely.

'Yes, please; black, no sugar,' he replied with equal courtesy.

'Of course. I remember,' she said. 'You're very early today, Stuart, is there a reason?'

'Yes, I have a wake to attend later, I'm afraid.'

A look of concern crossed her face.

'I'm sorry,' she said.

'It's alright. It's not anyone close. Just someone I used to work with. Don't worry, this job should only take a couple of hours. There'll be plenty of time for me to freshen up and change.'

'You didn't have to come today. It could have waited until another time.'

'I promised you I'd come, and I never break my promises.'

She smiled, and he felt his heart beat faster.

Everything was already out of sync, thought Phil Maddox. He'd woken too early, eaten too early and dressed too early. Now there was too much time to kill before setting off.

For all that, he was looking forward to the day. Martin Walker called him back twenty-four hours after they'd spoken on the phone. He'd stressed how important it was they tried to keep their contact to a minimum. His tone was condescending. It was easy to forget how up himself the man could be and the passing of time clearly hadn't changed that. Then the invitation to the wake came through the door and Walker called a second time. He'd slept on things apparently, and decided it would look more suspicious if Adesh Kaul's old crewmates *weren't* there to pay their respects. Maddox couldn't have been more delighted.

He'd always found forming relationships difficult. He'd loved the camaraderie of being a firefighter and with it the sense of being part of a team who looked out for one another. He knew they weren't necessarily best mates, but the feeling of an unshakeable bond hadn't left him. They may not have the job any more, but they shared something else now. They shared a secret – and if there was someone out there, someone who'd discovered it, they'd need each other again.

His reverie was interrupted by the sound of a ringing phone and he recognised the number immediately.

'Mads!' said a booming voice. It belonged unmistakably to Gary Elder and hadn't lost its volume in five years.

'Gary . . .'

'Don't sound so surprised, mate! Just wanted to see if you were going today?'

'Of course I am.'

'Thank fuck for that. I got a call from Marty last night, pretty much ordering me. Cheeky bastard still thinks he's in charge.'

'Yeah, I got that call too.'

'What about Stu, is he coming?'

'Yeah, I spoke to him yesterday. He's devastated.' He heard Elder blowing through his teeth.

'Horrible business though, eh? Poor old Adesh, who'd want to do that to him?'

'That's what's worrying me, Gal.'

'You what?'

Surely it'd crossed his mind, thought Maddox. It *must* have.

'We shouldn't talk about it, not over the phone,' said Maddox quickly.

'Christ. You're sounding as paranoid as Walker.'

'I just think we ought to be careful.'

'You really think it might be connected?'

'I don't know what I think.'

'It was probably just an accident, mate. Adesh went for a crafty fag and it all went horribly wrong. How many scenes like that did we deal with back in the day, eh?' Something about his tone didn't quite convince.

'Maybe. I'll see you later, Gary. It'll be good to catch up.'

'Yeah, you too, mate.'

The line went dead. Maddox glanced up at the clock on his wall but it was only 8.15. He was starting to feel sick.

Martin Walker knotted his tie and looked in the mirror. He looked tired and there was a jaundiced pallor to his skin. He'd experienced a mixture of emotions since Adesh Kaul's death. There'd been fear, first and foremost. He fancied himself as someone who could smell when trouble was brewing, and his every instinct was telling him this was the first domino to fall and more would follow. Then there was Adesh himself. He could remember his first day, taking him to one side, looking him in the eye and liking what he saw. There'd been a quiet willingness about him with plenty of raw courage. All the ingredients were there, and he'd matured into a fine firefighter. He should still be doing it. Fighting blazes, saving lives. They all should.

'Marty! Do you want a cup of tea before you go?' It was Christine, calling from downstairs.

'Love one – be down in a sec,' he shouted back.

He wondered how it would go today when he saw the rest of them. Part of him was almost looking forward to the reunion. They'd been through so much together, but he hoped they'd use their brains. What happened to Adesh was terrifying. If someone *knew*, then they'd need to tread carefully. But how could they have been found out? It was impossible.

Despite the wedding venue in deepest south London, the Kaul family home was north of the river in Harlesden. Finn found himself outside a large five-bedroom house in a quiet suburban backstreet. The front door was wide open when he arrived. Mourners largely dressed in white were milling in numbers around the front garden. The sense of shock in the air was still palpable. If he felt awkward, there was no need; nobody seemed to even notice him.

Ordinarily there'd be a body, and traditionally there'd be a cremation within twenty-four hours. But the manner of death robbed the family of both body and dignity. What remained of Adesh Kaul was still with the coroner and would be for some time. With so many people having travelled far and wide for the wedding, the family wanted to proceed with *something*. Guests who'd come to London for a wedding now found themselves at a wake.

As he entered, Finn could hear a long, slow moan of anguish. He found his way into the living room and was greeted by a sight which in any other context would be beautiful. There were flowers everywhere; expensive ornate vases and bouquets festooned the room. A large framed picture of the victim surrounded by a number of small religious icons took pride of place on a large table almost completely covered by flora. Adesh Kaul stared out at Finn from the photograph. He'd been handsome in life, sharp boyish features with charismatic brown eyes, topped with a glossy mop of black hair. An image of Stephanie Kaul lying like a broken doll in her hospital bed flashed though his mind. He remembered what he'd felt then and the same thought struck him again – they should be on their honeymoon.

It took him a moment to notice the agonised howling had finally stopped. He turned and saw an elderly woman with long grey hair sat in an armchair, sobbing. It wasn't hard to deduce that it was Adesh's mother Neeta. A younger man and woman were trying to console her, but she could only raise a hand limply at them. Finn wasn't sure if she was acknowledging their sympathy or trying to tell them not to bother.

'Thank you for coming,' said a quiet voice behind him. He turned and was surprised to see Stephanie dressed in a traditional white saree. The state she'd been in on the previous day, he doubted the doctors could possibly have sanctioned this. She was as pale as a ghost and moved slowly and deliberately, clearly in great pain. Her face and hands remained wrapped in dressings. There was an ugly red weal on the side of her head where her hair was burnt away, and he couldn't stop himself recoiling.

'Nothing was going to stop me coming today,' she said, as if reading his mind. 'I had to be here, do you understand?' Her voice trailed off and Finn didn't argue. He understood only too well how lonely she would have felt lying in a hospital bed while her husband's family gathered.

'Is there any news?' she asked. Finn nodded and asked if there was somewhere they could talk privately.

She led him through the house and as they walked, he noticed a trio of well-built men talking together in the conservatory. His eyes lingered on them as a fourth man arrived and was warmly greeted. They were the firefighters, he was sure of it. He'd worked with enough of them over the years to recognise the type. The oldest, a burly man with greying hair, caught Finn's eye and sized him up in return.

Stephanie was at the foot of a staircase. She turned awkwardly and asked for his help, and they slowly went up a step at a time. She led him across the landing to a small bedroom, which seemed to be doubling as a cloakroom. Finn moved some of the coats on the bed and she sat down, visibly grateful.

'The woman in the chair – that's Adesh's mother. The young man with her is Ajay, Adesh's brother, and Gurpreet, one of his nieces.'

'How are they all coping?'

'They're not. Ajay's not right. He broke down last night, drank a bottle of whisky and slept on the floor under that picture of Adesh. He's only got his act together today because his mother's in an even worse state.'

'I can't imagine how they're feeling.'

'This is what I wanted you to see. How loved he was.'

'How are you bearing up? You really should be at the hospital, you know.'

He said the words gently but firmly and she nodded in acknowledgement.

'I'm taking it hour by hour. But please . . . tell me how your investigation is going?'

There'd been some fresh updates earlier in the morning and Finn was grateful to have something concrete to relay. None of it was likely to make Stephanie feel much better though.

'The preliminary pathologist report has confirmed traces of an accelerant on Adesh's body.' Stephanie looked confused, and Finn took a deep breath. 'We think he was doused in it. We'll know for certain by the end of the week.' She closed her eyes, and he continued. 'Despite the fire there's also some minute traces of blood on the toilet cubicle wall. Forensics believe it *could* be consistent with signs of a struggle. We're still working on that. We've also got a witness statement from one of the hotel staff, who thinks he saw someone follow Adesh into the toilet. We're formally treating his death as suspicious now.'

There was a long pause, then she slowly shook her head.

'Why? I just don't understand why . . . ?'

Finn didn't know what to say. Not because of the question; it was one he'd been asked many times over the years. He felt paralysed because it was exactly what he'd been asking himself since Karin's death. The look on Stephanie's face was the same one he'd seen in his bedroom mirror earlier.

They spoke a little longer, and Finn promised to keep her updated. She thanked him, and then he pleaded with her to return to hospital. She assured him she would soon and he escorted her back out on to the landing. She was immediately greeted by another mourner who began to console her. Finn went to follow them downstairs but then something strange happened.

He stopped.

Stephanie turned to see where he was and he quickly made an excuse about needing to make a phone call. He retreated back to the bedroom where he stood with his back to the door, propping it shut. He felt sick; sweat was forming on his brow. His breathing was laboured. Was this a panic attack? He went over to the window and pulled it open. There was a welcome breeze across his face and he took several large gulps of air. It was Stephanie who'd brought this on. Her raw emotion, the pain of her loss . . . he could feel his own tears welling up now and he tried to get a grip. '*Not now*,' he said under his breath. He needed to go downstairs and talk to those firefighters. He just didn't want to. He didn't want to do anything, he felt paralysed. He just wanted Karin back, to talk to her, for everything to go back to how it was. The unfairness of it was overwhelming. He was a man who believed he could solve any problem in life, but he couldn't solve this one. He slammed his fist against the wall and tried to steady himself again. Was this rock bottom and if so, what came next? He wondered what Karin would say and tried to summon her, but this time the voice at the back of his head was quiet.

He'd deceived them, he thought. Skegman, Ojo, Paulsen – his whole team. Stephanie Kaul and all the people in this house too. He wasn't remotely ready for this. He shouldn't have come back. He slid down on to the floor and closed his eyes. After a few minutes he heard voices outside the door and he picked himself up. He couldn't go on like this, he thought. For the first time in a long time, perhaps for the first time ever, he wasn't sure he was fully in control of himself. And when he finally went back downstairs, the men he'd come there to talk to were gone.

15

'He was police, I'm telling you.'

Martin Walker looked nervously around the pub as he whispered the words to the other three men at the table.

'Seriously, Marty, you need to chill,' boomed Elder, taking a swig of his pint and bringing it back down with a bang. 'Obviously the cops are interested. A bloke dies in a fire at his own wedding – you think they're not going to be looking into it? There's no reason to think it's anything to do with us.' He said it with more bravado than he felt.

'Keep your fucking voice down, Gary,' hissed Walker.

'Oh, for God's sake. It means nothing to anyone here. And look around you – the place is deserted,' said Elder.

They'd left the wake early after Walker saw Finn with Stephanie Kaul. He may not look like a typical copper, but Finn's bearing gave him away. Walker knew police when he saw them. The brief moment their eyes met, there'd been mutual recognition, service to service, and it was enough to spook him.

The small backstreet pub they'd found was quiet and usefully out of the way.

'The skipper's right,' said Maddox. 'We don't know enough yet. We need to be careful.'

'He's not the skipper any more, Phil,' said Elder.

'We need to stay calm. Since the weekend I've been trying to figure this out,' said Walker.

'You think I haven't?' said Maddox.

'Phil – please. Just listen for a minute.'

Walker leant in, keeping his voice low.

'We all went into this with our eyes open. We all knew there was a possibility someone might work it out.'

'How? It all *burnt*,' said Elder. 'There was nothing left. Unless someone's opened their mouth?' He looked around the table. 'Well?'

'Don't be stupid,' said Maddox. Portbury and Walker both shook their heads.

'That just leaves Adesh, and I doubt he'd have said anything,' said Elder.

'We can't assume anything,' said Portbury.

'Exactly,' replied Walker. 'We have to accept it's possible someone knows what we did. We can't bury our heads in the sand.' There was silence as the words sank in.

'Jesus Christ,' said Maddox, shaking his head as he took a sip of his Diet Coke.

'What are you suggesting, Martin?' said Portbury.

'Where we have to be careful is in not panicking. Because if what happened to Adesh was nothing to do with it, then we don't want to draw attention to ourselves either.'

'So what *are* we going to do then?' said Elder.

'I'm going to set up a WhatsApp group for us.'

'Oh, brilliant. Genius. That'll sort everything out,' said Maddox.

'*Phil . . .*' Walker's tone of voice was the sort usually reserved for errant toddlers running amok in supermarkets.

'You were the one who always said we needed to stay away from each other!' Maddox protested.

'Listen to me,' said Walker, channelling his old authority. 'That's changed. We've all been to the wake now. We've been *seen* together. If anyone comes knocking, then we're just a

bunch of old workmates who reconnected after a terrible tragedy. It's fine. We can use the WhatsApp group to stay in
contact. There's nothing suspicious about it but use your
heads. If there's anything the rest of us need to know, use the
group – but be careful what you say on there.' He looked
around the table. 'Agreed?' Slowly they all nodded.

'Thanks, Dad,' said Elder, rolling his eyes.

'I'd like to say something,' said Portbury suddenly, 'while
we're all together.' The other three turned to look at him. 'I
think we should all raise a glass to Adesh. Don't you?'

The drive back to Cedar House helped focus Finn's mind. He
was trying to bury the memory of what happened at the wake.
He'd managed to pull himself together but was now feeling
ashamed. Like so many of the emotions he'd been feeling in
the past few weeks, it was unusual and unwelcome. Losing
those firemen – and he was certain that's who they were – was
a schoolboy error. He'd immediately rung the London Fire
Brigade and requested a list of the other firefighters who'd
served with Kaul at Earlsfield Fire Station five years ago. It
didn't make up for the mistake, but at least there'd be some
names to chase.

They'd emailed him the list by the time he returned to
Cedar House. It made for interesting reading. There'd been
roughly sixty people staffing Earlsfield when Kaul retired. But
four other firefighters left within a few months of him. With
one exception – the crew manager Martin Walker – they were
all relatively young men. What caught his eye was that all four
were from Red Watch – the same watch as Kaul. A coincidence? Or a team within a team? The men he'd seen at the
wake were three youngish men and an older man. Now he
wanted to know who they were, and he kicked himself again
for missing the opportunity.

Paulsen intercepted him with an awkward smile as he walked back into the incident room.

'I've been through Kaul's accounts. There's nothing out of the ordinary. The figures show a steady turnover. He seemed to get a lot of his work through word of mouth. He was turning a decent profit with plenty of repeat business.'

'Enough of a profit to pay for that wedding out of his own pocket?'

'That's where it becomes interesting. Sort of. Looks like he'd been regularly paying in small sums of cash into his account over a fairly long period.'

'Exactly how long?'

'Certainly for the duration of the three years of accounts the bank supplied. I've asked them to send me more from further back.'

'Good. Maybe he liked to be paid cash in hand. It's odd though. When the opportunity arises let's try and raise it with the family. How are the other interviews coming along?'

'Uniform have now spoken to everyone who was there, including the hotel staff. The trouble with a wedding is it's hard for anyone to know if someone *was* out of place. People just assumed if you were in the room, you were entitled to be there.'

'Doesn't have to be someone who was out of place – could have been anyone with a grudge. Someone we've already spoken to.'

'Now the wake's out of the way, we're going to start re-interviewing the family. I was going to go back through them and make a shortlist of who we should be following up on. And there's one other thing: I spoke again to the waiter who thought he saw a man follow Kaul out of the banqueting hall just before the fire started.'

'Did he see enough to get a description?'

'Said he was a white man with dark hair wearing a grey suit, but that was about it. We're talking to him again later and we'll see if we can get enough for an e-fit. How was the wake?'

Finn ignored the question, instead sharing what he'd learnt about Kaul's former teammates from the LFB. Paulsen frowned as she tried to read the relevance of it.

'What do you make of it?' she asked.

'It's unusual. With one exception they were all relatively young men.'

'How were they at the wake?'

'We need to talk to them individually, but it's just a line of inquiry at this point – among quite a few. First we need to track them down,' he replied.

'But didn't you get that information at the wake?' Paulsen persisted.

'They came and went. I was busy with Stephanie Kaul and they'd gone by the time I went to find them. It's my fault – I should have kept a closer eye; I didn't think they'd leave so soon,' he said briskly. 'The brigade's been helpful with contact details though. Let's start with the senior guy – Walker.'

Paulsen nodded, but kept her eyes on him for just a second too long before heading back to her desk. Finn watched her go, knowing he'd just about skirted it. Now he was back in the incident room everything felt normal again, but he knew he couldn't afford a repeat of what happened earlier.

'*You're allowed to grieve,*' said Karin.

'They all quit at the same time?' asked DI Andy Warrender standing over Mike Godden's desk, more irritated than intrigued by the information. Godden flashed a smile.

'No, not exactly the same time. Staggered over a fairly short period; the last one was . . .' he peered at the LFB email on his screen, squinting at the small typeface, '. . . a Stuart Portbury – eighteen months or so after the Pacific Square fire.'

Warrender, still wearing the expression of a vegan being presented with a steak pie, shook his head dismissively. He hadn't been the first to lead the Stansted investigation; he was the third senior investigating officer in total now. The first was discreetly moved on as the inquiry stalled, while the second retired unexpectedly. The role was seen as a poisoned chalice, but he'd been determined to treat it like any other investigation. It could be solved; he'd been convinced of it. And he still clung to the belief. But it was an inquiry that tended to throw up unexpected wrinkles – just like this one.

'It's too peripheral. What's your feeling?' asked Warrender.

'Whitlock was already dead when the fire teams went in. The body was trapped and they had more important things to deal with at the time. I don't see what they could have done. If he was alive, what motive would they have had to harm him? They didn't even know who he was.'

'And what was the SIO's thinking at the time about why he was there?'

'You know all this, guv.'

'Humour me – I want to get it straight in my head.'

Godden shrugged.

'We thought he'd probably gone there to meet someone. It was as private as neutral ground can be. Wrong place, wrong time though – but no one thought the fire crews who dealt with the blaze were an issue. Still can't see it myself if I'm honest.'

Warrender mulled it a bit more to be certain, then cemented his opinion.

'I agree, it's just coincidental. We've got enough wild goose chases to juggle without adding this to the list, and that's what I'm going to tell Cedar House. If they want to pursue it, good luck to them.'

Godden nodded in agreement and waited for Warrender to go. Once he was alone again he looked back at the email from the LFB.

'What was that all about?' said a voice behind him. It belonged to DC Jim Farmer. Godden jumped as if touched by a live current.

'Jesus, Jimmy, would you stop creeping up on me like that, I'm too old for it.'

While he made a meal of his indignation, he surreptitiously minimised the email on his screen. Farmer entered his line of sight with a wide grin, which turned immediately into an expression of curiosity. Again, the sense of a Labrador retriever struck Godden. He remembered a neighbour of his who owned a terrier. It got run over, he recalled.

'Just the boss following up on that DC from south London yesterday.'

'The one with the dark hair?' said Farmer excitedly. Godden winked at him conspiratorially, privately wondering if he'd been like that at that age – and if so, why no one ever chinned him.

'Chill your boots, Jim. There's nothing to see. A dead body way out of our patch – they're trying to link it to Stansted.'

'Really? Why? What's the connection?'

'There isn't one. You might as well link it to Lord Lucan or the Great Train Robbery if you want to play that game.' Farmer looked disappointed and Godden smiled smoothly again. 'When you've been on the job as long as I have, you get a nose for flabby bollocks. And that's what this is, trust me.'

'You think?'

'Certain. Warrender's sending them packing.'

'Suppose you're right. Just thought a new lead might, y'know . . . liven things up?'

'Liven things up, James? *Liven things up?*' He pulled a face of mock horror. 'If you want to liven things up, come and find me when you go on your break, and I'll buy you a cheeky half in the Royal Oak. That's if you promise not to tell the boss.'

'I'll hold you to that,' replied Farmer with a toothy grin, tapping Godden lightly on the shoulder as he turned to walk away.

'Liven things up, my arse . . .' muttered Godden.

Farmer laughed as he went, but the smile on Godden's face froze, then vanished. He waited for the door to close behind Farmer, then reached into his top drawer for the phone he kept there.

16

It was early afternoon when Martin Walker took the call from the young woman with the lilting accent. He was now sitting in the quiet of his garden, sipping some cold mineral water while Christine took her afternoon nap. He'd been churning over the morning's events in Harlesden when DC Paulsen called. His former workmates hadn't changed one iota. Elder was still loud, irritating and in your face. Portbury was the diametric opposite; quiet and thoughtful, always holding a little something back. And Maddox was the one you worried about – the potential weak link he'd always been. But Walker felt he'd got through to them and conveyed the right tone. They needed to keep their heads; that too was something which hadn't changed over the years, he thought ruefully.

Perhaps because of that, Paulsen's call didn't overly alarm him. If the police suspected something, then they surely wouldn't have phoned in advance. She'd been polite, courteously explaining her reasons for ringing. She was investigating Adesh Kaul's death and hoped he could fill in some gaps about his time with the LFB. He'd been only too willing to accommodate her. Walker wanted to look the police in the eye and get a sense for himself where they were at. Putting it off would only add to his mounting worries, so he'd told her to come that afternoon. It was the right move, he thought, as he listened to the birds tweeting from the apple tree next door. He took another sip of water and enjoyed the cold burn at the back of his throat, then closed his eyes and took himself back. If they did ask about One Pacific Square, he'd need to have his story straight.

An hour later, Walker was surprised to find two people on his doorstep. He instantly recognised one of them as the man he'd seen earlier at the wake. He was tall, with horn-rimmed glasses and cheekbones you could cut yourself on. He wore what looked like a white designer shirt with dark cotton trousers. Walker suppressed a slight sense of disapproval. In his day, plain-clothes police were more concerned with solving crimes than how they dressed. Sign of the times, he thought. The young woman next to him, whose face was breaking into an engaging smile, introduced herself as DC Paulsen.

Christine was now awake, and he'd already warned her who was coming and why. He led them through to the garden, where she'd laid out a jug of iced tea with a couple of glasses.

'Ooh – you've caught me out there. I was only expecting one of you. Let me fetch another glass,' she said as they emerged. She began to wheel herself back up the specially constructed ramp that led into the house. Walker glanced at Finn and Paulsen as they watched her go. People always seemed fascinated by the various ramps and handrails that were installed around the place. Perhaps sensing they were under scrutiny, the two officers sat down on the rattan chairs at the garden table, as Walker grabbed a spare from the patio and joined them.

'I saw you earlier at the wake. I should have spoken to you then, really. It would have taken up less of your time,' said Finn. He seemed curiously awkward for a senior police officer, thought Walker.

'It's okay. We . . . I . . . didn't stay too long.'

'The other men you were with – they also worked with Adesh?'

'Yes, it's been something of a shock for us all, as I'm sure you can imagine.' Finn and Paulsen both nodded sympathetically. 'So, what can I do for you?' said Walker.

'Can you think of anyone who might have wanted to hurt Adesh?' asked Finn.

'I haven't seen him in five years. Why ask me; there must be more recent people in his life?'

'We're looking into all areas of his world – his recent past and a bit further back. We noticed he quit the fire service quite suddenly. In and of itself that's no big deal, I know it's a high-pressure job. But several of you left around the same time: you, Adesh, Gary Elder, Phil Maddox and Stuart Portbury,' said Paulsen.

Walker noted immediately she'd rattled the names off without referring to her pocketbook, and he didn't like it. She'd done more than just look them up; she'd committed those names to memory.

'All within months of one another. It caught our eye,' said Finn, impassive as he spoke. That was one failure already, Walker thought. The whole point of their staggered departures was to *stop* anyone spotting a pattern. Now, here were two police officers in his garden questioning him directly about it. Before he could reply, Christine emerged from the house brandishing a glass tumbler. She wheeled herself over and passed it to Finn, who returned her smile with a pleasant one of his own.

'Pour yourself some tea, before it gets warm in the sun. There's just a squeeze of lemon in there too.'

'Lovely,' said Finn, helping himself to a large glass as she watched approvingly.

'I won't be a gooseberry. I'm in the living room catching up on *The Archers* if you need anything,' she said, before wheeling herself back towards the ramp again.

Walker waited for her to go before continuing.

'I can't speak for the rest of the boys . . . but I was fifty-one and Chrissie had just been diagnosed with MS. It was the right time for me to go. If something had happened to me on the job . . .' He shrugged. 'Well, you can imagine where that would have left her.'

'Do you know why Adesh quit?' said Paulsen. 'September of that year, wasn't it?'

Again, she possessed the information at her fingertips.

'I heard second hand it was something to do with his family, that they wanted him to stop. It's not uncommon. You two must know it for yourselves; we're in professions where you put your life at risk every day. And we're probably the ones who worry about it the least.'

'What was he like, Adesh?'

'Quiet. Dependable. He learnt fast and was gutsy. If you're running into a burning building you want someone like that watching your back. That's the highest compliment I can pay.'

'As a person? Did he have any enemies?' Finn continued.

'No. He wasn't the type who drew attention to himself. He was a good kid – a bit impressionable maybe, but essentially sensible. He certainly didn't deserve what happened to him.'

'No, I'm sure,' said Finn.

'One other thing we noticed – you all left in the months after the blaze at One Pacific Square. You were first responders there, weren't you?' asked Paulsen.

Walker could feel his heart thumping now, the sun suddenly feeling twice as hot on his skin. He pulled a face as if trying to recall merely what he'd eaten the previous evening.

'Yes. It was a hard night. Not one for rookies, not that any of us were. It was nothing to do with why I left though. But if it was a factor for the other fellas, I could understand it. You'd have to ask them.'

96

'According to the police interviews done at the time, your crew handled the area where Erik Whitlock's body was found. The third floor?' said Paulsen. Walker nodded but didn't reply.

'Tell us what you found.'

'It's all on the record, I said it all at the time.'

'Humour us, please,' said Finn. 'I'd like to hear it from someone in person. You actually found Whitlock's body, didn't you?'

'Yes. He'd inhaled a lot of smoke but must have fallen when he passed out. He'd got trapped in some of the construction gear. We tried to free him, but we couldn't shift it. It was too late.'

'Too late to save him or to get the body out, you mean?' asked Paulsen.

'Both, I suppose. He'd been there too long, and there was no pulse. It's as I said at the time – we were running short on air. It was all logged on the control boards, so you can see for yourself. We didn't know if there was anyone else in there either. What you've got to understand is that the fire was above us. We were searching for potentially trapped people who shouldn't have been there. There were teams who needed to get in and set up a control point to tackle the blaze itself. And you know how that turned out . . .'

'Do you know who Erik Whitlock was?' asked Finn.

'Yes, I read the papers like everyone else. Some heavy who worked for . . . what did they call him? *The Handyman?*' He said the name with disdain.

'I don't know about that, but he was certainly someone with strong links to the underworld. The people he associated with were exceptionally dangerous. Not the types you'd want to cross, put it that way.'

'I'm not sure I understand where you're going with this. Are you saying it was arson that night?'

'No, we've no reason to doubt the fire investigation team's findings. But the way Adesh Kaul died – if it was deliberate – was nasty. The sort of thing the people we're talking about might just do,' said Finn.

Walker shrugged and held out his hands.

'I can't see why they'd have a problem with Adesh. Like I say, Whitlock was dead when we got to him. My only regret is we couldn't retrieve the body for his family.'

'And you saw nothing else unusual that night?' said Paulsen.

'No. Nothing at all.'

'Then we won't waste your time any longer. Thank you for talking to us. It's been helpful,' said Finn.

The three of them stood and walked back through the house. As Walker showed them to the front door, Finn reached into his pocket and produced a small card.

'If there's anything else that comes back to you – particularly regarding Pacific Square – then call us. This is my number.'

Walker was still stood there a full ten seconds after the door shut behind them when Christine joined him.

'So what was all that about then?'

'Nothing, love. Just good people doing their jobs. We won't be seeing them again.'

But even as he said the words, he could feel his shirt sticking to the sweat running down his back.

17

Paulsen spent her tube journey home re-reading the witness statements taken from the wedding guests. She kept the crime scene photographs of Adesh Kaul's burnt remains carefully folded in her bag. They weren't the sort of images you wanted slipping out on public transport. When she'd first seen them she'd been more curious than horrified. Kaul looked like he'd died in the middle of a fight. Which is precisely what they suspected *did* happen, but the posture was deceptive. The boxer-like pose of flexed elbows, knees and clenched fists was caused by the shrinkage of body tissues and muscle in the heat. It wasn't an uncommon phenomenon apparently. One of the older male DC's caught her studying the photos at her desk earlier, and immediately mansplained.

'I bet I know what the post-mortem will say. I've dealt with a few fatal arsons in my time, so I know the drill,' he'd begun. 'The skin shrinks, then the fat starts leaking out. Your own lard basically stokes the fire – it can go on for hours if there's no one else about. If your man was lucky he was already dead at this point – doubt they'd have heard him screaming in the bogs though.'

Paulsen wasn't sure if he was genuinely trying to be friendly or just patronising her. She'd felt like deciding it was the latter.

'No shit,' she'd responded, and he'd taken the hint.

She hadn't been under the illusion Cedar House would be hugely different to Dunlevy Road, but the almost identi-kit men occupying the place was depressing. She felt the undercurrent in the room; the sideways glances she was receiving and the exchanged looks they thought she couldn't see. She didn't feel any great impetus to ease their discomfort either. Some of these men just wanted a wide-eyed young woman they could take under their wing and share their great experience with. There was nothing explicitly sexist about it. If anything, it was just their clumsy way of getting to know her. But she didn't like it. It wasn't who she was. Either she was accepted on her terms, or she wasn't bothered about being accepted. She walked out of the exit from Tufnell Park tube station and began the fifteen-minute walk to the small one-bedroom flat she shared with Nancy.

They'd met on a canal boat party in Islington a couple of years before, both dragged there unwillingly by friends of the boat's owner. The party was awful and they'd stood in a corner bonding over a shared line in acerbic humour. Mattie, as was her way, hadn't held back. They'd snogged on dry land next to the boat and by the time they left, a day, time and place for a drink was agreed.

The date itself proved eventful. It started with a quiet glass of wine, and after an hour of small talk, Mattie suggested moving on somewhere else. Somewhere else, it turned out, was several more places, and they'd ended up getting hammered before collapsing back at Nancy's flat. By the following morning they'd both begun to understand some-thing fairly fundamental was taking shape. Mattie was brutally honest about some of her previous relationships, and was equally blunt in inquiring about Nancy's past. She wasn't a woman who seemed to care how she came across. It seemed more important to Mathilde Paulsen to be herself than spend time worrying about how she wished to be perceived. It was a quality Nancy found sexy as hell, but then she'd already decided that back on the canal boat.

In turn, Nancy was the one person Mattie confessed everything to. She'd been a rock in a situation where others might have been tempted to cut and run. There'd been a price though. Their previously tight relationship buckled at times under the weight of it, the doubt in Nancy's eyes occasionally breaking Mattie's heart. Some things could be forgiven but not necessarily forgotten.

Almost a year on they were still struggling to find a way through it. Nancy worked as a trainee social worker, and at times Mattie felt more like a client than a girlfriend. Nancy was endlessly trying to put a smile on her partner's face, determined not to let her wallow in the past. Mattie often found the constant effort wearing. Then she'd see the hurt look on Nancy's face and would feel a whole new wave of guilt.

Mattie was already on her second beer when Nancy came through the door.

'Smells nice – what is it?'

'Spaghetti margherita.'

'That's a pizza . . .'

'Not now it isn't . . .'

Nancy smiled.

'Well, it smells good – and I'll have one of those if you haven't finished them all off?' She pointed at the beer. Mattie retrieved two more bottles from the fridge and passed one to Nancy, who collapsed on a chair at the kitchen table.

'So how's work been? You haven't really talked about it,' Nancy said.

'It's exactly what you'd expect. Half the room looks at me with utter disapproval, the other half ogles me.'

'And what about the men?'

Mattie found herself smiling despite herself. Nancy grinned back – it was rare her efforts to produce a smile actually worked these days.

'Seriously, there must be some decent people there?'

'Yeah – a few.'

'Made any friends yet?'

Mattie glared and Nancy held her hands up in mock surrender.

'It'd do you good to let a few new people in.'

'Believe it or not I've been busy.'

She explained the outline of the Adesh Kaul investigation, and its connection to the Pacific Square fire. It was one of their shared rituals. Nancy liked to follow the mechanics of police procedural work, while Mattie enjoyed sharing the details.

'I remember reading about the Stansted robbery, it was huge. Do you really think there's a connection to that?'

'Probably not. You should see the team investigating it. Talk about dead.'

'So why do you reckon this guy was set on fire?'

Mattie took a thoughtful swig of beer.

'You go to someone's wedding. You wait for your victim to get married, then you douse the bloke in petrol and set him alight. How much do you have to *hate* someone to do that?'

There was a silence. They both knew what the other was thinking. In the end it was Nancy who said it.

'You tell me, Mat.'

Ten minutes later they were both devouring large bowls of pasta, and the spotlight of the conversation was now on Finn.

'To be honest, he doesn't seem all there. His wife's just died. I don't know why they let him come back so soon.'

'Why's he back then?'

'Short-staffed, and he's clearly bright. Bit up himself though.' She looked guilty. 'Maybe that's harsh, could just be the bereavement.'

'You need to get on with these people, Mat.'

'It's early days. We're all still sussing each other out. It's what happens in nicks. Cops can be a bit like dogs, sniffing each other's arses by way of hello. Though—' She broke off suddenly, looking thoughtful. 'Feels like I've been given to this bloke as a bit of a project.'

'Are you sure you aren't being paranoid? What do you think he knows?'

'What could he know? No one knows the whole story. Except you.'

Mattie finished her meal and pushed the bowl away, tossing her fork into the middle of it.

'I just want to be treated like any other police officer, what's wrong with that?'

'Because you're not, Mattie. How can you be? Not now.'

Nancy grabbed the dirty plates and began loading up the dishwasher, as Mattie stretched out on the sofa.

'All I'm saying is, why not let a few people in for a change? I just get a feeling you might need them, one day.'

'Give it a rest, Nance,' said Mattie lightly, but the warning tone underneath was unmistakable.

'I'm serious. I'm worried about how this will end . . . that something really bad's going to happen. Again.'

'You're being melodramatic. How is what going to end?'

'That if you keep things bottled up, then . . . they'll start *leaking*. It's human nature. And then people will start looking at you. They'll smell something isn't right, if they haven't already. You work in a building full of people trained to do exactly that. And once they start looking . . . then where does it go, what's the endpoint?'

This time she was met with silence.

18

A bit of retail therapy always helped, thought Gary Elder. He looked at the rectangular shopping bags lined up on his kitchen island. Prada, Hugo Boss and Emporio Armani were all helping to distract him from the events of the morning. Strolling down New Bond Street in the sunshine, he'd tried not to think about the uneasy reunion with his former crewmates. But this surely is what it was all about. Why they'd all quit. He'd genuinely thought they might be grateful too, but there'd been no warmth from anyone, no word of thanks.

It'd all been a bit melodramatic. Walker hadn't changed though; he was still a condescending gobshite. The man was a hypocrite too. He'd played his part, but now wanted to wag his finger at them like naughty children. As for Maddox – once a spineless little weasel, always one. He'd looked like he was going to crap himself in the pub. At least Portbury hadn't whinged. Stuart didn't count though; he was a bloke who relied on flying under the radar. He'd never liked people looking too hard at him – probably because there wasn't that much to see.

Elder helped himself to a beer from the fridge. He wasn't going to be frightened or intimidated. He'd no doubt things would settle down, but he hadn't enjoyed how they'd made him feel earlier. Frankly, if he never saw any of them again then he'd be quite happy. He rubbed his arm absently; it was pink from walking in the sun earlier. The slight sting made him shiver, made him think of Adesh again. His flesh boiling and burning in the flames. Gary's eyes fell on the shopping bags. What he needed, he decided, was a night out.

Elder parked the Maserati as he always did, a couple of streets away. Troy's nightclub in Purley could get a little fruity of an evening, which was part of the fun. It wasn't the sort of car you brought to the front door. Besides, it played into the game he liked to play when he got a girl interested. *'Come outside – I'll give you a lift home in the Maserati'* – they'd always laugh disbelievingly. Then as they left he'd pretend some of the old bangers parked up nearby were his, until they turned the corner and he played the double bluff. It usually guaranteed him at least a snog at that point, with the promise of a bit more later.

Elder liked the fact a fast car still impressed the girls. He increasingly found the twenty-somethings who frequented Troy's a bemusing breed. In his day, you went out on a Friday night, sank a few beers and tried to get lucky. He smiled wryly as he remembered the pulling power of telling someone you were a fireman – almost up there with the Maserati. Now they all sat around in clusters, sipping their fancy cocktails, heads in phones, hardly talking to one another. And you needed to be careful – spill someone's drink these days and you might get a squirt of acid in your face for your trouble.

He'd also got used to going out on his own. At first it was a bit of a leap into the unknown, and he'd felt a bit of a Billy no-mates. As his friends settled down with families, nights out like these had seemed to lose their allure. But it was like going to the cinema on your own, he reasoned; there was no shame in it. On arrival he'd always pop into the toilet and put on his Franck Muller watch (never to be worn out on the street unless you were really stupid), then sit at the bar sipping a cocktail and waiting for things to liven up. It was easy mingling then, and the watch would do the job of catching someone's eye. If you were lucky it'd be the right eye; a girl looking for some adventure with someone who was clearly a man of the world. If James Bond were real, then surely this is how it would feel.

He'd been there around forty-five minutes when he saw a blonde staring at him from the other side of the bar. She wore a dress that was more like a belt, with legs which went up to her armpits. He blazed her a smile. Ten minutes later he'd established her name was Sam and was being introduced to some of her mates – two rather giggly girls and a couple of suspicious-looking lads. He couldn't work out if Sam was with either of the boys, but he wasn't bothered. He had the clothes, the car and the watch. The battle, if there was one, was already over – they just didn't know it yet.

His early optimism was quickly punctured. As the night wore on, he began to feel the two decades or so which separated him from this generation. He remembered as a teenager monosyllabically answering his parents' questions, and this felt exactly the same. The difference was he was now the old fart whose presence was embarrassing and unwelcome. The Maserati didn't even engender any interest. When he'd described some of the specs they'd nodded politely and changed the subject on to some reality TV show involving celebrities on an island.

He looked across at Sam to see if she was still interested, but even the idea of taking her home suddenly repelled him. It felt like it would be bordering on paedophilia. To rub insult into injury one of the lads – Al or Alfie, something like that – asked him if his kids knew he was out, and shouldn't he be getting back home to them? They'd fallen about laughing, and Elder decided enough was enough.

He felt strangely unsettled and niggled as he walked back to the car. He hadn't enjoyed the day. Poor old Adesh in the morning, then the uncomfortable reunion at the pub, and now a humiliating evening in Troy's. A good night's sleep is what he needed and then he'd go again. He unlocked the car but didn't notice the man in black padding up behind him. The same man who'd followed him from his house when he'd set off for Troy's earlier in the evening. The same man who'd sat in his own rather more modest vehicle, patiently waiting for him to return. Elder felt something strike the back of his head and everything went dark.

When he woke, he could feel the lump on his skull starting to rise. He was in the Maserati, he realised quickly – in the driver's seat. He was buckled in and as he looked down saw plastic flex wrapped around him. Something wet splashed down his face. Fumy and oily; he recognised it immediately as petrol. Confusion turned to fear. He wriggled at the bonds. He couldn't move. A dark figure loomed over him holding a plastic bottle. Elder strained to see the face but was stuck fast.

'Who are you? What is this?'

But he already knew what was going on. What was happening. What was going to happen. How was this even possible? He strained to look out of the open door of the car. It was dark, but he could see they were on a concrete forecourt outside what looked like some lock-ups. There were loads of places like this in the area, deserted even in the middle of the day. His terror was only matched by the impossibility of the situation. Randomly an image of his mother came into his mind. How she'd looked when he was a boy. He was crying now with fear, the tears mingling with the petrol dripping down his face.

'Come on, mate . . .' said Elder, the words coming out in a hoarse whisper. The man was now walking steadily backwards, emptying the plastic bottle in a long straight stream until he was a safe distance away. Elder couldn't take his eyes off him. The man tossed the bottle aside, and pulled a silver Zippo lighter out from his pocket, together with a piece of paper. An orange glow lit up the darkness and Elder saw the paper was actually a twenty-pound note.

'Don't do this. Please, I can help – whatever this is about.'

The figure held the note to the flame and waited for it to catch. His face became part illuminated, a set of teeth baring a wolfish grin. He held the note up, the flame already eating its way through, then parted his thumb and forefinger and let it drift slowly to the ground.

19

There was no getting away from it, thought Finn, the evenings were a trial. He was watching an M&S Moroccan meatball ready meal slowly rotate in the microwave. He and Karin always made time to cook after work. She always believed it was important to sit around the table and eat together, however late in the day. They'd enjoyed some of their best conversations over a chicken curry at half past ten at night, and they were moments he used to anticipate during the day. Without her, a ready meal with a glass of wine was enough to fill his belly and take the edge off the fact she wasn't there to share it. He uncorked a half-drunk bottle of Rioja as the microwave beeped at him. He looked over at it resentfully and felt his heart sag. He put the cork back in the bottle, checked the time then reached for his phone. Perhaps tonight there was an alternative.

Finn walked into the familiar lounge of The Red Cow and saw who he was looking for straight away. Sat in the corner nursing a glass of wine was Jackie Ojo. It'd been a hopeful call; with a six-year-old boy to look after, he didn't think she'd be free at short notice. He was delighted when she said she was. He ordered himself a single malt and brought her over a second glass of red.

'You managed to get childcare then?'

'Yeah, my mum. Always complains when I ask, then complains when I don't.'

'Sorry for the late call.'

'So what can I do for you, guv? I was expecting a night in front of the telly.'

'You can drop the guv tonight for a start, Jacks.'

It was true to say Finn actively went out of his way to avoid making friends at work. Ojo was the exception to the rule, but even then it was complex. In the early days their working relationship hadn't been so close. As a middle-class white male DI with a Cambridge education, she'd quickly formed a very particular view of him. In turn, he'd found her cool exterior both frustrating and unhelpful. That all changed after one particular investigation: a woman battered to death by a boyfriend with years of form for domestic abuse. They couldn't prove he'd killed her, and he knew it. Finally, they'd found a way in. It'd been Ojo who'd spotted it first; their suspect was an abuse victim himself, only he'd never recognised it. Once they'd teased that out into the open, the confession followed quite quickly. Afterwards they'd gone for a drink to celebrate. That's when they'd discovered how wrong they'd been about one another, and a bond was formed. There was nothing remotely romantic to it, just two people talking shop and finding themselves on the same wavelength. It became an infrequent tradition. Once or twice a year, rank would go out of the window and they'd work their way through a few bottles putting the world to rights. They were nights they both enjoyed, because sometimes it takes a cop to understand a cop. Even Karin had understood that.

Finn found Ojo's worldview refreshing. She didn't tolerate bullshit and didn't hold back when it came to giving her views on the hierarchy of both Cedar House and the Met. One thing he respected about her was she didn't use these infrequent blowouts to simply bitch about people. That could be because he was the DI and she saw it as unprofessional, but his instinct was that she simply didn't like backstabbing. So, when she made a criticism, he knew it came from a constructive place, however bluntly expressed.

'These are slightly strange times, and I thought I owed you an explanation,' said Finn. She looked at him searchingly and he got a sense she was biting her tongue. As a detective sergeant she'd regularly been Finn's number two, the bridge between the DI and the DCs. Now all of a sudden, she'd been displaced by a moody DC who'd been dropped in from nowhere.

'I take it you're referring to Paulsen? I assumed she'd been dumped on you by Skegman because I was working the Thornton Heath stabbing.'

'Well . . . there's certainly something to that.'

'It's alright – my nose wasn't out of joint. I don't mind taking a step back on this one.'

'Really?'

'Yeah. I've worked with you long enough. If there was a problem, you'd tell me. I reckoned you were putting her through her paces. To see what she's all about.'

'That's about the size of it. So now you've seen her in action – what do you make of her?'

Ojo smiled enigmatically. Finn was beginning to recognise that expression when it came to Paulsen. He'd seen the same look on Skegman's face in YoYo's at the start of the week.

'She's different, I'll give you that. Are you asking me because you want to know what I think or because you want to know what the hairy-ear brigade are saying?'

'If by that you mean your middle-aged male colleagues – of which I count myself one – then yes . . .'

Ojo took a sip of her wine.

'Honestly? They don't like her.'

'Do I need to have a chat with her?'

'Not yet. It might just be some defensive bullshit. It is her first week. See how she beds in before you start getting heavy.'

'I'm assuming the problem's her attitude rather than her gender?'

'It's a nick, not some hipster coffee shop. There's a few . . . shall we say . . . reformed dinosaurs in there. There's also a few idiots like Dave McGilligott who react like pubescent schoolboys when a young woman comes into the mix.'

'How did you deal with all that when you started?'

'I didn't. Hated every minute of it. At one point I was almost ready to give up. But I didn't, and that's the point.'

Finn was surprised. Ojo was always so unflappable, with a nice line in acerbic put-downs for anyone who overstepped the mark. It upset him he hadn't recognised how distressed she'd been. It also immediately strengthened his resolve not to let the same thing happen to Paulsen.

'I'd no idea it was that bad.'

'Don't get me wrong. I don't want to make a meal out of it. I don't think anyone meant anything genuinely malicious. It was more the daily accumulation – being patronised, not trusted as much as the male DCs. Comments about the way you're dressed, your make-up and all the rest.'

'What happened?'

'You think there was some great moment? Some big blow-out where I put them all in their place?' She took another sip of her drink and shook her head as she remembered. 'Nothing like that. They just got used to having me about and it calmed down by itself. It's as simple and empty as that.'

'I'm sorry, Jacks. I'd no idea.'

'The one thing about men you can rely on is their short attention spans. It's crap when it comes to relationships, useful when it comes to workplace bollocks.'

'Is there anything you can do to help Paulsen?'

'Help her? She's got to help herself. She needs to stop sitting there like a duchess not talking to anyone, for a start. They can take it from you – they know you're a moody bugger – but if she doesn't change her ways, things will start to get nasty, trust me.'

Finn absorbed what he was being told, but it was more a confirmation of what he already knew. It was good getting Jackie's perspective. He'd spent too much time alone in the flat.

'So how are you then, guv? Sorry – *Alex* . . .' She said his name with a deliberate layer of awkwardness and they both smiled.

'Let's stick with guv. I'm . . . managing, I suppose.'

'There's a lot of concern among the team.'

'Concern? Really? Or do they think I shouldn't be back?'

'Now you're being paranoid. It's just very soon to be back, is all.'

'How do I seem to you?'

'Honestly? Not one hundred per cent and I've known you a while. If you were on my team, I'd send you home again.'

Finn wasn't expecting that, and the answer rocked him. It's why he valued her so highly though. It vaguely irritated him they didn't talk like this more during the working week.

'I wouldn't put myself in this position if I genuinely thought I couldn't do it.'

'How many times have you thought about your wife today?'

The honest answer was she was always there. On his journey to work, at the wake in Harlesden, in Martin Walker's garden . . . He didn't expect it to be any different tomorrow either.

'I'm guessing a lot. And if you hadn't been thinking about her, what would have been filling your head? The investigation, most likely. And you and I both know, jobs like this get solved in that thinking time; that's where the real work gets done.'

'I reckon I was at about eighty per cent today. And that's the truth.'

Ojo gave him an old-fashioned look.

'That's a big twenty per cent. Just saying . . .'

The barman brought over a far-from-appetising-looking hamburger and went to put it in front of Ojo. She pointed at Finn, barely hiding her disgust at the steaming, greasy pile.

'You don't mind, do you? I'm starving,' said Finn. This, he noticed, was another side effect of bereavement; days of no appetite at all, followed by junk food binging. He took a bite and washed it down with a swig of whisky. He offered her a chip, and despite herself she took one and began chewing on it thoughtfully.

'So are we really chasing the Handyman then?' she asked.

Finn, mouth full of burger, just rolled his eyes and carried on munching.

'I'll tell you something about the Stansted robbery,' Ojo continued. 'Someone I trained with at Hendon was working up there at the time. Two days after the robbery, the security guard they dumped in the field with the van driver comes forward. His three-year-old boy's been talking about a "funny man" at school.'

'Two days afterwards? They must have balls the size of—'

'Exactly,' cut in Ojo. 'Some bloke gets into the nursery school unnoticed and somehow manages to get this kid alone. He gives the boy a bag of those chocolate coins and a note for his dad; it's a warning to forget what he saw. They were making a point – we can get to your kid whenever we want. If they ever do make an arrest and need him to ID someone, I wouldn't hold your breath.'

'What's your point?' said Finn.

'Would people like that think twice about burning a man alive?'

'But why? What could these guys have possibly done?' Finn's brow furrowed and he stared into the middle distance for a moment. Ojo shrugged. Finn carefully put his burger down and wiped his hands with a napkin.

'Alright. Let's play a game.'

Ojo smiled and shrugged. She knew that expression, when his brain was properly assaulting a problem. She also wondered if that wasn't the point of the drink – that he needed a sounding board and there was no one at home now to bounce off.

'Go on then.'

'Why would the Handyman – or whoever he is – come after Adesh Kaul? The only link is Whitlock . . .'

'. . . who was a money launderer.'

'Exactly, so maybe he brought money with him to Pacific Square, and went there to meet someone. The place was deserted and central – the perfect place for an exchange.'

'But Whitlock's remains were the only ones that were found.'

'So perhaps he was there early, or someone else didn't show. Either way, the fire breaks out. We know the cause of the blaze was a builder's kettle. That was proved categorically by the fire investigation. The crew wouldn't have known they were even going until the first 999 call is made.'

'So if they crossed paths with Erik Whitlock it would have been accidental,' said Ojo.

'And if Whitlock *did* bring money with him, then the first crew that goes in – before the building goes up in smoke – would find Whitlock and his money.'

Ojo mulled it over for a moment, looking for holes.

'Kaul's wedding was expensive – we know that. And there's that cash he was paying into his account.'

'Suddenly not so implausible, is it?' said Finn. 'I'll tell you something else – Martin Walker's house has had some serious money thrown at it. There were chairlifts, ramps, extensions all over the shop. I might be reaching – but it looked a lot for a man living on his pension.'

Ojo was nodding now as she followed his logic.

'It fits. If it was the Stansted money, then it gives the people who originally stole it a decent enough motive to kill Kaul. But why do it now? Why so long after the event?'

'Because they've only just found out?' He shrugged. 'Or I'm making patterns out of something that really isn't there and he was barbecued by someone whose pint he spilt last week.'

'No, it's a decent explanation. If Kaul was sitting on a pile of money, he must have been keeping it somewhere.'

'I hope I'm wrong. If they did take the Stansted proceeds and the robbers now know . . . then they're way out of their depth.'

'You think the other four men could be in danger too?' said Ojo.

'I keep coming back to the way Kaul was killed. The setting, the method – it was done for a reason. What if that reason was to very visibly punish him?'

Finn suddenly felt very tired and shook his head. Ojo smiled sympathetically.

'Get some sleep, guv. We aren't going to solve it tonight. But it's a good theory.' She checked her watch. 'I ought to be going too – my boy will be doing everything he can not to be going to bed.'

'Thanks for coming out, Jacks, I appreciate it.'

'No problem – we'll do it again this time next year.'

Her expression suddenly turned serious.

'Make sure you look after yourself. I know how difficult it can be when things aren't great at home; you start going in early, coming back late. Using the job as an umbrella to hide under.'

'You're sounding like Karin. She gave me pretty much the same lecture before she died.'

'Should have guessed she'd already marked your card.'

The barman walked past, another two burgers plated up in each hand. Finn signalled to him for the bill.

'She left me something, by the way. Only found it on the day of the funeral. A riddle.'

'You what?'

'Seriously. A note. In her underwear drawer.'

Ojo arched an eyebrow.

' *"How far will a blind dog walk into a forest?"* She said it was important. Any idea?'

'Haven't got a clue! Can't you look it up?'

'No – can't do that. Be cheating . . .'

'And asking me isn't?'

'I thought, y'know, the female perspective. You might have an insight.'

Ojo shook her head, nonplussed.

'You're asking the wrong girl. I reckon she knew exactly what makes you tick. My advice: try looking at yourself through her eyes.'

He looked back at her helplessly and she chuckled. Ojo stood up and swung on her coat.

'But maybe not tonight. Do yourself a favour, give your brain a rest. It'll help – with all of it.'

She patted him on the shoulder and left. Finn sat at the table on his own for a while as he finished his drink. The empty flat waiting for him wasn't enticing. Ojo was right –

his head felt full. There was far too much spinning around it; Adesh Kaul, Mattie Paulsen and a blind dog in a forest.

'*Gotcha,*' said Karin.

20

Five Years Ago

The top four floors were now ablaze. Walker could taste his sweat dripping on to his lips as they made their way up the concrete staircase. The heat was stifling, the smoke swirling around them ominously now. It was getting hazier the higher they went, but there was no sign of flames yet. They were now on the third floor – a large grey hangar-like area – and began hunting for the man they'd seen at the window.

Maddox and Kaul took one side, Walker and Elder the other. Construction equipment and builders' materials were strewn around them. Walker reached for his radio.

'Crew now on the third floor – smoke logging, but no sign of fire.' Even through his protective layers he could feel the temperature rising sharply now, and once the heat was inside your suit there was nowhere for it to go. The smoke was getting noticeably thicker too. Experience trained him to shut out the discomfort, concentrate on what he could see. He and Elder were both scanning for the same thing, but there was no sign of movement, no sign of life.

Elder gestured to the far corner, where a small room was mid-construction. The smoke was slightly less dense there and Walker followed Elder through. Inside were twelve wooden pallets each stacked with large canvas sacks. Elder went over and peered inside one of them.

'Jesus! Marty – come and have a look at this.'

Walker went over and looked into the nearest one. Instantly he saw the unmistakable design of currency.

'There must be thousands here,' said Elder.

More than that, thought Walker. Millions. The size of the bags, the number of notes, the number of bags . . . it was easily millions. But what was it doing there? He focused again, annoyed – distractions like these are what got you killed.

A shoe was poking out from behind the pallets and Walker ran over to find a body lying face down.

'Casualty!'

Turning it over, he saw the face of a lined, heavily tanned man in his late forties. There was something of the ageing rock star about him. Walker thought he looked *exactly* like the kind of guy you'd find unconscious next to several million pounds in a burning building. He removed his glove and put his hand on the man's chest. He reached for his radio.

'We have a casualty. Probable smoke inhalation.'

Kaul was now coming through the small entrance to join them.

'There's no sign of anyone else on this floor, skip. Phil's still checking though.'

'Good. Help me with this one. I can't tell if he's breathing,' Walker replied.

Elder was still standing by the canvas sacks.

'Just wait, before we rush into anything.'

And Walker *knew*. He didn't need to ask. He knew exactly what Elder was thinking. Because he'd been thinking it too.

21

Today

It took Finn a while to find them, but the whispery thin fingers of smoke still just about visible above the rooftops were a clue he wasn't too far away. The burnt-out remains of the yellow Maserati GranTurismo were found smouldering in the early hours of the morning by a builder who owned one of the nearby lock-ups. He'd called 999 and it hadn't taken long to identify who the car belonged to.

Finn spent the drive from Balham taking in the implications of it. While he'd been out drinking with Jackie O, a second member of the Pacific Square fire crew was burning to death. One of the five men who'd retired so soon after that night. Suddenly the theory he'd shared with Ojo in the pub seemed less like conjecture and now a hard line of inquiry to be pursued. Was the Maserati, like Kaul's lavish wedding, visible evidence of a very bad decision they'd made in the heat of a blaze? One thing at a time, he thought.

He parked up in the street that gave way to the cordoned-off cul-de-sac. The sunshine from the previous day was long gone, replaced by a windy, grey morning. The rank smell of burnt-out metal, plastic and flesh hit him straight away – a variation on a theme from the stench he'd experienced at the hotel. He saw uniformed officers doing door-to-door inquiries at the nearby row of terraced houses. The other side of the cordon he could see the silhouette of DC Paulsen talking to what looked like a uniformed inspector. Behind her was the charred skeleton of the Maserati.

A black scorch line extended around twenty yards from the wreckage, and it wasn't hard to deduce how the blaze began. There was nothing accidental about this. Scenes of crime officers in blue gowns were working within the cordon, and there were numbered markers dotted around them. The fire investigation team would be on scene shortly too.

Paulsen turned, saw Finn approaching and ducked under the tape to join him.

'There's the remains of one body inside – I'm going to go out on a limb and say that's what's left of Gary Elder,' she said.

'How much do we know?'

'Well, there's no doubt about this one.' She pointed at the scorch line that snaked away from the car. 'You can see where it started. Whoever did it wasn't worried about making this look like an accident. Uniform think Elder might have been lured here. There won't be any CCTV or ANPR though – this cul-de-sac's completely blind.'

Finn quickly looked around and could see it was the perfect location. There were no properties backing on to it, and he could already tell the chances of any useful witnesses would be slim to none.

'So, we've now got two of the retired firefighters who attended Pacific Square in the morgue. What's your instinct, guv?'

Finn looked at the smoking funeral pyre which once was Gary Elder's pride and joy. Images of the abandoned banqueting hall in Morden, the scorched scene in the toilet and a distantly remembered television report of the Pacific Square blaze passed through his mind. He felt a note of caution.

'Let me tell you something about coppers' instinct; it's what bad police use as an excuse to cut corners. Egotistical chancers throw it out when they want to chuck procedure out of the window and do their own thing. If I had a quid for every monumental cock-up that happened because some idiot wanted to follow their nose, their gut, their sphincter or any other part of their anatomy, I could probably retire now.'

'Yeah – but what's your instinct?' said Paulsen, and he smiled.

'I think it's possible this fire crew stumbled on something five years ago. Clearly we need to look at protecting the other three members of that team. But there's one question I always ask myself, because it always comes back to this . . .'

His eyes were alive now, Paulsen thought. For the first time since she'd met him the deadness there was gone, replaced with a new vitality.

'. . . *Why now?*'

The bespectacled man in the waistcoat looked up at the charcoal grey sky with a disdainful sneer. The weather was so unpredictable at the moment, and he was a man who deeply disliked unpredictability. Seven minutes later he arrived on the dot of nine twenty-five outside a small shop on the other side of the village green. He unlocked the front door and walked inside.

The small, almost Dickensian interior was lined with varnished wooden floors. There was a vintage panelled mahogany counter at the far end which spanned the width of the entire shop. Behind the counter were boxy wooden shelves offering a variety of gentlemen's shoelaces, Zippo lighters, metal house numbers and brass door knockers. There was a sign on the wall written in ornate font, declaring:

Shoe Repairs, Key Cutting and
Engraving Services. Inquiries welcome.

The man sat down on a worn leather stool behind the counter, and extracted a mobile phone from his waistcoat pocket. He tapped on it and waited for the call to connect. Outside on the street he could see a middle-aged woman with a King Charles spaniel. The dog was defecating on the pavement and he watched as she went through the meticulous process of scooping and collecting the deposit into a small plastic bag. If ever there was a metaphor for life, he mused to himself. Finally, his call was answered.

'Good morning,' he said. 'Things are gathering some momentum and we need to talk face to face.'

The shop door opened with another tinkle, and he calmly returned the phone to his pocket, smiling pleasantly at the young woman who'd entered.

'Dear me. The weather's quite the disappointment today, isn't it?'

To his surprise, Finn discovered there'd been an early breakthrough. A teenage girl who'd seen Elder driving his car around the area before told one of the uniforms she'd seen him in the local nightclub the previous evening. He'd apparently tried it on with a group half his age and left, tail between legs, just after eleven. It gave them something to work with and the beginnings of a timeline. As he and Paulsen drove over to the club, Finn decided to do some gentle probing.

'You haven't told me yet what made you put in for a transfer.'

She turned and looked at him coolly. He thought he'd been subtle. The brief silence was broken by the satnav and he focused on the road.

'A bad experience. The first really bad one I've had in the job.'

'What happened?'

'I'd rather not go there, if that's okay.'

In the rear-view mirror, she saw his jaw tighten. Paulsen was starting to recognise it as a sign of irritation. She felt a flush of anger herself; the question was intrusive and she owed him no explanations. 'I know how things can sometimes linger,' Finn persisted. 'If you ever do want to talk . . .'

. . . *I'll talk to Nancy*, she thought, but didn't say. 'Thank you, I'll keep it in mind, guv,' she said instead. The words were respectful, but the tone emphatic. She wanted to ring-fence the subject, then build a wall around the fence. It was important people understood what was off limits, even superior officers. The fewer people who looked in that direction the better as far as she was concerned.

'And how are you, sir? This can't be an easy time for you,' she asked, deliberately changing the subject. *Have some back*, she thought, as she saw his jaw tighten again.

'I'm not brilliant,' he replied after a moment. 'I mean, don't get me wrong, it's really helpful getting back to work, but bereavement's like an iron grip around your heart. It's always there and sometimes that grip tightens.' Paulsen suddenly regretted her earlier brusqueness.

'I can't imagine . . .'

'Then don't try. It's not a headspace you want to get into. But no, in answer to your question, I'm not quite myself yet, or at the least the man I like to be. I hope you can forgive me any unintended insensitivity.'

She wondered if he was making a point – she hadn't wanted to share with him, and then he'd shared with her. She wasn't sure if he was playing with her or whether something important just happened. For the next few minutes they sat in awkward silence, the only words coming from the satnav.

The nightclub manager was helpful. Elder was a regular at the club and a bit of an oddity by all accounts. An older man, who tended to frequently come there on his own. There'd never been any complaints about him and he tipped heavily, which made him popular with the staff. The manager also provided them with the hard drive for the club's security cameras.

'It's possible the killer mingled inside the club, the same way as at the wedding – assuming it's the same person. If we're lucky we might get a match,' said Finn as they left.

'Do you want me to look at it?' replied Paulsen.

'No, I'll get uniform to do that. There's something else I want you to do as a priority. DS Ojo's been putting in some calls at my request. There's a few pieces of the jigsaw missing, and I think I know someone who can help us find them.'

22

An hour later Paulsen was driving through an area of dense woodland on the London–Surrey borders. As the trees gave way to the countryside, her satnav directed her down a well-maintained approach road. A few minutes later she caught a first glimpse of the building she'd been sent to visit. HMP Brazely was a sprawl of grey blocks. From a distance it could have been a factory, but the razor wire that topped the fence around the perimeter hinted at its true nature. She drew up at the security gate, produced her ID, then focused on the reason she was there, and the man she was going to meet.

Jane Prentice, the governor, was pleasant and easy-going. Her office was all modern greys and minimalist furniture, with some eye-catching abstracts on the walls to add a splash of colour. Paulsen imagined it was probably some contrast to the living quarters of the five hundred and ten inmates housed inside the nearby cells. Prentice pulled out a couple of chairs and they sat in front of her desk.

'Kenny Fuller's from Liverpool originally, came down to London around fifteen years ago. He lived in Edgware and worked as a scaffolder before he was arrested. But I'm guessing this is more to do with the Handyman, isn't it?'

Paulsen nodded.

'My DI thinks Fuller's the nearest thing we have to someone with a direct link to him – if he exists – and that he might be prepared to talk about it.'

'I suppose that depends on who you believe the Handyman is? Fuller worked as hired muscle for a number of gangland figures. It gives him a certain power in here so be careful he doesn't try and play you. He's got good reason to keep that going.'

'Does the name Raymond Spinney mean anything to you?' said Paulsen.

'Yes, he's one of the names constantly linked with the Handyman.'

'Fuller worked with Spinney on a post office raid in Holloway a few years back. He was quite chatty on the subject after he was nicked, which was unusual. Most of his associates are too petrified to give up a thing.'

'Why are you so interested in Spinney?'

'Because of two deaths on our patch. There's a chance we can connect them to him. It's possible they're the work of a professional and if anyone can recognise the signs it's probably Fuller.'

Prentice thought about it for a moment, then nodded in agreement.

'For the most part he's been quiet and cooperative. But he's very . . . how can I put it? *Distinctive*. His nickname in here is "Smiler" – do you know why?' Paulsen shook her head and Prentice continued. 'He spent some of his early twenties sleeping rough. One night he got in a fight and was attacked with a machete. They left, literally, a dent in his scalp. He calls it his "other" smile – you'll see why when you meet him. He can get frustrated very easily, and just occasionally spectacularly loses his temper. It's only happened once here when he was accused of cheating during a game of table tennis. It took four men to restrain him. Two of them were hospitalised, and one's still not back at work.'

'I'll be sure not to take him on at table tennis then,' said Paulsen. 'Has he asked for a solicitor?'

'We told him someone was coming to see him and he waived his right. I think he's just curious to know why you're here.'

Fifteen minutes later, after a seemingly endless walk through the prison complex, Paulsen found herself in a small, sparse room with a table and a couple of chairs. There was a mounted security camera in the corner, and the prison officer who'd escorted her waited by the door as she took a seat. Shortly afterwards there was a knock and a second officer entered with a tall shaven-haired man. He wasn't wearing handcuffs and studied Paulsen with interest as he walked in.

'Blimey. You didn't tell me she was a student?' he said with a toothy grin and a thick Scouse accent. To Paulsen's chagrin his escort flashed the ghost of a smile back, before ushering him to the chair opposite. The escort exited and took up a position outside the door, while the other prison officer remained in the room with her. Both of them, she noted, carried tasers.

'You writing a paper on me or something, love? For your *diss-ur-tay-shun*?' He grinned again and Paulsen smiled curtly back before going through the necessary formalities. When she'd finished she produced her notebook and placed it on the table in front of her, and pulled a biro out of her bag. Fuller was watching it all closely.

'Shall I tell you what I know about you, DC Paulsen?' he said with a friendly smile. She needed him to talk, so at this point allowed him to control things a little – or at least gave him the illusion of control.

'You're on edge. You keep looking down. Stop doing that, I'm not a threat. Treat me like an adult and I'll treat you like one.' He crossed his arms. 'Alright, love, I'm going to do this – but we're just going to see how it goes, for the minute. What can I do for you?'

'Raymond Spinney . . .' she said. The words came out of her mouth like cut crystal.

'Oh. Him.' His smile broadened.

'What can you tell me about him?'

'Nothing I haven't already said. Go back and read the statements I gave when I was nicked.'

'I'm investigating the murder of two men. One was burnt alive at his wedding. The other was also burnt, in his car.' Fuller was unreadable as he took the information in. 'Is that the sort of thing Spinney might have asked you to do once?'

'Jesus Christ, love, I don't know. He's the kind of man that likes to make a statement, certainly. He wants people to know that he has a reach – because he *does*. Is fire now his thing?' Fuller shrugged non-committedly. 'I haven't seen him for a good many years – how would I know?'

Again he was inscrutable, and held her gaze for a bit too long. She referred down to her notebook instinctively, irritated with herself as she did so. She didn't like being intimidated. Especially by men.

'I told you not to do that,' he said.

'Do you think it's likely he was involved in the Stansted robbery?'

Fuller laughed.

'Ah . . . the Handyman. You want to know if Ray Spinney's the Handyman? Bloody hell, love, you really are writing a paper, aren't you? Do you want me to tell you if the Loch Ness monster's real while I'm at it? Don't you think I've been asked this about a million times? I can't be arsed, love – sorry. "Interview terminated", as you people like to say.' He turned to look at the prison officer in the corner as if ready to leave.

'Alright,' said Paulsen quickly. 'What about Erik Whitlock?' At this Fuller slowly turned back to face her.

'What about him?'

'We know he was an associate of Spinney's. We know you used to work for Spinney. Did you ever meet Whitlock?'

'Half the criminal fraternity of London probably dealt with Erik Whitlock at some point. He was a middleman. Or at least that's where he always positioned himself. A money launderer, a link man – a go-between, whatever you want to call it. He was the buffer between a buyer and seller. And a good one, but I could also tell you about a dozen people who lost everything because of him. Including people I know, by the way. He was a flash bastard too. I hope he felt every fucking minute of it when Pacific Square burnt.'

'Do you think the proceeds of the Stansted robbery passed through his hands?'

'Don't be stupid, love – you don't come across as stupid. Every newspaper in the country claimed he was involved with that when he died.'

'But do *you* think that?'

There was a pause. Fuller was choosing his words carefully now.

'Do you know how difficult it is to deal with that quantity of money? You need someone who knows what they're doing. Back then Whitlock was the *only* bloke you'd go to for that.' Fuller stopped. He seemed to be thinking very hard. Paulsen waited for him to continue, but he didn't.

'Go on . . .'

'I'm pretty sure he'd dealt with about seventy-five per cent of the Stansted proceeds before he died. I don't think you'll ever find it. Most of it, if not all of it, will be abroad now. Disseminated. As they say.'

'And what about the remaining twenty-five per cent?'

'Well, now, there's a question . . .'

Now it was Paulsen's turn to think – all this was almost confirmation of Finn's theory.

'Do you think . . . *whoever* was behind the Stansted robbery would ever forget about that twenty-five per cent? Be happy with what they did get? I mean seventy-five per cent of what they stole was still a huge amount.'

Fuller grinned, but there was no humour to it.

'Not in a million years.'

'Even after all this time?'

Fuller looked at the prison officer again.

'I'm done.'

The officer looked over at Paulsen. Fuller's expression was intense, the earlier good humour well and truly gone. There was a glint of something menacing there now. Paulsen decided she'd gleaned as much as she judged useful and nodded at the officer. Fuller stood and turned, and Paulsen saw the back of his head for the first time. About a third of the way down there was a dent, a long cavity that resembled a grotesque grin which curved horribly inwards. For a moment Paulsen felt her stomach turn. Prentice's words came back to her: *'He calls it his other smile.'*

The officer led Fuller to the door and then he suddenly stopped and turned back to Paulsen, well aware of what she'd been staring at.

'I should tread carefully, love. When people in your profession start asking questions, Ray Spinney always knows. *Always.*'

What scared her most was that he sounded like he was doing her a favour.

23

'For fuck's sake!'

DI Andy Warrender was puce, thought Godden. He was a man with a natural pinkness at the best of times, but this was the first time he'd seen him actually go the full beetroot. The fleshy jowls around his face were literally shaking. He looked like an angry holidaymaker furiously complaining about a delayed flight at the departure gate.

'What's the matter?' Godden asked patiently.

'Another member of that fire crew's been murdered. Same as before – someone torched him.'

'Jesus. The crew that attended Pacific Square?'

'Yeah. I just spoke to Cedar House. They ever so politely told me to keep my nose out of it. Arrogant tossers.'

'You're thinking it's something we should be looking at? I thought you weren't interested?'

'I am now. If there really is a link to Whitlock, then there's a link to Stansted, and that makes it ours.'

'Was it on their patch again?'

Warrender nodded.

'Well, I can understand why they're circling their wagons then. They'll pool what they have. It's like you said earlier, let them do the legwork then it's a win-win for us. If they find something that's relevant we can send someone to join their investigation. If not, we've saved ourselves some bother.'

Warrender grabbed a chair next to Godden's desk and slumped into it.

'You know what's really pissing me off, Mike? People don't take us seriously. They think they're better off keeping us out of the loop. But they don't understand the big picture and it's lazy. More than that, it's fucking unprofessional.'

'So what can I do to help?'

Warrender was calming down and drummed his fingers on Godden's desk for a few seconds while he thought about it.

'Dig out the interviews that were done with the fire crews after Whitlock's remains were found and go through them. I'm sure Cedar House are doing exactly the same thing, but I'm not being caught with my pants down. See if there's anything that strikes you as odd.'

'Sure.' Godden's face creased into a frown. 'But this particular crew may have served together for years. We're all focusing on Pacific Square, but it could be something else they dealt with. Some private bollocks they were dabbling in.'

'Exactly. Have a look and see what you can find out. That DI I just spoke with – Finn – was so far up his own arse, I'm surprised he's able to walk in a straight line. Nothing would give me greater pleasure than to tell him he's wrong.'

Pleased with the insult and with some modicum of good humour restored, Warrender left. The man was an imbecile, thought Godden. A well-meaning imbecile, but an imbecile nonetheless. Not that he was complaining, because right now, more than ever, he needed Warrender to be predictable.

It seemed obvious to Godden what was happening. Both Cedar House and Raymond Spinney clearly believed the fire crew stumbled on to something five years ago. Money probably. Spinney must have received proof from somewhere and was now ensuring some loose ends were being tied up. The greedy sods should have just let it burn. Spinney's summons

135

earlier must be connected to this. At a guess, he was needed to mop up behind the murders and ensure any potential threat was nipped in the bud. Godden sighed – there were still three more members of that fire crew to go. Dead men walking. This was nowhere near over yet. It was going to be a ball-ache.

He'd long ago come to terms with the reality of what he was: a dirty cop. For the most part, anything he'd done was small fry balanced against the weight of his career as a whole. His career still mattered to him too. He'd done a *lot* of good work over the years. He'd been a good thief-taker who'd achieved some notable results in his time. It was there in black and white. Not that anyone would see it that way if he was ever discovered. He'd be disgraced – his name known and vilified. It's just how it was and he'd worked too long and too hard to allow it to happen.

When he'd first graduated from Hendon he'd never have countenanced taking a bribe, let alone being on the payroll of a criminal. His father came from a generation that grew up respecting the police, and he'd been passionately proud of his son's career choice. His old man would turn in his urn if he could see him now. He wouldn't understand – this was about pragmatism. A failed marriage, maintenance payments and a stupidly high mortgage on a flat he'd bought when love prevailed over common sense. It all meant he'd been left with little choice.

The first contact came six years ago – Godden had since worked out that Spinney must have been planning the Stansted heist at the time. They'd been watching him for a while. He'd taken to treating himself to a regular Friday night balti at his local curry house, and that's where the approach was made. A bespectacled man in a black waistcoat came and sat opposite him and said just one word:

'Franny.'

Francesca was his daughter. She was eleven at the time, and the man proceeded to describe in fine detail the sequence of her day; from leaving home in the morning to go to school, to the moment she returned to the small terraced house she shared with Godden's estranged wife. The man in the waistcoat then outlined in equally meticulous detail Godden's outgoings and expenses. He balanced them against his monthly pay cheque and the likely cost of Franny's future education. Godden would have been pushed to find an accountant who could have produced a better audit of his finances. The man he'd come to know as Raymond Spinney offered him a cash supplement, regular, for as long as his assistance was needed. All that was required in return was information. He need hurt no one and no one need get hurt.

It did not stay like that; the terms of the deal subtly changed as his demands grew over the years. If any of Spinney's associates came under scrutiny, then Godden would nudge the investigation down another path. On some occasions he was asked to ensure minor bits of evidence were contaminated so they couldn't be used in court. Sometimes he was asked to talk to potential witnesses. He never threatened anyone, it was more about cajoling. Using his easy charm to suggest giving evidence in court wasn't in anyone's interests: *'You don't need that kind of aggravation. It's you I'm thinking of . . .'*

The trouble was, one of the men Godden helped protect was Erik Whitlock. Someone smart could potentially make the connection if they knew what to look for. He'd hidden his tracks well over the years, but it was always a tricky line to walk. Make it too obvious and an absence of information could be just as incriminating. Some pieces of the puzzle therefore needed to be left in play. It was about risk management, and Godden fancied himself as rather good at that.

After the Stansted heist it hadn't been hard to get on to the investigating team. The robbery was on his patch which was why Spinney targeted him in the first place. Even then, Godden felt he was no more than an insurance policy, a backup if the post-heist plans unravelled. He did just enough. Small nudges and swerves which allowed Spinney to slip under the radar and eventually go off grid altogether. He might forever be in the frame, but proving it was now almost impossible – thanks to Godden. When Warrender took over as the team's senior investigating officer, the two men quickly formed a friendship. The man was an idiot, yes – but there was an earnestness to him that Godden rather liked. The fact he too was emerging from a messy divorce helped cement the bond. Their friendship made steering him away from Spinney that bit easier too.

Now two former firefighters were dead and Erik Whitlock's name was once again on people's lips. It meant those little pieces of the puzzle Godden deliberately left in the system could form a potential path to his desk – if the right person came looking. He needed to clean up and it needed to be done fast.

24

Finn, Paulsen and Ojo were holding an impromptu summit in YoYo's. Momentum was starting to build now, even if it was all rather unfocused. There was forensic evidence, witness statements from two crime scenes and new information flying in from all angles. In these situations, Finn liked to take things out of the incident room and bounce it off a few trusted heads. To his own surprise he now seemed to be including Paulsen in that.

'The fire investigation team have now confirmed both blazes were arson. The same accelerant was used at each crime scene,' said Ojo, passing Finn a piece of paper from the pile gathered on the table in front of them. The news was hardly a surprise, but Finn was pleased to see it in black and white. He scanned through the report and then took a sip from one of Yolande's industrial-strength filter coffees.

'Let's start with Adesh Kaul first. Are all the interviews complete now?'

Ojo nodded. 'We've taken statements from everyone who was at the wedding, including the hotel staff and guests who weren't part of the wedding party. There's conflicting descriptions of a man a few people say they didn't recognise – but none of them tally. We're in the process of trying to go through the photos, that were taken on the day. Just in case someone caught him accidentally. We've also been through Kaul's phone records and digital forensics haven't found anything on his laptop. We've also looked into Stephanie quite intensively. There's nothing out of the ordinary there either. No recent ex-boyfriends or dodgy workmates to speak of.'

'What about his finances? Did you dig any deeper?' said Finn, looking at Paulsen.

'I still can't account for how he paid for the wedding,' she replied. 'The gold Stephanie wore on the day cost nearly thirty grand alone. You'd expect to pay a sum like that for the entire event. His business was doing well – but not *that* well. There was nothing in his savings which would have covered it either.'

'What about those cash sums of money he'd been paying in to his account?'

'They go back about four years. To begin with, they were quite large – as much as a thousand pounds each sometimes. By the time he died it was roughly a couple of hundred every month.'

'It's possible some of his clients paid him in cash?' suggested Ojo.

'Enough to pay for thirty grand's worth of bling, and a wedding on top? I'm not convinced,' said Finn. 'What about Elder – was he doing anything like that too?'

'No, but he owned his house outright and the same goes for the Maserati. All paid for up front,' replied Ojo.

'If these guys did get their hands on some of the Stansted money, they haven't exactly been discreet, have they?' said Paulsen.

Finn took his glasses off for a moment, revealing uncharacteristically bag-lined eyes. He held the frames absently for a moment, gesturing with them as he spoke.

'They aren't career criminals though. Most people wouldn't know what to do with cash sums like that. You'd probably put it somewhere safe, wait until you think you've got away with it – then start enjoying yourself.'

'I did discreetly ask some of Kaul's family if they'd seen

anything unusual regarding his money. They all said he was never short of a few notes, but that he kept the business close to his chest. I saw no reason to disbelieve any of them,' said Paulsen.

Finn blew through his teeth as he considered it. 'I know it was my theory – but let's just all be careful of unconscious bias with this, eh?'

It wouldn't be the first time an investigation team fell into the trap of bending the facts to fit an attractive explanation. Part of him was also desperately hoping these men really hadn't been so fucking stupid.

'It does hang together though – especially if there's still twenty-five per cent of the Stansted cash unaccounted for, as Kenny Fuller claims,' said Paulsen.

'What did Chapel Row say when you told them about that?' said Finn.

'DI Warrender was sceptical. Reckoned you had to take anything Fuller said with a pinch of salt.'

'He's right, but you can't just dismiss it outright.' Finn looked deeply unimpressed.

'So what direction do you want to go in now then, guv?' asked Ojo.

Finn stirred his coffee, then carefully laid the spoon down next to the cup.

'If we think these guys took money from Pacific Square then let's try and stand that up and see if there's any actual substance to it.'

'That won't be easy. We'll never be able to prove there *was* ever cash in that building. The firefighters are the only people who'd know. Whitlock's the only other potential witness and he's dead. It's almost the perfect crime,' said Paulsen.

'They'd still have to account for any cash we find. Do you want me to apply for search warrants?' said Ojo to Finn.

'Not yet, I want to talk to these men first. Besides, I doubt they're keeping it in shoeboxes under the bed. And after five years who knows how much of it they've still got? Do we know what their precise movements were on the night itself?'

Ojo nodded and reached for a folder in her bag. She added it to the pile of papers on the table.

'They were part of Red Watch at Earlsfield Fire Station. From the official report, Walker led a breathing apparatus team in just after they arrived on the scene. They'd seen some-one – presumably Erik Whitlock – waving at the window.'

'Walker told us when they reached him on the third floor he was already dead, and they couldn't retrieve the body,' said Paulsen. Finn shook his head.

'Was he though? If we're saying they're potentially unrelia-ble witnesses, then can we trust anything they've said from the point when they went in? If they stumbled on Whitlock and twenty-five per cent of rather a lot . . . how do we know they didn't kill him for it?'

There was a pause as they each thought through the implica-tion; the speed of decisions which would have been taken – literally – in the heat of the moment.

'It might not have been a collective thing,' said Paulsen. 'Maybe one of them acted and the others had no choice. Or maybe it's like Walker said – it was too late and there was nothing they could do for Whitlock. If the cash was just sitting there . . .'

'Before you both run away with this, there is one other thing,' said Ojo. 'I spoke to Gary Elder's mother. She claims he went into business with Adesh Kaul for a short time after they both retired. Only for about eighteen months. So the business has been dead for quite a while, but she seemed uncomfortable talking about it. I got the feeling she was hiding something.'

'What kind of business was it?' said Finn.

'They provided bouncy castles for hire. Children's parties, that kind of thing.'

'They wouldn't be cheap to buy,' said Paulsen.

Finn nodded.

'Dig a bit deeper, Jacks, see what else you can find out. Anything which links those two is important. It might be what funded the wedding and the fast car.'

'Or it might be a business they set up with the proceeds of cash they nicked from Pacific Square,' said Paulsen.

'Exactly. So first things first. We've heard Walker's explanation; now let's see what the other two have to say. I'll interview Maddox. DC Paulsen – you go and speak with Stuart Portbury.'

'And if our murderer *is* the fucking Handyman – you know, a bloke you described as a fairy story earlier this week – with all due respect, guv, how are we going to bring him in?' said Ojo.

Paulsen found herself warming to the Detective Sergeant. She was starting to get a handle on Ojo's relationship with Finn and was enjoying it, just as she was enjoying the smile on Finn's face. It vanished though as he focused on the question.

'We don't know what happened in Pacific Square once those men found Erik Whitlock. But two of them are dead, and the other three may now be targets. If they're not telling us the whole story, then we may need to protect them from themselves.'

25

Phil Maddox
The police want to see me. Does anybody
know why?   07:08

Martin Walker
Stay calm. They're just asking about Adesh.
They've already talked to me. Be honest –
tell them you hadn't seen him in years.   07:12

Phil Maddox
FFS – you didn't mention they'd been to see
you.   07:13

Martin Walker
It was just a DI and a junior DC who asked all
the obvz questions. Nothing you can't handle. 07:16

Phil Maddox
What if they ask about Pacific Square?   07:17

Martin Walker
Tell them what you can . . .   07:19

Phil Maddox
Gary, Stu – have they spoken to you yet?   07:19

Phil Maddox
Come on guys – I need some help here?   08:20

Stuart Portbury

They're coming to see me too. The skipper's
right – tell them as much as u can. It's the
best way of getting rid of them. You've got
to stay calm.   08:34

Phil Maddox

I am calm. But there's potentially someone out
there who KNOWS about us. Doesn't that
concern you?   08:36

Stuart Portbury

What good will worrying do? We don't even
know what happened to Adesh yet. Keep a
grip mate.   08:39

Phil Maddox

FFS!   08:42

Phil Maddox

Gary – are they coming to see you too?   08:44

Phil Maddox

Gary?   09:02

26

It was an odd choice, thought Finn.

One Pacific Square gleamed before him in the late morning sunshine. It was now an established part of the London skyline, alongside the Gherkin, the Shard and the Cheesegrater. The angular dark blue tower hadn't managed to acquire its own unique nickname, partly perhaps due to its troubled origins.

The choice he found so puzzling was the location of Phil Maddox's flat. It was only a mile or so from the tower. It was hard to understand why he'd want to live so close to a place that surely held difficult memories. Or maybe that was the point – sometimes the best places to hide were in plain sight.

Maddox's flat was at the top of a new build, a clay-coloured oblong of a structure, criss-crossed with shiny glass balconies. Finn didn't like it. Give him a period building any day. His eyes unexpectedly began to prick. Another of those random guerrilla attacks of grief. Somewhere in an alternate reality, he and Karin were living in a Victorian townhouse raising the family they'd never talked about having. This time the assault on his senses was mercifully brief. One of the bizarre things about bereavement, he was beginning to notice, was you couldn't anticipate how acute these moments were going to be. He cleared his thoughts and headed for the entrance.

Inside, the flat looked expensive. It offered a stunning view of the Thames from the huge windows at the end of the living room. Everything looked new. Formica furniture and chrome fittings abounded. Finn casually asked if Maddox owned the place, and he nodded awkwardly. Awkward to the point of embarrassed, thought Finn.

There were a pair of sofas close to the windows. Finn sat on one that looked as if it'd never been used. Maddox sat opposite, arms crossed, visibly nervous. In the circumstances it wasn't surprising.

'Gary was burnt alive as well . . . just like Adesh?'

For a moment Finn saw the misshapen thing at the wheel of the burnt-out Maserati. A hunk of blackened meat, peeling strips of burnt flesh fused to scraps of charred material. The accompanying smell of gristle, toxic and plastic. He remembered too the sour-sweet smell which permeated the corridors of the Manor Park Hotel.

'I'm afraid so. Have you any idea why someone would target either of them?'

'No, none at all. I haven't kept in touch with anyone from those days since I left.'

'Why did you quit, if you don't mind me asking?'

'I'd had enough. Simple as that.'

'That's it?'

'It sums up a lot of boring reasons, but yes.'

'I know Adesh Kaul and Gary Elder left around the same time. So did Stuart Portbury and Martin Walker. Was there any specific reason you all went more or less together?'

'No. It wasn't something we talked about. It's just how it panned out.'

He looked tense. Finn was already recalibrating his approach. Go in too hard and the man would clam up.

'It was all within months of the Pacific Square blaze . . .'

'So?'

'Was it connected?'

147

'And what if it was? It's hardly something I should have to explain. You have heard of PTSD, haven't you? We went through a hell of a lot that night.'

He made a good point and Finn felt ashamed for not thinking of it sooner. The pressures on firefighters attending major incidents were immense. It was a perfectly valid explanation for why all these men had left so soon after Pacific Square.

'I'm sorry, you're quite right. Was that the reason?'

'I can only speak for myself, but yes, it certainly played a part in my thinking.'

He ran through his version of what happened that night. Finn couldn't help notice it tallied exactly with Walker's account. He wondered if that's because it was precisely what happened, or whether they'd colluded on it. The surviving men may not have seen each other in the intervening years, but he'd seen them talking amicably enough at Kaul's wake. It was entirely possible they'd settled on an agreed narrative.

'So what have you been doing since you retired? It's nearly five years, isn't it?'

'Freelance IT work mainly. It's a lot safer than fighting fires.' He gestured at a smart workstation in the corner of the room.

'And that's paid for all of this?' Finn gestured at the rest of the room and Maddox looked awkward again.

'I inherited some money too. It's partly why I quit the job, my mother died shortly before. You can check that if you want,' he added somewhat unnecessarily.

'Doesn't it worry you? Two of your old colleagues dying in these circumstances? Aren't you concerned you might be targeted too?'

'Obviously it's worrying. Mainly because I don't know *why* they died. You must have some idea?'

'Not at this point, no.'

148

'Do I need protection?' His foot was tapping nervously now.

'It's something we can talk about. If there's a genuine threat to life, we've a duty of care towards you.'

Maddox shook his head.

'But I've done nothing wrong. I've nothing to hide.'

Finn decided to stop dancing.

'Phil, the man you found inside Pacific Square – Erik Whitlock. You know who he was, don't you?'

'Yes, I read the papers at the time.'

'Good. Because we think he might have taken some money in there that night. A lot of it. I'm trying to get to the truth, because if I don't know the full picture then it makes protecting you very difficult. So, if there's something you want to tell me . . . now's the time to say it. It might just save your life.'

Maddox breathed out with what almost sounded like a whimper. Finn was certain the man was about to break, but then for the first time since they'd begun talking, he looked him in the eye.

'You asked me why I quit. There was a job we did a few years back. A house fire near Streatham. Some kid was playing with matches in the back garden while his parents were watching telly inside. It was autumn, so there were a lot of dry leaves on the ground.' He looked out of the window, the sun reflecting brightly off the river below. 'The leaves were like tinder and this kid set himself alight. He can't have been much more than nine. His parents never heard a thing. The first they knew was when they saw the orange glow reflecting off the TV. I carried him out of that garden myself, his skin melting on to my uniform. He died in hospital a few days later. You talk to a firefighter, a paramedic, a cop . . . everyone's got a story like that. I'm betting you have too. So don't ask me why

I quit, because you know why – it *all* catches up with you in the end.'

And just for a moment, Finn heard the authenticity in the man's voice.

'Does it look like I robbed a bank?'

Stuart Portbury seemed more mildly amused than terrified for his life, thought Mattie Paulsen. The small one-bedroom flat in Greenwich where he lived was modest. She was looking for signs of excess spending, but nothing was jumping out. If anything, it reminded her of her own boxy flat that she shared with Nancy. There was a kitchen diner on the ground floor with a small bedroom at the back, and a cupboard-like shower room in between. He lived alone and the whole place, unlike hers, was spotlessly clean.

'If you don't mind me saying, you don't seem too bothered that two of your former colleagues have been murdered?'

'What gives you that idea? Of course I'm upset. It's more that I can't get my head around it. I don't understand why.'

She led him through the flow of their thinking: *One Pacific Square – Erik Whitlock – stolen money – the Handyman*. Portbury just looked bewildered.

'I was *outside* One Pacific Square – I never went into the building on the night. I was manning the pump. Whatever went on in there you'll have to ask the others about. The other two now, I mean.' He corrected himself and looked away for a moment.

'I'm sorry, but I had to ask.'

'And this is a genuine line of inquiry? That Adesh and Gary were killed for money they're supposed to have stolen that night? Cash you think I took too?'

'You tell me.'

'All my money's in a NatWest savers account, which you're welcome to go through. You won't find much.'

'I'll take you up on that. And if we take a *really* close look at your accounts over the last five years, what will we find?'

'Too much shit bought off eBay? Look, if you do want to do that, then knock yourselves out. I haven't got anything to hide. Search this place too if you want – there's nothing under the bed. I'm a tradesman these days, spend most of my time with my arm up a U-bend. I earn enough to live a quiet life and that's how I like it.'

He seemed genuine enough, thought Paulsen, but something nagged at her about him. She'd felt exactly the same about Walker in his garden, she realised.

'Did you ever get a sense that something strange had gone on? Were the other guys different afterwards, like they were hiding something?'

'No. We were all absolutely shattered for ages after. We didn't really talk about it. Nights like that you're just grateful to come away in one piece. You do realise there were more than just the five of us there that night? There were firefighters from all over London.'

'Yes – I'm aware of that. But you quit afterwards. You and the other four you drove there that night. Why?'

He shrugged.

'A lot of firefighters quit after Pacific Square. I'm sure the LFB have all the details – ask them how many needed help with PTSD as well.'

'Did you?'

'No. Like I say, I was lucky, I was outside the building.'

She noticed he tensed slightly as he remembered. The memory seemed to bother him.

'You still haven't told me why you left the job?'

'I can only speak for myself. For me it felt like the end of an era. And those guys *weren't* my mates; I haven't stayed in touch with any of them since I went. But we served together for a long time. When the team began to break up, the job felt different to me. I didn't like it. It just seemed like a natural time to make the break.'

'Alright, Stuart. But if there is something you're not telling me – and maybe you don't want to break that circle of trust with your old crew – just remember it didn't help Elder or Kaul.'

This seemed to register, and for a moment Paulsen thought she saw something else in Portbury's expression, a cry for help in his eyes. Much later she'd remember that.

It was Ojo who broke the news of Elder's death to Martin Walker. The former crew manager was visibly shocked. He'd said all the right things, offered his assistance, but she'd still come away with an impression he was holding something back.

'They all are,' said Paulsen as she, Finn and Ojo regrouped at Cedar House.

'What did you make of Portbury?' asked Finn.

'Cool as a cucumber, but that's because he thinks all this has nothing to do with him. There's no obvious signs of unexplained wealth. He's the only one whose finances seem to fit his circumstances.'

Finn turned to Ojo.

'Jacks, have you found any more on that business Kaul and Elder set up together?'

She went over to her desk and grabbed some paperwork.

'I pulled this off the Companies House website earlier.' She skimmed down the sheet. 'Gemini Leisure – incorporated on March 9th 2016, dissolved on April 16th 2017. Lists Elder as Company Secretary and Kaul as a director.'

'That puts them in business for a year. That's a lot of time for them to have made some enemies,' said Paulsen.

Ojo was still glancing through the paperwork she was holding.

'There's more, hang on . . .'

She went back to her computer and scanned through her emails.

'Fuck . . .' she said under her breath, before tapping at her keyboard. She went over to the printer, waited for it to judder into life and then pulled a slowly emerging sheet of A4 from its jaws.

'When I Googled Gemini Leisure earlier, the only other thing I found was a brief newspaper report about a legal proceeding involving them. Turns out some woman suffered a life-changing injury on one of their inflatables. She broke her back and was paralysed from the waist down. She and her husband tried to bring an action against them, but Gemini were cleared of any liability. I emailed the local paper earlier to see if they had any more and they've just replied – it turns out she committed suicide earlier this year.'

Finn and Paulsen exchanged glances.

'A husband, you say?' said Finn.

27

Kevin Pender was looking old, Paulsen thought. Which was odd, because she'd only just met him. He possessed a mop of unkempt black hair and a face which looked permanently stern thanks to a pair of thick-set black eyebrows. There was weariness too. You could easily knock off five years and picture the younger, warmer iteration of this man. Before tragedy changed him. She and Finn were in the front room of his three-bedroom house in Sutton. It mirrored its owner's state of disrepair. She guessed this was a home once, rather than just a living space. Expensive-looking furniture sat neglected, chipped and stained. The living room was scattered with miscellany – papers, books and mugs piled in corners, gathered on chairs. There were prominent wedding pictures too on the mantelpiece. A self-conscious, smiling brunette posing with that younger, friendlier version of Kevin.

'It was my brother's birthday. He was the one who actually booked the fucking thing.'

The words themselves were angry but the voice was toneless. He looked like a man in urgent need of help, thought Paulsen.

'Take your time,' Finn said.

'You still haven't properly told me why you're here?'

'We're looking into Gemini Leisure.'

Pender reacted immediately.

'Good. That pair of fucking chancers deserve to burn in hell for what they did.' Finn and Paulsen exchanged a look.

'Just tell us what happened, if that's okay,' said Paulsen.

'Vinny – my brother – he's got two little ones. He'd invited half the street round for a barbecue, so we knew there'd be a lot of kids running around. We all thought a bouncy castle in the garden would be a good idea. Debs loved kids. We wanted lots.' He smiled tightly. 'Anyway, she was jumping on it with some of them. But you could tell it hadn't been properly inflated. I mean, I didn't like it from the moment I saw it.'

'Were they there, Elder and Kaul?' asked Finn.

'No, they'd installed it the day before.' He took a deep breath and resumed. 'So Debs is trying to get off it, and she's doing that stupid walk you do on those things, you know, like you're on the moon or something. She gets to the end and I see her foot slide as she tries to jump off, and she falls forwards on to the grass. We all laughed. I mean, it *looked* funny – but then she doesn't move and the kids think she's playing, so they're all jumping around. But she's not moving . . .'

'How quickly did you learn the severity of it?' asked Finn.

'Almost straight away, once they'd done their X-rays and stuff. Her spinal cord . . .' He shook his head, and suddenly brought a closed fist down hard on his own knee in frustration.

'I'm sorry to make you revisit this—' said Finn.

'Everyone thinks there's always going to be some great story of redemption. That she'll start doing these inspirational things – become a Paralympian or something. But that's not how it was. She was talking about suicide from day one. She just didn't want to go on.'

'Why did you take legal action against Gemini Leisure?' asked Paulsen.

'Do you know what the safety regs are on bouncy castles? They're supposed to be tested on an annual basis, they're supposed to come with a unique number that proves they've been tested. That number's meant to go on a database. It's got to conform to British standards of safety.'

'And did it?'

'Officially, yeah, but that's because those two conmen managed to get themselves on the list of approved inspectors. In effect they approved themselves. It's an absolute joke.'

'Do you hold Elder and Kaul responsible for what happened to Debbie?'

'What do you think? That bastard Elder tried to buy me off. Can you believe that? He actually offered me money. Can you fucking believe it?'

Finn and Paulsen glanced at each other.

'How much?' asked Paulsen.

'We didn't get that far, because I told him what he could go and do.'

'Was he serious?'

'Oh, yeah. Muttered something about a five-figure sum if I backed off. It's a good job he said it over the phone. If he'd said it to me in person . . .'

His anger was rising again. Paulsen wondered if it would ever really leave him; wondered just how far it might take him or *had* taken him.

'I know this is difficult—' began Finn.

'*Difficult?* Do you know what it's like to lose someone you love before you've even got started? To watch her slipping out of reach? Have you any idea, mate?'

Paulsen glanced at Finn and could see he was controlling himself. He glanced at her and briefly caught her eye, catching her concern. There was a flicker of awkwardness on his face, and he turned back to Pender.

'It must be hard.'

'You've no idea.'

'I'm sorry to ask you this, Kevin, but where were you the night before last?'

'What's that got to do with anything?'

'Just answer the question, please?'

'Am I being accused of something?'

'Can you just clarify where you were?'

'Here. My wife took an overdose four months ago, what do you think I'm out doing – partying?'

'Were you on your own?'

'Yes.'

'So there's no one who can corroborate that?'

'No. Are you going to tell me what this is about?'

'Where were you on Saturday afternoon?'

'Same. I was here on my own.'

Finn looked at Paulsen, and then spoke.

'Adesh Kaul and Gary Elder are dead. They were both murdered.'

Pender shrank back into his seat. You could read it as either guilt or shock, thought Paulsen, but it was impossible to tell.

'And you think I did it?'

'You have a motive and no alibi for either day. What would you think if you were us?' said Finn.

'Mate . . . I haven't got the energy to make a cup of tea right now, let alone murder someone. Is this some sort of piss-take? Can't you see I've been through enough?'

'Kevin, please, is there anything you can tell us about those two dates? Something which can help us eliminate you from our inquiries?' said Paulsen. For a moment he was unfathomable, and then he laughed.

'I'll give you something – I'm *glad* they're dead. I hope they died in fucking agony and I hope anyone they ever loved feels exactly the way I do.'

It was enough for Finn.

'Kevin Pender, you are under arrest on suspicion of murder. You do not have to say anything, but it may harm your defence if you do not mention when questioned something which you later rely on in court. Anything you do say may be given in evidence.'

Paulsen half expected him to explode, but instead he shook his head as if almost amused by what was happening. He sagged back into his chair, the fight ebbing out of him. As Finn handcuffed him, Paulsen tried to make sense of it. He'd all but invited arrest. But could the small wiry man in front of her really have overcome Adesh Kaul? Overpowered Gary Elder and torched him alive in his own car? This felt like it was just raising more questions than answering anything. Looking at Finn, she could see in his eyes that that was precisely what he was thinking too.

28

Godden logged out of his computer and grabbed his jacket, preparing for his appointment with Spinney. Across the corridor he saw Jim Farmer, head down in some paperwork. He crept over and gave the young DC a sharp tap to the ribs. To his satisfaction, Farmer jumped halfway out of his seat.

'Jesus, Mike! You scared the shit out of me.'

'Yeah, well. Now you know what it feels like.'

Farmer's face opened out into a broad smile.

'The gaffer wants us to go through all this,' said Farmer, motioning at the small tower of paperwork on his desk. 'It's everything we've got on Whitlock – I thought I'd make a start. I've got hard copies if you need them. I know how much you hate reading off a screen.'

'Good lad. Very enterprising. You get stuck in – I've just got to nip out for a few hours.'

'*Hours?* How long are you going to be?'

'How long's a piece of string? Chasing up a lead, aren't I.'

'What lead?'

'You may well ask, old son,' he said, being deliberately cryptic, giving the younger man a wink. 'If the boss asks, tell him I'm in the bog.'

'What, for several hours?'

'Like he'll notice.'

Godden grinned, and Farmer laughed. He seized his moment,

and made for the door. Farmer watched him go, but the smile didn't last for long as his face clouded with uncertainty.

It was Skegman who made him do it. Finn hated press conferences but the media interest in the investigation was now at a point where it needed addressing. Two former firefighters burnt to death within days was always going to make headlines. It wouldn't take long for some bright spark to start digging and find the link to Pacific Square. The latest development was now front page news. The *Standard* splashed with:

'Firefighter deaths: police arrest man'.

Finn was aware the press office was keeping reporters informed, as they did with every major investigation. Their job – in the finest traditions of policing – was to provide the facts, and nothing but the facts. Media releases were written in simple, clear terms without embellishment. But factually accurate as they were, they were often an art form in how to suck the drama out of something. The gruesome way Gary Elder died, reduced to *'Officers are investigating the sudden death of a man in his thirties'*.

Journalists knew this and would always pressure the media team for more flesh to put on the bones of a story. Often though, for operational reasons, it was important to hold some information back. There were plenty of times you didn't want to jeopardise a live investigation by giving away details of a suspect or a location. More importantly, you didn't want to put someone's life at risk. An off-the-record chat explaining the situation to a trusted journalist was usually enough. It was the small minority who chose to break those unwritten rules that Finn had a problem with.

Now that there was someone in custody, Skegman judged it the right time to feed the pack. They hadn't found any hard evidence at the two crime scenes to link Kevin Pender with either murder. An appeal for witnesses and information at this point made sense. If someone came forward who'd seen him at the Manor Park Hotel or in the vicinity of Troy's nightclub, then everyone's jobs would become that much easier. There was an art to these things though. Finn knew what was needed to bring the story alive – the difference between a few shots on the evening news or a full report given more time and greater prominence.

He'd made the call to Stephanie Kaul as soon as he'd informed the press office they were calling a news conference. She'd been released from hospital and was now recovering at home. He knew her shocking appearance – together with the emotion she'd undoubtedly bring – would provide good pictures and audio. He was honest and up front about it when they spoke. If the coverage was memorable, it might just help provide the critical piece of information they needed. She'd agreed without hesitation.

Stephanie arrived in a taxi around an hour before the press pack was due to get there. Finn's first impression was that she was looking slightly better than when he'd last seen her. She still moved painfully slowly and the dressings remained in place over her burns, but there seemed to be a bit more colour to her complexion. He quickly realised it was an overly optimistic estimation. The deadness in her expression was still there, the shock still audible in the reediness of her voice.

Crime scene photographs of her husband's burnt corpse adorned the incident room walls, so he took her over to YoYo's instead where they could talk privately.

'Thanks for coming in, Stephanie. You didn't have to do this, and I appreciate it.'

'Have you got him then? The man who killed Adesh?' He noticed it was the only time she seemed to come alive – when the subject of her husband's killer came up.

161

'I don't honestly know and that's the truth. We'll know more when we've interviewed him.'

'And you really think it's connected to the bouncy castle business?'

'That's what we're looking into. Does the name Kevin Pender mean anything to you?'

She frowned.

'Vaguely . . . he made a complaint or something. Can't remember the details. Adesh said it wasn't very important.'

Nice, thought Finn.

'Do you remember much about that period?'

As she considered it, a couple of uniformed PCs in the corner laughed raucously, and she winced. Finn recognised that – the way grief seemed to magnify the senses. The way *everything* hurt.

'Not really. Adesh always kept everything to do with his work to himself. He loved coming home and telling us all the stories when he was in the fire brigade. It changed after he left.'

'Any reason why?' Finn asked carefully.

'No. Different kind of work though, wasn't it? When you're risking your life every day, it's more exciting, I suppose.'

'Did you ever meet Gary Elder?'

'Yes, but I wasn't wild about him. I didn't *dislike* him . . . he just wasn't really my cup of tea. He didn't deserve what happened to him any more than Adesh, though.' She faltered. 'Please . . . can you tell me why? I need to know *why* my husband died.'

'The man we've arrested – it's only on *suspicion* of murder. We haven't charged him. He might be completely innocent. That's partly why you're here – we need hard evidence. I'm hoping this appeal might be able to help with that. But you don't have to do this if you don't feel up to it.'

'I'm doing it.' Her voice was barely audible but her face said it all.

A short while later Finn led her through to a large room in the basement of Cedar House. There was a long table at the front adorned with microphones and recording devices. Behind it was a backdrop emblazoned with the large blue branding of the Metropolitan Police. Finn poured Stephanie a glass of water from a jug, then sat down next to her. Around thirty journalists were there, with several television cameramen positioned at the back and sides of the room.

Finn opened proceedings by talking through what everyone already knew. A thirty-eight-year-old man had been arrested earlier that day in connection with both murders. He was now in custody and would be questioned shortly. Finn explained that there was still a lot of work to do and there remained a lot of gaps in their knowledge. He made the standard appeal for information and witnesses, then introduced Stephanie. She began strongly; her voice surprisingly clear and confident, shorn of that earlier weakness. She described her husband, what kind of man he'd been – a loving son, brother and partner. Someone who'd helped others, someone who'd made a difference. Finn's face was impassive as she spoke, but as he listened he thought about Erik Whitlock, and the different scenarios that might have unfolded inside that burning building. Would they ever really know what role Adesh Kaul played that night?

It was only when Stephanie started talking about her husband's hopes of becoming a father that she lost it, her head dropping into her bandaged hands to disguise the tears that were starting to fall. Finn was well used to what happened next – anything with a lens zoomed in and focused. There was a deferential silence; not out of sensitivity, but from a desire to capture every last tortured sob on their recording devices.

Worse still, he knew it wouldn't hurt, aware it would become the defining image – the tears of the widow. He briefly let them get what they'd come for, then took the focus off Stephanie by opening up the floor to the usual questions.

'Are you looking for anyone else in connection with this?'

'We're keeping an open mind on that.'

'Is the threat still ongoing?'

'At this stage, I can't rule that out.'

'Given both victims' history, is there a connection with the Pacific Square blaze?'

'We're investigating all possibilities – but you'll understand why I can't answer that question at this point.'

Then, just as Finn was ready to wrap things up, it came. The BBC London reporter asked it.

'Is this connected to Erik Whitlock's death in the Pacific Square fire?'

'Again, you'll understand if I can't go into detail.'

'So you're not ruling it out?'

'I repeat, we're keeping an open mind about the motive and investigating all possibilities.'

Finn could see realisation dawning on the faces in front of him. One of the tabloid reporters followed up quickly.

'Whitlock was the Handyman's money launderer – is that a line of inquiry?'

'Is what? The Handyman? Come on, guys – how many times do I have to say it? Until we know what happened to these men and why they died, we're keeping an open mind.'

The questions continued to come, and Finn continued to bat them away. It was irritating but ultimately he understood the link to the Handyman was always going to be made. At least this way he'd been able to address it head-on. It might just keep the headlines the right side of lurid. It would be interesting to see what Walker, Maddox and Portbury made of them.

'I'm sorry if that was difficult,' Finn said to Stephanie as he escorted her to a waiting taxi afterwards.

'Don't be. I'm sorry about the waterworks. Actually I'm not – I don't mind the world knowing how I felt about Adesh.'

Finn thought of Kevin Pender and the hatred he'd spewed towards both Kaul and Elder. One way or another, by the time this was over Stephanie was going to learn things about her husband which she wouldn't like. He smiled gently at her.

'I'll let you know if there's any developments. Thank you for today – I hope it does some good.'

That much he was sure about.

29

Martin Walker

I've just had a call from the cops. They've
made an arrest.   16:02

Phil Maddox

Yeah – just saw it on the news. Who is it?   16:04

Martin Walker

It's something to do with that bouncy castle
business Gary and Adesh set up. Some bloke
with a grievance apparently.   16:05

Stuart Portbury

Good. Let's hope that puts it to bed.   16:06

Phil Maddox

But they're also linking it to the Handyman . . . 16:06

Martin Walker

No they're not. It's just the media doing that.   16:09

Phil Maddox

I don't like it. Don't think we should
assume anything.   16:10

Martin Walker

Let the police investigation run its course. I'm sure
they've got a good reason for nicking this guy. 16:11

Stuart Portbury

Either way, maybe we should give this group a rest
for a bit? Don't want to arouse any suspicion!   16:13

Martin Walker

Agreed.   16:15

Phil Maddox

Well I don't. That's nuts. Until they charge this
bloke, the threat's still active IMHO.   16:16

Martin Walker

Fine – then let's only use this group if it's
absolutely critical. Does that work for you Phil? 16:18

Phil Maddox

Sure. I just want to make sure we've got all our
bases covered. Like I always used to . . .   16:19

30

Raymond Spinney enjoyed his excursions into London. They were increasingly rare because of the virus of CCTV cameras around the capital. An associate once told him there were over four hundred thousand of them in the city, which worked out roughly at one for every fourteen people. They were everywhere these days – in the streets, on the underground, on the buses, even in the taxis. He wore a long dark coat with usefully long collars, which he wore up. Just another old man, mingling among the throng.

He caught the tube to Tottenham Court Road then made his way to a small coffee shop which sat equidistant between New Oxford Street and the British Museum. The Italian-run cafe was often overlooked by the youngsters who preferred their syrup-filled monstrosities. He was pleased to see Godden already there waiting. He ordered an espresso, then joined him at a small table at the back.

Godden rose to greet him, smiling awkwardly.

'You could have warned me in advance what you were planning. It's difficult to help you when I'm finding things out second hand from that idiot Warrender.'

Spinney ignored him and took a sip of his coffee, a flicker of appreciation on his face as it went down. Godden always found him impossible to read. You could never gauge his mood. His voice gave little away either, always even and precise. Spinney fixed him with a lizard-like stare.

'Just tell me concisely what they know.'

At Chapel Row, Jim Farmer was struggling to find his focus. Sifting through historic paperwork was monotonous work. He'd signed up for the car chases and dawn raids. The material on Erik Whitlock – most of it reams of thick court transcripts – was dry as a bone. But he knew if he missed something important, Warrender would chew him out. Worse still, Godden would be angry at his sloppiness, and he hated the thought of that. Mike Godden was someone whose respect mattered to him. He'd looked out for him, steering him clear of the usual rookie mistakes. In turn Farmer saw the older man as something of a mentor. Today though, he couldn't shake the feeling something was amiss. The DS was lying about where he was. He was sure of it. For the first time the banter between them hadn't felt genuine. It was possible he was dealing with a personal issue, but if so, why not simply tell him that? He'd been odd ever since that DC from south London came to visit. On a whim Farmer logged into the PNC. He opened a new search box, and cross-checked the name *'Erik Whitlock'* with *'Mike Godden'*. He expected nothing, but to his surprise a small list of results appeared. As he began to read them, so his eyes began to widen.

You didn't actually have a conversation with Ray Spinney, thought Godden. He spoke in short staccato sentences, and you ended up responding with long detailed explanations in return. Your own questions were only answered with a question back. Godden was smart enough to know it was probably a deliberate strategy; in its own way, no different to the

169

techniques you might use in the interview room to break a suspect down.

Try as he might, he never seemed to come away from their meetings feeling anything other than unsettled. It was always a relief when he could get away, and that went beyond the simple concern of being spotted together. The man made you feel uncomfortable. As he made his way on to the concourse at Liverpool Street station, he scanned the departure boards and was grateful to see the next train was only a six-minute wait. By the time he got back to Chapel Row it would have been a three-hour round trip. Long enough to look legit, short enough that a covering lie would keep people at bay if they asked.

He reflected on his conversation in the cafe. Spinney was after information about the fire crew – more specifically, the police investigation into the two murders. It was surprising given they had someone in custody now. It was also unlike the so-called Handyman to show signs of unease. Perhaps after holding such control over the Stansted investigation, the idea of an unknown team digging into his affairs was rattling him. Or maybe it was because his name had come up at the press conference at Cedar House. He'd specifically asked Godden to bring information on the officers leading the inquiry. It was as close to a red line as Godden was prepared to draw, and it certainly hadn't been part of the original brief. He was fairly certain Spinney would never kill a police officer. The man was smart enough to know it would change the tempo of everything. But he was an inveterate collector of information, and Godden was hoping he just wanted to know who the main players were in south London. Someone must have done the same due diligence on him once upon a time, he realised.

Before leaving for London, Godden found the details of

DI Finn, who'd so wound up Warrender earlier, and the young DC – Paulsen – who'd visited Chapel Row. The nature of Spinney's interest said it all; he'd wanted to know about their personal lives – where they lived, who they lived with. A little digging on the net showed Finn appeared to be in a relationship with a local solicitor. Paulsen's Facebook profile suggested a gay relationship with a trainee social worker. That'd disappoint Jimmy Farmer if he ever found out. Godden crossed his fingers he was right about Spinney's motives regarding the pair. He could only care so much though; it was hard enough keeping his own arse out of the fire.

His train of thought was disrupted as he felt a mobile phone vibrate in his pocket. It was the one he used uniquely for Spinney. He read the text and stopped in his tracks.

Someone's looking into you. Find out who and shut them down.

He tried to fully assimilate the implications. Who the hell would be doing that, and why? What could they have discovered? And how did Spinney even know? At least that one he could guess at; there must be another inside man somewhere. How naïve was Godden to think he was the only one? They could be at any station in the country. All it needed was someone with the necessary IT skills to set up an alert if Godden's name was being run through the system. His mind was racing now; if he was compromised then so was Spinney and his life wouldn't be worth a thing. He glanced up at the departure board clock, and saw he now only had three minutes to catch his train. The station was starting to fill with rush hour commuters. He sprinted for the barriers with a growing fear his life might just depend on it.

Forty minutes later he arrived back at Chapel Row. He'd almost expected to find anti-corruption officers waiting for him at the front desk, but things seemed fine. As he walked back in, he glanced around carefully. Farmer was where he'd left him, still at his desk, working at his computer. Godden popped his head round the door and produced a casual grin.

'Everything okay, Jim?'

Farmer looked up, but there was no returning smile.

'Did you ever meet Erik Whitlock in person?'

The question felt like a steel blade to the guts. Godden raised an eyebrow as if it struck him as odd.

'Don't think so. Why do you ask?'

'Are you sure?'

'I don't know, mate. I can't tell you how many people I've interviewed this week, let alone way back when. What's this all about?'

'I found a report of a meeting you had with him here six years ago.'

Godden felt his stomach heave. Nothing good could possibly come from this.

'Maybe I did, it's possible – like I say, I can't remember every conversation.'

'And you can't recall this one, or what it was about?'

'Nope.' The word hung there, and Godden knew exactly what Farmer was thinking. That the man he'd met an hour earlier – Raymond Spinney, the Handyman – possessed officers on his payroll; bent police who were derailing the very investigation they were there to pursue, and Mike Godden might very well be one of them.

'There's no record of what was discussed, just the date and the time. Why wouldn't it have been recorded?'

Godden knew full well why. Police in north London were

investigating the post office raids Spinney was thought to be behind. They'd followed the money and drawn a line between Spinney and Whitlock, one of the first occasions the connection was made. The Handyman hadn't been prepared to lose his prize launderer and asked for Godden's help to shield him. Godden had found a pretext to bring Whitlock in for a chat. By feeding back his own version of that interview, he'd been able to temporarily steer the investigating officers away. It was enough for what was needed at the time. Later, when Whitlock's notoriety grew, nobody questioned that early brief intersection with the law. Godden hadn't taken to the man though. He was arrogant and seemed to think his very particular skillset made him an underworld celebrity. Or maybe he just knew that when you were protected by men like Ray Spinney you could afford to be confident. He'd treated Godden with disdain that day. Later when it emerged he'd died in the Pacific Square blaze, the policeman hadn't shed any tears. The real question was how a record of that meeting remained in the system. He thought he'd removed it a long time ago. That was the trouble with the electronic age, nothing's ever really deleted or destroyed any more.

'Must have just been an informal chat, mate, so there was no solicitor present. If it was something important I'd have remembered it. And if you're saying six years ago – that was before Stansted, so not really relevant, eh?'

Farmer looked far from convinced.

'Look, I better crack on, I've wasted enough of the afternoon already. It's honestly nothing to worry about, Jim. We could have been talking to him about anything. He was constantly on our radar at the time.'

The younger officer's face relaxed into a smile, and Godden fought the urge to fist pump.

'Thanks, Mike, I knew it had to be something like that.'

Godden finally allowed himself to breathe out as he walked to his desk. He looked back over at Farmer, now happily engrossed again in his paperwork. This would need watching.

31

Nancy Deen stifled a yawn. She'd spent her morning with one of her favourite clients, a young mother who was just finding her feet again after being released from prison. Now she was back at her Shoreditch office ploughing through the paperwork which came with the case. Her flow of concentration was interrupted by a call from reception – there was someone waiting for her downstairs. Nancy was bemused, because her diary was clear for the afternoon. She went down and was greeted by a large, well-set man in builders' overalls. He smiled pleasantly at her.

'Nancy Deen?'

'Yes?'

'Don't worry, it's nothing serious,' he said, maintaining the smile. 'DC Paulsen sent me.'

'She did?'

'Yeah, she said you needed some work doing at your flat?'

'Not that I'm aware of . . . ?'

Now it was the man who looked confused. He pulled a slip of paper from his pocket and read from it.

'Flat 2, 56 Batsford Road, Tufnell Park? That is your address, isn't it?'

'Yes, but I honestly have no idea what this is about. What kind of work? Why have you come here?'

The man continued to beam at her.

'It's alright – I can see there's been a misunderstanding. Why don't you ring Detective Constable Paulsen and tell her I paid you a visit? She'll explain everything, I'm sure.'

His broad smile extended wider.

'He said what?' said Paulsen. She was at her desk in the incident room, phone clamped to her ear as she strained to hear what Nancy was saying.

'He was adamant. Said you'd know what it meant.'

'And he had our address?'

'Yeah – he read it out to me.'

Paulsen digested this then forced a quiet calm into her voice.

'It's nothing to worry about, Nance. It's like he says, a misunderstanding. I just wanted to get a quote. We've always talked about getting the kitchen done, I rang someone this morning – they must have got the wrong end of the stick.'

'But why come here? Why would you give them my work address?'

'Just as a point of contact. I'll explain later. Listen, I've got to go. It's really nothing to worry about. We'll speak later – love you.' She ended the call and looked up to see Finn waiting for her.

'Are you ready?' he asked.

'For what?'

'Kevin Pender's interview. His brief's here.'

He turned to leave but she hesitated.

'What's the matter?'

'It's my partner – she's just had a visit. At her office. Some bloke claiming to be a builder – said I'd rung him, which is bollocks, I haven't rung anyone.'

'What happened?'

'This guy told her to check with me ... said I'd know all about it.'

'So what was it – some sort of mix-up?'

'Not exactly. When she asked who he worked for, he said "the Handyman" ...'

32

Kevin Pender gave a 'no comment' interview. It was no more than Finn expected given the lack of hard evidence against him. When he returned to the incident room, he held a quick briefing to update the team and focus minds. He was well aware – as he'd been from the start – that their biggest problem was the method of death. Fire was every investigation's worst enemy. If *he* was planning a murder, it would be his weapon of choice. Fire destroyed everything. It was the ultimate cleanser. Now the clock was ticking – and they needed to find something or they'd have to turn Pender loose. The appeal they'd made at the press conference was generating calls, albeit none of the particularly helpful kind so far. Work was continuing at Pender's home and the two crime scenes and they'd just have to hope an apple would fall from the tree.

Finn found something else waiting for him after they'd emerged from the interview room; a message from the firm of solicitors where Karin used to work. As it turned out they'd received a remarkably similar message to Nancy Deen. A phone call in their case, asking to speak to Karin, also casually mentioning 'a handyman'. Finn and Paulsen were now in Skegman's office bringing him up to speed with developments.

'It's a warning shot – nothing more. The fact they called Karin's old office shows their information's out of date. They clearly weren't aware she ... doesn't work there any more,' said Finn, checking himself.

'They found Nancy easily enough,' said Paulsen.

'Don't let it unnerve you. The press conference probably ruffled some feathers, that's all,' said Skegman.

'But I thought the Handyman didn't exist?' she said, looking at Finn.

'I said the tabloid cliché didn't exist, I never said there wasn't someone fitting the profile. The Handyman – whoever he actually is – wouldn't have liked seeing his name back in the headlines. I'm willing to bet this is just a message, but it's very old school,' said Finn. Paulsen looked unconvinced.

'The timing of this is interesting. Right after we've made an arrest, especially of somebody with no links to organised crime.' Skegman realised what he was saying as he said it. 'I take it Pender *doesn't* have any links to organised crime?'

Finn shook his head. 'None as far as we're aware. But everything's still on the table right now. Pender's got a decent motive, that's for sure. But we still need to find something solid before we can charge him.'

'The appeal hasn't produced anything?' said Skegman.

'Just time-wasters so far, but nothing else.'

'With respect, you're all making a lot of assumptions, aren't you? What if it's *exactly* what it looks like – that the Handyman's making threats because he *is* behind Kaul and Elder's deaths? Because they took his money,' said Paulsen.

'You're not convinced by Pender?' asked Skegman.

'Whoever committed those murders knew what they were doing. I spoke to the fire investigator earlier. He thought the toilet at the hotel might well have been a deliberate choice of location. The cubicle kept the blaze contained. The sprinklers and the alarm system made it difficult for the fire to spread. Elder was killed in his car. Odd as it sounds, it's like the killer was being careful, as if he didn't want anyone else to get hurt.'

'I'm not sure I understand?' said Skegman.

'The point I'm making is these were carefully planned. I'm not sure Pender's that man. He's emotional, and a bit broken. Is it credible his reaction to his wife's suicide is to work up such a detailed plan of revenge? Does he even have the skill-set?' Her voice was raised to make the point, just about the right side of passionate. She looked at them both as if it was obvious.

'If it's the Handyman going after these firefighters, why draw attention to yourself by making clumsy threats – to your partner, my wife?' said Finn. 'It's not how people like that work. If anything, it feels like a protest – their way of saying this has nothing to do with us.'

'But why Nancy – how did they even know about me?'

'Maybe the jungle drums were beating after your trip to see Kenny Fuller? We know he's got links to Ray Spinney. I'm willing to bet he relayed the details of your little chat.'

The memory made Paulsen shiver. The idea of someone of a similar ilk to Fuller paying Nancy a visit turned her stomach.

'Doesn't it worry you how they managed to get hold of our details?' she persisted.

'There's any number of ways. I'd recommend getting off social media though – or changing your privacy settings,' said Finn. 'It's not that hard to find out information these days.' Paulsen looked ready to argue, and Finn held up his hand in a conciliatory gesture. 'You can't allow yourself to be knocked out of your stride – that's what these people want.'

'I've not been knocked out of my stride,' she said with visible irritation now. 'But how would you have felt if they'd done this to your wife?'

It took a second for Finn to react. He was so used to every-one tiptoeing around the subject of Karin it was jarring to hear someone refer to her like that.

'Fair point.'

He looked away awkwardly but if Paulsen was embarrassed, she wasn't showing it.

'We can put an officer outside your flat tonight if you're concerned?' said Skegman. He'd been watching the entire exchange with fascination. Paulsen shook her head.

'That won't be necessary, sir, but thank you.'

'What have you told Nancy?' said Finn.

'That it was just a mix-up. She thought it was odd but noth-ing more.'

'You did the right thing. DI Finn's right – I'd try and ignore it,' said Skegman.

'I'd rather not ignore it. I'd prefer to find the spineless piece of shit who's trying to intimidate me, and give some back. *Sir*.' The final word dripped with sarcasm and Skegman's previ-ously sympathetic smile hardened.

'And the best way of doing that is to direct your energies into the investigation, DC Paulsen. Thank you, that will be all for now.'

She looked ready to say more, but checked herself. Her participation in the conversation was clearly over. She glanced briefly at Finn, then took the hint and left the room.

'Are you okay?' Skegman asked Finn.

'I'm fine. She's just a bit shaken up – it's understandable.'

'She was out of order.'

'It's okay . . . honestly.'

Finn look slightly more ruffled than he was making out. Skegman could tell, because in the normal run of things Finn very rarely allowed his discomfort to show – and God knows Skegman had enjoyed trying to provoke some over the years.

'There's one other possibility we can't rule out,' said Finn, changing the subject.

'Which is?'

'We might be looking at two completely separate investigations. Even if Pender is our man, we might have stumbled on a robbery no one ever knew occurred.'

Skegman digested this, his little beady eyes darting around the room for a moment.

'I'd be happier if there was a bit more hard evidence to back up some of these theories. We've got until half past three tomorrow afternoon to charge Pender – what's your next step?'

'Jackie Ojo's gone over to his property to supervise the searches. There was nothing in Kaul's post-mortem that puts him at the hotel and Elder's PM is taking place on Saturday. There's a cell site analysis being done on his phone which should tell us more about his movements. The appeal is still generating calls as well – let's see if something falls out of the tree.'

'What about the other firefighters? If we think they've committed a crime, shouldn't we be investigating it? And if we think they're in danger, shouldn't we be looking to protect them?' said Skegman.

Finn thought about it for a moment.

'We know this investigation is under some scrutiny now. The more it looks like *we* think those firefighters did something, the more someone else might too. We could end up endangering them inadvertently.'

'. . . and then it becomes a self-fulfilling prophecy. Alright, let's see where we are tomorrow afternoon and re-assess.'

Finn nodded.

'And how are you coping, Alex? I am going to keep asking that question.'

'I didn't know you cared, dear,' said Finn quickly, though neither man smiled. There was genuine concern on Skegman's face, though Finn knew it was as much for the investigation as it was for him. 'If I said I was taking things one day at a time, that'd be an exaggeration, but I'm still walking and talking. That's got to be a win.' He checked his watch. 'I better get a shift on – I want to talk to the forensic team over at Pender's place.'

'Do me a favour – take the night off. Leave the searches to Jackie O, and deal with it in the morning.'

For once Finn didn't feel like arguing. If there was evidence to be found, Jackie would find it. Besides, he suddenly felt very tired.

'*Rest, you silly man,*' whispered Karin.

'Alright, boss,' said Finn, not entirely sure he was talking to Skegman.

33

It turned out to be a good choice. That evening Finn managed to allow himself to relax properly for perhaps the first time since Karin's death. He wasn't a man who pursued hobbies as such, but he did have interests. Sport was one of them. He treated it the way other people treated fine wines; he wasn't interested in the cheap stuff at the lower end of the market. What absorbed him was the tactical battle. He loved watching the finest minds pit themselves against each other – it was the strategy that held his interest. He spent the evening sipping on a single malt, reading the biography of legendary American football coach Chuck Noll. Karin's favourite album – Nick Cave's *The Boatman's Call* – played quietly in the background. That was another first, as he began to feel comfortable again filling the silence at home with music. As he made his way to bed it all felt a bit odd. There was almost a sense of betrayal, to have put Karin out of his mind, if only for a few hours. He was also aware it was the kind of evening that had so concerned her in Berlin – one spent enjoying his own company a bit *too* much.

It turned into a hot and muggy night, and he didn't sleep well. Random images of Karin resurfaced as he tried to get cool. He found himself dwelling on memories of their earliest dates, moments of domesticity, and worst of all, the sight of her at the end ravaged by chemotherapy. He tried to distract himself by solving her riddle about the blind dog in the forest, but still couldn't divine its meaning. He wondered if in part that was subconsciously deliberate. A little piece of her he was keeping alive by not solving it. His thoughts drifted on to the investigation, but it wasn't Kevin Pender who preoccupied him. There was something about those former firefighters that wouldn't leave him. The dead look behind Martin Walker's eyes, matched only by Phil Maddox's haunted expression as he'd told the story of the child he'd failed to save. They weren't just men hiding a secret, they were being consumed by one. He decided if the searches at Pender's house were still ongoing in the morning he'd visit Earlsfield Fire Station first thing instead. He'd read the reports of the Pacific Square blaze several times now. He wanted to talk to someone else who was there. Someone who wasn't part of Walker's crew.

Paulsen spent her evening fielding more questions from Nancy about the man who'd visited her at work. Mattie batted them away, but her irritation with Skegman and Finn wasn't so easily banished. It didn't sit with her to be passive in the face of intimidation. If someone was sending a message, then you sent one back. *'Try and ignore it,'* Skegman had said. It felt patronising.

They'd spent the evening slumped on the sofa in front of the television irregularly distracted by their phones. But as she watched Nancy, cross-legged and studying her handset, Mattie could only wonder why she and Finn were targeted. It can only have come from someone inside – again, the possibility didn't seem to unduly bother her superiors. It should have. The idea of a corrupt police officer handing over their details turned her stomach.

The unease stayed with her through the evening and that night Mattie Paulsen dreamt. She was somewhere high, the cityscape spread out in front of her, and she was angry but couldn't remember why. There was a face too, the face that was always there. The one with the affable smile, gleaming white teeth and clear blue eyes. Somewhere there was a liquid brown voice, which began every sentence with the word 'mate'. And she was advancing towards him. Again.

She woke with a start, soaked in her own sweat, and stared up at the ceiling. She and the man in her dream weren't done with one another yet.

34

The next morning Finn felt surprisingly refreshed despite his lack of sleep. He checked in with Ojo, but there'd been no evidence uncovered at Pender's house overnight to link him to the crime scenes. No new witnesses had come forward either. It was a concern, but he'd half expected it. If they couldn't charge him, then they'd have to release him at two that afternoon or apply to a magistrate for an extension. But at eight o'clock in the morning, he wasn't worried – there was still plenty of time for something to happen. It would almost be a break with tradition if it *didn't* come at the last minute.

He decided to follow his overnight instinct and go directly to Earlsfield Fire Station and talk to the station manager there, Sarah Connelly. He'd recognised her name from the reports he'd read on the Pacific Square fire, and knew she'd worked directly with Walker's crew on the night. There was just a chance she might remember a small detail which could unlock something, even if she didn't realise its relevance herself. Finn was shown up to a small second-floor office where he was introduced to a no-nonsense woman in her mid-forties.

'I was at Lambeth Station at the time. I transferred to Earlsfield a year or two after Pacific Square. Been here ever since and it's worked out well.' She said the words factually rather than with any great emotion, and Finn sensed a degree of suspicion. It didn't surprise him – the two services didn't historically mix brilliantly. There wasn't a good reason for it, and in his experience it never got in the way when things mattered. He often felt it was like watching two dogs eyeing each other up in the park; same animal – two entirely different breeds.

'Did you know Adesh Kaul and Gary Elder?'

'I knew *of* them. In this job you often come across fire-fighters from other stations in the course of events. One Pacific Square certainly wasn't the first time we'd worked together.'

'What about Walker, Portbury and Maddox?'

'Same again. I used to see a lot of Martin Walker in particular. He was a crew manager, like me. Proper old school – I liked him.'

'I should imagine the news about Kaul and Elder must have come as something of a shock to people here?'

'Yes, there's still a lot people here who worked with them back then. So, before we get into anything else, I'd like to know where you're at with your investigation?'

'Of course. At this point it looks like it might be connected to a business Kaul and Elder set up after leaving the job. We've made an arrest and we're holding someone in custody.'

'Have you charged them?'

'Not yet.'

'Are you confident it's this bloke?'

'Not a hundred per cent,' said Finn honestly. Connelly nodded, appreciating his candour.

'So what is it you think I can help you with?'

'I'm after information in the first instance. There are gaps in our knowledge, and I'm trying to build up a picture of who these men were.'

'That's fair enough, I suppose.' She sat back in her chair, with an almost resigned expression.

'Were the five who retired particularly close?'

188

'Why's that relevant? I thought this was just about Kaul and Elder?'

Again Finn could feel resistance. He was trying to build up some trust with Connelly before he broached Pacific Square. She was blunt and uncomplicated, which he liked. The wariness was getting in the way though, and he needed her to get past that.

'Like I say, the more I know about them the better. We've spoken to the others but they haven't given much away.'

'From what I remember, and from what I've been told by people here, they were very much a gang of five. They were part of Red Watch, but tended to be a team within a team. It happens, and I've got no problem with that as long as it doesn't become a clique.'

'And did it?'

'A little bit by the sounds of it. Like I say, a tight team isn't necessarily a bad thing. When you're in a life or death situation you want people around you who you trust. I'm sure it's the same with police. I don't mind it as long as it doesn't exclude others.'

'So why do you think they all left within such a short space of time of one another?'

'As I understand it, they didn't leave en masse. You're making it sound a lot more dramatic than it was, if you don't mind me saying.'

Finn decided to get to the point.

'The Pacific Square fire seems to have been the catalyst. Did you not think that was odd – seems quite a coincidence?'

'Not really. We know a lot more about PTSD now. Or to be more accurate, the job is a lot more sensitive to it than it used to be back then.'

'And you think that's what it was?'

'I was there at Pacific Square. It took me a long time to shake it off. No firefighters died, but sometimes you don't measure these things by numbers. I saw people with severe burns, others with life-changing injuries. There were experienced men and women in tears afterwards. Plenty of people suffered from trauma after it, and quite a few left the job too.'

It didn't quite tally for Finn. He wasn't insensitive to the point Connelly was making – far from it. He'd seen it in police officers too. But he'd talked to Martin Walker and Phil Maddox himself, looked them in the eye. He was sure they were hiding something. He also couldn't get away from his suspicion that Erik Whitlock was alive when they entered the building. He decided to chance his arm.

'So tell me about the rumours?'

'What rumours?'

'That something changed with them after the Pacific Square fire,' he lied.

'Who told you that?'

'Did you ever hear anything like that?' She hesitated, which pretty much answered his question. 'If I'm going to keep them safe, then I really do need to know everything. Until we've charged someone, I have to cover all bases.'

She sighed and looked out of the window for a moment as if pondering the wisdom of what to say next.

'There was something. It was before my time so this is second hand. Apparently Elder once drunkenly claimed he could retire whenever he wanted and didn't need to work again. Said he'd Pacific Square to thank for that.'

'What did you think of that?'

'Sounded like the usual Gary Elder bollocks. He was well known as someone with a mouth on him. But you know what . . . he never did work again, did he?'

190

For a moment she looked troubled, as if there was something else. Finn pushed on.

'According to the report I read, you arrived pretty much at the same time as Walker's pump.'

Connelly nodded.

'So did anything strike you as odd, either on the night or afterwards?'

'I can only tell you what I remember. I was in radio contact with Walker when he led the breathing apparatus team into the building. They found a body, but reported it trapped. They wanted to bring it out but were running low on air.'

'What happened next?'

'After they came out, the next BA team went in to try and establish a bridgehead. The aim at that point was to try and stop the fire from spreading, but you know how that turned out.'

'So, Walker's team were the first BA team to go in. They only went up three floors and were already running out of air. I mean, I'm not a firefighter but I've worked with enough crews, been at enough scenes to know that sounds a bit premature.'

'What's your point?' Again she looked uncomfortable.

'Was it?'

'There were stretches when they were up there when they weren't responding. I'm not talking about losing radio contact, but not responding. Ordinarily that's no biggie, because things obviously happen in those situations and you can't always talk—'

'But given what Elder was mouthing off about later, it's stuck in your mind?'

'Yes, but I didn't see or hear anything which gave me cause for concern.'

'Was there enough time for something out of the ordinary to have happened up there?'

191

'I don't see how anything *could* have happened. They tried to get Whitlock's body out, but couldn't. Their air was running out, and when they came out they were empty-handed. I saw that with my own eyes.'

'You're sure?'

'Absolutely. It's not like I was on my own either. There were plenty of other witnesses.'

Again, she looked as if there was something on the tip of her mind she was struggling to access.

'What is it?' he asked.

'To lose contact with one of them – okay, that happens. But there was a brief window where they *all* went silent. The signal should have been fine. I should have questioned them about it afterwards, but as you can imagine there were more pressing things to deal with at the time.' She paused, then continued. 'Let me ask you something, DI Finn. What are you gaining from pursuing this?'

'How do you mean?'

'You tell me you've got someone in custody, and that you're one piece of evidence away from charging them. But you come here – why?'

The question was a valid one and it'd been nagging at him since the small hours; a suspicion slowly digging its way out and forcing its way to the surface.

'Because I'm not sure the killing's over yet.'

35

Detective Sergeant Mike Godden was enjoying a reassuringly uneventful morning. Warrender was holed up in his office doing God knows what, while Farmer was still quietly ploughing through his paperwork. Things with him still weren't quite right following their uneasy confrontation the previous day. There'd been an awkward greeting as they'd passed each other on the stairs first thing, a wariness behind his eyes which hadn't been there before.

Today wasn't a day for more conflict though. He was more than happy to keep his head down at his desk and let things calm down after the previous day's dramas. There was plenty to get on with too. He was surprisingly diligent about his work, given his divided loyalties. He genuinely didn't know where the proceeds of the Stansted heist were. He'd never asked Spinney, and he'd never been told. It protected them both. He didn't *need* to know and thus was free to investigate with freedom. One day he'd write a book – probably from a prison cell – on how to screw a police investigation from the inside because there really was an art to it.

There were two principal ways the cash was probably laundered. The most likely method with sums of money so large was to have smuggled it abroad. From there it would have been deposited into some foreign financial institutions whose laundering enforcement was likely less than rigorous. Needless to say Erik Whitlock was the undisputed master of the tactic.

He was known to have contacts inside some of the Albanian and Romanian gangs in London. Eastern Europe was therefore the most probable destination. Those connections would have allowed him to act quickly in the immediate aftermath of the heist. It was always the critical period in a robbery of that nature. The faster it could be split up, the faster it could be moved, and the harder it was to trace. It was a bit like going on holiday, Godden thought. You spread your cash around your body; some in your back pocket, some in your front, and a few notes in your shirt pocket – just in case.

The other method Whitlock often used was commonly known as 'smurfing'. Here, the money was broken up into much smaller amounts then passed on to a large network of different people. They'd then pay it in to their own bank accounts without arousing suspicion. Later, it would be a simple matter for Whitlock to set up a shell company which each person would then invest in. The technique earnt its name from the famous cartoon characters, who would move around their village each doing their own small share of mindless work. It was the smurfing network that Godden was pursuing. Ever the thorough detective, he'd actually made some headway in uncovering the identities of Whitlock's associates. Just as diligently as he'd tracked them down, he'd then made sure no one else could or would. With Spinney's consent, he'd arrested a handful of them who he was sure knew very little about the wider operation. Enough to keep the investigation moving, to satisfy Warrender, but achieving precisely nothing.

Godden thought he'd identified nearly three hundred people across the UK in the laundering network. There were undoubtedly many more, but it gave an idea of the breadth and scale of the operation. He was able to regularly snoop on their financial records as well as monitor their emails. It was a giant act of running on the spot, but with Warrender breathing down his neck he needed to at least be seen to be working up a sweat. It was also work he'd neglected for the past twenty-four hours and there was plenty to catch up on. As he scanned the routine reports, something caught his eye. He double-checked, instantly feeling the hairs on the back of his neck starting to rise. It served him right for thinking things were under control again. Stupid, stupid, stupid . . .

A properly functioning laundering network should operate without any of its component parts being aware of one another; the whole system rotated around that principle. But now Godden was looking at two separate records; they belonged to a roofer in Chorley and an office manager from Maidstone. They'd both received calls from the same mobile phone yesterday – and the chances of that happening were astronomical. He'd check it out in case it was some bloody PPI firm, but he already knew in his heart it wouldn't be. The only thing these two people shared in common was Erik Whitlock. And he was dead, wasn't he?

36

It was a puzzle, thought Stuart Portbury, and it was irritating him. He was standing in Mei Tsukuda's bathroom staring at a wall. He'd solved the problem of her leaking toilet, but now there was peeling paint on the other side of the room. It didn't make sense. He took a step back and looked at it again. It was like one of those pictures on the internet where you were supposed to spot a camouflaged leopard hidden on a mountaintop. The answer was there if you could only see it.

'So what do you think it is?' asked Mei.

'There,' he said after a moment, pointing at the wall. 'You can just about see them: tramlines.'

'Tramlines?' she repeated uncertainly. He walked up to the wall and pointed more closely at a small grey shadow that was discolouring the bright white paint job.

'It's only happening between these two points,' he said as he moved his finger to a peeling patch of plaster a few inches lower. 'I reckon there's a condensate pipe behind there.'

Mei looked with bemusement at him.

'It's good news. Now we know what it is, we can do something about it. I'll need to bash in the wall but I'll have it looking right as rain by the time I'm done.' She smiled and he felt his heart light up. 'It is going to take a while though . . .'

Then, as was their tradition, she offered him a drink before he began work. A few minutes later they were sat in her kitchen drinking perfectly steeped sencha tea.

Portbury loved spending time in this house. There was an ambience to it he'd never experienced before. It always felt like a place of perfect calm. It took him a while to work out why, but then he'd finally seen it. There was nothing symmetrical. His own flat was perfectly symmetrical – a picture hung either side of a bookcase, shelves lined the walls either side of the fireplace – but there was nothing like that here. He'd even Googled it – it was called *wabi-sabi*; the lack of symmetry within a space, emphasising the form and beauty of the objects inside. The kitchen was a perfect example. They were sat around a long wooden kitchen island with a simple sink and a glass hob at its far end. There was virtually no clutter on the black marbled counters behind them, apart from a tiny indoor garden enclosed in glass. But most of all, it was quiet. The hustle and bustle of London might as well be on a different planet, and for Portbury that meant everything. He liked to think after all this time he and Mei were as much friends as odd-job man and client. She lived alone with her fifteen-year-old son Riku. His father died when he was young, and Portbury sensed she didn't have many friends she could talk to about the difficulties of raising a teenager on her own. As a single man in his late thirties with no children, it wasn't as if he brought a wealth of experience, but they'd enjoyed long conversations in this room which he'd come to value.

'He's constantly bored. He's always complaining he doesn't know what to do,' she said as she sipped her tea.

'He's a teenager, Mei. I was exactly the same at that age. There's almost so much occupying your mind it paralyses you. Like a bottle so full of water when you hold it upside down nothing comes out.'

'No, it's more than that. It is about . . . *enterprise*.' She looked at him uncertainly, as if not sure about her choice of vocabulary. 'He is not self-sufficient. A young man should have interests to pursue, pastimes . . . but he does not do the things other boys his age are doing.'

'You'd rather he was glued to his phone? Or slouched in front of the TV all day? Sounds like he's got a bit more about him.'

'I worry it's because he has no father figure. No one to set him an example.' She looked at Stuart hesitantly for a moment. 'I was hoping that maybe you might be able to speak with him? You are very wise. I know this from our conversations. I think you might be able to help him.'

'I lost my father when I was young. I know how hard it can be. My dad was an accountant, spent his whole life with his head buried in work. Every weekend he was in his study working. It made me sad because I never got to see him. Then one day his heart gave out. He'd been warned by the doctors – they said he worked too hard. I was only fourteen.'

'Younger than Riku – you poor man,' said Mei. He smiled gently back at her.

'I was close to my mum, just like Riku is to you. So I wasn't alone, and I wasn't unloved. But I wish my dad hadn't worked so hard, wish he'd spent a bit of time with us instead.'

'I'm sure he loved you.'

'Yeah, he did. In his own way. I'll happily talk to Riku, if you think it would help. I'm not sure what I can say, but I'd be more than happy to try.'

'I know you will find the words. Thank you, Stuart.'

She reached across and held his hand for a moment, meeting his eyes with her own. There was nothing romantic in it, but the heartfelt look of gratitude made him feel like a giant. He drained his tea.

'Can't sit here all day – your bathroom needs sorting out.' He stood, took his empty cup over to the sink and washed it out. 'Don't worry about Riku, he's going to be just fine.' He smiled reassuringly at her, then headed out to his van which was parked out the front. He picked up his toolbag from the boot and turned to go back inside. Just for a moment he thought he saw someone on the other side of the road watching him, but when he looked again he was alone. Nerves, he thought. Just nerves.

Martin Walker was working up a sweat. As a firefighter he'd always kept himself fit and he'd never lost the habit. He was at the gym in a rowing machine, focusing on the rhythm of the belt and the wheeze of the fan as he pushed and pulled. It was one of the few places where he could truly clear his thoughts. As he felt the sweat soak through his vest he went through the logic of the situation again. He was fairly certain Christine was safe now. Someone was now in custody for the two murders. Typical that it should all be tied up with one of Gary's idiotic business ventures. The only concern now was how deeply the police looked into Elder and Kaul themselves. He was being paranoid, he told himself. The future would look after itself, and he would look after Christine.

After he finished, he picked up his hand towel, wiped his brow and headed back to the changing room. There were two other men in there. The first – overweight and old – looked like he should be sat in the park with a blanket over his legs. The second was naked and towelling himself down. In his forties perhaps, he was muscular and heavily tattooed. Walker relaxed and walked towards the showers. Paranoia again, he thought. He was seeing potential threats every-where now.

Five minutes later, he emerged with a towel wrapped around his waist. The fat man was gone and the tattooed man was now dressed, checking his hair carefully in the mirror. Walker went over to his locker and pulled out his clothes. The man blew through his teeth and Walker could see powerful shoul-ders with thick-set muscular arms.

'It's too hot for this malarkey . . .' the man muttered under his breath.

Walker looked at him suspiciously – was that aimed at him? Or just a general comment to the world? He slipped on his boxer shorts and started searching for his socks. The man turned to walk past him. Suddenly one of those muscular arms shot out and grabbed Walker's throat. He heard a strange high-pitched gasp, and realised it was coming from his own larynx. The man picked him up like a doll and slammed him up against the lockers. He tried to speak, but all that came out was more strangulated air.

'But then you'd know all about heat, wouldn't you, Martin?'

He seemed to be squeezing even harder now, and Walker flapped pathetically at the giant arm extending out in front of him. He was too old for this, he realised. He'd gambled and lost, and now Christine was going to be alone.

'We know what you did. And now it's time to pay the price . . .'

Instead of squeezing the life out of him, the huge fist around his throat unexpectedly released its grip. Walker sucked in a deep gulp of air with an involuntary whoop and collapsed on to his haunches. His assailant looked down with barely disguised contempt and pulled a piece of paper from his pocket. He screwed it up and threw it in Walker's face.

'The man I work for wants to talk to you. Be at that address at the time specified. If you don't, then I'll break your wife's spine with my own hands.'

He walked out, and all Walker could hear was the sound of his own gasping breath.

37

Pinning her brother down, Mattie Paulsen decided, was like nailing jelly to a wall. Jonas Paulsen was two years older than her, but they shared several characteristics. There was the same wide mouth, jet black hair and light accent. Like his sister, there was a quiet thoughtfulness to him, but he'd always carried far less angst than her. It made for an interesting dynamic between them, his relaxed approach to life often at odds with her intensity.

A teacher at an inner-city school in east London, his job kept him extremely busy. It meant midweek drinks weren't the easiest to arrange, so they tended to keep in touch via text and email, with only the occasional meet-up. Despite this they were close, and she often found herself worrying about him. Jonas historically found relationships difficult to maintain, and Mattie was careful not to ask too much about his personal life. She'd been surprised, then, when she'd received a text requesting they meet. It seemed pressing, and he'd suggested an early morning coffee before she headed into work. Intrigued, she'd agreed, and they'd settled for a cafe in Highbury.

When she arrived, he was sat by the window in a black polo-neck jumper sipping a cappuccino, reading from his iPad. He wasn't normally the most tactile, but he greeted her with an unexpected hug. They sat and he signalled to the waitress.

'An Americano, please, with a splash of soya milk.'

'Very good,' said Mattie, impressed. Her conversion to soya was only a recent development and Jonas smiled.

'Like I'd forget. So how have you been? How's the new job?'

'You know. Pretty much like the old one.'

'And Nancy?'

'Fine. You?' she said.

'Muddling along.'

'Seeing anyone?'

He smiled tightly.

'Muddling along.' This time she smiled.

'Nothing else you want to tell me?'

'Not really,' he said, and she shrugged. She knew there was a reason she'd been summoned, but clearly he'd get to it when he felt like it. Some things never changed.

'You never really explained what happened at your last station. In fact, you never explained it at all.'

'Oh, I see. You tell me nothing about your life, but you want to know everything about mine?'

'Why change the habit of a lifetime?'

'It's just work stuff. You're really not missing anything,' she lied.

'Mum and Dad were worried about you, said you weren't in touch for a long time.'

'So *that's* what this is about? They've sent you to interrogate me?'

'Don't be stupid, no, they haven't.'

'So it's you who's getting nosey, is it?'

He recoiled slightly, and his voice became quieter, as it always did when she went on the attack.

'Why are you being so defensive?'

'Because this is unusual, Jonas. You don't often go out of your way to arrange an early morning coffee with me. What's up?'

'A boy can't see his sister?'

'I'm guessing there's a deeper reason for it?'

'Why do you always have to strip every conversation down to the bone?'

'Saves time.' She pouted at him. It was a familiar dynamic; her argumentative, him weary.

'Alright – it is about Mum and Dad. Well, Dad, actually.'

'Has something happened?'

'Sort of. A few weird incidents.'

'Such as?'

'He took the dog for a walk but forgot the dog . . .'

'What do you mean?'

'He put his coat on, grabbed the lead, then drove to the park but forgot to take the dog with him.'

She grinned.

'It's not funny,' he said.

'Isn't it?'

'No, he also tried to make a cup of tea by putting the electric kettle on the gas ring.'

This time Mattie laughed out loud, then stopped when she saw the sober expression on his face.

'Lighten up, he's always done things like that. He's got a brain the size of a planet, but can't figure out how a washing machine works.'

'It's more than that. Mum's worried.'

'Has he seen a doctor?'

'No, but I'm trying to persuade them he needs to.'

'Really? It sounds like nothing.'

'Go visit them, see for yourself. You might not find it so funny.'

'You think it might be something serious?' She tapped the side of her head. 'In there?'

'He's lost a lot of weight and he's quite gaunt. It takes him a while to understand things too. You talk to him for a bit, then you find he's still about three sentences behind.'

'He's just getting old.'

'Maybe. Mum needs some help. She could use a hand, Mattie.'

She saw the worry in his eyes and for the first time began to take the implication fully on board.

'If you rang her a bit more, you'd know,' he said.

For once the reprimand wasn't met with a sharp retort. She knew she'd neglected her family for the past year. She'd wanted to protect them from what happened at Dunlevy Road. It would only have deeply upset them. As the sunlight shone through the window of the cafe, her nightmare the previous night came back to her. The vista of London, the man with the affable smile standing with his hands outstretched.

'Mattie?' said Jonas, snapping her back into the room.

'I'll ring. Soon, I promise. I'm sure it's nothing, but you were right to tell me.'

She smiled reassuringly as she always did when her big brother was troubled.

Finn's day hadn't particularly improved after he'd left Earlsfield Fire Station. The searches at Kevin Pender's property were now complete. They'd found no evidence to link him with either crime scene so he'd been released on bail. It didn't take long for Skegman to summon Finn to his office for an update.

'Pender's still very much in the frame,' Finn insisted with more conviction than he felt. 'Both crime scenes are large and complicated and it's still very early in the forensic investigation. The cell site analysis on his phone shows it was at his home at the time of both murders. Doesn't clear him though, just proves he didn't bring his phone with him.'

'But you've got nothing so far which puts him at either scene. Have SOCO wrapped up at the hotel yet?'

'Yes, we've spoken to everyone who was at the wedding now. There are several vague descriptions of a man in the main banqueting hall shortly before Kaul's murder who nobody was able to identify. But they all contradict each other. One says he's tall, one says he's short, one says he had brown hair, another says he was blond – that kind of thing. No one seems to have caught him on camera either. As far as Elder's concerned, we've got nothing from the nightclub that's useful. We've interviewed the people he was with and they've all confirmed he left on his own. CCTV shows him walking back to his car – but there's no coverage in the side street we know he parked in. We've checked his phone records and he didn't use it after leaving the club so it doesn't look like he was lured.'

'So how did he and his car end up at the murder scene? Come on, Alex, the bloke was driving a Maserati around Purley, for God's sake. How visible do you have to be? Someone must have seen something?'

'Either Elder knew the killer and drove them both there, or the killer overpowered him and drove them both there.'

'What about the link with Ray Spinney?'

'I think we have to keep it on the table.' He shrugged. 'I still can't rule it out.'

'That's unfortunate,' said Skegman tightly, and Finn knew why he looked concerned. It meant there was still a threat to the surviving firefighters – that this wasn't over. 'Do you want to put surveillance on the other three?' Skegman continued. Finn blew through his teeth.

'At this point, I think the likelihood is we're looking at two separate crimes. Pender still looks a good fit for the murders. As much as we haven't got proof he did it, we haven't found anything that clears him either. He doesn't have an alibi for either day.'

'And the theory about the stolen money?'

'The station manager at Earlsfield told me Gary Elder was mouthing off about being wealthy enough to never have to work again. Pender claims Elder tried to buy him off. But here's the thing – it might be that the money didn't come from Pacific Square, but that the press conference has flagged up the idea they stole that money from some dangerous people.'

Skegman nodded, remembering their earlier conversation.

'And if we're not careful we might end up putting the other three in the line of fire ourselves. What do you want to do?'

Finn pursed his lips. 'Let's hold off for now. I'll take responsibility if it goes tits up.'

He suddenly stifled an unexpected yawn, his sleepless night catching up with him. Skegman arched an eyebrow.

'Keeping you up, are we?'

Finn looked sheepish.

'Nothing a week on a beach wouldn't . . .' He checked himself. The words came automatically, without thought. Finn wouldn't be going on any beach holidays any time soon. Without Karin he wasn't sure if he'd ever go away again. He held up a hand to acknowledge the slip.

'You know what I mean.'

Finn turned on his heels and left, feeling Skegman's gaze burning into the back of his head. He knew what the man was thinking; that he really *should* be on a beach somewhere, resting and healing. Anywhere but here leading a murder inquiry. The constant scrutiny was becoming tiring though. From Skegman, from Ojo, from his whole team.

'*Fuck 'em*,' said Karin.

38

Phil Maddox
The cops have released the guy they arrested
without charge. 16:07

Stuart Portbury
Where did you hear that? 16:10

Phil Maddox
I rang the police to find out what was happening.
It's been 24 hours since they nicked him. 16:12

Stuart Portbury
Doesn't mean he didn't do it – just that they
didn't have the evidence to charge him. 16:15

Phil Maddox
Are you taking the piss? If it isn't him, then
it's the fucking Handyman isn't it? 16:17

Stuart Portbury
U r being paranoid. 16:18

Phil Maddox
Fuck off Stu – how blind do you have to be?
Martin – I know you're reading these
messages, what do you reckon? 16:21

39

The only thing Martin Walker hadn't understood was why he was still alive. Then he'd worked it out and felt even more scared. He was driving down the M2 motorway nervously eyeing the time. The address on the piece of paper he'd been given simply stated:

Tankerton Beach, Red Beach Hut, 8pm <u>tonight</u>.

It was now nudging four and he felt sick. It wasn't hard to deduce the man at the gym worked for Kaul and Elder's killer. He might very well have *been* the man who'd murdered them. His throat still felt sore from the grip of those giant hands. What he was also now sure about was that Kaul and Elder's deaths were warnings. Their graphic murders, together with the incident at the gym was a message: *we can hurt you at any time*. So why was he still alive? There could only be one answer. Money. He'd spent the drive doing the sums. Working out how much he could get through selling the house. He'd have to strike some sort of a deal with whoever he was about to meet. Make them understand about Christine. He felt his nausea rise again as he remembered the threat made by the man at the gym. It hadn't been an idle one – those giant hands could snap her back like a twig. He'd done some Googling before he'd set off, reading everything he could find out about the Handyman. There was certainly plenty of speculation about his identity. The best bet seemed to be this Raymond Spinney. Everything he'd read didn't suggest a man blessed with the milk of human kindness.

Walker recognised the address immediately. His parents used to take him to Whitstable when he was a child, a regular pilgrimage on a sunny bank holiday. He didn't have warm memories of the place though. He couldn't stand seafood, for a start, and preferred his beaches golden and sandy. The thought this was a lure to simply isolate him couldn't be ignored either. It was precisely the sort of situation those two police officers warned him about. If it was a trap, then he was walking into it eyes wide open, but what else could he do? Would they find his remains in a burnt-out beach hut tomorrow? Then why not kill him in London – why hadn't that man simply choked him to death at the gym? Round and round the questions went.

An hour later he arrived at the seaside town. At just after five in the afternoon, it was still basking in the hot summer sunshine. He parked in one of the small side streets and walked towards the seafront. It was an ordinary weekday afternoon, so despite the fine weather there weren't the mass of day trippers milling around like he remembered from his youth. He could see hardy-looking fishing boats and an ugly metal-clad asphalt plant across the harbour. He'd forgotten how industrial the place felt. He carried on, and found himself facing the three rows of black clapboard huts which comprised Whitstable Harbour Market. It all felt eerily surreal to him, the cheery blackboards offering whelks and oysters, the marine art, ironwork and driftwood curiosities. It was the last place on Earth he'd expected to be when he'd got out of bed that morning, and now it might just be the last place on Earth he'd ever see.

He went over to one of the huts and bought a pint of beer, sitting down at one of the trestle tables. He sipped his drink, ice cold and welcome, and looked out at the green-blue sea. He put aside his childhood prejudice – if this was it, there were worse places to die. He'd run into enough burning buildings back in the day, so whatever awaited him here he'd go head-first into without fear. He turned his phone off. Christine would be worried about him, but he couldn't let that distract him. For the next three hours he basked in the peace of the place, allowing the sun and the sea to calm his nerves. Then just before eight o'clock he stood, ready.

Tankerton Beach was exactly as he remembered it. As he made his way over he could see in his mind's eye his mother sat on a deckchair wearing a sun hat and oversized sunglasses, engrossed in a book. His father would be laid out on his front next to her, soaking up the sun's rays in an era when no one thought anything of it. The shingle beach and wooden groynes which neatly segregated it looked like an England from an old-fashioned picture postcard. Walker surveyed the beach from the top of the steep grassy bank on the promenade that overlooked it. He quickly identified the red hut he was looking for, and made his way down. Reaching the door, he stopped. Behind him he could hear the laughter of people enjoying themselves in the late evening sun. He lifted a hand as if to knock, then lowered it again and grabbed the door handle and walked inside. A rush of warm, sour air hit him and he gagged for a moment. The tiny, shed-like space was empty except for a small wooden table. A man in a waistcoat with old-fashioned spectacles was sat on his own, and Walker's first reaction was one of relief. He'd been expecting someone similar to the thug from the gym. This little guy didn't look dangerous, more like a bored lawyer waiting for his next client. He recognised him though. The same man from the familiar mug shot used by the tabloids when they wrote about him. This was Raymond Spinney.

'Please, have a seat, Mr Walker,' he said, motioning at a small chair. 'Before we talk, I need you to understand something very clearly. The gentleman you met this morning at your gymnasium is currently parked outside your house in south London. There are also associates of mine waiting on the beach outside. I've no desire to make graphic threats, but understand what could easily happen if you make some unwise choices.' He spoke as if explaining a small caveat at the bottom of an insurance document.

'You're the Handyman, aren't you?' said Walker. 'Why *do* they call you that anyway?'

Spinney ignored him, but turned his head very precisely and looked him in the eye. Walker felt his early confidence draining away. The eyes scrutinising him were devoid of emotion. This wasn't a man you could negotiate or bargain with.

'I want to know – in your own words – what happened at One Pacific Square.'

Walker was ready for him. He'd spent the previous three hours anticipating this, so didn't hesitate with his answer. He described in comprehensive detail the chain of events. What he'd been doing when they'd got the call, the sighting of the man he now knew was Erik Whitlock, and the decision to lead a BA team in on a search and rescue mission. He told him of the discovery he and Elder made inside; the stacks of money on the pallets next to Whitlock. And he told him what they did next.

When he finished, he sat back. It felt good to have finally said it all out loud. It struck him he'd never done that before, and the irony of who he was saying it to wasn't lost on him. Spinney absorbed it all with the same unmoving expression.

'Aside from your former colleagues, have you ever told anyone else what happened? Your wife, for example?'

'No one.'

'You understand that I will require you to return what you took?'

Again Walker was ready for him, the answer rehearsed on the seafront earlier.

'I don't wish to see my wife get hurt, so I'll do that willingly and without argument. But I have a question . . . how did you know?'

'If you do as I've instructed, then neither you nor your wife will be hurt. If you tell the police about this conversation, on the other hand—'

'You haven't answered my question. How did you find out? There were only five people who knew.'

'Do we have an agreement?'

A growing suspicion which was forming in Walker's mind coalesced, and he laughed out loud.

'*You didn't know*, did you? Right up until this moment you didn't know for certain we took your bloody money?' Spinney was silent, unreadable. 'If you didn't know, then why kill Kaul and Elder? Why wait until now to have this conversation?' Walker could see he wasn't used to being on the back foot. He certainly didn't like being laughed at.

'You literally brought me to Whitstable for a fishing trip!'

Raymond Spinney roared with fury and brought his hand smashing down on the table. Immediately the door to the hut opened, and a heavy set man dressed in a T-shirt and jeans stepped inside. It was enough to refocus Walker's mind on the jeopardy he remained in – Spinney hadn't been bluffing about his associates outside, which almost certainly meant he hadn't been bluffing about the man watching his house in London either. 'Get out,' said Spinney simply and the heavy in the T-shirt did as he was told. Walker used the interruption to think. All the things which hadn't made sense to him on the drive down from London were now becoming clearer.

'This isn't about us, is it? If you didn't kill Kaul and Elder, someone else did, and you don't know who it is, do you?'

40

Finn was in the car park outside Cedar House hoping no one was watching him. Across the road, YoYo's Cafe was relatively quiet, with just a couple of DCs on a tea break. Notwithstanding the riddle she'd set him about a blind canine wandering a forest, there was still one outstanding obligation to Karin he hadn't fulfilled. He'd been putting it off for long enough. He opened his car boot and looked at the object inside. It was wrapped in several plastic bags and he picked it up, feeling its heft in his hands. He removed the plastic wrappings to reveal a small, dark blue urn.

Finn didn't know how he felt about Karin's remains. Try as he might, he couldn't draw a line between the object in his hand and the woman he'd shared his life with. It wasn't as if there weren't some suitable places to scatter the ashes either. There were plenty of locations which Karin herself suggested before she died. She'd been fairly ambivalent on the subject though, very much of the view that once she was gone, she really didn't care. *'You'll find somewhere. I trust you.'* But it was a misplaced trust. He found he couldn't actually bear to have the urn in the flat. It upset him wherever it sat, just another jagged reminder of her absence. The idea of scattering all that remained of her into the wind was just as difficult though. The thought of there being nothing left of her at all was too much to bear. He'd wrapped it in plastic, in part so he wouldn't have to think about it. Out of sight, out of mind. Except that it wasn't. He'd brought it in to work, because he thought earlier he might just have the willpower to finally do something about it.

Morden Hall Park was somewhere in the early days of their relationship they'd spent a lot of time together. Sunday afternoons where she'd skilfully pushed past his defences and got to know the real Alex Finn. 'Scatter me there, if you must,' she'd said. It was, ironically, only a short distance from the hotel where Adesh Kaul was murdered. As he felt the object in his hand, Finn realised he still couldn't do it, his earlier impetus gone again. He carefully wrapped the urn back up and returned it to the boot of the car.

Feeling unsettled, he walked back towards the station pondering his other problem: DC Mattie Paulsen. She'd barely said a word all day, glaring at her screen as if daring anyone to approach her. Even by the standards she'd set in her brief time at Cedar House it was off, if not downright hostile. It was safe to say plenty was being said *about* her and none of it very flattering. She'd been angry the previous day at Finn and Skegman's reaction to the incident involving her partner. He understood the emotion – her point about Karin not entirely misplaced. But was there something else, deeper and more troubling, bubbling beneath the surface? If so, then what? Was it connected to the reason she'd transferred to Cedar House? He needed to lance the boil, and although he could make some discreet calls to Dunlevy Road, instinct told him it should come from her own lips. They were overdue a conversation.

At her desk, Paulsen was struggling to focus. She'd been preoccupied all day by her conversation with Jonas earlier. As a family they'd never dealt with serious illness before. The spectre of it was terrifying. She may have distanced herself from her parents over the past year, but it didn't diminish her feelings for them. She'd been trying protect them, but now she realised she'd done quite the opposite. As ever when she was struck by guilt, it morphed into anger. She'd slowly deteriorated into a filthy mood.

Then there was Nancy. She'd texted her several times, to check everything was okay after the events of the previous day. The replies were terse and infrequent, a familiar sign she wasn't happy with Mattie. It was just adding to her growing sense of isolation. To compound things, the shadow cast by the man in her nightmare didn't seem to want to leave her either. As usual when she fell down the rabbit hole of that particular memory, it produced a combination of emotions – none of them good. She could feel her eyes pricking and hated herself for it. She wasn't going to cry – not here, not in this office, not in front of some of these people. They'd never, ever let her forget it. Her head was starting to gently pulse; give it another hour it was going to be a skullsplitter.

'Mattie, have you got a moment?'

It was Finn, and the use of her first name jarred. She hoped this was to do with the investigation and not those side glances he'd been giving her all day. She could tell he'd picked up on her mood. A patronising lecture would just about be the cherry on the icing on the top of the cake. He led her out of the incident room and into one of the general meeting rooms. It all felt needlessly furtive. She gave him a look like a patient mother expecting an errant toddler to explain themselves.

'What's the matter?' he said simply.

'What do you mean?'

'You don't seem right. What is it?'

Paulsen struggled to control her irritation. It was a demand, not a question – what business was it of his?

'With respect, sir – it's nothing for you to worry about.'

'I need everyone with their heads focused on the job, so I'm entitled to ask. You haven't said a word to anyone all day. What is it?'

Again, he repeated the question with the same blunt entitlement. She was fighting hard to contain a low simmering rage.

'If I was a male DC, would you have taken me out here and asked me that?'

'Don't be ridiculous.'

'You'd give them the benefit of the doubt.'

'That's utterly ridiculous—'

'And that's twice you've used that word. A woman who challenges you is ridiculous, is she?'

Finn could feel his own temper starting to rise now. Enigmatic he could tolerate. Rude, in-your-face insubordination was a whole other thing.

'A friendly word of advice, Detective Constable Paulsen. If you want to be part of my team, you need to change your approach. These are good people here; they know what they're doing. You're treating them like something you trod in. Now you're talking to me like I'm beneath you . . .'

Her head was throbbing now as he spoke. She was back on top of that building with London spread out in front of her. The man with the pleasant smile was holding out his arms trying to reason with her while she inched ever closer. It was his face she could see, Finn's voice she heard.

'. . . you are a junior, new member of the team who's yet to show anyone here what you can do. Frankly, you seem to have your head up your arse at times,' Finn snapped. Paulsen seemed lost, but then her eyes focused on his. Later he'd remember that look.

'Yeah, I'm every inch the temperamental *bitch*, aren't I? Young and female means I've got my head stuck up my arse, obviously. Whereas all those middle-aged men next door—'

Finn was about to respond, but she didn't let him. 'Let me give *you* a friendly word of advice.' She was almost shaking with anger. It was out of all proportion to the moment. He could feel something important was unfolding, but couldn't quite understand what. Suddenly she was in his face, the words being screamed. 'You shouldn't be here! You're cheating everyone in this building! Worse – you're cheating the victims. I'm sorry your wife died, but you're a mess. You're broken. The whole room's watching you stumble through this and it's embarrassing. None of them have got the balls to say it to your face. Well, I have. And you've got the fucking nerve to lecture me?'

It seemed to echo around the small space they were standing in. For an instant they stood face-to-face in silence, almost as if they were both too horrified to know how to respond. Finn waited for her anger to give way to something else, a self-awareness of where she was and what she was doing, but it didn't come. If anything, her frown of contempt intensified. Still shaking with anger, she turned and walked away. He tried to call out, knew he *should* say something, but couldn't. It was exactly how he'd felt in that bedroom at Kaul's wake. He was paralysed, couldn't speak and felt a rush of humiliation. What she'd said cut through to the core of him. Every last insecurity going on beneath the surface vocalised and thrown in his face. In normal circumstances he'd have dealt with it comfortably. God knows he'd handled enough gobby DCs over the years. But these weren't normal circumstances. He'd lost his authority to a junior officer only half way through her first week and he'd have to find a way to claim it back. For both their sakes.

Paulsen stormed down the corridor and straight into the toilets. She found a cubicle, locked it shut and took some deep breaths. She could feel her heart beating; there was almost white noise in her ears. Instantly she hated how she felt – she could only remember one other time she'd experienced such instant self-revulsion. Walking away from a multistorey car park, listening to the screams coming from the other side of the building. For an instant she was back in that moment. She shook her head, banishing the memory. It was the present she needed to worry about now.

Finn didn't chase after her. When he walked back into the incident room Paulsen was back at her desk working quietly, and he decided not to pursue it there and then. He was fairly sure that, once the red mist cleared, remorse would set in and then they'd talk. He glanced over again as he walked through, but her gaze was fixed firmly on her screen. If she was worried about the consequences, she wasn't letting it show. As he sat at his own desk, Ojo came over to join him.

'Guv, one of the firefighters called in. It's Maddox, he wants to talk to you.'

'Any idea what about?'

'No, but that's the thing. He wants you to meet him in person tonight – says there's something you need to know.'

41

Mike Godden was sat on a park bench watching a young mother feeding the ducks with her toddler. He'd give his soul to be that child, he thought. To have a clean slate, a chance to do it all again. He'd left the office to try and clear his head following the discovery he'd made earlier. Could Erik Whitlock really be alive? Ask any police officer and they'll tell you *nothing* is ever impossible. It really wouldn't have been beyond Ray Spinney's means to have faked Whitlock's death all along. There were plenty of advantages in having a man like that able to operate under the radar. Then again, there could be another explanation. Could Spinney be laying a trap for him? He'd surely know Godden would spot the identical phone numbers and draw these conclusions. It felt like bait dangling on a hook. But why?

The possible endgame of his association with the Handyman was something Godden frequently thought about. His options were limited but he possessed one ace up his sleeve. It was very much a nuclear option; to use it might well provoke mutually assured destruction. They weren't quite at that stage though. He checked his watch and sighed. He needed to tell Warrender about the phone numbers. If there was a possibility Whitlock *was* still alive and it hadn't been thoroughly investigated, then some serious questions would be asked.

Jim Farmer was lying in wait when he walked back into the office.

'Where've you been?' he asked.

'What's it to you?'

'I don't know where you are half the time these days, Mike, you never tell me.'

'Didn't realise we were a married couple, Jimbo,' said Godden. 'I've found something, as it happens, come and have a look at this.' He showed Farmer the paperwork with the two phone numbers and explained their significance. The DC's eyes almost bulged out of their sockets.

'What are you saying – that Whitlock's still alive? That's mad . . .'

'Not necessarily. It could be someone else has inherited his network, or is trying to reactivate it for their own use. Whitlock worked for a lot of people, remember? Any one of them would see that network as a very useful mechanism for laundering money. It's not like it's a service you can buy on Amazon.'

'So who do you think it could be?'

'That's what we need to find out.'

'So is this what you were chasing yesterday?' Farmer asked cautiously.

'Yeah. Sorry, mate – I couldn't tell you, there wasn't time. I needed to verify a few things.'

Farmer looked unconvinced.

'Where did you go?'

'Harlow, if you must know.'

'You're sure about that?'

Christ, he knew something, thought Godden. A nasty thought seeded itself at the back of his mind.

'Absolutely. No offence, Jimmy, but what's with all the questions?'

'You wouldn't lie to me, Mike. Would you?'

'Bloody hell, mate, where's that coming from?'

'Just tell me where you were yesterday.'

'I just told you, Harlow. What's going on, Jim?'

Farmer looked hesitant, but hesitant was good as far as Godden was concerned and he took full advantage.

'I promise you I'll explain everything in due course, but right now I'm asking you to keep the faith. We're close to something and it needs careful handling. Right now I need you to trust me.'

'I do. But why can't you tell me now?' There was a different tone to Farmer's voice. Insistent. With a sinking feeling, Godden realised this wasn't going to go away.

'Because of these numbers. We've got to find out who made those phone calls. Don't you think that's the priority? Especially if there's a chance Whitlock's alive.'

Slowly Farmer nodded.

'What are you doing today?' said Godden.

'Why?'

'Because I could use a hand with this, if you're done playing twenty questions.'

'Alright, sarge, if that's what you want.'

Godden grabbed his coat and walked over to the door.

'Where are we going?' said Farmer, picking up his own jacket.

'St Albans. One of Whitlock's network works near there. He's the closest to us and doesn't know we know. It won't hurt to lean on him a bit and see what he can give us.'

Ten minutes later Godden was driving them both into the depths of the Hertfordshire countryside. Farmer hadn't said a word since they left Chapel Row, and as Godden glanced across he could see the younger man was lost in thought. Thinking too hard was the last thing he wanted him doing.

'Listen, as we're going on a bit of a road trip, how's about letting me ask you a few questions and then I'll answer some of yours. How's that sound?'

'Alright, sarge, fair enough.'

'And what's with the "sarge" all of a sudden? Loosen up, mate. Why don't you tell me how it's going with . . . what's her name? Julie, wasn't it?'

'Julia. And yeah, it's going well, thanks.'

'What's she do again? HR?'

Farmer nodded.

'Didn't you say she had a kid as well?' Godden persisted. It was like getting blood out of a stone. Usually he couldn't shut him up.

'Yeah – Emily, she's a little cracker.' Farmer's face finally broke into his old goofy grin. Hallelujah, Godden thought.

'So how are you finding all that then?'

'Brilliant, as it goes.'

He was embarrassed, but the tension between them seemed finally to have broken. For the next half hour they chatted casually as Farmer regaled his experiences of the local soft-play areas. Just after they passed Hatfield, Godden took a sudden turn-off.

'I thought you said we were going to St Albans?' said Farmer.

'Almost. This guy runs a landfill business about a mile from here.'

They drove down a long curling approach road. A few minutes later they were greeted by something resembling the set of a science fiction film. It was a huge bowl of a place which looked as if the world's largest dustbin had been tipped over it. It stank in the heat and they both winced as the stench hit them. Godden pointed at a large Portakabin overlooking the main expanse.

'Come on, let's try the main office.'

There was rubbish as far as the eye could see. A yellow crane stood in the middle, as if abandoned mid-manoeuvre.

Everything was eerily quiet as they left the car and began walking.

'What are we doing out here, Mike?' asked Farmer.

'You know what we're doing here; I told you what we're doing here.'

'Yeah, you showed me a phone number on a piece of paper and you also said that's what you were chasing yesterday.'

'Which I was.'

'Except you only found out about that phone number today. The print-out you gave me was timestamped.' Farmer stopped. 'So what are we *really* doing out here?'

'I don't understand, Jimmy,' Godden replied with affected irritation. They were standing on the lip of the steep bank which overlooked the dump below them, and there was just the faintest of echoes now as they spoke.

'Then I'll make it clear. I ran a cell site analysis on your phone yesterday and got the results fast-tracked this morning. You weren't in Harlow; you were in central London. You went to a cafe near the British Museum and were there for exactly forty-two minutes then caught a train back from Liverpool Street station. So why are you lying to me?'

Godden felt his stomach heave. The puppy-dog Jim Farmer he was used to was gone, and in his place was a Rottweiler. He'd never seen Farmer like this before, strident and sure of himself. For a second he wondered if he'd been played. Was this the real Jim Farmer and the puppy dog act just that – an act?

'Who did you meet in London?' asked Farmer.

'Jimmy, if you went to the effort of doing a cell site, why on Earth didn't you say something to me back in the office?'

'Because I wanted to know what this little trip was really all about. And I also wanted to get you alone, somewhere neutral. I'm really hoping there's a good reason for all this. Because you're someone I respect, and I wanted to give you a chance to explain yourself.'

'Explain myself? Maybe I should remind you, mate – I'm a detective sergeant, you're a DC. I don't have to explain myself to you.'

'Save it. Either tell me the truth or I can only assume you're lying to cover your arse. The question is why.'

'What reason would I have to lie?'

'You know the rumours, Mike. People have said for years there's a bent cop on the Stansted investigation team. You go off-grid yesterday and can't tell me why. I find evidence you met with Erik Whitlock before he died and you claim you can't remember it. A man at the centre of our investigation and you can't remember whether you met him or not? Do me a favour.'

Godden shook his head. 'If all that were true, it would make me a very dangerous man. So coming out here alone with me wouldn't be the smartest move, would it?'

'I'd like to see you try something, Mike. I'm almost half your age and twice your size. Trust me, I've calculated the risk.'

Godden held his hands up in a conciliatory gesture.

'Hold your horses, Jimmy, this is all getting a bit out of hand. You're bending the facts to fit your theory. That's what bad police do. What you should be doing is altering your thinking to fit the available facts.'

For the first time Farmer looked unsure.

'How do you mean?'

'I had some private business to take care of yesterday. That's what I was doing in London.'

'What kind of private business?'

'I met a lawyer, okay? I'm having a few problems with Elaine, my ex-wife. I know I shouldn't have done it in the middle of the day like that, but I didn't have much choice. I needed to see him; it's to do with Franny.'

'Be more specific.'

Godden motioned at the Portakabin with his hand.

'Look – why don't we do what we came here to do, and then I'll tell you all about it over a coffee. Or we can have a fist fight right here. It's up to you.' He flashed his trademark quicksilver smile. The wind whistled around them for a moment, and Farmer nodded guardedly.

When they reached the Portakabin door they found it unlocked and entered. The place looked like it'd been neglected a while. Papers lay randomly scattered over tabletops, and there were the dregs of old cups of tea which appeared to have been ignored for months. The smell inside was no better than it was outside.

'Looks pretty dead to me,' said Farmer.

'I don't understand,' said Godden.

'Yeah, you do. You knew this place would be deserted, that's why you chose it.'

'Chose it? For what?'

'You tell me, Mike.'

'This is madness. I told you why we're here.'

'Do you know what I did yesterday after you told me you couldn't remember meeting Whitlock? I went through every-thing. Not after Whitlock died, but from *before*.'

Godden nodded slowly, almost approvingly; it's exactly what he would have done. 'Before Pacific Square burnt down you were in contact with a Polish guy, Jan Gacek. I traced his number from your desk phone; there were multiple calls in the week leading up to the fire. Turns out he was employed by Densmead Construction, the contractors who were building Pacific Square. Fancy telling me what that was all about?'

'Jim . . .' Godden took a step forwards.

'Back off, Mike,' said Farmer sharply. 'I'll tell you what I think –
I think you were arranging access for Whitlock at the construction site. I think Gacek was the guy who let him in that night.'

Godden nodded, as if there was a simple explanation.

'Jim. It's like this . . .'

Without warning he threw a punch, sending Jim reeling. He
followed it up with a second, and moved in for a third but
Farmer was back on his feet almost immediately. He grabbed
Godden before he could strike again and subdued him with
ease, the older man blowing hard at the exertion.

'Don't make me hurt you, Mike. Because if I hit you, you
won't get back up. Do you understand?'

Godden stood stock-still. He felt sick as a dog. Everything
he'd worked for was unravelling. He looked around the room,
desperate to find some means of turning this around. Farmer
could see what he was thinking, and slapped his face with his
open palm.

'Jesus!' said Godden with surprise.

'I said, do you understand?' repeated Farmer. Godden
nodded. Farmer pushed him up against the wall.

'Fuck's sake, Jim!'

'Give me the key fob for the car.'

Godden reached into his pocket and held it out. Cautiously,
Farmer took it from him.

'Now hold out your hands.'

Godden did as he was told. Farmer pulled some handcuffs
from his jacket pocket and snapped them on him, leading him
out of the Portakabin.

They walked back the way they'd come, along the steep
bank overlooking the huge site below.

'How long have you been fucking this investigation over?
Since the start?' He gave him a shove and Godden stumbled forwards.

228

'Tell me something, Jim . . . this little girl of your girlfriend's – Emily?'

'Shut up about her, just walk nice and slow back to the car.'

'When you look into her eyes, wouldn't you do *anything* to make sure she was okay?' Godden stopped and turned. 'Trust me, it's no different when they get older. I did all this for Franny.'

He looked Farmer bolt in the eye and for a moment there was vulnerability. It gave him the opportunity he needed. He threw himself forwards with a roar, head down. Farmer staggered backwards, and his foot gave way underneath him. He tripped and fell back over the brow, somersaulting down the steep clay-coloured embankment until finally coming to a halt at the bottom. Godden peered cautiously over. The body was quite still for a second and then it twitched. Farmer seemed to be slowly trying to prop himself up with one hand but couldn't make it and fell back again. There was a winding path around the side of the site which led down there, and Godden quickly started to pad round it.

He'd known about this place for a few months now after visiting it on another job earlier in the year. The company who ran it were in administration and he knew it was unmanned. He'd hoped to try and persuade Farmer to back off, maybe even meet Spinney for himself and make his own arrangement with him. But there was clearly no chance of that, and he'd been left with little choice.

As he got closer he could see the pain etched on Farmer's face. Shock was setting in and he was white as a ghost. He'd sustained a cut to his forehead and blood was streaking down into his eyes but it was his leg which made Godden wince. The angle was all wrong, folded and bent, and blood was pooling beneath him.

'Mike . . . call an ambulance. I think my leg's bust.'

'How can I?' He held up his handcuffed wrists. Farmer fumbled in his pocket and managed to slowly extract the key. Carefully Godden lowered his wrists close to the injured man's hands, and Farmer unlocked the cuffs.

'I'm sorry, Jim, I really am.'

'It's okay, just call an ambulance.'

It wasn't what Godden meant. He walked round behind him and placed his hands over his mouth and nostrils. Farmer flailed feebly at him, but Godden easily held him off. He kept his grip tight enough to do the job, light enough not to leave any marks.

'Shhh, Jimmy. Shush now.'

When it was over he gently let the head fall back on to the ground. When the body was eventually discovered, everyone would assume there'd been an accident and he'd slipped. He picked up the discarded handcuffs and their key and carefully put them back into Farmer's pocket, wiping his fingerprints off them with the dead man's shirt. He took back his car key fob and straightened up. The walk uphill in the heat seemed to take forever, and not once did he look back at the broken heap of a body he'd left behind.

42

'She said *what* to you?' asked Jackie Ojo. Finn and Ojo were in YoYo's. She'd been updating him on a line of inquiry she'd been following when she noticed he was barely listening to a word. That's when she caught just how angry he was. Finn was frequently irritable or tetchy, but furious was unusual. It'd been her suggestion to take it out of the building, and so once again her mother was on emergency child-minding duties. Ojo sipped her tea and listened with incredulity as he explained his confrontation with Paulsen earlier.

'You can't let that go. You've got to bring her in tomorrow and read her the Riot Act.'

'That's just it. I'm not so sure that is the way to handle it. I think it was a cry for help in its own way.'

'Funny way of showing it. Grinds my gears a bit . . .' she said, looking irritated.

'It's alright, I'm a big boy. I can handle a child DC having a temper tantrum.'

'With respect, that's not what I meant. Do you know how careful I have to be about showing any excess emotion? If you're a bloke, it's fine. If you're a woman, it gets commented on. If I'm happy, if I'm sad, if I'm angry – I can't bring it to work. First, they poke you and want to know why. Then they don't let it drop: "*Jacks – what was up with you yesterday?*" And finally, they spend half their day talking about it among themselves. Most of them are actually decent blokes – yet a

231

female colleague shows a bit of emotion and it's like a Martian's landed. It's not like half of them don't have wives, girlfriends or daughters either. If Paulsen speaks to any of them the way she spoke to you, it will kick off big time – trust me.'

Finn looked at Ojo guiltily. He'd always made certain assumptions about her, he realised. He thought she was naturally demure. Now he realised how much she was actually suppressing her true personality, her cool reserve merely a front.

'I'm sorry—'

'Don't be,' she cut in. 'That's just how it is in the Met. Sometimes I wonder if I worked in a bank, whether it would be the same. Not so much institutional sexism, as institutional pubescence.'

Finn smiled, despite himself.

'I've never noticed. If anything, I've always thought you command a lot of respect in the room.'

'Now I'm a DS I do. They've all worked with me for a bit too, so they know me. But Paulsen's new, junior and doing everything she can to piss everyone off. It's not a good mix.'

He considered what she was saying. Whatever Paulsen's problem was, it clearly went deep. It would be easy to ignore it, write it off as a personal issue that he didn't need to worry about. Or, he could treat her outburst as a moment of indiscipline and bollock her for it, but that didn't feel right either. His every instinct was telling him that to turn a blind eye would be negligent.

'How do you get on with her?' he asked.

'She's curious about me – I can see that at times. The opportunity for a proper chat hasn't come along yet. In fairness, most of the time she's been as off with me as she has with everyone else. I can try and grab her at some point though, if you'd like.'

'Might be an idea. She's got a first-class brain. She's not frightened to take the initiative, and having somebody who stands a little bit apart from everyone else . . . I quite *like* that,' said Finn.

'Course you do – because that's exactly what you're like.'

Finn smiled.

'She doesn't fit a mould. She thinks a little bit out of the box. We can get jaded, old dogs like us.'

'Thanks.'

'Pleasure. I mean it though – she's brought an extra dimension to this investigation, something fresh, but what I saw earlier was disturbing. She didn't care about my rank or hers. When she was yelling at me all I saw was raw pain.'

Ojo shook her head. 'I don't care how good she is – you can't let that stand. She has to know it was unacceptable. When you do talk to her, maybe you could use what happened as an excuse to delve deeper. I tell you one thing – you'll see something different tomorrow. Give her a night to sleep on what she did and she'll be bricking it by the morning.'

Before Finn could reply, his phone started ringing. The name *Mattie Paulsen* was flashing up.

'Maybe sooner,' he said.

'For fuck's sake, Mattie,' said Nancy as she took a bite of the slightly soggy stir-fry she'd made for them. It wasn't the greatest meal, but then she hadn't really been concentrating on what she'd been doing. They'd been too busy arguing while she was cooking. Mattie told her about the argument with Finn pretty much as soon as she'd come through the door. It was Nancy who'd pushed her into calling Finn to apologise. The fact Mattie acquiesced so easily suggested she'd known how stupid she'd been, even if she couldn't admit it. She was now sat on the opposite side of their round glass dinner table, holding her phone with a pensive look on her face, her food untouched.

'He's not answering.'

'What did you expect?' said Nancy, trying to contain her own anger. History showed getting angry with Mattie achieved precisely nothing. Despite all the talk of learning and changing, here they were again.

'You could lose your job for this.'

'I won't.'

'And you know this because . . . ?'

'Because Finn's not that kind of bloke. He won't make a big deal out of it. He'll wait until tomorrow, I'll apologise, then he'll bollock me, and then we'll get on with it.'

'You seem pretty sure of that.'

'He's not petty. He'll be pissed off, and he's not answering his phone because he wants to make me sweat.'

'Looks like it's working.'

'I don't need this, Nance.'

'What if you're wrong about him?'

'Then I'll be wrong, won't I?'

'Just tell me why you did it?'

'I already have – he was patronising me. He'd been doing it all week. I got angry because . . .' She looked lost for words.

'What?' Nancy asked gently.

'. . . he got to me. I kept thinking about being on that roof . . .'

'Jesus wept, Mat – I don't need to say it, do I?'

Mattie bowed her head.

'You can't lose your temper there. Besides, do you know how it looks? The woman who gets emotional when things get difficult?'

'That's not fair, and you know why.'

'The point is, no one else does. The point is, you don't want anyone else *to* know. Unless they already do?'

Mattie shook her head. 'How can they? If anyone at Dunlevy Road suspected something, it would have reached Cedar House by now. And I can tell – with Finn, Skegman, Ojo, *all* of them – they don't know anything. They're too busy working the investigation or trying to figure out what makes the new girl tick, but they know nothing.'

Paulsen prodded her food around her plate for a moment, and then lifted a forkful to her mouth.

'I fucked up, didn't I? I think he probably was trying to help me and I misread it.'

'Can I say something, without being shouted at?'

'Can't guarantee it . . .'

'Maybe you do need to tell someone what happened.'

Mattie stared at her incredulously.

'Are you off your fucking head?'

'Maybe there's someone you could trust. Get some advice from.'

'No one would understand, *no one.*'

'You can't control yourself. So you need people around who'll protect you, if you can't protect yourself.'

'I barely know anyone. I've just started there.'

'What about this guy, Finn?'

'No. He's the last one who'd understand. Haven't you been listening to a word I've been saying about him? There's something a bit damaged about him.'

'Come on, Mat, didn't you say his wife had just died? I just think . . . someone like that might just be the right guy at the right time. You could use what happened today as an excuse. Show some humility, try and get his trust.'

Mattie pulled a face.

'Look the word up,' said Nancy.

'Which one? Trust or humility?'

'Both.'

'Alright, I'll make things right with him. But telling him what happened . . .' She shook her head. 'I don't think you've thought that through. What that would mean for me. What it would mean for *us*.'

Finn left YoYo's shortly after eight in better humour than when he'd arrived. It felt like he'd spent most of his day thinking about Mattie Paulsen and he'd been starting to bore himself. It was time to refocus on the task in hand. He wondered why Phil Maddox needed to talk to him so urgently. Was the pressure starting to tell? He remembered how fragile he'd seemed when he'd visited him before. There was also the Handyman to consider. As much as Finn dismissed him at the start, he was hanging over this investigation like a spectre. And right at the back of his mind, there was still that damned blind dog in the forest nagging at him. He smiled to himself. He didn't need to be doing any of this – he could still be at home on leave. But he'd wanted it, and it still felt like the right choice.

He made his way to the tube and caught a train to Vauxhall for his rendezvous with Maddox. One Pacific Square caught his attention as it always did now in this neck of the woods, and he made the ten-minute walk past it to the large oblong of a building where Maddox lived. He could see people dotted around the exterior, sat in small boxy balconies on a warm summer's night. He approached the main entrance and saw it was ajar. The locking mechanism was broken and the door swung open as he pushed it. Quickly running up the staircase to Maddox's flat, the smell of fumes hit him immediately – a suffocating petroleum cocktail. He reached the front door and banged his fist on it. He could hear a fire alarm shrieking inside.

'Phil! It's DI Finn!' he shouted.

To his surprise the door opened suddenly and he almost fell

forwards. Smoke poured out and he found himself face-to-face with a man in black leathers wearing a dark motorcycle helmet. He started to cough violently as the smoke and fumes hit his lungs. The black-clad figure was holding what looked like an iron crowbar, and there was barely time for Finn to react as it came swinging round and the world went black.

43

Five Years Ago

'It's a no-brainer, what are we waiting for?' said Maddox. He was like a little boy hopping with excitement at Christmas. Elder ignored him and focused on Kaul.

'Adesh, there's thousands here, millions possibly . . .'

'So? Not our problem, is it?'

'Isn't it? We've got time. There's a skip outside, next to the west side wall. I saw it from the window. All we have to do is take the sacks down a level and chuck them out.'

'Then what?' said Kaul.

'We'll worry about that later, let's just get them out first.'

'Have you lost your fucking mind?' said Walker. He would replay these moments in the years that followed, and this was the instant he knew he should have stopped it.

Elder turned and strode over, gesticulating as he spoke.

'It's just a big building site, Marty. There's no one else here . . . we wouldn't be putting anyone at risk.'

'You don't know it's empty,' said Walker.

'What are we saving here? Some office space a few Russian oligarchs have spunked their rubles on? Let it fucking burn.'

'What's happening, guys – you've gone very quiet?' said Connelly over the radio.

'We've cleared two floors,' replied Walker. 'Has the ambulance arrived? I think the casualty might still be breathing.'

238

'It's here. You need to get him out fast, Martin – we've got to start tackling the fire itself. We're waiting on you. You're okay for air, but you need to get moving.'

'Understood. We're on our way,' said Walker.

'Just wait, skip,' said Elder. 'Think about Christine. Her MS. There's enough money here to take care of her for the rest of her life.'

Walker was silent.

'What about Stu?' asked Kaul quietly.

'He's one of us. We deal him in. He'll be fine with it. Why wouldn't he be?' replied Elder. Walker looked over at the unconscious man again.

'And him? We've got to get him down.'

'We can't,' said Elder.

'What do you mean we *can't*? We've got time to get him and the money out.'

'Think about it,' said Elder. 'Who is he? Where does that money come from?'

'He doesn't need to know – if he asks afterwards we tell him it went up in smoke. We don't even tell him we saw it.' Walker could hear the words coming out of his mouth, even if he couldn't quite believe he was saying them.

'And you think he, or whoever this cash belongs to, will believe us? You think they won't notice when we start spending it? If we're going to do this, then no one can know.'

'How long's he been out – ten minutes?' said Maddox. 'I'm guessing there's already brain damage, if he isn't already dead.' He checked for a pulse.

'Martin – what the hell's going on? Are you guys okay?' said Connelly over the radio.

'We're fine,' said Elder quickly into his radio. 'The casualty's dead and the body's trapped. We're just trying to move it now.'

239

Walker bit his tongue. Something else he'd reflect on later.

'*You're starting to run low on air – if it comes to it, leave the body and get out.*'

The heat in their suits was becoming unbearable. Whatever they were going to do, they needed to do it now.

'We're not leaving this man,' said Walker.

'How many people have we *had* to leave over the years? The ones we couldn't save?' said Elder.

'We owe it to his family to get him out.'

'Do you want to change the rest of your life, or do you want to carry on risking it every day?'

'He's dead. I'm telling you,' said Maddox.

'Adesh, have you got anything to say?' said Walker.

'What are we waiting for? I'm in.'

'It's a win-win, Marty. No one loses,' said Elder.

Walker looked at the body and Maddox shook his head again. He thought about every trip he and Christine had made to the hospital, those moments in front of the TV at night when he'd caught her staring pensively into space, the fear etched on her face.

'Alright. Let's do this.'

44

Today

It was a myth that when fire sprinklers were set off in a flat, they went off in the whole building. Jackie Ojo was stood in Phil Maddox's sodden front room and realised many of the other residents would probably have little idea of the horror that'd taken place here. In the end it was the young couple in the flat below who'd called 999. Smelling smoke, they'd gone up to investigate and found Finn's unconscious body on the stairwell.

'We thought he'd burnt his dinner,' they'd said in their statement. Ojo could understand why; the stench of roasted meat and burnt fat still hung heavy in the air.

The irony was Maddox hadn't forgotten his roots. There was a carbon dioxide fire extinguisher still hanging in the hallway, smoke alarms, and carbon monoxide detectors on the walls. Much good any of it was to him in the end. Two SOCOs in white protective suits, both wearing masks, were working in the bathroom. Ojo braced herself, gagging at the smell and coughing as she turned the corner. She used a handkerchief to cover her mouth and entered. One of the SOCOs glared and Ojo held up a hand to acknowledge she knew why. Even though she was wearing the full protective apparel it was a tight space and they didn't want her going any further.

Her eyes were immediately drawn to it; the twisted lump of barbecued meat in the tub. Whispers of hair sat in tufts on a charred bald skull, grinning with yellow teeth. Strips of bright red flesh hung out of the blackened torso, while greasy white ribs were visible where the midriff was completely burnt away. The body lay curled up in a layer of sooty black water. What interested her was that the firefighters hadn't actually put anything out. They'd found the carcase still steaming. The inference was clear; someone took care to stop the flames from spreading. Forensics and the post-mortem would confirm it later, but it looked like Maddox was set alight in the tub, then the shower used to extinguish the blaze. Like Kaul and Elder before him, he must have been overpowered. For a moment she tried to imagine the battle. After the first two he'd have known what was going to happen. Why the intruder was there. She tried to imagine his fear in those last, desperate moments. The bathroom, all antiseptic whites, would have felt like an execution chamber. Finn must have arrived barely minutes too late, just as the attacker was finishing up. She took one last look at the blackened eye socket of the dead thing in the bath and left.

Finn's head was thumping. He'd been lucky, but it certainly didn't feel that way. The worst of the damage was just a nasty cut on the side of his head. He'd been taken to nearby St Thomas's Hospital where they'd stitched him up. The X-rays showed no signs of concussion, and he'd finally been released not long after three in the morning. Now, six hours later, after very little sleep, he was sat in his kitchen downing painkillers. His front doorbell chimed, and he found Mattie Paulsen unexpectedly waiting outside with an awkward expression on her face. He gave her a thin smile and let her in.

'How are you feeling, sir?' she asked.

He noted with private amusement the chastened use of the word 'sir'. They hadn't actually spoken since their confrontation the previous day. It felt an eternity ago.

'Like a truck hit me.'

'Actually it was a Halligan bar. We found it outside, Maddox must have kept his after he left the job.'

'No wonder I feel like I've gone ten rounds with Anthony Joshua.'

She looked bemused, clearly unfamiliar with the reference.

'What have I done to earn a home visit?'

'The DCI was concerned about you; he wanted to know if you were alright.'

Finn knew that wasn't true because he'd spoken to Skegman on the phone earlier. He could guess her real motive for coming over. The reality of what she'd said to him the previous day was clearly now biting at the young DC.

'I'm fine. Before anything else – I take it we've paid Kevin Pender a visit?' said Finn, in no hurry to give her the opportunity to apologise. Paulsen nodded.

'We sent officers directly to his address the moment we heard what happened. He wasn't there, but we tracked him to his parents' house. He went straight to them after he left the station yesterday. They've both given him an alibi for last night and it looks solid.'

Finn digested the information, but he'd already been certain it wasn't Pender who'd attacked him; the man in the motorbike helmet was taller and broader for a start. It wasn't just his head making him feel nauseous. From the moment he'd regained consciousness he'd been haunted by the realisation they should have given Maddox protection. He'd told Skegman in his office not to do it, that he'd take responsibility if things went tits up. Well, a man was now dead. He also remembered what he told Ojo in the pub – that he felt he was functioning at eighty per cent. He'd thought it was enough.

'*That's a big twenty per cent,*' she'd said to him. It was feeling like that now. Somewhere in that twenty per cent he'd failed Phil Maddox. And even then, was he using his grief as an easy excuse or was he simply not doing his job properly? It was the very point Paulsen had screamed at him the previous day. Self-doubt was something new to him. He was a man of certainties and police work was the area of his life where he felt most certain. He didn't like how he felt one iota; it was bordering on self-loathing. He saw Paulsen looking at him curiously, as if sensing what was going through his mind.

'I want a thorough search done of Maddox's flat when SOCO and the fire investigation team are finished there. There was something he wanted to tell me which he thought was important.' He said it firmly and quickly, hoping the weakness he felt wasn't showing. She nodded in acknowledgement, but still seemed awkward. It wasn't just him feeling awful, he realised. She looked sheepish. He hadn't seen that before.

'Is there something you want to say, DC Paulsen?'

She looked up, finally meeting his gaze properly.

'Yes. I wanted to apologise for what happened yesterday. It was inexcusable. I'm dealing with some personal issues at the moment. I let them get to me and it won't happen again.'

He considered his response. The fact she might have had a point when she'd been yelling at him didn't change or excuse the shocking nature of her outburst. Or his need to address it. The apology was a good try as an opening gambit but he wasn't going to let her off the hook that easily.

'As I recall, it was asking whether there *was* something else on your mind which triggered the whole episode yesterday. I don't suppose you feel able to tell me what it is?'

'I'm sorry, but no. It's difficult and very personal,' she said stiffly.

'Okay. If we weren't up to our eyes in what's now a triple murder inquiry we'd have a longer and blunter conversation. But make no mistake, if you're going to continue on my team then you'll have to explain yourself fully to me at some point. Not today, not tomorrow but when this is over we'll have that conversation. I'll decide then what disciplinary action is appropriate.'

Whatever she privately thought, she contained it well.

'There's something else you should know.' Her tone was brisk again. 'I've received an email overnight from a sergeant at Chapel Row – a DS Godden. I haven't looked properly at the detail yet, but he thinks he's got evidence someone might be trying to reactivate one of Erik Whitlock's smurfing networks. He's suggesting the only person with the capability would have to be Whitlock himself.'

Finn almost forgot the banging pain in his head for a moment.

'That's impossible. They identified Whitlock by his teeth. Have you looked at the records?'

'I'm still trying to establish who the forensic dentist was, but the remains were returned to the next of kin.'

'Then see if you can track them down, we may need them back.'

'How much credibility do you want to give this?'

'That Whitlock's alive? It's nuts . . . but he worked for some pretty serious people. So could his death have been faked? Your guess is as good as mine, but talk to this Godden by all means and see what he's got.'

'There's one final thing, guv: DCI Skegman's authorised round-the-clock surveillance for Walker and Portbury.'

Finn nodded, but said nothing.

'Shouldn't we be pushing those two harder about the money now?'

'What money? We've still got no hard evidence they took *anything*.'

Paulsen nodded, then stood up.

'You know they found you on the stairwell? You'd been placed there, presumably by the same man who attacked you. DS Ojo says it looks like Maddox's killer was careful to keep the fire contained so it didn't spread.'

'Just like the other two. Whoever did it just wanted Maddox hurt. He was targeted. These are professional hits. The only question now is who's next? Walker or Portbury?'

Stuart Portbury followed Mei up the stairs and stopped on the landing. Like every other part of the house it was spotless, and upstairs it smelt of freshly washed clothes. Mei pointed at the door at the end of the corridor. She brushed his arm with her hand, then turned and went back downstairs. He walked over to the door and knocked. A quiet voice responded, inviting him in, and he went on through. The room was nothing like the usual cliché of a teenager's bedroom. The bed, all crisp white linens, was immaculately made up with an expensive-looking velvet throw at the end. An ornate antique lamp sat on the bedside table, and the brilliant white walls were lined with shelves stacked with books. At the far end was a wooden desk, where a young man was sat studying a laptop screen intently. He turned and Portbury was greeted by a boyish face with a fringe of floppy black hair and John Lennon spectacles.

'Riku? I'm Stuart, I'm a friend of your mum's.'

The boy stood up, almost to attention.

'Please, sit down. I'm sorry if I'm disturbing you.' Portbury gave him a reassuring smile and Riku sat down again. He knew what he wanted to say, but he suddenly realised he hadn't a clue how to begin the conversation. The boy solved the problem for him.

'I guess Mum must be worried about me then ... ?' He smiled shyly.

'She's just being a mum. It's what they do.'

'I'm fine. She worries too much.'

'I don't think it's anything specific she's concerned about. It's ...' Portbury faltered, aware of how atrocious he was at talking to anyone under the age of twenty. 'Well, my dad died when I was young. So I know what it's like to grow up without one. Especially when you hear all your mates talking about their families. You feel different, like you're some sort of freak. But you shouldn't.'

Riku's eyes flicked involuntarily down and Portbury realised he'd hit a spot.

'There's loads of people just like you. Why don't you tell me all about your dad? I want to hear all about him.'

He hadn't even liked Gary Elder that much, Martin Walker mused as he tended to his roses. But it was the strange thing about that job – he'd probably have given his life to protect him once, knowing Elder would have done the same for him. You had each other's backs, that's just how it was. So soon after Adesh's wake, there'd be another funeral now. He'd met Elder's mother once – a genuinely sweet lady who'd been so proud of her boy. She was old then, so she must be nearly in her eighties now. It wasn't fair.

It was another beautiful day and the garden couldn't have felt calmer. He looked up and saw Christine through the kitchen window. Something wasn't right with his wife. Something hadn't been right with his marriage for a long time though. Not since he'd retired if he was honest. There was a hairline crack beneath the surface, and it was getting larger every day. He'd always thought she understood the bigger picture of their lives, that everything he did was for her. But

247

there was no doubt she'd been shaken by the deaths of Kaul and Elder. She'd met them back in the day, so could put faces to the names. The horrific manner of their murders prompted a deluge of questions he couldn't answer. More than that, there was real fear now. It lurked beneath the surface as they ate their meals, stalked them while they were out shopping, hung over them as they silently watched television at night.

He'd never told Christine about the events inside Pacific Square, but she wasn't stupid. However hard he tried, she knew him well enough to know *something* significant took place that night. The unspoken secret was the elephant in the room of their relationship. She'd withdrawn into herself, giving him a small melancholic smile whenever he caught her watching him.

He'd been particularly non-communicative about the reason he'd disappeared the previous day. He'd told her it was just some admin work related to a charity walk he was planning, but they both knew that was a lie. He *always* told her where he was just in case she needed help, and he always kept his phone switched on for the same reason. To break such fundamental unwritten rules of their marriage signalled something was seriously up.

The uncomfortable atmosphere was now stifling after his day trip to Whitstable. The truth was he didn't quite know where his conversation with the man in the beach hut left them. If the Handyman – the man who'd stolen the bloody money in the first place – wasn't behind Kaul and Elder's deaths, then who the hell was? He'd pondered moving out of London for a while, but with Christine's condition it simply wasn't practical at short notice. What would he tell her? Where would they go? More importantly, they'd have to come back at some point. He didn't see any point in running and was reluctant to get too close to the police; when the dust settled he didn't want to end up in a prison cell. But he also knew he needed to do *something* because someone, somewhere, was coming for him.

He'd messaged Portbury and Maddox on the WhatsApp group as soon as he'd returned from the coast. He knew Portbury read the message but hadn't received a reply. Maddox on the other hand called straight away. Walker told him everything – about the man in the gym, the trip to the beach and the conversation with Spinney. Phil predictably began to panic. He was talking of going to Spain and maybe staying there. He'd also talked of telling the police *everything*. It'd taken a lot of persuading to get him to see sense. He just hoped what he'd told him would stick and the idiot wouldn't do anything stupid. The camaraderie of the old days seemed a long way back in the past.

He heard the doorbell ring and turned around; Christine was waving at him from the conservatory to indicate she'd get it. He emptied the remainder of his watering can into the soil. The sky was a cloudless blue and he leant in, inhaling the gentle fragrance of the flowers. Everything was actually perfect right now – that was the irony of it. He heard the conservatory door open, and saw Christine emerging. She was accompanied by a uniformed police officer and he felt his heart sink.

45

Mike Godden slept remarkably well and woke with a clear sense of purpose. There were things to do with the day. He knew Farmer's body would eventually be found, and Chapel Row's own CCTV cameras would show them leaving together. An explanation would be needed, but he was sure he could come up with something. He was equally confident the evidence at the scene would point to a tragic accident. The fact no one would even suspect him of being responsible would help carry the lies a long way. He'd spent the previous evening at the same Indian restaurant where he'd first met Ray Spinney. He didn't fancy a night in on his own given the day's events, and a curry felt a reassuringly normal thing to do. It also gave him a chance to think.

He was certain now it was Spinney behind the calls to the two members of Whitlock's smurfing network. He'd never really bought into the idea Whitlock was still alive, largely because the timing was so suspicious. The sense he was being toyed with wouldn't leave him, and the question remained: why? Farmer's inquiries may have disturbed Spinney more than he previously thought. If he genuinely believed Godden was compromised, then there was no telling what he might do next. This was a man known for his abhorrence of loose ends, and Godden didn't fancy ending up in a ditch with a screwdriver sticking out of his skull. He briefly considered informing Spinney about Farmer and the steps he'd been forced to take the previous day. It might be a reassurance to know the source of the problem was now eliminated. Alternatively, a dead police officer might freak him out even more and that was the last thing he wanted. It was a gamble he decided against.

Godden possessed one piece of leverage on Spinney, and again he mulled it over. It was the nuclear option, but then sometimes the way to take control of events was to seize and shape them yourself. In the course of their six-year association, Spinney had always used prepaid burner phones to make contact. He used a different one each time, but that didn't matter – if anything it'd helped. As a contingency, Godden had ordered cell site analysis done on three separate phones in succession. Naturally he didn't explain why he'd wanted them, or who he was pursuing – but the results gave him what he needed. He knew where Spinney was, down to the street number, and now was the time to use that information.

Feeling better after a chicken madras and a beer, he'd gone home and started to put his plan into action. First, he rang an old snout. Someone usefully pliable, perfect for what he needed. He instructed him to send an anonymous email the following day from a newly created account. A small internet cafe without security cameras would do the job. He talked him through the detail of it and then when he was satisfied his instructions were understood, he'd finally gone to bed. The memory of what took place at the landfill site resurfaced unbidden as his head hit the pillow. Somewhere along the line he'd become a monster, he thought, but what shocked him the most was how little he cared.

The following morning, he had arrived at work early and emailed DC Mattie Paulsen the information he'd uncovered regarding Whitlock's network. Alerting Cedar House to the possibility Whitlock might still be alive was as good as tossing a small stick of dynamite into their investigation. He could imagine the conversations they'd now be having down there. If the body of a young DC turned up in Hertfordshire, then it'd be just another twist in an already evolving inquiry. As he sat at his desk sipping on a coffee, he felt things were starting to come back under his control a little. He looked across his office window at the empty seat at Farmer's desk, and shivered involuntarily.

'Mike – you got a sec, mate?'

It was Warrender.

'Sure, guv.'

'I've just seen the paperwork you left me on Whitlock's network – what's your take?'

'It's taken us literally years to track down the people on that list. Even now, I'd say we've only probably got about sixty per cent of the whole network identified. I honestly don't know who else other than Erik Whitlock would or could be ringing any of them up. The whole point of the network is its anonymity. None of them know each other. The only common denominator *was* Whitlock.'

'You can't really believe he's still alive?' Warrender's face was taking on that pinkish hue again. The one it tended to when he was working himself up.

'No. I'm just presenting you with the facts.'

'So why did you tell Cedar House he might be?' He was definitely turning puce now.

'I didn't tell them that. I just presented the facts to them as well, because it might be connected to their investigation. Surely they need to be notified of anything connected to Whitlock?'

'They've got their hands full as it is. Another one of the Pacific Square firefighters was murdered overnight.'

'Jesus,' said Godden, genuinely surprised.

'Something's going on, Mike. I don't what it is yet, but the wheels of something are turning. Have you seen Jimmy, by the way? He hasn't come in and he's not answering his phone.'

'No, but he was coughing and sneezing all day yesterday. Probably a summer cold.'

'Fuck's sake. If he's not coming in, he needs to pick up the phone and—' Warrender was interrupted by a ping from his computer signalling the arrival of an email. As he always did mid-flow, he cast an eye across it in case it was something important. Now it was his turn to look surprised, and this time Godden knew *exactly* why.

'Someone's given up Raymond Spinney?'

Finn was looking out of the incident room window, with his phone tight to his ear. He hadn't particularly warmed to Andy Warrender the first time they'd spoken, and the sense of a well-meaning blunderer was only intensifying. The sound of elation in the man's voice was only matched by Finn's own natural caution.

'I've just been sent an anonymous email. You ever heard of Sandbury?'

'It's in Kent, isn't it?'

'Yeah – a small village, south of Ashford. The email claims that's where he's been hiding out. He's been using the alias George Caldwell, and apparently even runs a small business out there.'

'That's all you've got? Just a tip-off?'

'No, more than that. There's a time stamped photograph attached, taken the day before yesterday. It's from Sandbury railway station's CCTV camera – it's blurry, but it's a good enough ID for me. There's also a sample of his handwriting, an invoice from Caldwell's business. It's a perfect match with the samples we've got on file for Spinney.'

'And you're tracing the email?'

'Obviously, but I'm not expecting to get much back. Anyone with the balls to do this isn't going to want to be found. I've contacted Kent Police and they're preparing a raid.'

'When?'

'As soon as; they're just getting their ducks in a row. If it is Spinney, then they don't want him slipping away. Christ alone knows what kind of protection he's got.'

If there were bent cops on the payroll, thought Finn, this would soon prove it. He wondered what the betting was that Kent Police would find nothing through the raid. He took stock, focusing on a shaft of sunlight coming through the window and watching the dust particles dancing in it. Something about all of this felt off.

'Don't you think this is all a bit convenient? All of a sudden some evidence appears implying Whitlock might have returned from the dead, then twenty-four hours later someone gift-wraps you the location of one of the most wanted men in the country?'

'What have you found on Whitlock?' said Warrender. He sounded irritated, unhappy at having his big breakthrough questioned.

'We've only just started looking into it. When he died he was identified by his dental records. So the question is – did someone get to the forensic dentist? We're getting hold of the original documentation and will take it from there. But I've got to say, I'm more interested in why someone might want us to *think* Erik Whitlock survived – and why they're chucking it into the mix now.'

'I'm going to need to interview Martin Walker and Stuart Portbury. I need to know what they know,' said Warrender.

'No,' replied Finn instantly.

'What do you mean "no"? You should have interviewed them days ago.'

'We did,' replied Finn testily. 'Is there reason to believe the members of that fire crew came into some money? Yes. But right now I'm more interested in keeping them alive. A secondary investigation can wait until we've caught the psycho who's trying to kill them.'

'Oh fuck off,' said Warrender with pure frustration.

'Pardon?' said Finn. There was another long pause, and when Warrender spoke again, it was with audible restraint.

'I have to focus on Spinney. If there's *any* chance of getting him into an interview room, I have to take it. You've got your investigation and I've got mine. If there's anything you need to know I'll be in touch – all I ask is the same courtesy back. And I *am* going to need to sit in a room with Portbury and Walker, sooner rather than later.'

'Sure, but I need you to back off until the killer's caught.'

'And what if you don't catch him – what if he kills both of them first? Where does that leave me?'

'They're both under round-the-clock surveillance. They're going nowhere, and we aren't going to let anyone hurt them. Once we've caught the killer, then you can have them. With any luck, you'll have Spinney soon and then the threat will be off the table anyway.'

Finn could understand why the other man was so on edge. After being the butt of so many jokes for so long, Warrender needed this. Hanging up the phone, he turned and found Paulsen patiently waiting for him.

'I've just been talking to Erik Whitlock's widow,' she said.

'What did you tell her?'

'Only that she might be able to help us with a live investigation. She's happy to come in and speak to me.'

'Good. Does she still have her husband's remains?'

'I thought I'd work up to that one . . .' said Paulsen.

That was going to be a conversation, thought Finn. Someone's ashes couldn't be reliably DNA-tested. But if the recovered dental remains were still intact they could be re-examined. If it could be proved they were definitely Whitlock's, then it would end speculation about a resurrection once and for all.

'It's in someone's interest to start a rumour that Whitlock's still alive, so let's knock that firmly on the head before it gains any more traction. When she comes in, tell her we're going to need her husband's teeth back.' He said it as deadpan as he could manage.

Paulsen gave him a look which said *are you sure?* and just for once, he didn't blame her.

46

Erik Whitlock's widow, as it turned out, was quite beautiful. The dark-haired woman in her forties waiting at the front desk looked anything but the stereotype of a gangster's moll. She presented more like a high-powered businesswoman. Her elfin features belied a hard pair of eyes though. She looked like someone well versed in keeping secrets, thought Paulsen.

'Thank you for coming in, Mrs Whitlock. I'm sorry it was at such short notice; I hope it's not been too much of an inconvenience.'

'I don't use that name any more,' she said, as Paulsen led her down one of the station's long antiseptic corridors. Mattie guided her to the soft interview room. A more relaxed and comfortable environment, it was normally a place where children or vulnerable people were taken to be gently questioned.

'So how can I help you?' the former Mrs Whitlock asked, with little warmth. She clearly wanted to get whatever this was over with as fast as possible. Paulsen could see it was going to be difficult. The barriers were up, but there was something about this woman which also made her feel sympathetic too. She sensed beneath the hard exterior was someone who'd suffered, and that was a combination she understood only too well.

'Someone appears to have gained access to information only your husband would have had any knowledge of. Has anything irregular occurred in the last few weeks or months? Has someone unexpected made any kind of contact with you, for example?'

'No. Nothing like that.' Again, the same dismissive tone.

'Perhaps an email, or an unusual phone call?'

'Nothing at all.'

'Can I ask if you've stayed in touch with any of your husband's friends or business associates?'

The ghost of a smile crossed the woman's features.

'Business associates? No. I can't say I was *in touch* with any of them when he was alive.'

'I'm afraid there's no easy way to ask this question, so I'm just going to ask it. Has anything occurred in the last five years that's ever made you question whether your husband might still be alive?'

There were any number of ways the woman might have reacted. She could have screamed, got angry, laughed, or even just walked out. She did none of those things. Instead she frowned and rolled her head for a moment. Paulsen persisted. 'We think it's possible someone might be trying to suggest he is. I can only imagine how distasteful you find that. We just want to put a stop to it.'

'And how exactly do you intend to do that?'

'We'd like to re-examine his dental remains – if you still have them?'

The woman arched an eyebrow; Paulsen wasn't sure if it was in surprise or disgust.

'You doubt the findings of the original examination?'

'We want to be sure they weren't falsified.'

'I'm sorry to disappoint you but I don't have them. What was left of Erik was scattered on a beach in South Africa a long time ago.' Paulsen tried to conceal her disappointment, and the woman looked faintly amused. 'There is something I will tell you though. Whether it will help or not, I don't know. For the past eighteen months, on the first of every month I've received a package through my letterbox. It must be delivered by hand overnight, but I've never seen anyone. There's no postage on it. It's quite anonymous and I genuinely can't tell you where it comes from or who's sending it. There's cash inside – you'll forgive me if I don't tell you how much. It's enabled me to live without worry. Why am I telling you? Because as far as I'm aware no crime is being committed.'

'That might be a premature assumption . . . but you think that it might be Erik that's sending you this money?' said Paulsen.

'I'm under no illusion of what kind of man my husband was, or of what circles he mixed in. I know that I loved him, and that he loved me. Do I find it conceivable that he might have made a provision for me in the event of his death? Yes, I do. Do I think it's possible his death might have been staged? As I say, I know what kind of world he operated in – and what he might have needed to do to protect me. What you have to understand, DC Paulsen, is that to me he's like Schrödinger's cat in that burning building. Both alive and dead at the same time, and I'm quite comfortable with that.' She smiled and kept her eyes locked on Paulsen's, and it felt oddly as if they'd reached an understanding of sorts.

Martin Walker poured the tea from the pot and then peered into his cup suspiciously.

'Sorry, love, should have let this steep a bit longer. I hate pissy tea.'

'I don't care about the fucking tea,' snapped Christine. It wasn't her language that surprised him, but her tone; the terror he could hear behind it. The mantelpiece clock seemed to be ticking louder than Big Ben.

'What's the matter, love?'

'I'm scared, Marty.'

'There's no need to be.'

He went over to the window and peered through the curtain. DCs Claire Lowton and Dave McGilligott were still sat in the car parked on the other side of the road. He'd taken them a flask of tea earlier, and apart from a few requests to use the toilet it was easy to forget they were there. Walker found them a reassurance even if his wife didn't. The police seemed more concerned with protecting them than questioning him again, and for that he was grateful.

'Are you sure you don't want some tea? It'll do you good.'

'I'd rather talk. It's time you told me the truth about a few things, Martin.'

'Such as?'

'All of it . . . starting with *this.*' She motioned at the room, the house that surrounded them. 'I've always left the financial side of things to you, but I know your pension's not that great. How did we afford all this? The chairlift, the ramps, the Harley Street consultants; it must have cost tens of thousands?'

'You don't need to worry about it.'

'Martin – please. People have died. There's so much you're keeping from me.'

'For your own good,' he snapped.

The words were followed by a long silence. It was the first time he'd actually acknowledged that truth.

'Why does someone want to kill you? You stole money, didn't you? And now whoever you took it from wants it back?'

She'd hit the nail on the head, and now he was trying to understand just why he was so reluctant to tell her. If there was anyone who deserved to know, it was her, but he couldn't do it. And deep down he *did* know why. To admit what they'd done made him a different man, a common thief. He wasn't sure he'd ever be able to look her in the eye again once the confession was made.

'I think we may need to move away for a while,' he said.

She put her hand to her mouth and from across the room he saw a silent tear slowly roll down her cheek.

Stuart Portbury looked more irritated than anything, thought Finn. Like he'd been told the afternoon forecast was for showers. He was sat opposite the former firefighter in his modest living room in Greenwich. Finn wanted to check for himself how Portbury was bearing up after the double whammy of Maddox's death and the decision to deploy round-the-clock protection. He was also the only other member of the fire crew he hadn't met for himself. Like the others, something wasn't quite right, even if he couldn't put his finger on it. Portbury seemed more put out by the surveillance units outside than the death of another former colleague.

'Does it have to be twenty-four seven? Really?'

'It's for your own safety.'

'I honestly don't think I'm in any danger.'

'I don't want you to take this the wrong way, but if I was in your shoes I'd be worried,' said Finn.

'I understand why you're saying that, but do you know how many firefighters attended Pacific Square? It's in three figures. Are you telling me they're all in the cross hairs of this psycho?'

'No. But we have reason to believe that your old crew are.'

'We've already been through this. I told your colleague – I didn't even go in the damn building. I certainly didn't take any money. You must have been through my accounts by now?'

'Whether you did or didn't take any money is irrelevant. What matters is whether someone else thinks you did . . .' Finn let it hang there as Portbury caught on.

'Until we catch them there's a very clear threat to your life. You won't notice the officers going about their work, but they'll be there if you need them. And you might just end up very grateful for that.'

'And how am I supposed to do my job? What kind of trades-man turns up with a police detachment in tow?'

Did this man need to be taken to the morgue to see the barbecued remains of his ex-colleagues? Finn almost said it out loud.

'It might be an idea to forget about work until this is sorted out.'

Portbury sighed.

'And how do I earn a living in the meantime?'

'I'm sorry, I really am. But we can't just ignore it. We have a duty of care.'

'Duty of care ...' Portbury repeated the words slowly as if hearing them for the first time. 'Now there's a phrase.'

47

DC Susie Gyimah hadn't slept well. She blamed the foxes who'd been shagging, fighting or whatever it was they did at three a.m. to make such a godawful noise. Now, at her desk trying to focus, she was paying for it. She quickly stifled another yawn as she saw Mike Godden making his way over. She wasn't his biggest fan; the arrogant bugger could use some manners frankly. He treated DCs and PCs like something he'd stepped in, then smarmed up to Warrender like they were joined at the hip. He was a lazy sod as well; always getting other people to do his legwork for him. She'd also seen him get just a bit *too* friendly in the bar with some of the younger female officers. Something smelt bad there, and she tried to avoid him where possible. Not today it seemed.

'Alright, Suze,' he said, flashing an irritating smile.

'Sarge.'

'What are you cooped up in here working on then?'

She tried to remember the last time he'd made small talk with her and couldn't. As a rule, he bantered with the boys and ignored the girls – in the office at least. Jim Farmer was his normal stooge, which was a shame because if you got Jim on his own he was a decent bloke. Godden seemed odd this morning, almost skittish. He normally swaggered through CID.

'Paperwork. I've got a shitload from yesterday which I haven't caught up on.'

'Well, that's one thing about the job that doesn't change. I don't want to sound like your grandad, but you lot have it easy. When I started out, we were using typewriters. The day they invented the word processor I nearly cried.' She squeezed out a tight smile. This wasn't just small talk; it was *painful* small talk.

'Since you're down here, sarge, don't suppose you want to confirm the rumours, do you?'

'What rumours would they be then? I'm not really up on who's shagging who around here these days.'

'People are saying you've found the Handyman? That's the word in CID, that your governor's received a tip-off.'

He grinned wolfishly back at her.

'I can't confirm or deny a thing but watch this space – it could be an interesting day.'

Now he genuinely did have her interest. Most of the rank and file at Chapel Row found Warrender's team as big a joke as the rest of the world. But catching the paparazzi's favourite bogeyman would be one way to shut the critics up. She could only imagine what state that idiot Warrender was in up there.

'Listen,' said Godden, leaning in. 'It might not be the worst idea to arrange some drinks in the Royal Oak tonight – for the whole station. Been a while since we all had a blow out together.'

'Interesting,' she said conspiratorially.

'Isn't it?' he replied with a wink, and began to walk on. He stopped again suddenly.

'By the way, you haven't seen Jimmy Farmer today, have you?'

'No, why?'

'Been no sign of him – probably laid up at home with that new bird of his, wailing about man flu.' He gave an exaggerated eye-roll and headed off.

264

That should help sell it, Godden thought. Jaunty and friendly; his usual self, in other words. If anyone asked questions later, people would say he'd been relaxed and normal. These situations were all about the marginal gains, you never knew how important they might become later. As he walked down the corridor he could see Warrender on the phone in his office. Godden could tell straight away something was wrong. The DI looked ashen, with none of the usual histrionics. He braced himself, and focused his thoughts quickly. It might be nothing, but if he was right about what was coming, he'd need to be word perfect. Warrender saw him looking over and immediately beckoned him in.

'Mike, there you are – I've been looking for you,' said Warrender. He looked shell-shocked and Godden pulled a concerned face.

'Something up, guv?'

'It's Jimmy.'

'What about him?'

'I've just had a call from a DS in Welwyn. There's a landfill site on their patch that's gone into administration. One of the people from the accountancy firm handling the job drove out there this morning, and found the body of a man in his late twenties. They called 999 and the uniforms who attended found Jimmy's ID on it.'

'*What?*' said Godden with a rehearsed mixture of shock and horror.

'He took a picture at the scene.' Warrender tapped on his phone and passed the handset over to Godden who slowly looked down at the image. It showed Farmer's head slumped to one side, his hooded eyelids shut as if simply dozing. Dried blood mingled with clay-coloured dust caked his face. The expression was exactly as it'd been when Godden left him the previous day. Not that there was any reason it could or would have altered, but it so closely matched the last image in his mind's eye it shook him momentarily.

'Jesus . . .'

'There's a full crime scene in place, I'm just about to head out there.'

'What are SOCO saying?'

'Early signs are that it was an accident. Looks like he went there for a nose around, then fell down a slope. I can't quite believe it, to be honest.'

'How long ago?' said Godden, still affecting shock.

'I've just been talking to his girlfriend. They don't live together so she doesn't know whether he came home last night. She texted him early this morning, but he didn't reply. She wasn't too worried because he doesn't always answer immediately. I haven't told her about the body yet, that should wait until there's been a formal ID. Mike – I hate to ask, but you may just have been the last person to have seen him alive. You went out on a job together yesterday, didn't you?'

'Yes, we were following a lead on Whitlock's network. The guy we wanted wasn't there, so Jimmy volunteered to try and track him down. I dropped him off just outside Hatfield.'

'Do you think that's why he might have gone to that landfill site? He'd found something?'

'Possibly . . .'

'How did he get there if he didn't have a car? I don't understand.'

Godden shrugged, affecting total bemusement.

'Okay. I've ordered a cell site analysis of his phone – hopefully it'll give us an idea of where he went after you dropped him off, then we can start to construct a timeline.'

Godden was anticipating this too. He'd looked at the map earlier and identified the place he'd claim to have left Farmer. It was en route to the landfill site, but far enough away to match the version of events he'd just given Warrender. It would also tally with the results of any cell site analysis. It wasn't watertight but would have to do.

'I've got to say I can't remember a landfill business coming up with any of the people we'd been looking into. What else do we know about it?' he asked Warrender.

'Very little at this point, but there is *something* which might give us a clue. The main office is a Portakabin with a mounted CCTV camera. The administrators have been maintaining it because the place has become a magnet for fly-tippers.'

Godden felt like he'd just been punched in the solar plexus. Once he'd made the decision he might have to kill Farmer there'd been very little time to plan anything, so he'd improvised. The landfill site seemed the perfect choice because it was secluded and neglected. It's not like he was born yesterday either. He'd looked out for cameras when they'd arrived and hadn't seen any. He'd clearly missed one and it was his ridiculous luck it was actually still working. Over the years he'd dealt with many thriving businesses who'd been hopeless at maintaining their security, let alone a firm which went bust months ago. His mind was racing. His carefully constructed cover story was now in tatters.

He thought it through logically. The footage was probably being transported back to some nick in Hatfield for a DC to go through. It would clearly show him entering the Portakabin with Farmer. It would also show the pair of them exiting, with Godden in handcuffs. There was no lie which would get him out of that. One careless oversight and his house of cards was crashing down. There were only two options now. Either confess to murdering a fellow officer and admit to being on the payroll of one of the most wanted men in the country – or go on the run. It was a no-brainer. Experience told him running was probably doomed to fail, but at least he'd have the glimmer of a chance. He didn't possess a fraction of the resources Spinney did. There was no network of contacts who could protect him, no carefully planned strategy to get him out of this. He'd improvised and improvised, and now he was all out of ideas. There was a vicious irony to it. He'd done all of this for his daughter; for Franny. Now either way, he'd probably never see her again.

'Mike?' said Warrender.

Godden snapped back into the room and saw the concern on his DI's face. He felt like plunging a steak knife into the middle of it.

'Sorry, it's so hard to take all this in.'

'I know, mate, tell me about it. Do you want to come out there with me? I know how close you two were.'

'It's alright, guv. Someone needs to manage things here; this is going to come as a massive shock for the whole place, and then there's the Handyman. We need to stay on top of that; we can't drop the ball, whatever else is going on. We owe it to Jimmy to see the job through. Do you know when the raid in Kent's going ahead?'

'Not yet, but imminently.'

Warrender sympathetically patted his arm.

'I've got some calls to make, and then I'll head out. Stay in touch, let me know of any developments.' He shook his head. 'What a business, eh? Poor Jimmy . . .'

Godden nodded gravely and waited for Warrender to go, then grabbed his jacket. He estimated he'd just enough time to go home, grab his passport and get to the airport. After that, he did not have a clue.

48

The timing was awful, but Finn didn't really have much choice. The crime scene was still very much live at Phil Maddox's flat, while the operation to arrest Ray Spinney could proceed at any second. It was hardly the time to be going AWOL, but some things – some moments – were simply too important to let pass. He'd experienced an epiphany about one of his problems and there was only a small window of opportunity to act. He was once again stood in the car park of Cedar House, staring down into the boot of his car at the object wrapped in carrier bags. He unwrapped it, and held up the urn containing Karin's ashes. This was important and he didn't want to regret it later. He looked at it closely just to be sure in his own mind, then wrapped it back up. He checked his watch and committed to the decision. With luck he'd be back within a couple of hours.

A short time later he parked up outside a small hotel in South Kensington. He walked past the reception desk and scanned the lobby until his eyes settled on a table at the far end. Sat, surrounded by luggage and sharing a pot of tea were Otto and Olga Bergmann, their pensive faces breaking into warm smiles of recognition as they saw him.

'Alex. We didn't think we'd see you again before we left?' said Otto with his heavy German accent.

'Nor did I, if I'm honest,' Finn replied.

'We were surprised to hear that you'd gone back to work. It's so soon,' said Olga. She noticed the bruising on his face and the stitches on his scalp and her expression turned to one of concern. 'You're hurt . . .'

'It's nothing, really. Just work.'

Olga and Otto exchanged a look.

'What brings you here?' said Olga.

'How have the last few days been?' he asked huskily, ignoring her question.

'We stayed to see London one last time. It's the city Karin made her home. And we are old, our travelling days are probably behind us now. We wanted to say goodbye, if you understand me,' replied Otto. Finn nodded. 'So please – what is so urgent you dashed here right before our flight?'

Finn pulled the urn out from the bags that swaddled it, and placed it carefully on the table. There was a long pause as the couple took it in.

'We can't take this,' said Olga. 'She should be with you.'

'No. It just upsets me,' said Finn. 'It's not her, not to me, anyway. I just can't connect with that object.'

Otto picked up the urn and turned it between his hands.

'Are you sure?' he asked.

Finn smiled sadly, then tapped the side of his head.

'She's in here. Everything that matters . . . please, take her home – scatter her somewhere special. I'd like that. I think she would too.'

Olga picked up the urn; her turn to look at it, to try and make sense of it. Then she unzipped her bag and carefully put it inside.

'Thank you,' she said.

He waited with them until their taxi arrived, helped them with their luggage, then said his goodbyes. After they'd gone, he returned to his car, and it was then the tears came. This time there was a flood, not just a passing shower; huge heaving sobs which left him gasping for air. Somewhere inside he felt a strange detachment, an awareness he urgently needed to return to the incident room. But he let the tears flow because even in his grief he understood they were necessary. When they finally subsided, he took a half-drunk bottle of water from the passenger seat and splashed some over his face. This was it, he thought, the final goodbye. She was on her way home now and she literally did not exist any more beyond the memories. And that bloody riddle, he remembered. The dog in the forest. He was starting to carry it around like a comfort blanket now, not actually trying to solve it. Not for the first time an unexpected smile forced its way through the sadness. He jumped suddenly at the sound of his phone ringing, snapping him out of the moment. A split second to regain a semblance of composure, and he answered.

'Finn, it's Warrender. You should know – one of my DCs, Jim Farmer, died overnight. I'm at the scene now.'

'Shit – what happened?'

'He went out on a job yesterday with DS Mike Godden, my right-hand man . . .' He faltered, and Finn could hear heavy emotion in his voice now. Grief just seemed all pervading at the moment. Was it always there? Had it taken Karin's death for him to notice how ever-present it actually always was?

'. . . it looks like Godden was involved somehow. We have CCTV of him with Farmer at the scene after he told me he hadn't been there. Looks like Jimmy *nicked* him for some reason. He was wearing handcuffs. Now he's gone missing. We've got a manhunt underway.'

'Why would Godden have killed Farmer?'

'It's early days obviously, so none of this makes much sense. Digital forensics are going through his computer as we speak. My guess is Jimmy must have got a sniff of something. They were investigating Whitlock's money laundering network.' Warrender paused. 'If Godden was working for Spinney, then everything we've done would have been going straight back to him. For years.'

There was a long silence as the implication sank in for Finn. An awful lot of things were starting to fall into place.

'That's what your thinking is? That Godden was in his pocket?' He asked it as carefully as he could. The whole world knew the rumours that the robbers were being helped by an insider. Finn remembered the attempt to intimidate Paulsen's partner, and the call Karin's old colleagues received. Was Godden the leak?

'Of course he was fucking bent,' said Warrender. 'You asked me earlier if I thought it was coincidence we got a tip-off about Spinney the same week we get a smell Erik Whitlock might be alive. I think we now know which tree all of that shit's been falling from.'

Finn wondered how many conversations Warrender was now rewinding in his head. He could only imagine the feeling; the stupidity, the betrayal and now the great cost.

'You get the tip-off the morning after Farmer's killed? You think that came from Godden?'

'Why this morning – of all mornings?' rasped Warrender.

'Why does Godden give him up then – as a distraction?'

'I think so. If Jimmy was on to him then maybe it became every man for himself. If it was a distraction, then it worked perfectly. Right now he's in the wind, and Mike Godden's a detective with decades of experience; if there's one man who knows every trick, it's him. He'll know *exactly* how to disappear. But I'm buggered if I'm going to let that happen, even if it costs me my career.'

Finn listened with some sympathy, unable to disagree with Warrender's assessment. He was right about his career prospects too; what happened in the aftermath of this was likely to be ugly even if they did bring Spinney in later.

'Listen, I've got to go,' said Warrender. 'As you can imagine, I've got my hands full. I'll be in touch if there's any news.'

The line went dead. Finn looked out of the car window trying to understand how these new developments tied in with his own investigation. This surely put paid to any notion Whitlock was still alive. Whether it came from Spinney or a bent detective, the source of the information was compromised. Finn was as certain as he could be Spinney *was* the man behind the murders of the fire crew. What was going on at Chapel Row, though tragic, was ultimately no more than a consequence of the net closing in. If Godden's betrayal led to Spinney's arrest, then some good might yet come out of this mess. So why did he feel so troubled? He watched as the hotel doorman greeted a smartly dressed businessman loaded down with bags.

'You're missing something,' said Karin.

49

In the event, Godden hadn't gone to Stansted Airport. Instead he'd walked out of Chapel Row, found the nearest cash point and emptied out as much money as his various cards would allow. From there he'd walked into town, hired a car and driven away from his life as he knew it. He'd formed the beginnings of a plan but knew he'd have to move fast if it was to work. He calculated there was just a narrow window where he might be able to rescue something from this.

There were two ways in which Erik Whitlock laundered money. The first was the smurfing network, while the second involved smuggling cash out of the country. Whitlock's links with a number of Romanian gangs meant Godden was confident he knew where most of the Stansted haul probably finished up. What hadn't gone to the network was now more than likely with various less-than-rigorous financial institutions in Bucharest. It now also seemed probable a chunk of it ended up in the hands of a luckless fire crew in south London, but they were the least of his worries. Romania was now a possible escape route; somewhere the Handyman's contacts *might* just be able to forge a new identity for him – if he could get to Spinney before the police did. The irony of that wasn't lost on him either.

He'd decided to try and fly from Gatwick; Stansted or Luton, although closer, would have been too obvious and too risky. He was parked up on a small side road only a few miles from the M25, which would take him round and down into Sussex. Somewhere a Territorial Support Group team were almost certainly getting suited and booted, ready to bring the Handyman to justice. It was less than half an hour since he'd walked out of Chapel Row, and he was betting even Spinney's insiders hadn't got wind yet of what was unfolding. It wouldn't take long though, and Godden smiled as an old saying came back to him: *every problem is merely an opportunity in disguise*.

He pulled out the burner phone he used for contacting Spinney. This time there wasn't the usual delay before the familiar gravy-rich voice answered.

'Where are you?' asked Godden.

'Why do you need to know?'

'Because someone's given you up. Warrender's received a tip-off.'

'From who?'

'I don't know; it was anonymous but you need to get moving – they're on their way.'

'There's no need to be melodramatic. They won't get here in time.'

'You're sure of that, are you?'

'You think I'd leave myself that open?'

Did he already know? It scarcely seemed possible in the time frame. He wondered again if Spinney had another insider – maybe even at Chapel Row.

'They know about me too – that I've been working for you. Whoever tipped them off must have known. There's a warrant out for my arrest and I need help.' It may have been a lie, but it wouldn't be too far behind the truth for long.

'What sort of help?'

275

'A passport. If I try and use my own . . . well, it may already be too late. I can't risk it; if the airports have been alerted then I'll get picked up before a plane gets off the ground. I need a new one, and I know you can arrange it.'

'Where are you planning on going?'

'Romania – so I'll need some contacts in Bucharest too, people who can help me.' He paused. 'I think you owe me this.'

'I owe you nothing. You were well paid for your services.'

'I've just tipped you off the police are on their way. That's got to count for something.' He said the words dispassionately, but desperately hoped the 'traditional English gentleman' persona Spinney liked to project bore some relationship to the man within.

'Very well, largely because I think it's in both our interests if you disappeared.'

'*Disappeared?*' said Godden.

'If I wanted you dead, you'd *be* dead,' said the voice on the end of the phone.

'Well, that's certainly true. Not a big fan of loose ends, are you? Those three dead firefighters are proof of that.'

'*Three?*' Spinney sounded surprised.

'Yeah, one more got toasted last night – don't tell me you didn't know?'

'Last night?'

There was a puzzlement to his voice, the earlier insouciance replaced with uncertainty. It didn't make sense to Godden; surely Spinney knew all this? Come to that, surely he'd want to get off the phone and get moving. Something wasn't right.

'I don't care if you're going after these men, that's your business. Right now I'm more interested in my own situation.

Can you help or can't you?' There was a pause. It felt like an eternity to Godden.

'Go to the Cobham service station between junctions nine and ten on the M25 motorway and be there at one p.m. Wait in the car park and someone will call you on this number.'

The line went dead and Godden slumped back into his seat. He wasn't sure if he could trust Spinney, but what else could he do? He couldn't stay in the country now. It could take a day, a week, or a month but sooner or later they'd find him and then things would swiftly get unpleasant. This was the only way out. The price would be high; he'd be looking over his shoulder for the rest of his life and he'd never be able to contact Franny again. That thought was killing him. He couldn't accept it – he'd find her again somehow, some way. The belief gave him renewed hope. He started the engine and moved off.

Raymond Spinney carefully poured the small jug of milk into his cup and stirred his tea. Going on the run was hardly a new experience, but being on the back foot was. Since his meeting with Walker in Whitstable he'd been trying to work out why those retired firefighters were being picked off. The advantage he possessed over the police was he knew for sure there *was* money in Pacific Square five years ago. He also knew why Erik Whitlock was there, and the identity of the Romanian contacts he was supposed to meet. Either the money burnt, or the fire crew stole it. When he'd read about Adesh Kaul's death in the newspaper, instinct told him it was important. When Godden told him about the line of inquiry Cedar House were following, only then did he really consider the possibility his money survived the blaze. Contrary to people's assumptions he didn't actually care about the missing cash, nor that he was the prime suspect for the murders. Instead it was the manner of the deaths – graphic and well executed – that disturbed him.

As he looked out of the window and gazed at the lake in front of him rippling in the dappled sunlight, he felt something unfamiliar. He was not a man used to being in the dark; his inability to understand all of this troubled him. The only people who knew about the money were *his* people. Therefore, these deaths suggested someone within his own circle was getting greedy. What he couldn't understand was why the deaths were so lurid. If it was about the money, you wouldn't over-egg it. He knew that better than anyone. You didn't need the extra theatrics of torching people alive. He'd spent much of his time since talking to Walker trying to deduce who it could be. At first he thought it might be the Romanians, but his contacts on the ground were certain it wasn't them. It also didn't make any sense – they stood to benefit far more from maintaining their relationship than by burning bridges. He'd deployed every method of information-gathering at his disposal, but nothing was coming back. The threat of violence or the inducement of money usually produced *something*.

A simple process of elimination therefore told him it could only be someone with a detailed knowledge of his business. Someone who knew about the fire crew too. The killer was exceedingly well informed – so where were they getting their information? Godden was the logical suspect, but why? Too many things were happening at once; the murders of the fire crew, the tip-off the police received about his location, the possibility Godden's cover might have been blown. Experience taught him the best tactic was to go on the front foot; apply pressure and see what happened next. People under pressure tended to make mistakes, and mistakes tended to yield information. Placing a call to two members of the late Erik Whitlock's money laundering network was a quite deliberate move. He'd wanted to see how Godden would react. Now he knew – the man was rattled, begging for help. It didn't strike him as the response of a man with a clear plan.

The conversation was instructive nonetheless. It took Spinney mere moments to tap his contacts and establish the detective sergeant was lying about some aspects of his story. He'd also learnt about the overnight discovery of a dead police officer from the Stansted unit. That at least was easier to understand – as he appeared to be the individual who'd been digging into Godden. It was too early to judge if that was a rash and hasty action, or a necessary act of house cleaning. Either way it accounted for Godden's sudden desire for a new identity and a one-way ticket to Bucharest. He'd receive neither, but Detective Sergeant Mike Godden could still serve one last helpful duty. A fall guy in these circumstances was just what was required. It'd keep the police occupied for the short term and the problem could then be terminated at Spinney's leisure. It didn't remove the greater problem though – who was killing these firefighters? He was quite certain of one thing; somebody, somewhere, would pay for this. The money was a side issue – a marker needed to be laid down. He drained his tea. It really was a beautiful day, and a walk by the water would be the perfect salve to his worries.

Godden arrived at the motorway service station around half an hour early. He'd bought a baseball cap and some cheap sunglasses on the way, which did the job as he drove past the security cameras mounted by the entrance. He chose his parking space carefully. He was far enough away from any CCTV cameras in the main restaurant area, but central enough to be close to the families meandering through. If this was a set-up, then it would be a very public scene, with no quick and easy way out of the congested car park for either party.

He was absolutely starving and reached down to a white carrier bag on the passenger seat, pulling out a cheese baguette he'd bought with the cap and glasses. He bit a chunk out of it, simultaneously keeping his attention on the people around him. A white van was doing a slow cruise of the forecourt looking for a space. When it turned to do a second circuit, Godden slowly put the baguette down and began to watch it more closely. There were plenty of parking options available, but it didn't seem to be in a hurry to take one. He'd sat in too many vans like that over the years and recognised that crawl. He looked over at the car park exit just in time to see a grey Honda turning to block it. It was a standard manoeuvre. A second after it was too late, he realised what the van was doing. The first sweep picked him up, the second confirmed his identity. Before he could react, the van accelerated and skidded to a halt in front of him. Four armed police officers jumped out of the back and swarmed around his car, screaming at him to get out with his hands up.

Very carefully he did exactly as he was told, only too aware of how these situations could go. The nearest of the armed men ran over, roughly spinning him round and pushing him down on to his front. He felt the cold metal of handcuffs tighten around his wrists as the officer continued to bark at him. He smiled. It was the only response that was logical. He'd been outmanoeuvred. Spinney could have just killed him, but no – he knew what going to prison would mean for a bent police officer. For a moment he wondered whether to charge at one of the armed men and let them put a bullet between his eyes. In light of what was going to come his way, they'd be doing him a favour.

'Hello, Mike,' said a familiar voice. He looked round and saw Andy Warrender walking towards him.

'I think we need a catch-up, mate, don't you?'

50

Sandbury was a picture-book village. It was also very small, a community built for centuries around a village green. Its size made it a difficult place to enter unnoticed, so the six police vans didn't even try. They came through separately; three of them from the main approach road, the other three via the network of back streets behind the green. The first team stopped by Raymond Spinney's shop, the second outside his house. Both were quite deserted. A notice hung in the door of the shop, which simply said *Gone fishing*.

'Got the bastard,' Warrender claimed ebulliently, when he'd called to break the news about Godden's arrest. It was a form of muscle memory, thought Finn. That's what you do after catching a big one; fist pumps, high fives and the promise of beers later. But there was a hollowness to this, an emptiness behind the words. A police officer was dead as a result of Warrender's incompetence. Celebrating the capture of the man who'd probably done it – the same man who'd been working under his nose for years – wasn't just a pyrrhic victory, it was laughable.

Godden was brought to south London to be questioned at Cedar House. Not only was he the prime suspect in the suspicious death of a police officer, he also possessed potentially critical information regarding Finn's triple murder investigation. Geographically it made sense, but Finn didn't trust the clearly porous walls at Chapel Row either. Warrender agreed only too happily. It would have been a further humiliation to have brought his own detective sergeant back in handcuffs.

They hadn't wasted much time. A duty solicitor was in situ, and Finn and Warrender were sat in the interview room awaiting Godden's arrival from the custody cells. It was an awkward wait and Finn could hazard a guess at what was going through both Warrender and Godden's minds. There was no police officer alive who hadn't played out this scenario at some time; just how would *you* handle being questioned by one of your own? Finn was interested to see what approach Godden would take. He'd read through his service record and it was impressive. He'd have sat in rooms just like this one and thought about the best approach to break a suspect down. He'd know *exactly* the kind of strategising Finn and Warrender were doing as he waited in his cell. He was probably down there doing precisely the same thing. The balance was fascinating to Finn in some ways, like those sporting contests he so enjoyed studying late at night.

Warrender was sat next to him breathing heavily, and his slow drags were the only noise punctuating the silence. Finn glanced over at him. The man was staring into space focusing on God knows what. Conversations past, or the one about to happen maybe.

'Are you going to be okay?' Finn asked. Warrender gave him a hollow smile back.

'I'll be fine. Don't you worry about me.'

A few minutes later the custody sergeant escorted Godden into the room. He flashed a smile straight at Warrender as he entered, and his former DI visibly flinched. Finn was reminded of a smooth estate agent greeting a would-be buyer. He waited for Godden to sit, then looked over at the solicitor who nodded discreetly and pressed the button on the digital recorder.

'This interview is being recorded,' said Finn. 'We'll provide you with a copy or a transcript if you require one.'

'Think I'll pass,' said Godden, winking at Warrender.

'That's noted for the record,' replied Finn. 'You do not have to say anything. But, it may harm your defence if you do not mention when questioned something which you later rely on in court. Anything you do say may be given in evidence. Do you understand that?'

'Yes. I'm familiar with the concept,' said Godden. 'Where to begin then, chaps?'

Finn saw Warrender's jaw tighten out of the corner of his eye, and tried to remind himself these two came to work that morning on the same side. It was already clear Godden was trying to get under Warrender's skin. He could only trust the other man was smart enough to understand why, and resist the provocation.

'Save us a lot of bother, Mike. How long have you been working for Ray Spinney?' said Warrender.

'About six years,' came Godden's instant response. 'He approached me shortly before the Stansted heist and offered me a retainer. At the time all he wanted was information. He promised no one would get hurt, but as time went by his demands got bigger, and the deception required from me increased as well.' Godden's solicitor leant in to say something in his ear, but he waved her away. The answers were loud, direct and blunt. There was no attempt to obfuscate or lie. He was talking with the freedom of a man who didn't need to deceive any more, Finn realised.

'Why did you do it?' said Warrender.

'I needed it,' said Godden simply. 'For my daughter. I'd gone through a messy divorce from her mother and I couldn't keep up with the maintenance payments. Not on our salary, you know how it is.'

'What sort of information were you passing on?' asked Warrender, ignoring the attempts to personalise the conversation. Watching the other detective was like watching someone self-harm, thought Finn. Each question provoking an answer which must have felt like a stab to the guts.

'Not as much as you might think. For a lie to succeed, you have to bed it in truth. An awful lot of the investigative work I did was genuine. It was only when things got a bit too close that I steered them away.'

Warrender's face was a volcanic red now, and Finn hoped the man wasn't going to compound an already awful day with another mistake.

'What happened with DC Farmer after you left the station together yesterday?' rasped Warrender.

Again Godden's solicitor tried to say something to him. Again he wasn't having it.

'Jimmy was a good cop. Better than I gave him credit for, as it goes. He'd begun to piece a few things together.' He flashed that irritating smile again at Warrender. 'Which is more than you ever managed, I might add.'

Warrender shuffled in his seat, and Finn shot him a warning look. Godden was grinning now, enjoying the moment. It wasn't hard to see how he'd gotten away with it. A linear, pig-headed senior officer, blindsided by a cunning subordinate only too aware of how to press his buttons.

'Let's keep this on point, shall we?' said Finn.

'Oh, there's nothing funny about any of it, trust me. I took Farmer out to that landfill site because I needed to shut him down. My first choice would have been to strike some sort of a deal—'

'But he wasn't a weak streak of piss, like you?' snapped Warrender.

'No. He wasn't. I tried to reason with him but couldn't, so I killed him and left him there. It wasn't personal, but I didn't have a choice. I'd hoped it would look like an accident, but then you told me about the CCTV this morning.'

He said it all in the same matter-of-fact way and it was only by a miracle Warrender hadn't leapt across the table yet. Finn was watching Godden carefully as he spoke. The man was neither a sociopath nor a psychopath. He'd seen both over the years and this was different. A cold-hearted man, boxed and coxed by his own choices.

'Why are you telling us all this?' said Finn. He was giving it all up far too easily and for the first time, there was a flicker of uncertainty on Godden's face. He paused before answering.

'Because I'm going to die. Spinney's playing with me, by selling me out to you. It might be next week, or in ten years – but he's coming for me.'

'But surely it would bother him, what you might be able to tell us about his operation?'

Godden laughed.

'Yeah, he's having sleepless nights about that. You don't know him beyond his reputation. I know the man, how he works. He wouldn't have given me up if he feared I could hurt him. How did the raid go this afternoon by the way? I assume it must have happened by now?'

'Was it you who sent me the tip-off?' asked Warrender.

'Indirectly, via a snout, yes. Don't suppose you caught him?'

Finn kept his face inscrutable, Warrender didn't.

'I'll take that as a no,' said Godden answering his own question, and despite his bravado there was some fear in his eyes now.

'Was it Spinney who reactivated Erik Whitlock's money laundering network?' asked Finn.

'I honestly don't know, but that would be my guess. He makes sure he knows everything about every part of his business, so he'd know the names. The timing was quite deliberate, you can be sure of that.'

'Meaning?'

'I think he was trying to smoke me out.'

'Why? I don't understand,' said Finn.

'Even he couldn't bloody trust you, could he?' said Warrender.

'He said something interesting to me earlier ... he genuinely didn't seem to know there'd been another murder.'

Finn leant in. It was entirely possible Godden was playing them. There was still every chance he was carrying out Spinney's instructions even now, but this felt important.

'What are you trying to say?'

'Listen, I've been dealing with this man for six years. He's got ice for blood. He doesn't raise his voice, doesn't show emotion, he's Mr fucking Spock. But when we spoke ... he sounded *scared* and I've never heard that before. I think he's as much in the dark about who's killing those firefighters as you are.' He let the words sink in. 'Don't you get it? Spinney isn't your killer – it's someone else.'

51

'So to clarify: there's one dead police officer, one bent one who says he murdered him, and Ray Spinney's disappeared. Again. On top of that, you're now telling me he's more likely to be the next victim than our prime suspect? If I didn't know you better, Alex, I'd say you were taking the piss.'

The expression on John Skegman's face was withering. It didn't sound great out loud, Finn was forced to concede, and the DCI was entitled to be a little sceptical. They were with Paulsen and Ojo in the incident room as they regrouped after Godden's interview. Warrender was on his way back up to Chapel Row. He'd barely said a word afterwards and Finn almost hadn't known what to say to him. A day which began with the expectation he might finally bring the Stansted investigation to a close was instead ending in yet more failure. Finn empathised – it was hard not to. By the end of the interview he'd wanted to wipe Godden's smile off his face too. There was a certain grim comfort in the likelihood someone would be doing that sooner rather than later.

The idea Spinney *wasn't* behind the killings left them all a little bamboozled. There was something about Godden which convinced Finn though. Looking him in the eye – one police officer to another – he was certain the man was speaking the truth. He'd nothing to lose, and even now was still thinking and reasoning like a detective.

Skegman turned his attention to Ojo and Paulsen.

'What do you two think?'

'If it's not Spinney, then logically who would have the motive to kill these men?' said Paulsen.

'Someone with a grudge?' offered Ojo.

'Obviously,' scowled Paulsen.

'I meant ... perhaps another firefighter from the same station – someone who found out about the money and was jealous,' Ojo retorted.

'Have we found anything which backs that idea up? I'd like a theory at this point which is at least rooted in something solid,' snapped Skegman.

'And I'd like a ponytail. Disappointment abounds,' said Finn, running a hand up his closely trimmed scalp.

There was silence for a moment. Ojo's face cracked into a broad smile. Even Paulsen's frown relaxed. Skegman glowered at Finn, who finally shrugged.

'Jackie's suggestion makes sense, actually. The only thing that connects these men is their former profession. It must be linked to that.'

'There's also the money,' said Paulsen. 'It could be someone with a specific grudge against Spinney.'

'How do you work that out?' said Ojo.

'An internal dispute between Spinney and some other gangster? If you wanted to smoke him out, you kill the fire crew and take the money. *His* money. It might be a way of provoking him. We all know the hardest thing with that man is simply finding him.'

Finn shook his head. 'The deaths have been too graphic, they feel personal. If it was a gang war thing, you wouldn't go to these lengths. The use of fire seems deliberate too, like it's important to the killer.'

'How are the other two men getting on?' asked Skegman.

'Walker and Portbury are both under surveillance,' said Finn. 'They've been given panic alarms, we've got high-speed pursuit vehicles standing ready by each of their properties, and there are firearms units on standby.'

'Are they coping with that?'

'Walker's comfortable enough – he just wants to make sure his wife's safe. But Portbury insists on pretending it's not happening, though I think the penny's finally dropping,' said Finn.

'Once we've resolved the direct threat to their lives, we're going to have to investigate them hard. There's still no admission they actually took any money, I take it?' said Skegman.

'We've still no hard evidence there ever *was* any money,' said Paulsen.

'Portbury's absolutely certain he hasn't done anything wrong,' said Finn.

'Could he be telling the truth?'

'He's a funny one,' said Paulsen. 'I've been to his flat – there's no visible sign of any unusual expenditure, and he's adamant – between the lines – that he wasn't party to anything the other four might have done.'

'How's he been earning a living since he retired?' asked Skegman.

'He's some sort of odd-job man. When we looked over his accounts there didn't seem to be that much going in. The business isn't registered on Companies House either. But what was *really* odd was that he only ever seems to have had one client. Not a single payment from anyone else.'

'Who is it?' asked Finn.

'It's a Japanese name – Tsukuda.'

Finn and Skegman looked blankly at each other but Paulsen reacted immediately.

'But she was here this morning . . .'

'What are you taking about?' said Finn. 'Who was here this morning?'

'Is the initial M?' asked Paulsen urgently, and Ojo nodded.

'It's Mei Tsukuda. She's Erik Whitlock's widow.'

52

With two officers in situ outside Stuart Portbury's flat they at least knew where he was. Skegman ordered a Territorial Support Group team to join them there and rendezvous with Finn and Paulsen. Part of the Met's Specialist Crime and Operations unit, they were the heavy-duty support you called in for a drugs raid or for calming a riot. Paulsen queried whether they were necessary, but Skegman reminded her of the attack on Finn at Phil Maddox's flat. The weapon of choice then was a Halligan bar – a standard piece of firefighter's kit, and they'd yet to prove it belonged to the dead man. Nothing at this point could be assumed.

'So are we now looking at Portbury as a suspect? That doesn't make any sense to me,' said Paulsen, as Finn weaved through the mid-afternoon traffic.

'Right now he's a potential suspect *and* a potential victim. We need to know what he wanted with Whitlock's widow, and why he felt the need to pose as a tradesman to do it.'

'He obviously wanted to get close to her, but I can't see any possible motive to it.'

'There's also that money she's been receiving through the door. Unless you believe her husband's returned from the dead – and I don't – someone's been looking out for her.'

'You think it might be Portbury?' said Paulsen.

'It could be any of Whitlock's associates. Someone he made a deal with in the event of his death. We know Stuart wasn't spending his cash on flash cars or poncey penthouses – so is that where his share is going?'

Paulsen looked bemused and stared out of the window for a moment.

'This is important though, isn't it – this link?' said Paulsen, and Finn nodded.

'I think so.'

He looked across at her as he spoke and her frown morphed into that now familiar lopsided grin. Not for the first time the transition caught him by surprise. It was strangely infectious, and he allowed a smile of his own back in return. She could *feel* the potential breakthrough, the significance of it, which pleased him. It was something he could work with, despite all the other baggage she seemed to carry. It was a sensibility you either possessed or didn't. Jackie Ojo was born with it, even Godden showed under interrogation he still possessed it, but fatally Warrender *didn't*. It struck Finn then just how scared he'd been he'd lost it since Karin's death. The extent to which losing her was changing him he couldn't yet gauge. As he turned on the unmarked car's flashing blue light and put his foot down, he sensed it was a needless fear. What he wasn't quite so sure of was whether it was the investigation or DC Mattie Paulsen that'd brought him back from the brink.

Twenty minutes later they arrived at the small road where Stuart Portbury lived. The O2 Arena was just about visible in the middle distance behind the rows of high-rise new builds. Finn parked up behind a red Vauxhall Corsa. Inside the Vauxhall were DCs Sami Dattani and Amy Hunt. Finn knocked on the passenger door and Dattani lowered the window.

'How are we doing, Sami?'

'All quiet, guv. He's been in all day. He nipped out to the shops to buy a loaf of bread and some milk at about midday, but he's been home alone since then.'

'Has he said anything?'

'Brought these out for us.' Hunt held up a packet of half-eaten custard creams. 'Very nice too – but that's about it.'

'What about the other occupants of the building?'

'There's one other flat above him but the owner's at work,' replied Hunt.

'And where are the TSG team?' asked Finn.

'They've parked in the next street and are waiting on your word to proceed,' said Dattani.

Finn pulled out his radio and gave the sergeant in charge of the TSG team the go-ahead to deploy. Finn and Paulsen waited with the two DCs as the six-man unit manoeuvred into position. One officer covered the rear of the building, while one each covered the two sides to ensure all possible exits were covered. Within a couple of minutes, the sergeant and the remaining two officers joined them by the Vauxhall. All three were dressed in their distinctive protective gear. They each wore stab vests and carried batons, pepper spray and tasers. One of them was carrying an Enforcer – the large battering ram used for smashing doors in. Given what happened the last time he'd visited one of these firefighters, Finn was pleased to see them.

'Let's do this. Hopefully you guys won't be needed,' he said, then waited, as the TSG sergeant radioed the rest of his team to tell them they were now deploying. Finn walked up to Portbury's front door and rang the bell. There was no answer. He waited then rang it for a second time. Again, no response. The TSG sergeant radioed the three officers surrounding the building, but none of them reported any movement.

'What if we've got this wrong, guv? What if the killer's already inside?' said Paulsen.

'How? We've had eyes on him all day.'

The TSG officer carrying the Enforcer was already stepping forwards. Finn nodded at him to proceed and after a couple of attempts, the door gave way with a loud splintering shatter. The three TSG men surged into the flat, shouting 'Police! Police!' It was standard practice – they were moving fast and loud so that they could overwhelm any potential resistance without the use of force. Finn stood at the broken entrance and took a deep breath while they waited, before turning to Paulsen.

'I can't smell burning . . .'

After a few moments the TSG sergeant walked back through and re-joined them. He shrugged.

'The place is empty. He's not here.'

53

Stuart Portbury
This is like solitary confinement! Fancy giving them
the slip and meeting up?   14:34

Walker smiled as he read the message. He wasn't fighting this
alone then. If there was one man left from the old days he'd
want in the trenches with him, it was Stuart. Quiet and
dependable Stuart. Walker more than fancied it – he desperately *needed* someone to talk to. They could message each
other, but the appeal of getting out was strong. Stuart was
right; the house was feeling like a prison cell. Things with
Christine were tense and the atmosphere was difficult. He was
also certain the threat was solely directed at him and Portbury.
Whatever else happened, the killer hadn't hurt anyone close
to Kaul, Elder or Maddox. The two cops outside would ensure
no harm came to Chrissie if it came to it.

He'd also been giving a lot of thought to where the danger
might be coming from. Spinney didn't seem to know in
Whitstable, so it begged the question, who else *did* know about
the money? Walker's best guess was someone must have
blabbed. Elder or Maddox were the likeliest candidates. Gary
could never keep his trap shut, especially if he thought it
would impress female company. Maddox was different, but
alone with his laptop one night, who knew what he'd posted
or emailed. It might even have been Adesh in an unguarded

moment; it was impossible to tell. But once the information was out there, who knew who'd picked up on it.

Stuart suggested going to a nearby hotel where they wouldn't be disturbed. There was no point drawing attention to themselves by meeting somewhere public. Ten minutes after the first message Portbury confirmed he'd booked a room at a Travelodge in Battersea and the meet was on. The irony of the location wasn't lost on Walker; all roads seemed to lead back to Pacific Square in some form these days. Hopefully they'd figure out a way to regain some control of the situation, and he'd be home before Stan and Ollie out the front knew he'd ever been gone. Christine was taking an afternoon nap. He'd noticed she was doing this a lot now. They were getting longer and longer too. He guessed she was finding some refuge in sleep.

Walker took a perverse pleasure in evading his police protection. He'd clambered into his next-door neighbour's garden, then shinned over the fence into the adjacent side road where the Uber he'd booked was obligingly waiting. Now, a short time later, he was walking down the bland corridors of the Travelodge. Arriving at the door he was looking for, he checked his surroundings, then knocked. There was a split second of anxiety when there was no immediate answer, but he was flooded with relief when he heard footsteps on the other side. The door opened and Walker smiled as he saw his old colleague's familiar face.

'It's good to see you, mate, I can't lie. Who'd have thought it would come to this, eh?'

Portbury said nothing and closed the door behind them.

'Stuart was *there* the night Erik died – are you sure?'

Mei Tsukuda, or Mei Whitlock as she'd once been known, looked a pale shadow of the battle-hardened woman Paulsen met earlier at Cedar House. She was bemused by the revelation regarding Portbury and visibly struggling to make sense of it. After finding Portbury gone, they'd called the officers waiting outside Martin Walker's home, but there had been no movement in or out. Mei was the next obvious person to visit once they'd considered their options outside Portbury's empty flat. They were now sat in her immaculate kitchen, where the full extent of his relationship with her was becoming clear.

To Paulsen's surprise, Finn was quite relaxed about Portbury's disappearance. He refused to judge it until they knew more. The man might simply have fled out of fear, with good reason too. Paulsen felt less generous though. There was something creepy about the former firefighter's interest in the woman sat in front of them. But she was learning to respect the way Finn's brain operated. He worked the permutations like no police officer she'd ever encountered before – sifting them, stress-testing them, constantly rotating them to see if a different outcome would present itself. It was like watching someone play chess on three different boards simultaneously. And all this, just days after cremating his wife. She shuddered with embarrassment, remembering what she'd said to him in that small room in Cedar House. The accusations she'd made, the language she'd used. She'd lost control of herself, and temporarily lost her moral compass too. It wasn't the first time and she felt ashamed. Yet here she still was, right next to him in the thick of a murder investigation, his faith in her seemingly unbroken. It was extraordinary, and she felt somewhere along the way a bridge of trust had formed between them. She'd also noticed earlier that he'd made a point of not bawling out Dattani and Hunt, the two DCs who were supposed to be watching Portbury. They'd been mortified at losing him, but he'd made it clear it wasn't their fault and that Portbury was responsible for his own actions. Paulsen saw the respect in their eyes. She'd underestimated him, but that conversation – those words she'd thrown in his face like a full-on fist – would still need addressing at some point.

'How did you first meet him?' asked Finn, and Mei breathed out as she tried to remember.

'He put a card through my door – advertising himself as an all-purpose tradesman. As it turned out I needed a plumber, and he said it was something he could help with when we spoke later on the phone.'

'Makes sense – he was hedging his bets, gambling you needed something he could offer. As a former firefighter, he would probably possess a pretty useful all-round skillset,' said Finn.

'He helped with a number of things around the house and his prices were very reasonable. But you're saying he did all that just to get close to me?'

'I think so. You were suggesting earlier a relationship of sorts built up with each visit?'

'Not like *that* – it was more a friendship. He didn't seem to want anything except to help. He never made any kind of advance towards me, or even gave the impression that's what he was interested in. He was the perfect gentleman, and I trusted him. He gave me good advice . . . I let him talk to my son. He *helped* my son.' She looked horrified by the thought now.

'There's no reason to think he meant either of you any harm,' said Paulsen.

'So why was he doing it?'

Finn stared for a moment at the ornate row of mini cactus plants on the black marbled kitchen counter behind them, as if they contained a secret. But he was working the permutations again – Paulsen was starting to recognise the signs.

'There's one explanation which makes sense, one that answers every question. But you're not going to like it.'

* * *

'So how have you been bearing up?' said Walker. He was sat on a chair next to a desk loaded up with leaflets advertising the hotel's amenities. Portbury was stood with his back to him, staring out of the window of the narrow room. Even sat down, Walker could see the outline of One Pacific Square looming over them.

'Do you ever regret it?' asked Portbury.

'Taking the money? All the time, every day . . . and not at all. Does that make sense?'

'Not really.'

'I'm a proud man, Stu. I'm proud of an awful lot of what I've done with my life. What *we* did. You, me, Adesh, Gary and Phil. Running into burning buildings, putting our lives on the line. Helping people, saving them. And we did a lot of that – we saved a *lot* of lives over the years. But taking that money was theft. It was wrong and I know it was. Do you know what multiple sclerosis does to a person though? There's muscle weakness, muscle spasms, problems swallowing, chronic pain, bladder and bowel problems . . . I could go on. I've watched someone I love slowly degenerate. But there was the money and it gave me a weapon; something to fight back at that disease with. So no, part of me has no regret at all. You?'

There was a long silence before Portbury slowly turned. The late afternoon sun was now pouring through the window, silhouetting him so that Walker couldn't clearly see his features.

'Was helping your wife worth murdering a man for?'

'What are you talking about? We didn't . . . Whitlock was already dead.'

'Is that what you tell yourself?'

'He was dead. There was no pulse.'

'I know that. I've heard it all before. Did you know that fool Maddox emailed me last year? He wanted to meet up and I agreed. I wanted to hear it out of his own mouth, because you see – I always *knew*. I never took it on trust.'

'You're losing me. Knew what?'

'If you're honest, Marty – you know the answer to that.' Portbury stepped forwards, and Walker could see now the cold expression on his face.

'You've got to help me here, Stu. I'm not sure what you're trying to say to me. What happened when you met up with Phil?'

'I got him drunk – it wasn't hard – and he told me the truth.' He shook his head, and Walker saw the contempt in his eyes. 'Pissed and grinning in the corner of a pub, he told me what really happened. Like it was all some funny anecdote from long ago.'

'I still don't know what you're talking about; you know what happened. We told you everything.'

'No, you didn't. Whitlock was *still alive* when you left him up there. They lied to you – Maddox and Elder – so you'd agree to the plan. You all left him to burn. And guess what? Turns out he was married with a kid. A woman was widowed, and a boy left without a father, and for what? A chairlift for your wife? Some nice property? A fancy wedding? A fucking Maserati? You couldn't even bring the body out to give them any closure.'

'Wait, just wait,' said Walker, struggling to absorb what he was hearing. 'I swear I've always believed he was dead. There's no way I would have gone ahead with it if he hadn't been.'

Portbury came closer, almost nose to nose with Walker.

'Don't tell me *you didn't know*.'

And Walker knew exactly what he meant. Of course he'd known. He'd always known, irrespective of what he'd been told by Maddox and Elder. It was a lie he'd been telling himself for over five years to justify what they'd done. Whitlock was still breathing – he could have been saved. It just made everything so much easier to believe he was already dead. Martin Walker was a thief *and* a murderer. He'd known alright, and buried it deep. Portbury was silent now, the sun still blazing behind him.

As time stood still, Walker remembered a fragment of a conversation from long ago. *'What about Stu?'* Kaul had asked. *'We deal him in. He'll be fine with it. Why wouldn't he be?'* Elder's reply had been almost dismissive. Realisation dawned on Walker – there in those nine words, something terrible was born.

'It was *you* . . . you killed Adesh and the others.'

'No, Marty, I didn't kill them. That's on you,' said Portbury, bringing his fist around and crashing it into the side of Walker's head.

'Stuart Portbury has insisted all along he never went into One Pacific Square the night it burnt, and that's been corroborated by the other members of the team,' said Finn.

'So? We know he quit later with the rest of them. We also know he's been able to support himself financially without much of an income. He's knee-deep in this,' said Paulsen.

'Which I'm not disputing, but that's not my point. He wasn't there when the decision was made.' He turned to Mei. 'We may never truly know what happened up there. Maybe they subdued Erik, maybe he was unconscious but I don't think he was dead, not when they found him. I think they killed him, or at least ensured he couldn't escape, then stole the money he'd brought in to launder,' said Finn.

'But what did Stuart want from me? Why pretend to be a plumber?'

'He went to One Pacific Square to help put out a blaze. When his crewmates came out of that building, they'd made him a thief and an accessory to murder – whether he liked it or not. I don't think that sat right with him. As the years went by, he wanted to put a human face on the man they'd killed in his name. He looked into Erik Whitlock, discovered he was married with a son and became curious. I think he's been the one sending you money. Literally paying you back,' said Finn.

Paulsen was nodding slowly in agreement. *'Why now?'* Finn had asked early in the investigation. Now it made sense – because that's how long it took Portbury to find, meet and befriend Mei Tsukuda.

'But he was so gentle. He was kind. I'm struggling to recognise him as the man you are describing,' said Mei.

'Don't underestimate the power of guilt. It's like a cancer. It eats you from the inside and can utterly consume you if you let it,' said Paulsen. And it took her a moment to realise Finn's attention was off Mei and now on her.

When Walker came around, the sun was still in his eyes and he couldn't move. As he refocused, he saw it wasn't the sun, but a round, white light fitting he was looking up at instead. He was lying in the bathtub of the hotel room's small bathroom suite, fully clothed with his hands bound with what felt like plastic ties. He was wet as well, but knew immediately it wasn't water soaking through his clothes. He was drenched in petrol. Portbury was sat on a chair by the sink watching him. He'd been waiting for him to wake, realised Walker. He wanted him alive when he did it.

'For pity's sake, Stu . . .'

'Pity? Is that what you're after?'

'Please. Think about Christine at least. If you kill me, she'll be on her own.'

'How does the hypocrisy of that not choke your throat out? What about Whitlock's widow? What about her son? What pity did you show them?'

'I told you – I knew it was wrong. I should have been stronger. I should have stopped it.'

'But you didn't, did you? And that's why you're worse than the others, because you always did think you were better than us.'

'Tell me something. When you've done this – then what are you going to do? Go back home tonight and get on with the rest of your life? How exactly is that different to what we did? Who'll be the hypocrite then?'

Portbury laughed.

'No, I won't be doing that. I picked this hotel for a reason. When I'm done here this ends . . . in the only place it can end. And I am almost done here.' He stood up and pulled out a worn, silver Zippo lighter from his pocket. Walker glanced up desperately at the ceiling.

'Looking for the sprinklers, skipper?' He pointed and Walker could see the sprinkler head was wrapped tightly in waterproof black duct tape.

'Don't think health and safety are going to like that. The fire investigation unit will have a field day, won't they? Mind you, that bath is enamel-coated, so no need for me to hang around and watch this time . . .'

Portbury flicked the lighter and a burst of yellow-orange shot up and steadied itself. Walker instinctively thought of Christine, as he'd always done back in the day when he ran into a burning building. Portbury stepped forwards then casually flicked his wrist at him. There was a whooshing eruption of flame and Walker screamed in agony. Portbury picked up the holdall he'd brought with him and calmly sauntered out. Fire tore up the left-hand side of Walker's body, and he could smell the sickly-sweet odour of his flesh burning. Whether it was through pain or a surge of adrenalin he didn't know, but he pulled at the plastic ties with a burst of strength and felt them stretch. They were looser now and beginning to melt. He focused all the pain and rage on to his wrists, pulling at the ties, and this time they came apart. He instantly reached for the shower tap in front of him, clamping his burning hands down and turning it. The water shot down and he staggered up to greet it, only to scream again.

54

It started not long after Godden stepped out of the prison van. Within minutes of entering the reception room at HMP Brazely, he'd understood how this was going to go. Another prisoner waiting to be booked in was staring at him while they stood in line. Godden's eyes were drawn inexorably to the tattoo of a severed clown's head which adorned his neck. The man slowly leant forwards and spat in his face. Godden, determined not to be intimidated, wiped the gobbet off on to his hand then literally threw it back into clownman's face. He didn't bat an eyelid, but raised his arm instead. A meaty fist connected and Godden felt it smash into his nose. There was a salty taste at the back of his throat, and a long stream of blood started to pour from his nostrils. The prison officers with them pretended they hadn't seen a thing.

That was a couple of hours ago. Word it seemed was already spreading that the new con on the block was police. The trustee who delivered his first taste of prison food spat in it as he left it at the cell door, shouting 'I'm feeding the pig, lads!' as he went. Spitting, it seemed, was the weapon of choice here.

'They'll probably smear shit on your bedding next,' said Ed with his distinctive Brummie accent.

'Probably,' replied Godden.

Ed was his cellmate, and Peaky Blinders he was not. A burglar apparently, though judging by the level of twitching going on, an addict of some sort too. But to be fair to the man,

306

anyone sharing a cell with the ex-cop would probably be twitching by now. Everything so far was straight out of the playbook, what you'd expect as a police officer on the wrong side of the bars. He'd been waiting for it, even if it began sooner than he'd been expecting.

What was worrying him far more was the spectre of Raymond Spinney. His reputation as a man who didn't leave loose ends dangling wasn't just tabloid gossip, it was borne out by the facts. Godden's betrayal wasn't going to be forgotten. It was just another problem to be solved. He'd been giving it thought ever since leaving Cedar House, and was already forming the early outline of a plan. Spinney was a pragmatist at heart; if you were of use to him then he'd protect you. Godden knew that from experience, and protection was exactly what he was going to need. His train of thought was interrupted by a bang on the cell door.

'Oi piggy – we know you're here – we're going to cut you up, mate. Can you hear me? We're going to fucking cut you up . . .'

Despite himself, Godden was rattled. Surely this would settle down. He was only on remand – he'd have a word with his brief tomorrow. Whoever the prison governor was here – some bleeding-heart, liberal slip of a girl from memory – he was damn sure they wouldn't want the embarrassment of his death on their hands. There were too many people who'd want to see him in the dock for a start. In the meantime he'd work up a way of getting some leverage back with Spinney. The answer was somewhere in his head, he was sure of it – some scrap of information he'd picked up during their association. He lay back on the hard metal frame of his bed. At least he'd have plenty of time to think about it.

'Everyone worries about getting stabbed in the showers. But they'll try and chuck you down the stairs. You'll have to watch yourself on the landings,' said Ed.

'Thanks, mate,' said Godden.

An hour or so later there was another bang on the door. Godden braced himself for another burst of invective, but this time it was one of the prison officers.

'Shower time – let's be having you both,' said a gruff voice. Godden looked up suspiciously as he heard the door unlocking.

'What, at five in the afternoon?'

'You're a new arrival – they always do that,' said Ed unconvincingly.

The prison officer led the pair along the landing to the shower room, and pointed at the door. Godden looked at it warily, then reluctantly followed his cellmate in. There were four shower cubicles separated by waist height walls. They gave a little privacy but not much. The changing area was completely open and the door they'd come through possessed a window open to the wing which anybody passing could see through. Godden stripped and walked briskly into the first cubicle – better to just get this over and done with. He felt reassured that the prison officer was still standing outside on the landing. If it was Ed who'd been nominated to try something, then the poor fella was more likely to put his back out than inflict any serious damage. Godden turned on the tap and a blast of freezing cold water shot down.

'Obviously,' he muttered, fiddling with the tap which was making no discernible difference to the water's temperature. Another figure entered the cubicle next to him, but when he looked it wasn't Ed. A tall, well-built man with a shaven head was standing there instead.

'Alright, pal,' he said with a strong Liverpudlian accent as he turned his own tap on. The newcomer started to whistle tunelessly, and it took Godden a moment to recognise the melody over the noise of the water. When he did, his blood chilled and his mind filled in the lyrics like a macabre karaoke.

'Who can rob at sunrise?
Sprinkle it with gold,
Cover it in diamonds and a miracle or two?
The Handyman. The Handyman can . . .'

Godden looked at the man and saw a grotesque smile vaguely reminiscent of a Halloween pumpkin grinning back at him. But it wasn't the man's face, it was the back of his head. He was looking over at the door, clearly double-checking they were alone. Of Ed there was no sign. Godden could see now the 'smile' was actually a deep lurid scar which stretched the entire width of his skull. The man turned round and flashed an actual smile at him. It wasn't much more pleasant.

'A mutual acquaintance asked me to say hello.'

It was then Godden noticed what he was holding; a prison-issue plastic knife, similar to the one he'd been given with his tray of food earlier. But he could see this one was different. It was altered, whittled down to a sharp point. There was a sudden jab and Godden saw blood spurt out from somewhere near his Adam's apple, and his last ever thought was that Ed had been wrong about the showers.

55

Stuart Portbury could remember when they'd first told him. They thought they'd been doing him a favour; that he was one of the team, one of *them*. He'd known something was up in the aftermath of Pacific Square. Most of the crews who'd attended needed extended downtime afterwards. It'd been ferocious; lives weren't lost, but it was a major operation by the LFB. The men and women attending risked their lives over two days and a number sustained severe injuries. So, the reaction afterwards by his crewmates didn't smell right. Elder and Kaul were full of private nods and winks while Phil Maddox, usually so uncomfortable when things became laddish, was also trying to get in on it. In the end, Gary and Adesh took him out for a drink.

'How would you like to quit all this bollocks and go and live by the beach in Malibu instead, Stu? Well now you can . . .' was Elder's opening pitch. Then they'd told him what they'd done. The money, and the unknown man next to it they'd been too late to save. Too late to even retrieve. Yet somehow, they'd found the time to remove sack after sack of pounds sterling.

He'd wanted to be a police officer as a child, or a doctor. Someone who helped. His father drummed that into him, wanting him to be someone who contributed to society, not took from it. In the end he'd settled on the fire service. An honourable career, up until One Pacific Square – when the very people he'd served with dishonoured it. He'd read the tabloid coverage surrounding Erik Whitlock with interest, and a throwaway line in a paragraph covering his funeral changed everything. A single sentence which mentioned the wife and son he'd left behind. Portbury went into work that day and listened to Elder's booming laugh, Maddox's weasling self-interest, and watched Kaul going along with it all like a puppy. He'd felt sick. He'd looked at Martin Walker, a man he respected, and saw in his eyes that *he* knew. As time passed it troubled him more and more. The fate of the wife and son who'd been left behind. Eventually he started to dig, seeking answers of his own.

Mei Tsukuda, it's fair to say, was *nothing* like his preconception of her. He found a graceful, honourable human being doing her best to raise her boy on her own. He wasn't sure he'd ever met anyone quite like her before. His feelings weren't sexual; he possessed too much respect for Mei to reduce it to that. But he felt an overwhelming sense of obligation. It was an easy choice – the *right* choice – to give her his share of the money.

Initially he'd wanted to try and persuade his old crewmates to do the same. He felt sure once they knew the truth they'd want to. It was a few years since he'd seen any of them. They'd made a pact when they'd left the job to go their separate ways. The fewer lines which connected them, the less likely someone might find their way to the truth. After all, no one could even prove there'd ever *been* money in Pacific Square that night, let alone deduce which firefighters might have stumbled on to it. Elder, in his infinite wisdom, described it as the perfect crime. A 'victimless crime', he'd called it, and that might just have been the moment Portbury made his mind up.

Discreetly he'd checked up on them all and found out what they'd each done with their share. Elder and that obscene car of his, Maddox and his penthouse flat, Walker only caring about his wife, never mind the woman he'd left bereaved. Kaul took a bit of digging into, and initially Portbury thought he might be the only one whose decency was still intact. A little online snooping though revealed his wedding plans, and the disgusting cost of it all. Greed and self-interest in each case. They'd paid the price for it, he'd made sure of that. Now it was his turn.

He watched as the office workers started scurrying home for their evening commute, stared up and remembered. It all looked so different to how it did five years ago. He put the holdall he was carrying down, unzipped it and satisfied himself he'd brought everything he needed. It began in flames here, now it was time to end it the same way. At One Pacific Square.

Walker had managed to clamber out of the bathtub, and crawl in agony through the small bedroom and out into the corridor, where he'd mercifully lost consciousness. Within minutes a horrified maid found him and called all three emergency services. The news had rapidly reached Finn, who was still at Mei Tsukuda's home and had only just been informed by the officers outside Walker's house that he wasn't there. He'd immediately directed Ojo to the Travelodge and she was now at Chelsea and Westminster hospital where Walker was being treated. The good news was his injuries, while severe, weren't deemed life-threatening. Aware Walker was likely to be sedated for some time, Ojo was now managing to update Finn on her mobile from the hospital's corridor.

'I've spoken with the ambulance crew who treated him. He confirmed it was Portbury who attacked him and mumbled something else to them that they couldn't make sense of. One of the paramedics said it sounded like a warning, but then he passed out again and they dosed him up.'

'When do we think he might be conscious again? How badly hurt is he?'

'He managed to turn the shower on just in time, but he's got some very nasty torso burns. He's lucky to be alive. As for when he might be able to talk, your guess is as good as mine. I'm going to stay here just in case.'

'I'll send a couple of armed officers to join you. If Portbury finds out Walker's still alive, he might be tempted to come and finish the job.'

Finn was standing in the street leaning on his car with one finger in his ear as he focused over the noise of the rush-hour traffic. Paulsen was stood next to him, listening closely to his side of the conversation. She'd pretty much got the gist of it as they got in the car, where Finn filled in the blanks.

'Portbury must have said something to Walker before he tried to kill him. It's important, otherwise why would he try and warn the paramedics?' said Paulsen.

'Portbury's killed – or at least *thinks* he's killed – every one of his former crewmates. Who's left for him to go after?' said Finn.

'What about the fire station where they worked?'

'I don't think his grudge is against the profession as a whole, just the people he blames for leaving Mei on her own.'

'Do you know what worries me? When he murdered Maddox, he stayed at the scene to make sure the fire didn't spread. Sounds like he didn't do that with Walker,' said Paulsen.

'You think he's stopped caring if other people get hurt?'

'He's motivated by guilt. A guilt which has been growing for years. I don't think he has any rational perspective left.' Finn turned to look at her and she saw an understanding in

313

his face. 'I know a lot about guilt and what it can do to you and we'll have that conversation later. But not now, because if that's what's driving this then I think I know where he's gone – and what he's planning to do.'

56

Getting into the building was easy, but then he'd planned this for a long time. Start with the ending and work backwards, was his logic. In total, twenty-six different businesses rented office space in One Pacific Square, mainly a combination of insurance brokers, investment companies and commercial banking institutions. The building was protected by front-of-house security, reception staff, a concierge service, CCTV and an alarm installation, together with round-the-clock monitoring. Breaking in was almost impossible, but Portbury was armed with one major advantage: he'd no intention of coming out again. He'd found one of the many fire doors and used his Halligan bar to break in, which in turn set off an internal alarm. The whole thing would be on camera and security would be swarming all over it in minutes, but none of that mattered. He was now inside and they'd be too late.

The break-in triggered a series of events. Responding to the alarmed door, the building's head of security – a former Royal Military Police officer called Charles Stacey – sent two men to investigate straight away. He also routinely alerted Wandsworth Police Station, who'd dispatched a couple of uniformed PCs to assist. The sergeant who took the call, aware of the links to their investigation, tipped off the incident room at Cedar House. The news was relayed to Finn who'd immediately ordered three things: a complete evacuation of the building, a clear instruction that no one was to approach the intruder, and a request for armed SCO19 officers to rendezvous with him outside the main entrance.

Just over twenty minutes later Finn's Volvo, a blue light flashing on its front, skidded to a halt just ahead of the large grey piazza which surrounded the skyscraper. A long semicircle of evenly spaced anti-vehicle bollards prevented them from getting any closer. The armed officers were already in place, prowling with their distinctive Heckler & Koch G36 assault rifles. The building's evacuation was complete, and Finn guessed it hadn't taken long because most of the office staff were probably already on their commute home. Around half a dozen uniformed officers were forming a perimeter outside the half-moon of the piazza. Only a few people were showing much interest in what was going on. Once such a scene would have gathered a small crowd, but it was a sign of the times that most Londoners seemed to take it in their stride now.

The SCO19 commander was talking to a man in uniform who Finn guessed must be the building's head of security. He and Paulsen flashed their ID at the nearest PC, ducked under the cordon and ran over to join them. Finn recognised the armed commander immediately as Devon Samuels. They'd worked together before, and Finn was pleased to see him there. At six foot five inches tall, Samuels was an imposing figure but he also possessed a natural calm. He spoke with quiet authority, whether it was in the pub or out in the field, and it was a quality Finn appreciated. There was a mutual nod of recognition as they approached.

'So what have we got then, Dev?'

Samuels introduced Stacey, who Finn suspected was ex-military from his bearing. Stacey smiled formally, and when he spoke it was with a cut-glass accent.

'We had a break-in just before a quarter to six this evening. An IC3 male used some sort of crowbar to break in through one of our fire doors. As per your direction, we've not engaged, but we've kept eyes on him via the security cameras. We also managed to pull off an image for you.' He produced a sheet of A4 from his pocket. On it was a black-and-white print-out of a man with a large holdall walking up a flight of stairs. Despite being a screen grab, the definition was excellent and the identity of the intruder unmistakable.

'That's Stuart Portbury, alright. Where is he now?' said Finn.

'On the roof. He forced another entrance and has been out there ever since. I've got a man on the door, but we haven't approached him,' Samuels replied.

'Good, so at least he's contained,' said Finn.

'What's he doing up there?' asked Paulsen.

'Nothing, as far as we can tell. Either he's admiring the view or he's waiting for something. Do you want to tell me what this is all about?' said Stacey.

'We think your intruder is responsible for the murder of three men and the attempted murder of a fourth man earlier this afternoon.'

'So what's he doing here? Does he want to kill himself?'

'Possibly, but what's in that bag? If you just want to jump, why bring that with you?' said Paulsen.

'And why here? If that's your objective, you're not exactly short of options in London,' said Stacey.

'Because he has history with this place. He used to be a firefighter – he was one of the first responders when the original construction site burnt down,' said Finn.

'Are you saying he has a grudge of some sort? That he might have brought a device with him?' asked Stacey. There was a hint of panic, thought Finn; maybe not officer class after all.

'I wouldn't rule *anything* out. His life was bent out of shape that night. He's killed, or at least thinks he's killed, everyone who was responsible for that.'

'It makes sense that the final act would be to come here. What we don't know is what his plan is,' said Paulsen.

'Whatever he's got in that bag won't bring the building down. It'd take a hell of a lot more than that, and the roof would be the least effective place to detonate an explosive,' said Stacey.

'If he's a former firefighter then he'll know where the weak spots are. We can't rule out the possibility he could have planted something earlier. Something we don't know about,' said Samuels.

'That's impossible,' said Stacey.

'Portbury's planned every step of this; he's not improvising,' said Finn. 'DC Paulsen's right – this is the endgame in some form, and we can't take chances.' He turned to Samuels. 'Extend the perimeter and pull your men back to be safe, and call in bomb disposal. They can get some sniffer dogs in there.' Samuels reached for his radio and relayed the instructions. Finn turned to Stacey. 'Are you sure the building's empty now?'

'As sure as I can be, notwithstanding any idiots.'

'Good. Okay – Mattie, you're with us.' Finn started to walk, flanked by her and Samuels.

'And where are you all going?' asked Stacey.

'To the roof,' said Finn, without turning.

They took the lift from the deserted reception and stood in silence as it slowly ascended. Samuels was still carrying his assault rifle, with one hand resting on the trigger, the other firmly over its midriff and the barrel pointing to the ground. He looked calm, but the weapon was increasing Paulsen's growing sense of unease.

'Shouldn't we be calling in a negotiator, guv?' she said to Finn.

'To negotiate what? Is he planning to jump? Does he want to burn the place down? Has he got hostages somewhere? I want more information before I make my next decision.' He turned to Samuels. 'And an armed officer might spook him too; it might be best if you stay out of sight, Dev.'

'Okay, but if there's a vantage point I can find up there without him seeing, then I'm taking it. And if I think there's a threat to life, I'll take the shot,' he replied.

The lift gave a small chime and the doors opened. They walked out into what appeared to be a service corridor. At its far end stood another armed officer by the entrance to the roof.

'Wait here. I want to know the lie of the land before we go any further,' whispered Samuels. Paulsen watched as he padded over to his colleague. Whatever Portbury was there to do he hadn't done it yet, and it was hard to shake the feeling he was waiting for something. For a moment she found herself back on another roof on another summer's day, where another man was waiting. In her mind's eye she saw that face again, with its charming smile and hint of a leer.

'Are you okay?' said Finn, noticing her expression.

'I'm fine, but why did you want me up here? Surely it makes more sense to have me controlling the situation on the ground.'

'Because I might need some support from someone *not* holding an assault rifle. Is that alright?' he asked, his own irritation showing now, and she realised he was as tense as she was.

'Yes, of course,' she replied.

Samuels seemed to have finished talking to his colleague and waved them over.

'The roof's split over two levels. Portbury's on his own at the top,' he whispered as they joined him.

'Are we okay to proceed?' asked Finn. Samuels instructed the officer on the door to maintain his position, then motioned at Finn and Paulsen to follow him as he stepped through the door. They walked out slowly and found themselves on a grey concrete concourse. The first thing which struck Paulsen was the loud hum of the electrical generators that surrounded them. There was a small corrugated iron staircase close by which led up to the top level. Samuels looked at Finn, ceding control of the situation to him with a glance. Finn nodded in acknowledgement, then turned to Paulsen, mouthed 'with me', and walked over to the steps. Samuels crouched and started scouting for a position of his own.

As she reached the top of the stairs Paulsen was greeted by an extraordinary vista of London opening out in front of her. Despite the circumstances, she couldn't help but be taken aback. The Thames rippled below in the sunshine, and she wondered just how many miles out into the suburbs the view extended.

'Gorgeous, isn't it?' said a voice.

It took them both a moment to register where it came from. He was almost dwarfed by the backdrop; Stuart Portbury standing at the edge by one of the railings.

'Wait here,' whispered Finn. 'If I need you, I'll signal. And remember what Dev said. You won't be able to see him, but he's probably found a vantage point.' Paulsen nodded and Finn walked out slowly towards Portbury, his hands outstretched with his palms facing up.

'Hello, Stuart.'

'That's far enough,' said Portbury and Finn stopped around ten feet away. Portbury reached down to the holdall at his feet, and pulled out a large plastic bottle. He unscrewed it and tipped the contents over his head. Even from a distance away Finn could smell the petrol fumes.

'What I'm about to give you is evidence. It's a dying man's statement,' said Portbury. He took his Zippo lighter from his pocket and held it up.

'Stuart, just wait a moment,' said Finn.

'What do you think I've been doing? I've been up here almost half an hour waiting for you to get your shit together,' he replied. 'Still, I'm glad it's you, not one of those kids you sent to my flat. Not the smartest cookies in the jar, are they?'

Paulsen watched from her position by the stairs. She could guess what was in the bottle and it was clear now what Portbury was intending. She concentrated, channelling her feelings and focusing them, because this time she was determined the outcome would be different. She began to walk forwards.

'Listen carefully, because this is evidence I want used in court later,' said Portbury. 'On the twelfth of August 2015 I attended a fire at this site as a serving member of the London Fire Brigade. Four of my crewmates – Martin Walker, Gary Elder, Adesh Kaul and Phil Maddox – contrary to their training and moral duty, deliberately allowed a man to die that night in service of their own greed.'

Portbury paused; there'd been just the hint of a tremor in his voice. This was nothing to do with some nonsensical idea of giving evidence, thought Finn. This was a confession. Wherever this was going, it was only moments away.

'They stole a quantity of money, a share of which I accepted in return for my silence. Until this moment I've kept their secret, but I'm both a thief and an accessory to murder.'

'We know.'

The voice cut through like a whip crack, and Finn spun around – part in shock, part in fury as he realised Paulsen was now standing behind him.

'I told you to stay put. Move back.'

Portbury held up the lighter.

'I'd do as he says.'

Paulsen held her ground and Finn recognised the look in her eye. Wild and blazing. He'd seen it before, earlier that week in Cedar House when she'd completely lost control. The situation was threatening to come off the rails, if it'd ever been on them.

'You do this, then the last thing you're doing is absolving yourself.'

'*Paulsen,*' said Finn, but she ignored him and Portbury smiled.

'I know what you're thinking. Some sort of reverse psychology? You believe if you can find the right words you can get through to me. Change my mind. You think if you hold eye contact, impress me with your courage, make a big speech, you and you alone can end this. Well you're wrong. You've been watching too many films.'

'I understand you better than you think,' she said.

'I doubt it,' he said, before turning back to Finn. 'You have everything you need now. You know what happened here five years ago, and you know why I killed those men. Make sure the truth comes out, make sure what they did is made public.'

Paulsen took another step closer, determined not to be ignored.

'You don't own guilt, Stuart. I know exactly what you've been living with because I killed a man once.'

The words echoed around the rooftop.

'Not the same thing, you're police,' said Portbury. He was still holding the silver lighter up; it dazzled occasionally as it caught the early evening sun. Paulsen took yet another step forwards.

'I didn't burn them alive, shoot them or stab them. But I was responsible. I wanted it to happen. And it did.'

Another step.

'I'm warning you,' said Portbury.

'Mattie . . .' whispered Finn. She ignored him.

'You know what I've learnt about guilt? It isn't always rational. It's just a weight you carry and if you're not careful it'll crush you in the end, whether you deserve it or not.' The words seemed to register. For the first time, Finn saw doubt in Portbury's eyes. 'You can still put this right,' continued Paulsen.

She was now almost within arm's length of him. Finn reckoned if he lit the flame she was close enough now to be caught in the resulting fireball. He looked around, desperate for some sign Samuels was close, but could see nothing.

'The way I see it . . . a man is a sum of his choices,' said Portbury. 'You made a choice once maybe, but *they* made mine for me. I never asked to have someone's death on my conscience.'

'Then face up to it and deal with it. Because to end it like this achieves nothing. It's just—'

'A coward's choice?' said Portbury. 'You say you understand me. If that were true, then why would you *want* to go on living?'

'Because we have to,' said Finn quietly. 'Because we owe it to the dead, to take responsibility for our actions.' He looked across at Paulsen. 'Don't we?'

For a moment all three of them stood there in silence. Three damaged people, Finn would later reflect. Portbury slowly shook his head.

'I'm sorry but *this* choice is mine, no one gets to take it away from me.'

He flicked the lighter's flint wheel with his thumb. Finn dived forwards, throwing his arms around Paulsen, swinging her round and pulling her back in a single movement. For an instant the flint wheel sparked, but before it could engage there was a crackle of automatic fire and Portbury buckled to the ground. Samuels was stood around twenty feet away at a diagonal to them, with his weapon raised. Blood started to pool under Portbury's head. Paulsen wrenched herself free from Finn's grip and sprinted over. She sank to her knees, her eyes fixed on the body in front of her, her face impassive.

57

Seven Days Later

The summer heatwave was well and truly over, the dry conditions and baking temperatures replaced by consecutive days of thick cloud and hard rain. After too many sleepless nights in the heat, Finn was enjoying the change. He held a plastic folder of paperwork over his head and ran across the road from Cedar House towards YoYo's as the heavens parted. He looked around the cafe and saw Andy Warrender in the corner nursing a mug of tea. Warrender was in London following up some leads on Ray Spinney's current whereabouts. He'd suggested popping in for a final catch-up on the mutual ground their investigations covered. Finn agreed, as much out of curiosity as necessity. There'd been a strange thaw in their relationship over the past week, and DI to DI, Finn found himself empathising with his counterpart.

Warrender greeted him with a friendly smile and they shook hands. Finn still didn't rate him, but there was an integrity which was hard not to respect. Whatever else you could say, he'd meant well. The double blow of Farmer's death and Godden's betrayal would have hit anyone hard. All things considered, he looked remarkably at peace with himself. Finn immediately suspected the reason.

'I've handed in my notice, and it feels bloody great, I can't deny it,' Warrender said as Yolande brought Finn the espresso he hadn't needed to order.

'What will you do?'

'I've got family in Devon. It's time for something different. Running a pub, or even a gaff like this, suddenly feels appealing.'

'I was sorry to hear about Mike Godden,' said Finn.

It was nothing to do with sympathy for the dead man. Godden's death would have been devastating for Warrender and everyone at Chapel Row. Getting him to face justice in the dock for what he'd done was probably the only thing keeping them going following Jim Farmer's death. Godden also possessed crucial knowledge regarding Spinney, which he'd taken to the grave with him. It was the worst of all possible outcomes. Warrender shook his head and stared down into his tea.

'I guess he fucked me right to the end, didn't he?'

'What about Spinney – any leads?' asked Finn, changing the subject.

'Nothing. Just spent a wasted morning chasing shadows. Current thinking is he's probably gone abroad. Romania possibly. He has contacts and the resources to create a new identity. Interpol have been informed, but then he was living in plain sight out in Kent for years, so your guess is as good as mine. Frankly, it's not my problem any more.'

'What's happening with the inquiry?'

'My entire team is under internal investigation now. A new SIO is being drafted in, with a new team. They'll start again. Every last piece of evidence we gathered is considered compromised. They're welcome to it.'

Warrender drained the last of his tea. He looked out of the window; the showers were turning into sustained driving rain.

'I won't miss London either,' he said, then glanced back at Finn. 'By the way, I was hoping to catch up with that DC of yours – Paulsen? Just wanted to thank her for her help. Thought she had something about her, that one.'

'Sorry but you've missed her, she's been taking some personal time,' Finn replied. A couple of young officers across the road were sprinting to the main entrance of the station as the rain pounded down. 'And yes, she is a bit different.'

58

The weather more or less matched her mood, Paulsen thought. Although no, that wasn't entirely true. Since Pacific Square, she'd just felt numb, as if she'd reached saturation point. She'd gone back to Cedar House with Finn directly after Portbury's death. The rest of the team went for beers that evening. She naturally shunned the invite. The last thing she felt like doing was celebrating with a bunch of men who hadn't actually been there when it happened. She wasn't sure what they were celebrating anyway. They'd failed as far as she was concerned, another man was dead. She imagined they'd be slagging her off in the pub. Or not. Either way, their thoughts didn't really matter. She'd told Finn she needed some time off and he'd granted it immediately. She thought he should do the same but held back from saying so, having learnt her lesson on that front. She'd hoped to slip away unnoticed. It was Ojo who'd intercepted her. At first Paulsen was expecting an attempt to try and make her come out, but the detective sergeant simply said: 'Go home. Get your head sorted. But if you fancy a drink – just you and me – text me.' Then, almost brusquely, she turned and joined the rest of them as they headed off to the pub.

Back home things improved that week with Nancy. In a funny sort of way, Portbury's death felt like the closing of two chapters in her life. Perhaps the numbness helped in a weird way. For the first time in months she didn't feel either angry or guilty. The love child of those two emotions – the self-loathing – wasn't there either. It felt strange not to be carrying those feelings after so long, and it all added up to an odd sense of detachment. Seeing Stuart Portbury's guilt consume him in his own personal blaze affected her deeply. Everything she'd said to him on that rooftop was true. She'd known exactly how he'd been feeling, why he'd wanted to die. Seeing it so vividly made her realise that's the direction of travel she'd been on too. It wasn't that she'd ever felt suicidal, but she now understood with clarity where she might have ended up. On a metaphorical roof of her own, with nobody able to get through to her. She was ready to change course now, she just didn't know how.

Nancy sensed it, and there followed the usual attempts to cheer her up. This time Paulsen didn't find them annoying. Instead she felt grateful. There was no big moment, they didn't do anything special. Nancy just gave her some space and it already started to feel like they were finding themselves again. She'd told Nancy about Ojo's suggestion of a drink and Nancy had virtually forced her on the spot to send a text accepting the offer.

Now here she was, in a wine bar in Clapham feeling strangely nervous. Jackie Ojo was one of those people who said little, but whose eyes pierced right through you. Paulsen imagined that sitting opposite her in an interview room would be quite daunting.

'I didn't think you'd take me up on this,' said Ojo with a brisk smile as she passed Paulsen a bottle of Leffe. She sat down and took an appreciative sip from her own large glass of red wine.

'I thought you'd probably been waiting to give me the girls together speech?' said Paulsen. She'd meant it slightly more sociably than it came out.

'Oh, fuck off,' said Ojo, and leant forwards. 'Why are you at war with *everyone*?'

'I'm not. Honest, I'm not. Just ninety per cent of the world.'

Ojo surprised her with a broad grin. She didn't smile often, Paulsen noticed. You needed to earn it with her, she thought.

'I hate saying it, because it makes me feel so old – but I used to be just like you once. Being black and a woman in the Met is a hard combination. But trust me, this aggressive thing you've got going on . . . isn't the way to work it.'

'You don't understand – it's complicated. I'm far less interested in what goes on at Cedar House than you think. There's other stuff. What happens at work is irritating sometimes, but it's small in the scheme of things.'

'Okay. Can I ask what this other thing is?'

'I'd rather not go there. No offence.'

'Fair enough. Anyway. Here it is then, the big speech . . .' This time it was Paulsen's turn to grin. 'Your workmates – they're not the enemy. Some of them are dicks, absolutely. Some of them don't care, and some of them are really decent people. You've got to work with them all, or at least find a *way* of working with them. What you've been doing isn't sustainable.'

'What do you care?'

'As I might have just said – fuck off, Paulsen. I care because . . . well, girls together, aren't we?'

Paulsen realised she was enjoying herself, enjoying the banter. That felt new too.

'Did you have to work hard to be accepted here?'

'What do you think? But I learnt a few tricks. Tricks I think I can pass on to you, if you're prepared to listen to me. Some of these guys, they really want to get on with you – you're just not letting them in. Give them a chance.'

'What about the DI?'

'What about him?'

'Do I need to win him over?'

Ojo took a deep sip of her wine, a playful look forming on her face.

'What do you make of him so far?' she said.

'Not fair. You and him clearly go back.'

'I'm interested, genuinely.'

'Alright – at first I thought he was up himself. But he's complicated. Then again, I dare say the last few weeks haven't been the easiest, have they?'

'That's not a bad analysis. A lot of people find him difficult to work out. When I first met him, I thought there was genuinely something a bit missing. But there isn't. He just turns off the social graces sometimes, because his brain hasn't got time for them. They get in the way. Sometimes with other human beings he can be stunningly stupid.' They both laughed as she said the words. 'But when it comes to the job, he knows what he's doing. People tend to underestimate him; other cops, villains, Skegman even . . . the public . . . it's a mistake, trust me.'

'I'd worked that out actually.' Paulsen took a moment, feeling Ojo's gaze searching her out. 'He's told you what I said to him, hasn't he?' Ojo nodded and she felt a rush of embarrassment.

'What was that all about?' said Ojo quietly.

'It was the way he was talking to me. It just . . . triggered something.'

'To do with this *issue* of yours?' Paulsen nodded. 'I suppose that explains it to some degree, even if it doesn't excuse it. What the fuck were you thinking? His wife's just died.'

'I know, I'm not trying to excuse it. It was appalling, I understand that. I lost control. I just don't know how to put it right. We were right in the middle of the investigation. Portbury attacked him that night so we've not really talked properly about it since.'

'Do you really need me to tell you what to do?'

Paulsen rolled her beer bottle between her hands for a moment.

'No. I just don't know *how* to do it.'

'You're almost as bad as he is. It doesn't matter how you do it, Mattie. Just do it.'

59

Finn was cooking lasagne. He was in the mood for comfort food. It was good to be slipping back into another of his old routines. Cooking felt strangely healing and if he never saw another microwave dinner again it would be too soon. Tomorrow he'd call the estate agents and get someone in to value the flat. It was time to begin the process of moving on, in all senses of the phrase. He'd just put the lasagne in the oven when the front doorbell rang, and he found a familiar face waiting outside.

'Hello,' said Mattie Paulsen. 'I'm not disturbing you, am I?' She looked strangely small standing there, and her Scandinavian lilt sounded particularly pronounced. 'Can we talk?' she said, and he nodded her in.

'You've rather caught me on the hop, I'm afraid, can I get you a drink?' he said, wriggling with slight embarrassment at the kitchen apron he was wearing.

'Whisky, neat – if that's okay,' she replied. A hint of a smile crossed his face – he'd been thinking more tea or coffee. A few minutes later they were sat on opposite sofas in his living room, both nursing a glass of single malt.

'I'd like to start with a question,' she said. 'You heard what I said to Portbury out on that rooftop. About being responsible for someone's death . . .' Finn nodded. 'And yet, you haven't asked me about it. You let me take a week off instead. Why?'

'Because I wanted to have *this* conversation with you, and I wanted you to have the time to think about it first.'

He'd thought it through, she realised. Obviously he'd thought it through.

'So start at the beginning . . .' he said.

'And then?'

'Well, there's a lot of whisky left in that bottle.' He smiled, and she realised then what he'd done. The bridge he'd been building between them since she'd said those awful things to him. Everything was about bringing them to this point; a conversation where she could speak freely, without fear. He'd played her, but in the kindest way possible. Again, she thought, what a very Finn-like thing to do.

'It was just over a year ago. I was part of an investigation into a series of suicides at a children's home – a number of teenage boys. We'd received a tip-off about one of the staff. His name was Christopher Riggs. It all came down to one boy – Curtis. I was tasked with building up a relationship with him so we could get a statement. It's not easy with a kid like that, when they've been let down by adults over and over. Finally, he told me his story; what Riggs did to him. Trust me, it was the kind of stuff . . .' She blew through her cheeks. 'The very worst . . . and just when we'd reached a point where Curtis felt strong enough to go on the record, I got a phone call. He'd taken a dive out of his bedroom window. The same day he'd spoken to me.'

'Jesus,' said Finn. 'I'm sorry.'

'He survived, but was severely hurt and needs round-the-clock care now. We'd no choice but to let Riggs go. There was nothing we could use against him.'

That part of the story was all too familiar to Finn and he could guess where this was going.

'So what did you do next?'

'I went after Riggs myself. I wanted to scare him, mark his card, let him know we wouldn't forget. One day, after he'd done his shopping, I followed him to a multistorey car park and that's exactly what I did. He tried to tell me I'd got it wrong, and that Curtis was confused.' She swallowed. '. . . And I lost my temper.' She stopped, frozen in the memory.

'What happened next?'

'I threatened him, made it clear everyone he ever came across would know what he'd done. That he'd be looking over his shoulder for the rest of his life. I told him he might as well jump now . . .' She gave Finn a small, sad smile. 'And he did.'

She could see it in her mind's eye, the look on his face as she'd been shouting. In those seconds he'd made the calculation, the difference between life and death. He'd said nothing, just turned silently and vaulted over the edge. There was no scream, just the crash of impact and the sound of blaring car alarms. She'd killed a man, or at least as good as. None of his victims would ever see him in the dock, no jury would get to hear a full account of what he'd done, no judge would ever pass sentence on him. She'd taken all that on herself and let Curtis down in the process.

'What happened when they investigated it?'

'I was lucky – there was no CCTV in that car park.'

'So everyone assumed he'd jumped?'

'There was no evidence to suggest otherwise. Given what we knew about him, it wasn't a huge stretch for people to think his conscience had caught up with him.'

'And that's why you disobeyed me on the roof with Portbury?'

'Yes. I wanted it to be different this time. But I failed again.'

'It was a completely different set of circumstances. A different man with different reasons.'

'That's not the point; I don't learn. When I lost it with you at Cedar House, it was exactly the same loss of control.'

'Have you always been like that?'

'No. Well, not to this extent, anyway. A man died, regardless of what kind of person he was. I'd never lost it like that before. I couldn't stop it. And for a second, after he'd jumped – I was *pleased*.' She looked disgusted as she said it and gulped some whisky down. 'There's a reason I keep myself to myself at work; it's because I don't trust myself.'

'Where does the anger come from? Originally, I mean?'

'That's a whole other conversation.'

'But you've an idea?'

She nodded.

'Good. Understanding it is a start.'

She didn't look convinced. 'I didn't come here to be psychoanalysed.'

'So why did you come here?'

'To say sorry.' She looked up, meeting his gaze. 'I am *so* sorry for what I said to you.' Her voice trembled with emotion, and Finn nodded gently.

'I know.'

The smell of lasagne was starting to waft into the room, and the only sound was the faint whirr of the oven fan from the kitchen.

'So what happens now?' she said.

'My wife – my late wife – left me a note. In it, she asked me a question: "*How far will a blind dog walk into a forest?*" It took me ages to work it out. It only made sense to me after listening to Portbury out on that roof. The answer's obvious, really.'

Paulsen looked nonplussed.

'*Until it comes out the other side.*' He smiled sadly and let the words percolate for a moment. 'It was Karin's way of telling me to get over her. To find a way through the grief, to push on, keep on living. I think you've been lost in the same forest as me. The same one Portbury couldn't get out of.'

'Except I'm not grieving for Christopher Riggs.'

'No, but you're grieving nonetheless. You feel responsible for a man's death and you've been suppressing it for way too long. You don't do something like that without losing a piece of yourself in the process.'

'So, what are you going to do about it?'

'Nothing.'

'And why would you do that? So you can have a hold over me?' Her face was clouding with suspicion now.

'No. Not at all.'

'Nobody does something for nothing.'

'Since Karin died, I've started to see the world a bit differently. In less straight lines, I suppose. I think you deserve a second chance.'

'And what if I lose control again?'

'We can work on that.'

'It could cost you one day. Cost us both.'

'Then I'll take the risk.' He smiled. 'Now, I'm about to eat what I happen to think is an exceptionally good dinner. I've made way too much and I'm sick of eating alone. You're very welcome to join me.'

She produced one of her unexpected smiles.

'I'd like that.'

As Finn followed her into the kitchen, he considered what she'd said. He'd seen Paulsen lose her temper close up. She hadn't cared where she was, or who she was talking to. It was genuine blind rage, and now he knew it wasn't a one-off. She was right to say it could cost him. What worried him more was how much it might cost her one day.

'*Careful, Alex . . .*' said a dead woman.

60

A few miles across south London, Martin Walker stared at the ceiling from his hospital bed. He'd got used to the constant beeping of the heart monitor next to him, the drip connected to his arm. The drugs being pumped through his system were keeping the pain at bay. Much of the left-hand side of his body was badly burnt, from his shoulder down to his thigh. There were dressings on most of it, and movement of any kind was difficult.

He'd received several visits from Christine, as much as she'd been able to manage on her own. What happened seemed to have brought them closer again. With Portbury's death, at least one of their worries was over, but another cloud was looming. He'd been made aware of Portbury's dying declaration by Finn. There was no doubt the police would now be investigating him hard over the missing share of the Stansted money. He was, after all, the only person still living who could answer their questions. The future he'd worked so hard to try and make easier for Christine looked daunting and uncertain.

'Good afternoon,' said a rich, velvet voice. 'I really suppose I should have brought some grapes, but it does seem a dreadful cliché.'

The last time Walker heard that voice it was in a beach hut in Whitstable. He turned his head carefully, wincing as his scorched flesh stretched beneath the dressings. A slightly built man wearing a pin-striped waistcoat and a pair of old-fashioned spectacles was stood by his bedside holding a sodden umbrella. There was a strong smell of aftershave too. The expensive sort, the type you'd get in a gentleman's club mixed with a cocktail of brandy and cigar smoke.

'Do you mind if I sit down?' said Raymond Spinney, pulling up a chair before Walker could answer. A nurse walked past and he smiled politely before turning back, the warmth fading from his face instantly.

'Did you really think there'd be no consequence for what you did? You took something that wasn't yours, you know.'

'Not yours either,' croaked Walker.

'That's not quite how I work. Once I acquire something – whether it is money, goods or even people . . . then they're *mine*. And they stay mine until I decide otherwise.'

'I told you in Whitstable I'd pay you back,' said Walker.

'Yes, you did. But it's not the money that bothers me. There's something about you, and your greed in particular, which I can't quite get past. If society can't trust a man like you, Mr Walker, then where are we?'

Walker felt helpless. Whatever was going to happen he was in no position to stop it. Spinney leant in, whispering now into his unbandaged ear.

'It seems to me you were presented with a choice five years ago. You could have done your job, saved Erik Whitlock's life and left that money alone. Then none of this would have happened. I'm guessing you've been thinking a lot about that recently, so let me give you another choice.' He paused and pulled a spotless white handkerchief from his pocket. He removed his spectacles with his other hand, breathed on the lenses and started polishing them as he continued. 'I'll be leaving the country soon, so this is the last time we'll meet. I'm happy to spare your life and let you keep the remainder of the cash you stole. But if that's your wish, then your wife *won't* be so lucky. One of my associates will pay her a visit. It'll be as quick and as painless as he can manage, but it's not a precise science, I'm afraid. Alternatively, one of them can come and pay *you* a visit and end all this . . . indignity.' He waved a hand at Walker's bandaged form dismissively, as if it were a child's bedroom in urgent need of a tidy-up. 'If you choose that option, you have my word Christine will live out the remainder of her life untroubled.'

Spinney put his glasses back on and stood up, pulling his waistcoat straight as he did so. Outside the rain thundered down, and next to Walker the even beep of the heart monitor continued. Spinney smiled pleasantly.

'So which is it to be?'

Acknowledgements

I honestly never thought about this bit. I never thought about it, because I never thought I'd get here. And now I am here, it's really rather humbling. So some words of thanks are definitely in order.

Before I do though, I'd like to pay tribute to the real life firefighters of the world. This is a book about five very particular men, fictitious characters in a story who make a terrible choice. It is no way a reflection on the courage of the true life men and women in that noble profession, who risk their lives every day.

And so to the thank you's – firstly to my brilliant agent, Hayley Steed at the Madeleine Milburn Agency. Thank you so much for showing faith in officers Finn and Paulsen and getting me here in the first place. It's safe to say without your confidence in them and me, this wouldn't have happened. It's hugely appreciated.

A big word for my editor Eve Hall at Hodder & Stoughton – you took my increasingly complicated story, and applied a fantastic sense of story and structure to make it clearer and better with each draft. It has been a fantastic experience working with you; thank you for both your faith in me and this story too.

Thank you to copy editor Joe Hall – who made some invaluable observations right at the end.

A huge thank you to my friend Nishat – don't worry, she knows why.

And finally, thank you to you, the reader. I hope you enjoyed reading this book as much as I enjoyed writing it – Finn and Paulsen will return!